"So, my good Lord Winterley," she said in saucy cheer. "*Do* you have a mistress?"

"Miranda." He looked at her flatly, then downed the rest of his wine. "I do not have a mistress."

"No? No wife, no mistress? I say, what *do* you have, Damien?"

"Just a brat of a ward to marry off to the highest bidder." He picked up the wine bottle and refilled his goblet.

"Well, since I have neither fortune nor family, I don't suppose anyone's going to want me."

"Yes, they will. You have something else."

"What's that?"

"Beauty." He stared at her for a second. "You have beauty." Studiously avoiding her gaze, he continued eating.

"You're too serious, Winterley!" She reached for a pillow. "I will beat you until you smile!"

He ducked out of his chair with a rakish grin as she swung at him, then tackled her flat on the soft bed, both of them laughing.

"You are . . . impossible," he chided with a gentle sigh.

"Difficult, but not impossible." She wrapped her arms around him, relishing the weight of him atop her. "It all depends on who's trying."

"That sounded distinctly like an invitation," he murmured.

"Maybe it was," she whispered, stroking his hair. "Are you going to accept?"

Her words made him go very still. "I don't know."

"Think hard," she breathed, but he offered no protest whatsoever as she slowly pulled his head down to her until their lips met. She cupped his cheek, begging him with her touch not to pull away. He did not.

By Gaelen Foley
*Published by Ballantine Books:*

THE PIRATE PRINCE
PRINCESS
PRINCE CHARMING
THE DUKE
LORD OF FIRE
LORD OF ICE
LADY OF DESIRE
DEVIL TAKES A BRIDE
ONE NIGHT OF SIN
HIS WICKED KISS

# LORD OF ICE

## A NOVEL

# GAELEN FOLEY

BALLANTINE BOOKS • NEW YORK

2006 Ballantine Books Mass Market Edition

Copyright © 2002 by Gaelen Foley

Published in the United States by Ballantine Books, an imprint of The Random House Publishing Group, a division of Random House, Inc., New York.

BALLANTINE and colophon are registered trademarks of Random House, Inc.

Originally published in paperback in the United States by Ivy Books, an imprint of The Random House Publishing Group, a division of Random House, Inc., in 2002.

ISBN 0-345-49067-3

Cover illustration: © Robert Osonitsch

Printed in the United States of America

www.ballantinebooks.com

OPM 9 8 7 6 5 4 3 2 1

*Georgiana's Brood:*
# THE KNIGHT MISCELLANY

# *Georgiana's Brood:* THE KNIGHT MI

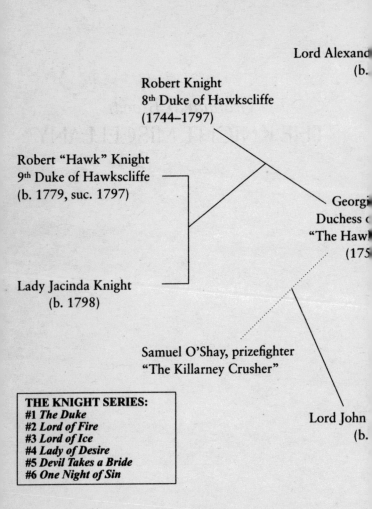

Lord Alexand
(b.

Robert Knight
8th Duke of Hawkscliffe
(1744–1797)

Robert "Hawk" Knight
9th Duke of Hawkscliffe
(b. 1779, suc. 1797)

Georgi
Duchess
"The Haw
(175

Lady Jacinda Knight
(b. 1798)

Samuel O'Shay, prizefighter
"The Killarney Crusher"

Lord John
(b.

**THE KNIGHT SERIES:**
#1 *The Duke*
#2 *Lord of Fire*
#3 *Lord of Ice*
#4 *Lady of Desire*
#5 *Devil Takes a Bride*
#6 *One Night of Sin*

CELLANY

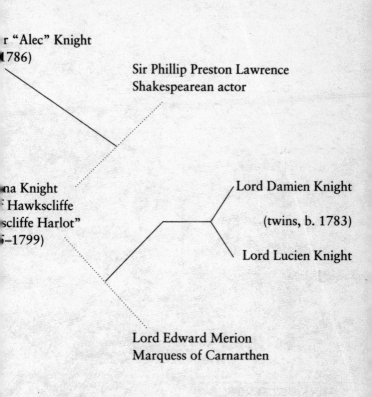

r "Alec" Knight
1786)

Sir Phillip Preston Lawrence
Shakespearean actor

na Knight
Hawkscliffe
scliffe Harlot"
5–1799)

Lord Damien Knight

(twins, b. 1783)

Lord Lucien Knight

Lord Edward Merion
Marquess of Carnarthen

Jack" Knight
1781)

Dotted lines denote Georgiana's lovers.

*'Tis bitter cold, and I am sick at heart.*
—SHAKESPEARE

# LORD OF ICE

# ⊰ PROLOGUE ⊱

*London, 1814*

"Look at you. Drunk again. You are pathetic," Lord Hubert said to his younger brother.

Major Jason Sherbrooke merely let out a low, insolent laugh in response. Staring into the fire, he sank more deeply into his tattered armchair and took another swig from his bottle of blue ruin.

Picking his way through the clutter of the major's seedy bachelor lodgings, Algernon Sherbrooke, Viscount Hubert, pulled out a fastidiously pressed and monogrammed handkerchief, veiling his nostrils from the dirt that hung in the air. "Heav'n preserve us, this room smells of rotted cheese or piss or some foul thing. Don't you ever clean up after yourself?"

"To be sure, I am the soul of industry," Jason slurred.

Algernon pursed his lips. The cause of his brother's malaise was obvious. He flicked a downward glance to the empty sleeve of Jason's disheveled, red uniform coat. The major had lost his right arm during the vicious cavalry charge at the Battle of Albuera. He had been lucky

1

to escape with his life. Pulling a coarse wooden chair over to the fire, Algernon gingerly lowered himself onto it. "Perhaps you should hire a maid rather than sitting around here feeling sorry for yourself."

"The devil I will. The last one stole from me," he grumbled.

"It is no wonder, considering your address." Indeed, Jason's lodging house was so ill-situated that it was not far from the slum tenements that Algernon owned— very secretly—in a treacherous quarter of the East End. Alas, that investment had not yet yielded the returns he had hoped, though he had raised his tenants' rents again last month. He did not care if Christmas was a fortnight away. He'd evict anyone who did not pay in full. "Why do you stay in this rat's hole? We both know you can afford better."

Jason looked at him dully. "What does it matter?"

"Have you no pride?"

"What the hell do you want, Algy? I rather doubt I owe this visit to a sudden rush of fraternal affection in your breast. Have you been infected with the bloody holiday spirit, or is there a reason you're here?"

Warily, Algernon scanned Jason's sun-weathered face with its scraggly copper mustache. He would have to proceed with caution. Even drunk, his sharp-witted younger brother was not a man to be trifled with, hardened as he was by his years of war. "Perhaps I came to stop you from drinking yourself to death."

"Waste of time." Raising his bottle again, Jason cast him a sidelong glance. "But somehow I doubt that was your motive."

Algernon held him in a penetrating stare for a long moment, then sighed, giving it over. "No. It was not."

"In the army, we respect a man that comes straight to the point."

"Very well." Algernon's narrow face tautened as he paused, his hazel eyes turning even colder. "I must have Miranda's dowry."

Jason's bleary eyes cleared with astonishment.

"My situation is grave—"

"Oh, no. No, you don't. Stop right there. Absolutely not."

"Hear me out—"

"There is nothing to discuss."

"Jason!"

"That money is not mine to give, Algy, and it is certainly not yours to spend. Richard left it for his daughter—"

"His by-blow! Damn it, Jason, it's not as though she's one of us."

"Miranda may be illegitimate, but that does not change the fact that she is our brother's child."

Their eldest brother, Richard, had been Viscount Hubert before the title had passed to Algernon, the second-born. An unmarried rake, Richard had died without legal issue, only a beautiful little daughter by his beloved mistress, the famed actress Fanny Blair. But Fanny had died with him on the lake that summer day when their pleasure boat had sunk. Only their then-eight-year-old daughter, Miranda, had survived, rescued by a fisherman.

"She is your niece and mine," Jason finished staunchly.

"Not by law," he said coldly.

"By blood."

"We owe her nothing. Let her find her own way in the world!"

"God, listen to yourself, Algy. You've always been such a coldhearted prick."

"How can you be sentimental about this girl? Her mother was little better than a whore!"

"Well, I happen to like whores," Jason said with a smirk, crossing his booted heels before the fire.

Biting back words he knew he'd regret, Algernon shot up out of his chair and paced across the cramped, filthy room, stepping over a broken footstool, empty bottles, and piles of soiled clothes in his path. He kicked a book out of his way and stopped by the far wall, blinking hard as he struggled to bring his vexation under control. Damn it, how was he to make this drunkard see reason? Within the folds of his lace cuff, his hand curled into a fist. "If I am ruined, the whole family will be disgraced, including you."

"There, there, Algy, you won't be ruined," Jason said, chuckling. "You've got the wits of a fox and the morals of a snake. I have faith in you. You'll find a way. But I will not hear you speak more against Miranda. It so happens I am very fond of that child."

"Oh?" Algernon pivoted. "Then when was the last time you went to visit her at school? A year ago? Two? Five?" he pushed on as Jason blinked, clearly taken aback. "Before Albuera, I warrant!"

Jason flashed him a warning look. "Miranda is being well cared for at school until she is ready for her debut."

"Debut?" he cried. "Firstly, she is a bastard and shall have nothing of the kind—"

"Yes, she will. That's what the money's for."

"Well, she'll get no help from me," he snarled. "I will make damned certain that neither my wife nor my girls acknowledge her in Society. Secondly, do you even realize that the time for this grand *debut* you envision is already passing? Miranda is nineteen years old. If you were so concerned about her welfare, you'd have realized that the appropriate age for her coming-out was a year or two ago."

Jason stared at him, looking rather aghast. "She's not nineteen!"

"Oh, yes, she is. Wake up, man! Put your bottle down and think! She is a grown woman—one you cannot mean to bring into our circles. Society will never accept her. Don't you see it would be cruel to thrust her into a situation where she cannot possibly succeed?"

"Oh, she'll succeed, Algy. You don't know Miranda. She's fearless. Besides, she's always shown the promise of her mother's beauty. A fair face can take a woman far in 'our circles.' "

Algernon forced himself to remain calm. "Listen to me. If it is indeed a good school, then Miranda will have been prepared for a position as a governess or some other respectable ladies' work befitting her station. I ask you—why must we be responsible for Richard's by-blow?"

"*We* aren't, Algy. *I* am." Jason shook his head in disgust. "Richard knew you'd treat her like dirt if he left her in your care."

"Where is your loyalty, damn it? I am your brother and I am facing ruin! Last year's harvest was poor. The 'Change is down—"

"And let me guess—you had to cover your darling Crispin's losses again at the gaming tables."

Algernon narrowed his eyes at him. "Crispin is my son, my heir. Am I to leave him at the mercy of cut-throat moneylenders?"

"I see. So, you'd rather take Miranda's dowry—her very future—away from her so that your fool boy won't lose face at the club. No, Algy. You and your son can both go to hell."

"Jason—"

"Algy, it's only five thousand pounds anyway. Crispin can lose that in ten minutes. This money will make the difference for Miranda's entire future."

"You *fool*." Algernon paced over and eased back down onto the chair beside him, intensely searching his brother's haggard face. "Five thousand pounds? Don't you put that bottle aside long enough to pay attention to your own accounts?"

Jason shifted uncomfortably in his chair. "What do you mean?"

"Before you went off to war, you invested the bulk of her inheritance money in a little company called Waring Iron Foundries. Do you remember?"

"Yes, what of it?"

"Jason." Algernon shook his head at him. "Waring Foundries landed so many war contracts that the company's become an empire. That five thousand is now worth fifty."

Jason's jaw dropped. He set his bottle down and stared at him in shock.

Algernon succumbed to a wry smile at his brother's stunned expression. Perhaps now the fool would listen to reason. There was a long silence, broken only by the whistling of the winter wind at the eaves and the popping of the hearth fire.

"*Fifty thousand pounds?*" Jason cried abruptly, regaining his tongue.

"Yes! You did it, Jason!" Algernon whispered feverishly. "You're the one who deserves that money. You see what you are capable of when your brain isn't soaked in spirits?"

"Damn me, fifty thousand pounds!" Tilting his head back, Jason slapped his thigh and began laughing drunkenly. He climbed out of his armchair, picked up his bottle again, and lifted it merrily. "Ho, Miranda, my lass! Fifty thousand pounds! By God, my girl, you'll buy yourself a duke!" He stumbled past Algernon, his face flushed with excitement. "Damn me, it's a bloody miracle." He pulled out his army haversack and, awkward with the use of his left hand, began packing a few articles of clothing.

"What do you think you are doing?"

"I'm going to Warwickshire to fetch the lass from school, that's what! If she's nineteen—is she really nineteen?" he asked, looking up from his task.

Algernon did not answer the question. "You're not going anywhere."

Jason straightened up warily, abandoning his task. "I beg your pardon?"

"Don't be absurd. There is no way in this world or

the next that we are placing that kind of fortune in the hands of a nobody."

"She is not *nobody*, Algy. Not anymore." His mustache tilted with his crooked grin. "She's Miss Miranda FitzHubert, heiress. You'd best remember that lest she cut you when she's a duchess."

Algernon rose from his chair, his expression turning dangerous. "Now, listen here, brother. You will hand that money over to me. I will not stand publicly disgraced over your misguided chivalry toward our bastard niece. Sign the account over to me. When I am on my feet again, I will replace the money, if you wish. Miranda will never be the wiser."

"Bugger yourself, Algy. Try the bank." Jason's laughter stopped abruptly as Algernon coolly pulled out a pistol and leveled it between his eyes.

"My dear brother, you do not seem to grasp the seriousness of my situation. I must have that money, Jason. And I shall. Bring me the documents and sign over the account. Now."

Jason stared incredulously at the pistol, then at him. "Have you lost your bloody mind?"

"We are kin. She is nothing."

"You son of a bitch," he whispered. "You'd do it, too, wouldn't you?"

Algernon cocked the gun with his thumb. "Just do as I ask, Jason. You're drunk. You're not thinking clearly. Indeed, you're not fit to manage the money or the girl. As head of the family, I will take charge from here."

"You would blow my brains out as I stand here for fifty thousand pounds, wouldn't you, Algy? Of course

you would. You'd do it in a heartbeat! After all—"
Jason paused, his face tautening with growing rage.
"—you killed Richard to get your hands on the title,
didn't you? *Didn't you?*" he bellowed as Algernon's
eyes flared with anger. "I don't know how you did it,
but you caused Richard's boat to sink on the lake that
day. You treacherous worm! I've always suspected it,
but not until this moment was I sure."

"I fear you have drunk yourself into lunacy, Jason,"
Algernon said in cold, deadly quiet. "Now be a good
lad and get me the documents."

"The hell I will! Do you think I'm afraid of that
gun? I've been looking down the barrels of French
muskets these past five years. What the hell do I care?
Go on, pull the trigger, Algy, you coward! I haven't
got a damned thing left to lose."

"Don't tempt me, Jason," he whispered. "It would
be such a waste. I am your next of kin, and I know you
made a will before you went to war. Killing you would
only make Miranda *my* ward; then her fortune would
come under my control, in any case."

"You're wrong there, old boy. Do you think I'm
daft enough to name you as her guardian?" His
lips thinned in a feral smile. "No, *brother,* I made
certain amendments to my will while I was in the
army—among men I could trust. Tell the truth, Algy.
Aye, admit you killed Richard and Fanny, and tried to
kill Miranda along with them, and I'll *give* you the
money."

Algernon stared at him for a long moment. His heart
was pounding, but his self-control was exquisite.

Slowly, he lowered the pistol, but not to his side. Instead, he stopped at the level of Jason's heart.

"Give my regards to Richard," he murmured.

The gin bottle fell; the shot rang out, the pan's flash illuminating Algernon's narrow face and soulless eyes. Reeling back, Jason crashed to the floor, clutching his chest. Algernon lowered the pistol to his side.

Gasping for air, Jason stared, aghast, at his brother's spotlessly polished boots as the viscount stepped over him, calmly went to the escritoire in the corner, opened the lid, and began searching through his private papers.

Reeling with pain and disbelief at his brother's sheer evil, Jason's first thought was that he was dying. His second was to curse himself for not protecting Miranda's inheritance as he should have through Chancery Court, but Richard had died so suddenly, and he, eager to be off to war, had eschewed the headaches of dealing with that lumbering bureaucracy, instead putting the money in the private investment fund in Miranda's name with himself as trustee.

She was in terrible danger. If Algy could kill his own brothers in cold blood, he would hardly scruple over his illegitimate niece. Helpless to stop him, Jason lay on the floor in a pool of his own blood.

"Ah, here we are . . . Miranda FitzHubert. Oh, dear. What's this?" Algernon paused. "Jason, Jason, what have you done? Well, this is most unfortunate."

Agonized, Jason looked up as Algy paced over to him slowly. The viscount tilted his head, peering down at him. His face was a blurry oval against the encroaching darkness in the room. His voice seemed oddly muffled, floating down crossly to him.

"You should not have put her name on the account, Jason. Now how am I to open it? You see what you have done? Now I shall have to get rid of your precious niece, too."

"No!" he choked out, but Algernon's shiny boots stalked away, returning to the desk.

Jason lay there watching his lifeblood pump out of his chest onto the floor, seeping into the dirty cracks between the planks. Through the horror, he realized his existence could now be measured in seconds, but at least he had done one thing right, he thought, picturing the severe, righteous face of the warrior he had named in his will as Miranda's guardian—the hardest, toughest man he knew, the fearless colonel of his regiment.

Damien Knight, the earl of Winterley. *Protect her.* . . .

Through the ethers, he sent out the desperate warning to his beloved brother in arms. He knew he had not erred in his choice. Damien Knight was a bloody war hero, for Christ's sake.

There had always been a mist of legend around the man—a mysterious glow of divine favor, as though he had been born for no other purpose than to fight for his king and to defend the weak, protect the innocent. Like some knight of olden times, he was as pure of spirit as he was ferocious in battle. Jason had entrusted Miranda to him because of the man's unassailable honor; he'd had no idea that Damien's terrifying, almost superhuman killing skills might be called upon in his role as her guardian.

As consciousness began drifting away from him, slowing the blood in his veins, he commended her to his friend; for himself, there was nothing more that he could do. He closed his eyes, knowing it was futile to fight the leaden coldness spreading through his limbs.

*"Jason?"* Algy's crisp voice sounded muffled now, as though coming to him from a growing distance or through some shimmering, watery veil.

*Beware of him, Knight. The only thing that can hurt you is a coward.* Then all thought dissolved in the peace settling over him. His fading eyes perceived an inward light of indescribable beauty. Powerless, weary, and wounded, he let it enfold him. In truth, death came as a relief to Jason Sherbrooke. The war had ruined him, disfigured him in body and soul, but now he felt no pain. He closed his eyes. *At last.*

He was going home.

# ❧ CHAPTER
ONE ❧

*Berkshire*

With a hard-eyed stare, Damien Knight, the earl of Winterley, swung the long-handled axe up over his head and slammed it down with savage force, cleanly splitting the upright log down the middle. The sharp crack of the blow ripped across the snow-frosted field like a gunshot, rousing the squabbling blackbirds that fed upon the frozen stubbled cornstalks. His movements were smooth, his mind blissfully blank as he threw down the axe, adjusted one of his thick leather gloves, and picked up the splintered halves of wood, stacking them on the fortresslike pile that had grown over the past weeks to looming proportions, as though no amount of fuel could build a fire capable of warming him. Positioning the next log on the tree stump that served as his chopping block, he dealt it, in turn, a death blow.

He repeated this ritual again and again, concentrating intensely on the task, allowing it to absorb his tattered mind, until suddenly, in the nearby field, he noticed that something had caught his stallion's attention.

His white warhorse was his only companion in this place. The stallion had been idly pawing through the frost, nibbling at whatever bits of grazing it could find, but now it lifted its head and pricked up its elegantly tapered ears toward the drive. Damien wiped the sweat off his brow with the back of his arm, rested his other hand on the axe's handle, and squinted against the white glare of the mid-December day, following his horse's stare.

The stallion let out a belligerent whinny and raced toward the fence, its ivory tail streaming out like a battle pennant. He watched the animal for a moment in simple pleasure. It must have been a month since Zeus had worn a saddle. Both of them were reverting back to a state of nature, he thought, scratching the short, rough, black beard that had grown in on his jaw. Without surprise, only a dim flicker of distress, he watched as his identical twin brother, Lord Lucien Knight, came cantering up the drive astride his fine black Andalusian.

Zeus raced alongside them on the opposite side of the fence, trumpeting challenges to the black for encroaching upon his territory. Fortunately, Lucien was too skilled a rider to lose control of his mount.

Damien dropped his chin almost to his chest and let out a sigh that misted on the crisp, cold air. He supposed his brother had come to check up on him.

He did not fancy the notion of anyone seeing him like this, but at least with his keenly perceptive twin, he did not have to pretend that he was right in the head.

Lucien and his bride of three weeks, Alice, were

living in Hampshire, a two-hour ride from Damien's ramshackle manor house, newly bestowed on him by Parliament along with his title. Not that he knew much about being an earl. His new rank seemed merely to have made him the servant of the bloody politicians. Picking up his last split logs and adding them to the woodpile, he cast an uncertain glance toward the run-down, overgrown mansion they had given him. Constructed of white-gray limestone, Bayley House, circa 1760, was modeled on a classical Greek temple with a triangular pediment atop four mighty columns. Damien thought it looked like a mausoleum.

It felt like one inside, too, sprawling hectares of empty floor bereft of furniture, cold enough to pre-serve a corpse. He half fancied the place was infested with ghosts, but he knew too well that it was only he who was haunted. He had neither the gold nor the en-ergy to see the house brought back to life and properly appointed, nor did he particularly care. Spartan that he was, he did not require luxury.

Upon arriving here in November shortly after Guy Fawkes Night, he had set up camp and had been bivouacking near the fireplace in what had once been the drawing room. His fellow officers from the regiment—what few survivors there were—had scat-tered and returned to their families, but at least he was still surrounded by his equipment, all sixty pounds of which he had carried on his back for hundreds of miles on marches through Portugal and Spain. It com-forted him: his trusty tent; his scuffed and battered tin mess kit and wooden canteen; his greatcoat for a blanket; his haversack for a pillow; a bit of cheese, biscuit, and sausage to sustain him; a few cigars. A soldier needed little else in life, except, of course, for liquor and whores, but Damien had given these up in an earnest effort to mend his fractured wits through the ascetic life.

'Sblood, though, he missed the lasses a hundred times more than the gin, he thought with a wistful sigh. Lucien could have his refined lady wife; Damien preferred low, bawdy wenches who knew how to handle a soldier. The mere thought of a soft, willing female roused his body's starved needs, but he ignored his agonized craving for release, coolly setting the axe out of the way as his brother approached. He could not risk anything that might upset his precarious equilibrium.

Snow flew up from under the black's prancing hoofs as Lucien reined in, vibrant and pink-cheeked with the cold, his silvery eyes sparkling with the aura of the newlywed. He sat back in the saddle for a moment, rested his right fist on his hip, and shook his head, looking Damien over in sardonic amusement. "Oh, my poor, dear brother," he said with a lordly chuckle.

"What?" Damien growled, scowling a bit.

"How charmingly rustic. You look like some hermit woodsman. Lancelot, maybe, after he became a monk."

Damien snorted. "So, she let you out from under the cat's paw for a few hours, eh? When's your curfew?"

"Only long enough for my sweet lady to remember afresh how desperately she adores me. When I return—" He flashed a wicked smile. "—the welcome home ought to be worth it." His luxurious black wool greatcoat whirled out behind him as he dismounted with an agile movement. Smart and elegant, full of Diplomatic Corps finesse, Lucien reached into his coat and presented Damien with a newspaper as he strode toward him. "I thought you might like to see what is going on in the world."

"Napoleon still under guard on Elba?"

"Of course."

"That's all I need to know."

"Well, burn it for fuel, then, though you certainly seem well supplied in that particular. Planning on burning a witch?" Lucien looked askance at the giant woodpile.

Damien regarded him wryly and accepted yesterday's copy of the *London Times* without further argument.

Lucien passed a shrewd glance over his face. "How goes it, brother?" he asked more softly.

Damien shrugged and turned away, abashed by his concern. "It's quiet here. I like it."

"And?" Lucien waited for him to report on his mental condition, but Damien dodged the unspoken inquiry, avoiding his twin's penetrating stare.

"Needs work, of course, this old place. Fences to be mended. We'll plant barley there"—he pointed to the fields—"oats there, wheat over there, in the spring." *If it ever comes*, he thought.

"God, grant me patience. Do not be deliberately obtuse, please. I didn't ask how your house is. I want to know how you're doing. Has there been any repeat of—"

"No," he cut him off, flashing him a warning look. He had no desire to be reminded of his hellish delirium—or bout of madness or whatever the devil it had been—on Guy Fawkes Night. He hated even thinking about it. The booming of the festival cannons and exploding fireworks had played a kind of trick on his mind, deluding him into thinking he was back at the war. For a full five or six minutes, he had lost track of reality, a horrifying state of affairs for a man so highly trained to kill.

When he thought of how easily he could have hurt someone, it made his blood run cold. He had exiled himself here since that night and did not intend to show his face in Society again until he had somehow cured himself, was no longer a threat to the very people he had sacrificed his innocence to protect, and had become once more the ironclad military hero the world expected him to be.

He noticed Lucien studying him, reading him in his all-too-knowing way, those silvery eyes flashing with formidable intelligence. "Still having nightmares?"

Damien just looked at him.

He did not want to admit it, but the ghastly dreams of blood and destruction were even more frequent now, as though his addled brain could not unburden itself of its poisons fast enough. The rage in him was a frozen river like the ice-encrusted Thames that wrapped around his property. He knew it was there, but the strangest thing was he could not quite . . . feel it. He could not feel much of anything. Six years of combat—of ignoring terror, horror, and heartbreak—had that effect on a man, he supposed.

"You really shouldn't be alone at a time like this," Lucien said gently.

"Yes, I should, and you know why." Avoiding his brother's scrutiny, he shoved some of the wood into a neater pile, then dusted a few stray bits of bark off his buff-leather trousers.

"At least you're still coming to London for Christmas with the family, I trust?"

He nodded firmly. "I'll be there." As long as the too-jolly prince regent could restrain himself from sponsoring another irritating fireworks show for the city, Damien saw little reason to worry. Christmas was a holy, tranquil night; it was New Year's Eve that tended to be raucous, accompanied by the usual rowdiness, noise, and explosives. He would return to his sanctuary at Bayley House by then. "Do you want something to drink?" he offered, belatedly remembering hospitality.

"No, thanks." Lucien slipped his hands into the pockets of his greatcoat and looked away, squinting toward the horizon. He seemed to hesitate. "There is . . . actually another reason I'm here, Damien. The truth is . . . ah, hell," he whispered, shutting his eyes. "I really don't know how to tell you this."

Damien looked over, taken aback by Lucien's stark tone. A prickle of dread ran down his spine as his gaze took in his brother's paling face and anguished stare. "Jesus, Lucien, what is it?" Abandoning the wood-pile, Damien walked over to him, drawing off his gloves. "What's happened? The family—"

"No, we're all fine," he said quickly, then lowered his head and spoke with difficulty. "I was in London on business earlier in the week when I heard. The news is all over Town. I'm so damned sorry, Damien." Steeling himself, he lifted his head and looked into his eyes. "Sherbrooke's dead. He was murdered Wednesday night."

"*What?*" He felt his stomach plummet with nauseating swiftness, but could only stare at his brother without comprehension.

"Apparently there was a robbery. The intruder shot him in the chest. I came as soon as I heard." Lucien gazed at him in distress. "I know—God, I know—you're in no condition to hear this, but I didn't want you to find out some other way."

Damien felt the air leave his lungs in a whoosh. "Are you sure?" he forced out.

Lucien gave a pained nod.

"Oh, God." He turned and walked a few paces away, then stopped, blank with shock. He dragged his hand through his hair and just stood there, at a loss, staring at the bleak horizon and the winter-bare trees of the orchard on the ridge, black and gnarled, and the cold glint of the frozen river. The sun had gone behind the clouds, and where there had been bright sparkles on the snow, now there was only a white, unforgiving glare.

There was a very long silence.

Behind him, he heard Lucien's black stallion snort and paw the ground in princely impatience. His brother murmured softly, quieting the animal, while Damien fought in silence to absorb the blow without falling to his knees in sheer despair. He had thought they were safe now. The war was over. How could he have forgotten that death, the ultimate victor, marched on?

He spun around abruptly, wrath darkening his face. "Do they know who did it?"

"No. Bow Street is still investigating. They suspect any number of known thieves in the area. I've taken the liberty of sending a few of my young associates to inquire into the matter."

"Thank you." He looked away, trembling, his face hard and expressionless, but even he was shocked by how quickly he adapted to the news. To be sure, this was an old routine by now, the death of a friend, he thought in deep, welling bitterness. There were courtesies to be carried out, rituals to be observed. He was the executor of Jason's will. There were duties to be fulfilled. He clung to them for his sanity's sake.

His men would need him, too, he thought. As their colonel, it fell to him to set the example of conduct, discipline, manly self-control. They still depended on him, as they had on the battlefield, to stand firm against the chaos and disequilibrium they all felt. Half a decade of their lives had passed in a roaring, blood-spattered flash of horror, and suddenly, here they were, dazed to find themselves in tranquil old England again, blooded savages thrown back into Society, where they must be gentlemen again. *By God, I have been selfish,* he thought, closing his eyes and damning himself for leaving them, coming out here to lick his wounds. If he had stayed in London, if he had looked after Sherbrooke better . . . *I should have been there.*

He bowed his head, agonized by the thought. Clearly, he had tarried in solitude long enough.

When he lifted his head again, his eyes were as cold and gray as stone, and when he spoke, his voice was the controlled, deadened monotone of a seasoned commander. "I will be needed in London for the burial, I presume. He was not close to his family."

Lucien passed an uneasy glance over his face, trying to read him. "There's something else." He reached into his waistcoat and took out a folded piece of paper, handing it to him. "Sherbrooke's solicitor has already tried to contact you. I told him I would deliver this. It seems Jason named you not only executor of his will, but guardian of his ward."

"Damn, I had forgotten," he murmured, taking the letter. He cracked the seal and unfolded it with a private shudder to recall the conversation after the Battle of Albuera when Sherbrooke, half dead from saber wounds, his right arm gone, had begged him to accept the guardianship of his little orphaned niece if he didn't survive. Damien had assured him that, of course, he would.

With a wave of loss that he quickly tamped down, he remembered how Sherbrooke used to buy souvenirs for the little girl, sending bits of Spanish lace and beads back to England for her from every town they conquered. Gaudy, colorful scarves, little dolls, satin slippers.

*What the devil was her name again?* He skimmed the solicitor's letter. *Yardley School, Warwickshire . . .*

He had never seen the child, but he knew she was the bastard daughter of Sherbrooke's deceased eldest brother, Viscount Hubert, by his mistress, who had been some sort of actress. Before Albuera, Sherbrooke had spoken often of the lively child, reading her earnest, little-girl letters aloud, to the hilarity of the officers at the mess, but after being maimed, he seemed to forget all about her, withdrawing into himself, drinking ever more heavily.

*Ah, yes,* he thought, scanning down the page. That was it.

Miranda.

Just like the girl in Shakespeare's *The Tempest.* A deuced fanciful name for an English schoolgirl, he thought with a stern frown. No doubt it was the actress's doing. He supposed the chit was fourteen or fifteen by now—or had she passed that age years ago? he wondered with a sudden flicker of uneasiness. He brushed it aside. Folding the solicitor's letter, he tucked it into his breast pocket.

Duty had a galvanizing effect on him. For a man of action, he had felt cut adrift since his regiment had been dissolved at the close of the war. He rolled up his emotions and tucked them away as quickly as a piquet could pull up camp and march. For the first time in weeks, he had some direction. After all, his demons could not haunt him when his mind was fixed on helping other people—his men, his new ward. He would hurry to London, arrange the memorial service for Jason, and steady his men after this difficult blow. With Lucien's background in espionage for the Foreign Office, the two of them would help Bow Street however they could in the effort to find the person who had done this; then Damien would ride to Warwickshire to break the news in person to the girl about her uncle's death.

*Damn,* he thought bleakly. That would be the hardest part. He would rather rush a fortified line of French earthworks than face a female's tears, no matter her age, but it had to be done.

He looked hollowly at Lucien, the silver-tongued, multilingual diplomat-spy. "How do you tell a little girl who watched her parents drown that the only person left in the world who loved her is dead?"

Lucien winced and shook his head. "Gently, my friend. Very, very gently."

"Jesus," Damien whispered, then looked away and let out a sharp curse under his breath. For Sherbrooke's sake, he vowed to give the girl the best of everything, even if it meant foregoing the purchase of the broodmares with which he had planned on starting his racing stock in the spring—his dream, such as it was.

Above all, he would find out who had done this.

"I'll go with you to London if you wish," Lucien offered, watching him closely.

"Thanks," he muttered, scratching his scruffy jaw with a barren sigh. "I've got to shave."

Ready or not, it was time to face the world.

*Warwickshire, a week later*

"The food is hideous. I hate Mistress Brocklehurst. I was never meant to be worked like a galley slave. I wish I was *dead*!"

"Oh, Amy, quit whining. I did three times more work than you today, and you don't see me moping." This tart reply issued from within the hollow of the unlit fireplace, echoing slightly, but only the speaker's drab, purple school uniform was visible, streaked with ashes, above a pair of prettily turned calves in black worsted stockings and battered half boots.

"But you have to do the most," Amy said, her blond curls drooping like the feather duster in her hand. "You're the eldest. And the strongest."

"And *you're* the laziest," Miranda FitzHubert retorted as she crawled backward out of the hearth with a smudge of soot on her nose. She stood, winced, gave her aching back a stretch, then elbowed the pouting twelve-year-old aside as she marched over to rinse her cleaning rag in the bucket of blackened water. "Hurry up, you lot!" she ordered the other dull, spiritless girls. "I've got to be out of here by five, and nobody had better make me late." It was the one, precious, magical night a month that made her existence bearable.

"Yes, Miranda," the others murmured at their tasks around the cold, drafty schoolroom.

The main body of the school's thirty pupils had left for the holiday break, but the four girls presently scrubbing the schoolroom—Miranda, Amy, Sally, and Jane—had no families to go home to and so had to spend their dismal Christmases at Yardley. They were a company of outcasts—by-blows, orphans, poor relations—forgotten and unloved. To pay for their keep between sessions, the headmistress, Brocklehurst, had put them to work with tasks that would have caused a scullery maid to shudder.

"What do you suppose the others are doing right now?" Sally mused aloud as she carefully wiped the baseboards.

"Oh," Jane sighed, standing on a chair to polish the

wall sconces, "I'll bet they're baking pies with their mothers or shopping for presents for their papas."

"Who cares what they're doing? I don't see why you all are so gloomy. It's a lot more peaceful around here without them," Miranda muttered, then attacked the caked-on dirt coating the brass fireplace grill.

Meanwhile, the clock on the mantel above her went on ticking relentlessly. She lifted her soot-smudged face and glanced at it. A quarter to five! God's knuckles, she would never make it in time! The curtain rose at six.

Mentally rehearsing her lines for the umpteenth time, she redoubled her efforts, vehemently scrubbing the brass gridiron until she could make out the reflection of her own green eyes blazing with determination in it.

She hurried the others along until, at last, they finished cleaning the schoolroom from top to bottom, put away their brooms and brushes. Miranda hushed Amy's chattering as the girls tiptoed past the headmistress's parlor, where Brocklehurst and Mr. Reed, the cheese-paring clergyman who had founded Yardley School for Girls, were having tea with the nasty old ladies from the Altar Guild.

The girls climbed the stairs to their cold, bare dormitory on the topmost floor of the old converted farmhouse. Moonlight striped the darkened room from the long row of windows on the wall. Striding down the long line of cots to the smoldering hearth at the far end of the dreary room, Miranda's step was light in anticipation of her long-awaited adventure.

She glanced out through the frosted pane and saw yesterday's snow still thinly covering the surrounding fields. Though it was scarcely past five o'clock, full darkness had fallen.

"How can ye have any energy at all, Miranda?" Jane asked wearily, falling onto her cot. "You worked like a dog."

"I'm too excited to be tired—and too nervous," she confessed. As the other girls lay inert on their cots or shut the curtains and began undressing with slow, weary movements, Miranda hurried to the crackling fire and pulled the cauldron out carefully on its metal crane. She ladled a washbasin full of the steaming water, then lit a few rushlights in the dark room.

They glowed like orange fireflies as she set them around her to light her task, her jittery anticipation growing by the minute. *Will there be many people in the audience tonight?* She hoped the playhouse was full to the rafters and bursting at the seams. The soldiers from the nearby barracks always loved her. Sometimes the travelers from the coaching inn came for the entertainments, as well. Maybe some fashionable Londoners would even be there. Maybe they would think she was even good enough for Drury Lane! she thought. Well, almost.

Soap in hand, she scrubbed her face, throat, and hands, scouring the dirt out from underneath her nails, dabbing the moist washcloth over her long, dark, wavy hair to get the soot out of it. The girls watched her in dull-eyed interest as they waited for Mrs. Warren, the cook, to bring up their tea and one slice of stale bread each.

Amy sidled up to her with a petulant look. "I want to come with you!"

"Absolutely not."

"Why?"

"They don't let children in."

"But I want to hear you sing in the burletta. I want to see you dance in the ballet!"

"Too bad," Miranda replied briskly as she plopped down onto the nearest cot and took off her sorry black boots and peeled off her smelly black worsted stockings. She put the washbasin on the floor and stepped into it with a giant sigh of pleasure; then she sank down on the edge of the bed again, savoring the luxury of letting her feet soak for a few minutes. She would be on them for the next six or seven hours, after all, mostly dancing.

"You're so lucky. It's not fair. I want to be an actress, too! You're going to run away with Mr. Chipping's acting troupe, and I shall die!"

"I wouldn't do that to you, Amy."

"Really?" The child sat down beside her and put her arm around her, leaning on her shoulder like the most devoted little sister, though her eyes sparkled with mischief.

Miranda cast her a wry smile. "If I ran off, how would my Uncle Jason know where to find me when he comes to fetch me?" *If he ever comes,* she thought, but did not utter the dismal words aloud.

"*Please* can I put on some of your rouge?"

"No."

"Why not?"

"Amy, you're twelve."

"Rouge is wicked," Sally announced, pushing herself up to a seated position from where she had sprawled on her cot.

Amy grinned at her. "Of course it is. That's why Miranda likes it. Miranda, when you're a rich and famous London actress, will you come and fetch me out of Yardley?"

Her long, dark hair slipped forward over Miranda's shoulders as she bent down to wash her soaking feet. "If you promise not to whine every day."

"I won't have anything to whine about!" Amy hopped up to sit on the heavy table by the wall, swinging her crossed heels prettily. "Just parties and balls and fine frocks and a hundred boys to swear they love me."

Miranda looked at her dubiously and lifted her feet out of the basin. She was hurriedly drying her feet and legs when all of a sudden, a bloodcurdling scream shot up through the floor. All the girls froze and looked around at one other, wide-eyed.

Amy jumped down off the table and began hopping about in panic. "Oh, no! Oh, no!"

Miranda whirled to her. "What have you done now?"

"Nothing! It wasn't me!"

"Amy!"

"FitzHu*berrrrt!*" Brocklehurst's roar zoomed up the stairs, followed in the next instant by marching footsteps that the girls knew all too well and feared like the advance of a Roman legion.

Miranda glanced in distress at the closed door of

the dormitory, then at the child. Amy's round face was pale and she was backing away from the door.

"Amy, what happened?"

"It was an accident!"

"Oh, blast, Amy. What did you break now?"

Amy's huge blue eyes filled with tears. "Her stupid Wedgwood doggy!"

Every girl in the room gasped with dread.

"Oh, *no,*" Miranda whispered, her heart sinking.

Brocklehurst's tirades tended to be lengthy. This could interfere with her slipping away tonight to reach the Pavilion Theatre in time. If she didn't leave in fifteen minutes, she would miss the curtain call. Mr. Chipping had given her the starring role as the heroine in tonight's burletta, *The Venetian Outlaw*. If she failed him, he might never give her such a large part again. He already thought all actresses were irresponsible. She didn't want to prove him right.

"Amy, you have to own up—"

"But Mr. Reed will flog me! Please, Miranda, I didn't mean to do it! I was only dusting it while you went to get another pail of water. It fell off the mantel."

"And you simply put it back?" she exclaimed.

"It didn't shatter—there were only four or five big pieces. I rested them back together and leaned it against the mirror."

"You were too busy primping at your own reflection, I warrant!" she said angrily.

"No, I wasn't, I swear! I didn't think anyone would notice it was broken! Or I thought maybe Brocklehurst would think she had broken it herself the next

time she went to pick it up! Please, Miranda, you have
to help me! She's going to kill me!" the child shrieked.
"Please!"

"Damn and blast!" Miranda cursed under her
breath, whirling around as the door slammed back on
its hinges. Her body tensed, well used to this fight.

Miss Brocklehurst towered in the doorway. The
candle in her hand illuminated the severe angles
of her mannish face, further harshened by wrath.
"*Fitz*Hubert."

The woman always emphasized the *Fitz* in her last
name as though to remind Miranda deliberately of her
illegitimate status, but she refused to be ashamed of
the lovely, flamboyant creature who had been her ill-
fated mama.

In her other hand, Brocklehurst suddenly held up
the decapitated head of her Wedgwood china doggy.
"You bad, cruel, horrid girl! I know full well you hate
me, but this—this is beyond the pale!"

Miranda summoned forth her acting skills and
forced her chin downward. She clasped her hands behind her back, the picture of contrition. "I apologize,
ma'am. It was an accident."

"'I apologize, ma'am. It was an accident,'" she
mimicked spitefully. "Do you think I shall let you off
so easily?" Bristling, Miss Brocklehurst prowled into
the room. She set her candle on the nearby table.
"Bad, proud, intractable girl! I have tried—oh, how
I've tried—to make something of you, but you will
never amount to anything."

Miranda's chin came up a notch. Her green eyes
narrowed with blazing defiance. *Oh, yes I will.* Bad,

proud, intractable—maybe that much was true. But she *would* amount to something. They'd see. She knew exactly what she wanted to be; she had dreams they could never crush. Dreams that would take her far, far away from here.

"Don't you dare glare at me, girl," Brocklehurst warned, but Miranda was too angry to obey, staring at her in simmering rebellion.

*Crack!*

The blow took her off guard. Miranda's head snapped to the side with the force of the headmistress's slap. Amy stifled a scream, clapping both of her hands over her mouth.

Recovering from the blow, Miranda insolently turned the other cheek, like a true Christian.

The headmistress glowered at her for it, but did not strike her again. "You insufferable baggage. You shall have no supper tonight, nor tomorrow night, nor the night after that. I'll starve you into submission, if need be! And you will be on slops duty—for a fortnight!"

*Ugh, not the chamber pots.* Miranda grimaced and looked away in revulsion.

"Miss Brocklehurst, if I may, do allow me to intervene," a nasally male voice intoned from the doorway.

Miranda instantly stiffened. Paling, she looked over as the Reverend Mr. Reed sauntered into the dormitory in all his pompous indecency, no doubt happy for an excuse to glimpse the girls wearing nothing but their shifts.

Jane grabbed her frock with a gasp, and Sally dove beneath the bedsheets in horrified modesty as his gaze flicked over them. Then, lingeringly, he eyed little Amy.

Miranda felt her blood run cold. "I said it was an accident," she forced out, drawing the pervert's attention to herself.

His gaze darted to her in warning. "What is this impertinence, FitzHubert? Do not speak unless you are spoken to."

She held his gaze in loathing. For all of Miss Brocklehurst's spite and bullying, far worse was Mr. Reed's inability to keep his hands to himself. And when it came to discipline, wielding the birch was his favorite pastime. It had been weeks since he'd had the opportunity to flog anyone. Miranda gulped silently, fearful that he was eager to keep his hand in play.

"This act of subterfuge indicates a serious lack of moral development," he remarked, stalking slowly toward her, his pale, long-fingered hands dangling at his sides. He had thinning hair, a bony beak of a nose, and shifty eyes. Tall and spare, he stood with a slight stoop that added to his air of furtiveness. "Are you proud of this act of destruction, FitzHubert?"

"Pride is her natural manner," Brocklehurst said in contempt.

"Mm, yes, vanity. Are you vain because men think you beautiful, Miss?" His stare raked her body and her face. "Do you forget that pride is first among the mortal sins, the very sin that toppled the angels?"

"I have tried for years to remove that stain from her character," Brocklehurst chimed in, nodding.

"As have I, ma'am, as have I. Alas, I see we both have failed," he said, staring at Miranda for a moment in lecherous malice. "In addition to what Miss Brocklehurst has indicated, you will come to my office tomorrow following the eleven o'clock service and take your punishment from my hand . . . privately."

Miranda flinched down into the core of her soul and closed her eyes, dropping her chin slightly, but she knew better than to argue with him. That would only make it worse. *It doesn't matter,* she told herself fiercely. She had lived through the humiliation and pain of a flogging before. Amy had been saved again. That was all that mattered—that, and tonight's performance. She could get through it tomorrow if only she could have her dream tonight.

When she heard Amy sobbing a few feet away, she feared the guilty child would confess. She shot the girl a sharp look askance. *Hold your tongue.*

In that moment, more than she despised Brocklehurst, even more than she detested Mr. Reed, she cursed Uncle Jason for abandoning her here and going off to war, forgetting about her. She despised him for it.

*Patriotism, bah!* she thought bitterly. He had gone for the adventure and had long since forgotten she existed. He had left her, his bastard niece, dangling here between two worlds—neither aristocratic, like her father, nor fallen, like Mama. He barely even remembered to pay her tuition anymore, as Brocklehurst frequently reminded her. She was little better than a charity girl, and that was even more humiliating than having to submit to the birch. Closing her eyes, she fought the feeling of it all crushing her. Only by remembering the last time she was onstage could she even breathe.

She struggled to remember the faces of the people who had watched her in delight and admiration and had listened to her singing with charmed looks. She knew of course that the rollicking entertainments and gaudy spectacles at the Pavilion hardly ranked as legitimate theater; Mama would have lifted her nose at the place with a diva's disdain. The amphitheater served another audience entirely—not lords and ladies, but the working people of Birmingham's factories, potteries, breweries, and mills, those who dug its canals, and the nearby garrison of soldiers. Miranda didn't care. Even if it was only a third-rate circuit theater, when the limelights gleamed and the applause rushed over her, she was someone else up there, someone beautiful and carefree, who made everybody happy, like her mother had. She made people laugh and forget their woes, and when they applauded and cheered and even threw flowers, for a fleeting instant, she was someone who was loved.

It was the closest she would ever come to recapturing those halcyon days in her father's glittering world of wealth and privilege, when she had been a little girl and would sing and dance to entertain her doting, wonderful parents. Life had been safe and warm then, full of Father's manly elegance and Mother's butterfly joie de vivre. How they had loved each other! If only they had been married, she thought in misery. If only tonight she could run away with the circuit company and never, ever come back to Yardley to be abused and beaten and called all manner of hurtful things.

But she knew what would happen to Amy if she left.

She had seen the way Mr. Reed watched the pretty child when he thought no one was looking. Miranda had made it her mission to see that he kept his distance, because she was the only person at Yardley School who dared defy him. Even if Reed and Brocklehurst ground out her spirit one particle at a time, she refused to abandon that vexing little girl the way she had been abandoned.

Having handed down her sentence, Mr. Reed and Miss Brocklehurst marched out in haughty procession. When the door had shut and the girls were alone once more, there was a terrible, hollow silence.

The only sound was Amy's soft, mournful crying, until Miranda's stomach grumbled indignantly, at which noise, Amy cried harder. "You can have my supper, Miranda. It's all my fault—"

"Oh, shut up, Amy. It doesn't matter. The food is wretched anyway." Miranda put her head down and quickly turned away to hide the tears smarting in her eyes. She lowered herself to her knees beside her cot and reached under the straw pallet, carefully pulling out her costume. She held it up and gazed at it in reverent silence. It made her heart ache, it was so beautiful, spun from ethereal gossamer muslin in the most delicate shade of pale lavender, embroidered with silver spangles.

The other girls gathered around, staring at the costume in wordless awe, as though it were a mysterious artifact from another world. It was a gown for a fairy princess, a changeling child caught between the mortal world and the fey one, belonging fully in neither. Miranda shrugged off the haunting thought. Having washed up prior to her sentencing, she sat on her cot and quickly donned the flesh-colored tights that all the dancers and actresses wore beneath their costumes, then lifted off her workaday purple dress, rinsed the rest of her body with a washcloth, shivering in the cold, and slipped into the sleeveless muslin dress. At once, she felt herself transformed.

Hurrying to the mirror, she tied her thick, wavy hair back with the matching lavender bandeau. The other girls looked on in growing wonder all the while. She dabbed a drop of rouge on her cheeks and rubbed it into her lips, then looked around for her slippers. She slid the sequined, satin dancing slippers out from under her cot, but pulled her worn, clunky half boots back on, for she still had a long trek through the snow to reach the Pavilion.

Amy looked at her morosely as Miranda donned her mantle over the skimpy lavender gown. Miranda gave her fellow orphan a brilliant smile that she hoped looked fearless. Amy smiled wanly and opened the window for her. Jane stood on a chair and looped the rope that Miranda had stolen to serve as her escape ladder around one of the exposed rafters.

Peering out the window, she assessed her escape briefly before climbing up onto the sill and grasping the rope. In short order, she shimmied down the side of the building, holding on to the line like one of Admiral Lord Nelson's ablest seamen. The light snow crunched under her boots as she plunked down onto the ground.

She signaled for the girls to draw the rope back in; then Amy tossed down her dancing slippers one at a time. The child waved woefully, her golden curls drooping.

"Don't forget to go down and unlock the kitchen door after everyone's asleep!" Miranda called to her in a whisper.

Amy nodded and waved. "Break a leg!"

Miranda blew her a kiss; picked up her slippers, one in each hand; and ran. The winter moon shone on the snow-frosted roof of Yardley School, which sat on Coventry Road about three miles outside of Birmingham, in sight of the River Cole and the Warwick Canal. It was a large, old, rectangular farmhouse of gray stone, with white-painted shutters and a slate roof. The school and all its miseries receded into the darkness behind her as Miranda raced away through the fields north of the village.

The clear December evening was so still it seemed to be holding its breath. The cold was sharp, but the silver gleam of moon and stars glittered magically on the snow in every direction as far as the eye could see. The only sound was her panting and her footfalls as she ran. Her misting breath streamed out behind her like a bridal veil.

She saw a band of deer pawing through the snow for forage. A startled hare darted across her path. At last, she came to a silent country road and turned left. A few minutes later, she skittered nervously across the bridge over the River Cole. She hated going over bridges. Having watched her parents drown, she wanted nothing to do with any body of water anywhere on earth. On the other side of the bridge, at Bordesley Green, her adventure took on its usual element of danger. The vagrants' bonfires were burning, out there on the distant green. She summoned forth a burst of speed and sprinted as fast as she could, skirting the large, dark, open expanse. They called it Mud City.

It was the blight of Birmingham—a growing squatters' village inhabited by criminals, beggars, pickpockets, thieves, and low, skulking rascals of every stripe. They had set up camp on the green and were so insolent that they had frightened the mayor and the town elders into letting them stay, lest they riot. The nearby garrison of soldiers had been stationed there to make sure the filthy creatures kept the peace. Miranda knew it was reckless of her to pass on the outskirts of their territory, but she was almost late and it was the quickest way to the Pavilion. She was freezing in her skimpy costume. Besides, she was not easily intimidated by anyone.

As she came away from the dark, open space of the green and approached the Pavilion, she saw the gaslights shining inside. Her heart leaped with rising excitement. Outside the theater, people were milling about everywhere, queued up to buy their entrance tokens, mostly men finishing their cigars before going in to find a seat. She raced up to the building, attracting numerous stares and half a dozen indecent propositions, but she ignored them and took no offense, for she knew full well how most of the girls in this business made extra money.

She pounded up the wooden steps of the back entrance, her heart racing with excitement. This night was special somehow. She could feel it.

Marching through the back hallway, she flung into the dressing room with a beaming smile.

"Miss White!" the players greeted her, using her stage name. She dared not use her real name, for her Uncle Jason would throttle her if he ever found out about this.

"You're late! We were beginning to worry!" the clown said anxiously.

"Oh, I'd never fail you, my dears," she chided gaily, giving his red, waxen nose a honk. Then she shrugged off her rough, woolen cloak.

"Hullo, beautiful," Stefano, the leading man, murmured, sauntering over to her with a suave smile.

Miranda dismissed his flirtatious look with a laugh and pulled off her snow-caked boots just as Mr. Chipping came bustling into the greenroom, hectic as a wind eddy. The lively little bald man was the manager of the circuit company, which traveled continuously between Birmingham, Coventry, Leicester, and Nottingham.

Mr. Chipping had often averred that her status as daughter of the late, internationally famed Fanny Blair would rocket Miranda to stardom, if she pursued it. He had already offered her the coveted position of juvenile lead, so that one day she might ascend to leading lady, just like her mother had been for a short time at London's Lyceum Theatre in the Strand, where Papa had first laid eyes on her. He lit up when he saw Miranda.

"Ah, there she is! My darling, my precious babe, my little gem! Not a moment too soon. You're on in ten minutes."

"I can hardly wait!" She threw her arms around the little man and hugged him with irrepressible spontaneity. A bit taller than he, she planted a playful kiss on his shiny pate. "I adore you, Mr. Chipping! I'm so happy. Thank you for this chance."

He chuckled, his eyes twinkling with affection. "You're welcome, my dear. I know you won't disappoint me." He turned to his actors. "Many people have a difficult time of it around the holidays. Let's give them our best." He squeezed Miranda around her waist, startling her out of her momentary brooding on the fact that nobody could possibly hate Christmas more than she did. It was the single most painful day of the entire year. "Are you ready, lass?" he asked in a jaunty tone.

She tossed her long locks over her shoulders with dramatic flair and turned on her most brilliant smile. "Always!"

# ⇥ CHAPTER ⇥
# TWO

Damien cantered his white horse up the sweeping, moonlit road from Stratford, arriving at Birmingham at around seven o'clock in the evening. He slowed the stallion to a trot as they entered Bradford Street and inspected the burgeoning town curiously as he rode through it.

Back in London, the memorial service for Jason had gone smoothly, but Damien had soon begun climbing the walls in his impatience for Bow Street to make an arrest. So far, they did not even have any firm leads. Lucien had finally persuaded him to leave the investigation to the authorities and to go break the news to his ward—the one thing Damien most dreaded. Still, even facing the little orphaned girl's tears was better than waiting around for something to happen.

Presently, he rode up to the impressive Royal Hotel in Temple Row and took lodgings for the night. The landlord turned awestruck when he read Damien's signature on the guest register and realized who he was. He gave him the best room in the inn and insisted that he stay gratis, but Damien declined, paying like any other customer. The kitchens sent up a grand dinner, which he ate alone in his rooms.

After bolting down his food as speedily as a starved wolf, he got up and drifted to the window, gazing out at the lights of the town and the dark countryside beyond. The glass panes mirrored his ghostly, hollow-eyed reflection back to him. He glanced longingly over his shoulder at the bed. He was so bored of his own company and, God help him, so starved for sex.

Now that he had ventured out into the world again, he could scarcely believe it had been six weeks since he'd had a woman. The hotel had a rule against bringing in whores, but hell, he was Colonel Lord Winterley, he thought cynically. The staff would surely turn a blind eye if the war hero wanted a lass to warm his bed on this cold winter's night.

*No,* he thought stoically after a moment. *Discipline.* No women. No hard liquor. Discipline was everything. Pushing away from the window, he paced restlessly in his room. He could not give in to temptation. As much as he ached for someone to touch him, he could not risk unleashing his emotions, could not let go of his rigid self-control. The problem was he could no longer trust himself, his own reactions. He would never purposely harm a woman, but what if he went mad again and lashed out without meaning to? After what had happened on Guy Fawkes Night, he dared not trifle with anything that had the potential to awaken the beast inside of him. The wild release of passion might prove just the sort of dangerous catalyst that he would be wiser to avoid.

Standing near the foot of the bed, he rested his

hands on his hips with a huge sigh. The night was still early, but perhaps he need not shut himself off entirely, he thought. It had been good to see his fellow officers at Jason's memorial service. He knew that his good friend, Lieutenant Colonel George Morris, was stationed in Birmingham. He decided to pay him a visit. There could be no harm in that. He quickly doffed his dusty traveling clothes and dressed in his uniform, deliberately leaving his dress sword and pistol behind. Though he felt rather naked going out at night in a strange city without his weapons, the world would be safer if he did not bring them. His mood improving at the thought of seeing old Georgie again, he jogged down the stairs and asked the concierge for directions to the local barracks, then set out on foot, heading east through the city.

As instructed, he made his way to Cole's Hill and down Belmont Row. 'Sblood, he seemed to pass a wench on every street corner, he thought, each one prettier than the last, murmuring soft invitations to him as he marched by, trying to lure him off the straight and narrow. He kept his stare ahead in staunch resolution. Turning right onto Duddeston Street, he saw the barracks and breathed a sigh of relief to have escaped the sirens' calls.

When he went in, the junior officers on duty greeted him joyously and made much of him. His cheeks flushed at their praise. Gruffly he asked for Morris.

"He's gone down to the Pavilion to watch the show," the subaltern said.

"The Pavilion?" Damien asked.

"An amphitheater down the road. The circuit company comes in once a month. Only blasted thing there is to do around here."

"Aye, but they've got the prettiest dancing girls in the county," the other sergeant added with a grin.

Damien stared at him. He swallowed hard. "Dancing girls?"

"Aye, Colonel. I can send a lad down there to fetch Colonel Morris for you."

"No, I, ah, think I'll go look for him myself," Damien said gingerly, already heading for the door. "Got nothing else to do."

"Enjoy, my lord!" they called after him, laughing, winking at each other knowingly.

A few minutes later, Damien bought his painted wooden token at the door and walked into the bright, noisy, chaotic Pavilion Theater, blinking against the light from the three large chandeliers that burned brightly above. Underfoot, a layer of straw had been thrown down to soak up the mud and melting snow from the audience's shoes. It rustled under Damien's boots as he stalked into the mobbed theater. At Bayley House, he had grown unaccustomed to so much color and clamor. It put him on edge.

He stood in the aisle with his back to the stage, scanning the double-tiered horseshoe of seats for his friend. He had hoped to pick Morris out easily by his uniform, but a full third of the audience were soldiers in red coats. With a distracted frown, he searched the sea of faces, brushing off an ale seller, quite indifferent to the exploits of the cape-and-dagger hero in the

Gothic musical playing out on stage. Indifferent, that was, until he heard the voice.

*Her* voice.

No shrill soprano, the woman's voice was a sensuous alto that brimmed with velvet warmth. Its rich, smoky timbre captured his senses and made him go still. From his vantage point, he saw the calming effect it had on the mob, as well. Intrigued, he turned around, saw the singer, and dropped his jaw.

His mouth watered; his eyes glazed over; his gaze swept the young beauty's tall, statuesque form. *Damn,* he thought, she was all . . . luscious curves. He had a vague impression of luxuriant, chocolate-brown hair cascading down her back, but was so enthralled with her skimpy costume, abundant breasts, and robust hips that it was at least two or three full minutes before his lustful stare traveled up to her face.

He felt his heart skip a beat. *Good God.* Heart-stoppingly lovely, she was, an angel's face to match that golden voice. Roses on snow, he thought. Ruby lips, creamy skin, sparkling emerald eyes. The bold beauty appeared to be in her early twenties. He scrambled to borrow a program from the fellow next to him and found the name of the actress playing the heroine in *The Venetian Outlaw.* Staring at her, he handed the broadsheet back to the man.

*Miss White.* But not pure, he fervently hoped.

That wasn't her real name, of course. They never used their real names, as he knew from his wide experience with women of her breed. He eased down dazedly on the nearest seat and watched her for the next two hours, mesmerized.

Whatever ailed him, he forgot it. She was a joy to watch, playing her part with good cheer, lusty confidence, and tart wit. With a provocative switch of her hips, she could make the entire male half of the audience roar with devotion. Damien shook his head in private amusement, but when she smiled, she dazzled him. He scowled when her silly musical was over, for the stage was a barren wasteland without her on it. He sank down, sprawling in his chair, and rocked his knee impatiently, waiting for her to come back. He bought a mug of ale and haughtily regarded the acrobats twirling this way and that. He saw no point in their gyrations, but their act gave him time to think. By the time they cleared the stage, he had made up his mind.

He had to have her. Devil take his vow. He was only a man. One of his closest friends had just died. Was that not a more-than-adequate excuse to seek comfort from a lady of the night? He would keep the liaison as brief as possible, leave the candles burning throughout his chamber—hell, he'd give her a gun if that was what it took to protect her from himself—but if he did not have her, he would die.

In his mind, it was already arranged. He'd call on his ward at Yardley School in the morning and visit Morris at the barracks tomorrow afternoon. Tonight, his sole mission was to coax that luscious creature back to his hotel and straight into his bed.

The competition was sure to be fierce. She would no doubt have many admirers, but he was prepared to pay more than he could spare and even to try out his new title if that's what it took to impress her.

She appeared next in the series of dances that ended the night's entertainments, the grand finale. There were a dozen girls dancing on stage, but he could not take his eyes off the dark-haired beauty. He sat, entranced, caught up in growing desire and anticipation. Biding his time until he could learn every curve of her face and body with his hands and his lips, he studied the lass from a distance. Her rosy cheeks had a youthful roundness that added to her air of charming exuberance. She had a strong chin and dark, highly defined eyebrows that stood out sharply against her creamy complexion, giving her face an expression of saucy willfulness. Aye, she had a bit of the devil in her, and there was nothing he liked better than a naughty girl in his bed.

Having lost all track of time, he was sorely disappointed when the ballet ended and the dancing girls flitted lightly off the stage, returning with the rest of the evening's cast to take their bows. Somehow Miss White became even more lavishly beautiful when the crowd applauded. She held out her hands gracefully, then curtsied as though to the queen. When she lifted her head again coming back up, her gaze traveled slowly, savoringly, over the audience.

Damien stared at the tears shining in her eyes, all at odds with her radiant smile. Tears, he realized, of gratitude. *You live for this moment, don't you, beauty?* She seemed to absorb the audience's outpouring of warmth and affection like a rose drinking in the summer sunbeams. As he sat there, very still, his chin resting on his fist, a part of his heart he had long presumed dead went out to her, he knew not why.

There was such sincerity in her face. He was trying to figure out the best way to approach her when her survey of the crowd suddenly came to him—and stopped. From halfway across the lighted theater, their stares connected with a force that nearly flattened him.

Damien couldn't move. His heart hammered. He could barely breathe, powerless under the spell of her emerald eyes.

She suddenly tore her gaze away, a bright blush rising in her cheeks. If his stare had flustered her, she recovered quickly, blowing the crowd one last merry kiss before striding off the stage with impetuous haste.

The curtain closed and the chase was on.

He was already on his feet, stalking down the aisle against the flow of the exiting crowd. He couldn't recall the last time he had bedded a girl who could still blush.

People jumped out of his path when they saw him coming, his fierce, single-minded stare fixed on the stage door as though it were a Spanish fortress town that he would take or die trying. When he noticed the men continually being turned away from the backstage area, a slight, predatory smile curved his mouth.

Perhaps they were content to take no for an answer, but he would not be denied his conquest. He left the crowd clamoring at the main door and went in search of another entrance.

Weary but exhilarated after the six-hour program, Miranda accepted the three shillings that were her night's pay, said her good-byes to Mr. Chipping and his players, and left the dressing room eating the last few bites of a sausage tucked into a split roll. She was starved after her night's exertions, having been denied her supper as part of Brocklehurst's punishments. Big Dale, the company's "heavy" or villain—who was actually a tender-hearted giant of a man—had let her take his little wine flask filled with good burgundy to wash down her sandwich and to warm her belly for the cold walk home.

Bundled up once again in her rough woolen mantle and battered black half boots, she walked down the cramped hallway to the back door of the theater to avoid the mob of men, mostly soldiers, demanding, as soldiers were wont to do, to be introduced to the girls. Though she still felt buoyed up with exhilaration after the show, the prospect of the long walk home made her sigh wearily, for her legs already felt like jelly from the strenuous demands of the ballet. There were any number of rogues clamoring to get backstage who would have gladly driven her home, but she could not risk anyone making the connection between Miss White of the Pavilion Theater and Miranda Fitz-Hubert of Yardley School.

A pang of dread darted through her to recall her appointment tomorrow with Mr. Reed and his birch, but she refused to let anxiety quash the warm glow of triumph she felt from the audience's generous applause.

*They adored me,* she thought happily, taking a large bite of her sandwich. She pushed open the heavy door with her hip and stepped out into the cold winter night. Stray snowflakes swirled around the wall-fixed lantern like moths. As she started walking down the theater's wooden back stairs, she suddenly stopped chewing and froze.

It was *him*.

The big, strikingly handsome officer who had been staring at her so intensely from the audience. He was standing at the bottom of the stairs, leaning against the post in an idle stance, one gleaming black boot resting on a low step. With his greatcoat draped over his arm, he drummed his fingers restlessly on the crude wooden banister; he looked up and saw her, and his fingers' drumming stopped.

Their stares locked. Again, as on stage, her body reacted with hot and cold waves of brazen thrill that rushed down her nerve endings and made her belly flutter. On stage, she had blushed all the way down to her feet, fascinated yet threatened by his stare. He reminded her of a great wolf who had crept up on a herd of sheep and had selected the one he wanted to have for supper—but Miranda had no intention of being devoured. What he wanted was no mystery.

She hesitated on the third step down, her heart booming. He was a formidable warrior of austere male beauty, over six feet tall and built of pure muscle. A man like that, radiating his aura of natural superiority, might prove severely tempting if she wasn't careful. She decided simply to ignore the magnificent creature, as she did all the others. It seemed risky to go any closer, especially since not another soul was in sight here behind the theater, but there was no avoiding him. Forcing down her last swallow of food, she summoned a brisk air of confidence and resumed her march down the steps.

"Excuse me, please. I would like to pass."

He slipped her a devilish little smile. Rather than standing aside, however, he stepped onto the bottom stair, rested his hands on the rails on both sides, and blocked her path with his body. And what a body it was, she thought, meeting his wicked half smile with an arch look. His giant shoulders were adorned with the gold epaulets of his proud scarlet uniform. Her gaze skimmed his massive arms and lean waist. The gray trousers of the infantry's winter uniform hugged his long legs, disappearing into shiny black boots. As physically intimidating as he was, though, she sensed no danger from him. Walking slowly down the steps toward him, she arrived on the step two above the one where he stood and found herself on eye level with him.

She raised her eyebrows and regarded him expectantly, waiting for him to move, but it was becoming clear that he was not about to let her pass until he got a little of her attention. He said nothing, but flashed her an angelic smile, their faces inches apart.

Fighting an answering smile, Miranda pulled the cork out of the flask and took a drink of red wine, inspecting him matter-of-factly. He had night-black hair, striking, chiseled features, and deep-set gray eyes. They were long-lashed, with an honest, penetrating gaze. Her glance slid downward to his beautiful mouth.

"Hullo, Miss White," he murmured in a low, sensual tone.

She flicked her gaze back up to his eyes. They glowed like polished silver. Rather pleased with herself

for having captured the attention of such a speci-
men, she corked the flask again with a guarded smile.
"Well," she said, "aren't you the forward one?"

"Only when I see something I want," he purred,
nearly grazing her jawline with the tip of his patrician
nose as he inhaled the scent of her skin. "I am your
slave, lady. Only say how I may serve you."

"Slave?" A tremor of excitement raced through her,
but she pulled back, holding him at bay with a challenging look. "Humph." She looked away with a toss
of her chin, her heart pounding. "You didn't even clap
for me," she said loftily.

"I didn't?"

"No, you just sat there. I saw you."

"I confess, I was too entranced by your beauty even
to notice the show had ended." His smile was indulgent; his gaze caressed her. His voice was soft, mellow,
and sweet as a sip of brandy. It had the same intoxi-
cating effect on her, as well, making her tarry to indulge in a bit of flirtation when she should have
been hieing herself home. He had the loveliest London accent with a hint of Tory Oxford in it—a real
gentleman, she thought, not one of these low "Brum"
squires. "I was entirely preoccupied with trying to
think of the words to tell you how . . . marvelous you
are."

"I see." Her eyes dancing, she uncorked the flask,
took another sip of wine, and licked her lips. "And did
these words finally come to you?"

He nodded slowly, staring at her mouth.

"Well? Let's hear them."

His inky lashes swept upward as he looked into her eyes. "You are an angel," he said softly.

Miranda promptly burst out laughing.

"Now, that is impolite," he scolded, laughing himself as he pulled back a few inches. To her delight, his manly cheeks flushed. "Tender words are not my forte."

"I daren't ask what *is*."

He leaned closer. "Come to my chamber at the Royal Hotel and I'll show you," he murmured.

Her heart skipped a beat, but she shook her head at his wicked invitation. "Now, there you go too far. Excuse me, sir. I must be on my way."

He did not budge; his smile turned sly. "Do I look like a man who gives up easily?"

She tried to slip past him, to no avail. "This may surprise you, but it so happens I am an honest girl."

"If I believed that, beauty, I would weep." He moved still closer, hemming her in. "Tell me your name, you delectable creature. Your real name."

"Miss White."

"No, it's not."

"Yes, it is."

"Oh, come."

"Come yourself. I'm going home."

"Tell me your first name, at least."

"Snow."

"Snow White?" he asked, giving her a long-suffering look.

"Adieu!" she said suddenly and started to duck under his arm with a mischievous grin, but he moved quickly, capturing her in the crook of his elbow, pulling her to him with a low, lusty laugh like a pirate.

"I do enjoy a challenge, sweeting." His hard, angular face was shadow-sculpted in the lantern's glow as he firmly lifted her chin with his leather-sheathed fingers. "I don't think you understand how much I want you."

"Sir!" Barely regaining her balance, she caught only a glimpse of his wolf-gray eyes before he closed them, lowered his head, and claimed her mouth. His lips smothered her gasp of alarm.

Hunger radiated from him, encircling her in a lightning-sphere of crackling electricity. He curled his gloved hand around her nape and deepened the kiss, coaxing her lips apart almost roughly. He groaned like a starved man as he tasted her in rich, intimate demand, his strong arms tightening around her waist. When she pushed against him in protest, he clenched her more firmly against his iron body, so hard and strong, so very male, subduing her feeble struggles with pleasure. She felt herself weakening as his tongue stroked hers and his hands petted her hair, her face, her neck. It felt so achingly good to be held, filling her with reckless exultation—half loneliness, half desire. His kisses and gentle caresses beguiled her, making her body throb until she could no longer hold herself in check. Reaching up with breathless uncertainty, she inched her hands over the broad planes of his shoulders and enfolded him in her arms.

A low growl of pleasure sounded in his throat, welcoming her embrace. He gently grasped two handfuls of her hair, letting it spill through his fingers. She ran her hand down his muscled chest and back up again, cupping his square, smoothly shaved jaw, too caught up in sensation to care that she didn't even know his name.

He paused just long enough to whisper to her between kisses. "Keep me warm tonight, beauty. You can do that for me, yes? I need you so badly, so very badly."

Miranda couldn't think, let alone answer, transported by sensation. Running her fingers through his hair, she simply pulled him down in a wordless demand for more kisses, which he gladly gave. A shiver of anticipation coursed through her when she felt him slip his right hand into the front of her cloak.

Lightly sucking on his tongue, she clung to him in scandalized delight, her body trembling with eagerness for his touch. She was acutely aware of his hand exploring the curve of her waist and her hip through the lavender muslin; then she let out a sharp gasp of desire as he squeezed the left cheek of her bottom. He began kneading her buttock in a rhythm that drew her pelvis even more deliciously snugly against his groin, while his kiss deepened with ravishing urgency. She nearly swooned when his fingertips advanced into the cleft of her backside and pressed lower, stroking the filmy muslin of her gown against the place between her thighs where she was helplessly wet. He pleasured her until she tore her mouth away from his and let out a wild groan.

"Oh, God, girl, you've got me so hard. I don't think I can wait," he panted.

She dragged her eyes open, dizzy and weak-kneed, her heartbeat galloping.

His chest was heaving, his angular face stark with need. He glanced toward the shadowy wall of the theater, then slanted her a speculative look. "It's dark beneath these steps."

"No!" she gasped, her eyes widening.

He gave her a dark smile, his lips still wet with her kisses. "Very well. The hotel, then." He kissed his way down her neck, then slowly released his possessive hold on her body. "I'll call a carriage," he whispered. "Wait here." He left the wooden stairs and dragged his hand through his hair, turning away.

Swaying dazedly on her feet, Miranda stared after him as he stalked toward the hackney stand.

It was several seconds before her head began to clear. *Oh, Miranda, what are you doing?* She squeezed her eyes shut briefly, struggling to regain her equilibrium. Ashamed of her wantonness all in a flash, she hurried away from the stairs toward the dark, snowy road home. She had to escape before the big officer came back. She feared she could not withstand much more of his persuading.

Trudging through the snow helped to cool her passion. Guilt and anger swiftly took its place. She could not believe she had let a total stranger do that to her—aye, and had relished it. Maybe Brocklehurst was right. Maybe depravity was in her blood. Was she a fool? she thought angrily. Could she not spot his type at twenty paces—the sort of highborn, pleasure-hungry rake who amused himself by chasing poor girls as though they were prey? Men only wanted one thing. Especially men in uniform.

What an utter egotist he was, she thought with a snort of disdain. She had never said yes to his indecent proposition; he had simply assumed her agreement. Call a carriage, indeed! It was just as well, she mused in a huff. If he had seen fit to keep holding her in his rock-hard arms, she might not have gotten away so easily.

"Hey!" It was only another moment or two before she heard his baffled shout. "Miss White!"

Thanking God that she had not told him her real name, she ignored him and kept walking.

"Miss White!" he bellowed again, sounding perfectly incensed. He had the voice of a man used to barking orders and being unquestionably obeyed, but she merely hummed under her breath, trying to pretend she was out of earshot.

Apparently, he was not fooled. "Damn it, girl, where the blazes are you going?"

"Home!" she yelled back, sending her would-be seducer a scathing glance over her shoulder. His powerful silhouette was outlined by the lights of the theater behind him.

"Why?" he roared, as though he could not fathom any woman saying no to him.

She whirled around just long enough to fling her reply grandly at him. "Because I, sir, am an actress, not a whore!"

"Oh?" he shouted sarcastically. "I didn't know there was a difference!"

She shot him a withering glare, pivoted forward again, and marched on toward Mud City.

Damien cursed under his breath, the expletive forming a steamy cloud on the night air. He could still taste her on his tongue, but he made no move to pursue her. Well, she had made a fine fool of him, he thought, realizing belatedly that she had been telling the truth—she was an honest girl. He had assumed she had merely been playing hard to get in order to wring more gold out of him. Denied his prize, he growled under his breath and turned away, narrowly recalling his vow. *No women. No liquor.*

Shrugging her off in irritation, he decided to go back to the barracks to see Morris, but thwarted passion made him steal one last, hungry glance over his shoulder at the girl. She was some distance away down the curving road, her strides long and vigorous, her dark cloak and long hair billowing out behind her. God, she was beautiful, he thought wistfully. *Honest, eh? Well, good for you, girl. See that you stay that way.* Out of long habit, he looked past her hurrying figure and scanned the horizon, when suddenly, a flicker of motion caught his eye.

His gaze homed in on the stand of trees by the bridge over the half-frozen River Cole. As he watched, a tall, dark figure emerged from the trees, stark against the snow. It stationed itself in the road as though waiting for her by prior arrangement.

*Bloody hell!* he thought, his expression turning to outrage. *Honest, my arse!*

Apparently, the wench had already scheduled a rendezvous for the night. She had chosen someone else instead of him. Why couldn't she have simply said so instead of letting him make a fool of himself? He shook his head, pricked by the rejection. Lucien was always warning him he was easily duped by women. As usual, his sly twin brother proved right. *Pleasure her well, my friend,* he thought in disgust, but as he started to turn away, he saw a second male figure materialize out of the cluster of trees. And a third.

Damien stopped, frowned, stared. There was something sinister about the furtive way the three men crept out of the darkness. Willing his gaze to penetrate the dark copse to see if there were any more lurking in there, he could just make out the dim outline of horses hidden among the brambles. The hackles on his nape rose in instinctual warning. Hadn't one of the subalterns at the barracks mentioned something about the criminal population that had taken up residence just outside of town?

Meanwhile, Miss White kept walking fearlessly toward them as though she knew who they were. Then Damien realized she could not yet see them because of the gentle ridge that rose up in front of her. His eyes flared with cold dread as the three men lined up across the road, as though preparing to ambush her. *They're not her friends.* Savage energy began pounding in his temples, in time with the thunderous pumping of his heart.

*They're bloody goddamned highwaymen.*

Already he was in motion, dropping his greatcoat, breaking into a run. He shook off the chains of the past few months' civility with a mental roar of release.

He had no weapon, but this posed little worry to a man who knew nine ways to kill with his bare hands. With each accelerating stride, his focus grew crisper, more sublimely clear, his mind already assessing the problem with mathematical precision, showing him his angle of attack.

As the girl neared the crest of the ridge, he poured on a fresh burst of speed, desperate to intercept her before the gang of criminals did. He felt his awareness heighten toward his battle state, then saw her freeze in her tracks at the apex of the rise. Finally she saw the men lined up across the road before her. Damien was too far away to make out what they said to her as they started toward her, but she whirled around and began running back toward the theater.

*Come on, come on,* he urged himself, pressing himself to sprint full-speed, but he was not fast enough to stop them from catching up to her. A fourth man on horseback came galloping out of the woods while the three on foot captured her within a few strides, grabbing her by her long hair. They tackled her to the ground in a plume of snow. She let out a scream that was quickly cut off when one clapped his hand over her mouth. Damien held back a roar of rage, for surprise was his only advantage. Murder in his eyes, he lost sight of her momentarily as he hurtled toward the rise.

When he came up over the ridge, he saw one man steadying the horse's reins, while the other two held the girl by her armpits and her ankles, struggling to hand her up to the man on the horse. She fought them fiercely, kicking and clawing—until the one who had hold of her upper body pulled out a knife and threatened her with it.

Damien felt something dark inside of him open its red, demon eyes, roused to wakefulness at the silver glint of the knife, the beast in him scenting blood. Jumbled memories flashed through his mind: nights on piquet, bayonet charges. His awareness was distant, yet crystal clear, controlled to the point of eerie tranquility; everything seemed to move slowly. The greasy brigand sheathed his weapon again in order to lift the uncooperative girl; then Damien was upon them.

Ignoring their Cockney shouts, he elbowed the man with the knife in the face, snapping his head back, seizing Miss White around the waist to catch her from falling as the man staggered back. The horse skittered sideways, but the terrorized beauty swiped at Damien's face with her nails, too panicked to realize it was him.

His eyes widened as her kick connected with the chin of the hefty man who was trying to hold onto her legs. Damien pulled her free of them and carried her two or three steps away, placing her roughly on the snowy ground behind him, swiftly positioning his body between her and her attackers.

The hefty man she had kicked in the chin was already back for more. Damien punched him in the face with such force that the big fellow reeled and fell, stunned. Damien glanced back for a split second to see if the girl was all right. On her knees in the snow, she looked up and met his gaze. Realization flashed in her eyes—who he was, that he had come to help.

Then a deafening shot exploded a few feet away. From the corner of his eye, he saw the pistol's flare, felt the bullet's bite as it grazed his left biceps, searing through the sleeve of his red uniform coat. He let out a curse and clapped his hand over the wound as the girl cried, "*No!*"

With sweat beading on his face, Damien slowly looked up from his bleeding arm at the one who had shot him, a wiry, unkempt man with a gold tooth. Deaf to the threats and shouts of the other men, Damien stared at the gunman in an icy silence for the space of a heartbeat, the pain in his arm diminishing into numbness.

The criminal lowered his gun and began reloading, but fear and haste made him clumsy. Lowering his hand from his wounded arm, Damien wiped the blood off his palm down the front of his scarlet coat, his pulse thundering in his ears like cannon fire in the distance. Reality wavered like the king's colors billowing slowly on the breeze. It buckled, split—and suddenly, fractured. He was back in Spain, the guns roaring around him, the French flinging themselves at his battalion. His confusion receded, narrowing down to one blissfully simple goal: *Destroy.*

"Run," he ordered the girl in a low, vicious growl as he stalked toward the gunman.

He did not want her to see this.

It all happened so fast.

Miranda hesitated, her heart pounding with dread to see the big, gray-eyed stranger walking straight toward the man with the gun. She had seen the chilling look that had come over his hard, angular face upon being wounded, though he had hardly flinched with pain. In that split second, she did not know what to do.

She felt she should obey his order—but how could she abandon him to save herself? He was outnumbered and already hurt. It was all her fault. Something like this had been bound to happen to her, venturing so close to Mud City.

She did not know what these cretins wanted or how they had known her real name. She only knew she was unutterably grateful to the big, handsome officer for so gallantly rushing to her rescue. In the next moment, however, any notion of him as her knight in shining armor turned to horror. He attacked the gunman, launching at him like a wolf. The man screamed, though the soldier had no weapon. Almost too quick for the eye to see, the soldier raised his fist, fingers curled in a savage hook, and struck the outlaw in his windpipe, fairly tearing the man's throat out with his bare hand, letting out the most terrifying, barbaric snarl she had ever heard from human lips.

The air left her lungs in a whoosh. She felt her gorge rise as he dropped the body and turned to the others with a mad glint of blood lust in his eyes. The others took the Lord's name in vain, backing away from him in shock.

Miranda needed no further instruction. She stumbled to her feet, tripping on the hem of her lavender gown as she began running back toward the lights and people around the Pavilion. Her mind was blank with shock. She had never seen anything so horrible in her life, but somehow, through her hysteria, she had the presence of mind to run in the right direction.

There was another scream behind her, but it was not the soldier's deep voice. She winced, realizing he had just killed another one, then ran faster until the man on horseback galloped his lanky mount past her, heading her off well before she reached the theater. Terror rose up in her anew.

Herded around like a wild filly, she turned on a six-pence and ran back the other way, bolting in the direction of the bridge over the River Cole—the way back to Yardley.

She ran until her lungs burned, taking a zigzagging path like a fleeing rabbit, but it only bought her a few extra seconds. She gave her terrifying rescuer a wide berth as she sprinted past him. There were two dead men sprawled on the ground, and he was at work on the third, beating the hefty one's face to a pulp, lost in a frenzy of violence. He seemed to be in his own world, barely even noticing her as she tore past him toward the bridge, trying futilely to outpace the horse.

"Aarrgh!" A wild, angry cry wrenched from her lips as she heard the dull cadence of hoofbeats sweeping up behind her.

The horseman was closing in. She could smell the horse, hear the creaking of the leather tack. Panting painfully with the air's sharp cold, she glanced over her shoulder as the rider leaned down from the saddle, steadying himself to grab her.

"Help me!" she screamed.

She could almost feel his hot breath on the back of her neck, when suddenly, the rider let out an odd shriek and pitched off the horse, hitting the ground, headfirst, a few feet in front of her. She heard the sickening crunch of breaking bones as he landed facedown with a knife jutting out of his back.

She skidded to a halt, nearly falling over the dead man, then stayed exactly where she was. The horse bolted on, riderless, tearing off over the bridge. No longer daring to move in any direction, Miranda covered her mouth with both hands to stop the ragged, animal whimpering that spilled from her lips. Her whole body was shaking. She turned slowly, forcing herself to look back at her wild rescuer.

There, on the moonlit ridge several yards away, a sword trailing from his grasp, he was the only man left standing, his giant shoulders rising and falling as he caught his breath. Like some berserker warrior out of Celtic legend, he stood in the cold white moonlight, his fury spent, dead men strewn around him.

He threw down the borrowed sword, dropped his head almost to his chest, and turned, wiping his brow with his forearm. The ground beneath his boots had been churned to bloodstained slush. His face was bloody, streaming with sweat; his smart uniform was torn, his hair disheveled. She had never encountered any creature more primal or more dangerous than this unbowed, elemental male.

She stood paralyzed. The quiet gurgling of the nearby River Cole was thunderous in the silence. As though feeling her awed, appalled stare upon him, the gray-eyed stranger slowly turned his head and met her gaze.

He looked inhuman in that moment, like the angel

of death: beautiful and terrible and utterly remote, his cool, silvery eyes devoid of emotion. A flicker of some distant response passed behind his diamond-hard gaze.

"What are you looking at?"

The sound of his voice terrified her, reverberating through her entire being with the force and raw, rumbling power of some mountain cataract. She picked up her skirts, whirled around, and ran. With a sense of disjointed unreality, she pounded back across the bridge and tore through the silent fields, stumbling through snowdrifts, fleeing blindly back to Yardley.

# ⇥ CHAPTER ⇤
# THREE

Late morning was bleak and eerily still as Damien's horse picked its way along the muddy, rutted drive to Yardley School, past the line of large, bare, gnarled trees with painfully twisted trunks. Dingy clouds hung low across the sky like a dirty woolen blanket. Arriving in the walled courtyard, he halted his stallion and stiffly dismounted before the thick front doors of the school. Aches and pains plagued his back, neck, and shoulders from the fight. His arm where the bullet had hit him stung like hell, but in a strange way, he was glad he had been wounded, because at least he could feel *that*. Otherwise there would only have been this terrible, cold numbness.

He led his horse over to the post beside the weathered mounting block, glancing at the gray stone farmhouse as he lashed the reins to the iron ring. He walked slowly to the front door, but behind his steely facade he was soul-sick with the hollow, shaky feeling that came as a predictable aftereffect of having gone on the rampage. He pounded out an implacable knock with the heel of his fist, since he had split his knuckles open during the fight.

As he waited for someone to answer, his thoughts drifted back to the events following the bloody melee. He had returned to the barracks after his damsel in distress had fled in horror of him. By that time, fortunately, his army chum, Morris, had returned. Damien had recounted the attack, how he had intervened and had, perhaps, overreacted. The officers had been outraged by the assault on the theater girl and had commended him for his quick response to her plight. While the regiment's surgeon had seen to his wound, Colonel Morris had sent a squad of soldiers out to patrol the area around Bordesley Green, another to remove the bodies.

Their subsequent search of the dead men's clothes had provided no clues to their identities but had revealed a strange tattoo on the left arm of the hefty one. The tattoo had depicted a bird of prey gripping a dagger in its talons. Morris had suggested that perhaps the outlaw had once served as a sailor. It mattered little now. They had shared a drink, toasting Sherbrooke, their most lately fallen comrade. Morris had ordered one of the men to drive Damien back to the Royal Hotel, assuring him he need not worry—the whole incident would be discreetly swept under the carpet.

"And tell that girl not to walk past there anymore," Morris had added with a scowl.

But even if Damien had known where to look for the mysterious Miss White, he never wanted to see her again. He was glad he had not told her his name. There was no need for her to know that the ferocious madman who had come to her rescue was the same

distinguished officer the nation had hailed as a hero.
No one in the civilian realm understood what it was
really like on the front lines, nor ever could; but that
girl, whoever she was, had gotten a taste of it last
night. He only hoped it did not scar her too badly—
but, no, he thought, staring at nothing. She'd be all
right. He knew a survivor when he saw one. Yet he
could not get her face out of his mind in that last moment before she had bolted—the way she had looked
at him, the terror and revulsion in her eyes, reflecting
back to him the full horror of the monster he had become. It made him wonder if he really should destroy
himself and do the world a favor.

Just then, the door opened behind him. "May I 'elp
ye, sir?" a ruddy, round-faced servant woman asked.

"Yes. I am here to see my ward, Miss Miranda
FitzHubert."

Under the ribbon brim of her house cap, the woman's
eyes widened. She quickly curtseyed. "Do come in,
sir! Major Sherbrooke, is it?"

The mistake pained him. "No, ma'am. I am Major
Sherbrooke's colonel and friend, Lord Winterley. I
have been appointed as Miss FitzHubert's guardian."

"Oh, dear," the woman murmured, taking in his
hard, meaningful stare. "Oh, dear me. Do come in,
my lord. Miss FitzHubert is at chapel with the others
girls. Shall I fetch her?"

"No, there is no need to hasten bad news. I will
wait." He stepped into the gloomy entrance hall. At
once he was aware of the cold, vaporous damp rising
from the flagstones. It could not be healthful, he
thought with a frown. He hoped the child had a hardy

constitution. "Is the headmaster available? I would speak with him."

"No, my lord, the Reverend Mr. Reed is our minister as well as headmaster. He is celebrating the Eucharist at chapel right now. Miss Brocklehurst, our headmistress, is there as well, minding the girls."

"As she should be, I'm sure," he replied with a forced, polite smile. "And you are?"

"Mrs. Warren. I'm the cook, housekeeper, laundress—I does a bit of everything." She opened a door to the right of the entrance hall and gestured to it with a kindly smile. "Would ye care to wait in the parlor, my lord? They shouldn't be more than ten minutes."

He nodded and started toward the parlor, then paused and glanced askance at her. "Do the children come in through the front, Mrs. Warren? My stallion is a bit high-tempered. It would not be safe if they took it into their heads to try to pet him."

"No, sir, the girls come in through the back. There's a nice stone path that leads from the church."

"Very good, then," he said with a curt nod, then strode past her into the modest reception room.

"May I fix you some tea?"

He nodded. "Thank you, ma'am. I'd be obliged."

She bobbed a curtsy and closed the parlor door, leaving him alone. Damien shrugged off his greatcoat, drew off his thick leather riding gauntlets, and waited restlessly. The fire burned feebly in the hearth, leaving a chill in the room.

Whoever ran this place had a cheese-paring soul, he thought, looking around at the threadbare carpet, faded furniture, and miserly coal fire, yet the tuition at Yardley was not cheap. Perhaps it was badly managed. Having run a regiment all too often without adequate food, shoes, or clothing for his men, let alone ammunition, he immediately recognized the signs of economies being practiced. But the hardships that soldiers could endure were certainly not appropriate for fragile young ladies. So far his opinion of Yardley was low, but he could not fault them on cleanliness. He scrutinized the parlor as though he were inspecting his troops' quarters. It was spotless.

He took a seat on the couch at length and sat ramrod-straight, his gaze fixed forward, his hands resting on his thighs. He spent a few minutes mentally rehearsing the painful speech he must make to his ward. He could scarcely believe that in a short while, he, who did not deserve to walk among civilized human beings, would have to comfort a bereaved child.

It was not long before the chapel bells began ringing, signaling the end of the service. Mrs. Warren came in with the tea tray and carried it to the small table nearby. He noticed her glance over her shoulder at the sound of the back door opening and the sudden chattering of numerous, high-pitched voices. A louder, pompous, male voice drowned them out, ordering them to be seen and not heard.

"That'll be 'imself," the housekeeper murmured, giving Damien an anxious look.

"Ma'am?" he asked.

Mrs. Warren pursed her lips with a determined air. "My lord, no matter what those two tell you, Miss

Miranda is a good girl, a fine girl. Aye," she whispered emphatically, "she is an angel, in her way."

"Mrs. Warren! Oh, Mrs. Warren!" the man's voice called from the hallway beyond. "Daft old woman, where are you?"

Damien's eyebrows drew together. He glanced toward the doorway.

The old servant clamped her mouth shut and gave Damien a conspiratorial nod, then hurried out into the entrance hall. "Yes, Reverend? You have a visitor, sir. His Lordship is waiting in the parlor—"

"Lordship?" the man exclaimed, then dropped his voice to a whisper.

Damien stood, contemplating the old woman's strange words. He heard several pairs of feet running lightly up the stairs that rose from the entrance hall, one of which, he imagined, belonged to his ward. Curious to see her, he walked to the doorway and looked up, but only glimpsed the swishing hems of some beige dresses and pale kid boots before the children vanished upstairs.

"My lord, welcome to Yardley School." The black-clad minister came toward him with an obsequious smile. "I am the founder and headmaster, Mr. Reed. How may I be of service?"

Damien's nape prickled with instinctive dislike. "I am Colonel Lord Winterley," he said with an imperious stare, taking the letter from Jason's solicitor out of his waistcoat and handing it to the man. "I regret to say that Major Jason Sherbrooke of the Hundred Thirty-sixth was killed in London last week. I have been named the guardian of his ward, Miss Miranda FitzHubert. I wish to see her."

"Of course, my lord," Mr. Reed murmured, passing a curious glance over his face before skimming the solicitor's letter. He looked up again a moment later and handed the letter back to Damien. "Forgive my hesitation, my lord. I have a duty to protect my girls."

"An honorable sentiment."

The clergyman's sallow countenance brightened at Damien's placated tone. "Won't you step into my office, then we will call her in? Do bring the tea, Mrs. Warren."

Tucking the letter back into his waistcoat, Damien followed him across the entrance hall into another room with a few bookshelves on the walls and an impressive escritoire in the center.

"Do make yourself comfortable, my lord." Mr. Reed gestured toward a leather armchair positioned across from the desk, but as Damien walked toward it, another piece of furniture blocked his path—one that released a bevy of old memories and sent a shiver of dread down his spine. He stopped and stared at it with anger leaping into his veins. It was a prayer kneeler with a book rest across the top, but the leather cuffs that hung down the sides betrayed its true purpose as the stand on which students were strapped down to take their lashes.

As a lad at Eton, he had been stretched across a similar device on a handful of occasions, usually due to his refusal to tell on Lucien for making mischief.

"Mr. Reed." He looked at the minister, who had gone to stand behind the desk. "If you have beaten my ward," he said calmly, "so help me, I will thrash you from here to kingdom come."

"Lord Winterley! Goodness," he said with a nervous little laugh. "You are indeed a man of arms. Rest assured, the prie-dieu serves only as a threat for our more unruly girls. It is never actually used."

Mrs. Warren sent Damien a sharp look out of the corner of her eye as she set the tea tray on the minister's desk.

"Thank you, Mrs. Warren," Mr. Reed said. "That will be all. Kindly ask Miss Brocklehurst to bring in Miss FitzHubert for me."

"Yes, Reverend." Sending Damien a last, worried glance, Mrs. Warren exited, leaving him alone with the headmaster. What a strange place this was, he thought, but he could not be sure if the tension he sensed lay in the atmosphere of Yardley School or if it was merely his own.

"Now then." The minister rested his bony elbows on his desk and interlocked his fingers. His pinched, sallow face was grave above his white collar. "About your ward."

"Yes. I have questions."

"As do I, my lord. After you."

Damien shifted in the large leather chair. "Is she in good health?"

"Oh, yes, she is hearty and hale, my lord. She is almost never ill."

"Excellent. Is she a good student?"

"To be sure, she is a clever girl, but . . ."

"Yes?" Damien prompted at the clergyman's hesitation. "Please speak freely, sir. I would like to know the truth of my ward's disposition."

"Well, in terms of temperament, Miss FitzHubert is, shall we say . . . strong-willed."

"Hmm."

Mr. Reed took a sip of tea. "She is quite intelligent, but does not apply herself with any great effort. You see, my lord," he said, leaning forward, lowering his tone, "what she lacks, in a word, is discipline. As an army man, I'm sure you can appreciate the value, nay, the necessity of that virtue."

Damien leaned his elbow on the chair arm and stroked his lips in thought, studying him. "Go on."

"She is prone to fits of temper. Defiance. Disrespect for her elders. Destructiveness. Dishonesty—"

"Dishonesty? I do not at all approve of lying females."

"Nor do I. Why, just yesterday, I'm afraid Miss FitzHubert deliberately smashed a porcelain figurine belonging to our headmistress, then tried to evade punishment by lying about it."

*Good God!* he thought, blanching. He had inherited the ward from Hades.

"Naturally, all of this is quite disturbing, Mr. Reed. Do send me a bill so that the headmistress's property can be replaced."

"You are very kind, sir, but it is the point of Miranda's actions that is the problem, not the property itself. I must say, I am relieved you have come to claim her, for Miss Brocklehurst and I are quite at our wit's end."

Damien looked at him warily. Claim her? Perhaps the man misunderstood.

"I am very sorry for the trouble my ward has caused you, Mr. Reed. I will address the matter with Miranda personally, and I assure you there will be no repeat of this behavior. In her defense, however, I would only remind you that fate has dealt rather harshly with the girl—her parents' deaths, her uncle's absence. I fear Major Sherbrooke neglected her for too long. It sounds as though she has run wild."

"Indeed, she has, I'm afraid, despite all our best efforts. We have thirty girls to manage. We cannot devote all our time and energy to minding one."

"Well, now that Miranda knows she is going to have to answer to me, I am sure you will find her more malleable."

Mr. Reed rose and rested his fingertips on the desk. He stared down at his ink blotter for a moment. "I'm afraid, my lord, that will not do."

"Pardon?" Damien asked in ominous foreboding.

"More decisive action is in order."

"What do you mean?"

"Just this: Your ward has broken the rules of our school so many times that under any other circumstances, she would have been expelled long ago. The only thing that stayed my hand was the knowledge that she had nowhere else to go. Now that you are here, I am sorry, but I cannot in good conscience keep Miss FitzHubert at Yardley."

"Surely you are not suggesting that I take her?" he exclaimed, his heart pounding.

"My lord," Mr. Reed said with an unflinching smile,

"I am insisting upon it. Your ward is a bad influence on the other girls. I must be responsible for them." With an air of finality, Mr. Reed sat down again and opened the lid of his desk, searching about for some papers while Damien sputtered in protest.

"You can't do this! I understand that you have other students to think of, but you are responsible for Miranda, as well!"

"Not anymore, sir." He glanced over the raised lid of his desk at him. "You are."

Damien leaped to his feet and planted his hands on the edge of the minister's desk. "Now, look here, my good man. I am only here to meet the chit and tell her the news about Sherbrooke. I apologize for her misbehavior, and I give you my word that it will stop as soon as I have spoken with her. But I cannot take her. It is out of the question. I am due in London to spend the holidays with my family."

"Well, if you wish to turn her out on the street, that is certainly not my affair. I am discharging her . . . to you." Scratching out his signature, Mr. Reed handed him a piece of paper that proved to be a writ of release. "There you are. Congratulations, my lord. I'm sure Major Sherbrooke would be very grateful."

"This is unconscionable! Do I look like some sort of nursemaid to you? I am in no wise equipped to take up the care of a child without so much as a moment's forewarning!"

"My dear colonel, whatever gave you the notion that Miss FitzHubert is a child?"

Damien stared at him in alarm, his heart pounding. "What is she, then, a banshee?"

"See for yourself. Miss Brocklehurst!" he called toward the door. "Bring in FitzHubert!"

Damien turned as the door opened. An older woman, pinch-faced and hard-featured, marched in and nodded to him.

"This is Miss Brocklehurst," Mr. Reed told him.

"Come along, then," the headmistress said sharply to someone in the hall.

"And this," Mr. Reed said in disapproval that verged on animosity, "is Miranda."

She walked in, her chin high, her green eyes blazing, ready for a fight.

Damien took one look at her and felt the solid earth fall away virtually from under his feet.

He stood rooted to the spot, his heart beating wildly. For a second he was not sure. It could not be—it was not possible. Her appearance was so changed. But when her emerald eyes locked with his and she paused in midstride with a gasp of shock, he knew there could be no mistake. It was the one woman in all the world he never wanted to see again: the indomitable Snow White.

She turned that very color, the roses draining from her cheeks as she gaped at him, panic-stricken. Damien trained his stunned gaze over her, scarcely able to believe his eyes at her transformation from scantily clad siren to this picture of demure innocence. She was dressed in a light beige walking gown with neat white gloves. Her luxurious mane of dark, wavy hair that had spilled down her back in such reckless profusion last night was plaited in two schoolgirlish braids with small white ribbons on the ends.

"My lord, allow me to present Miss Miranda FitzHubert," Mr. Reed intoned. "Miss FitzHubert, this is Colonel the earl of Winterley. Your new guardian."

"My *what*?" She gasped, looking from the minister to him, but Damien could only stare at her, at a loss.

His thoughts whirled, the puzzle pieces falling together with a fateful clang. *"An honest girl."* Her refusal to tell him her real name. Her actress mother, lost to her. Mr. Reed's report of her rebellious behavior. The school sat only about a mile from the Pavilion. He thought of the way she had soaked up the applause last night.

God help him, the truth was inescapable. This luscious, headstrong, impossible creature, who had flaunted her sweet body on stage before him and half the men of Birmingham; who had melted in his arms, then ditched him the moment he turned his back; who had nearly gotten him killed, traipsing blithely past a colony of criminals; this angel-faced disaster waiting to happen—was little Miranda FitzHubert.

Totally his and totally forbidden.

*Oh, my God,* he thought. *I nearly debauched my own ward.* For the first time in years that he could remember, the task before him gave him pause. The ravishing image of her in her gauzy lavender gown flashed again through his mind along with the memory of her warm, satiny lips parting for his kiss in hungry innocence. He trembled with dread at the agonizing temptation she presented.

"Will somebody please tell me what is going on?" the little deceiver cried in fright.

Damien steeled himself and glanced at Mr. Reed. "Leave us," he ordered.

Miranda's heartbeat was a panicked staccato. She had walked in braced for a flogging, but this was possibly worse. She could not believe the gray-eyed beast had tracked her down, but after what she had seen last night, she was half convinced he possessed supernatural powers granted him by the devil. An earl! she thought in dread. She knew what that meant. *Earl* meant a man who could do what he pleased to whomever he pleased, slay lowlifes without compunction. *Earl* meant rich. Rich enough to buy or bribe his way into possession of a girl who had dared to refuse his advances.

She had a terrible feeling in the pit of her stomach that Mr. Reed had just sold her down the river to this deadly creature—and why should he not? she thought wildly. Her Uncle Jason was nowhere on hand to protect her.

The headmaster slunk by like a cringing dog, obeying Colonel Lord Winterley without argument. Miranda bit her lip against the temptation to beg the vile creature to stay. She was scared to death to be left alone with her terrifying rescuer, but it was not as though she could reveal to Mr. Reed that they had already met, had already kissed, had already been guiltily bonded by blood. She feared it was time to pay the piper.

When the door closed, they stared at each other in wary silence.

Miranda trailed her gaze over him, marveling, for

by daylight, he was even more severely beautiful than she remembered, with his striking combination of jet-black hair and pale gray eyes. In their crystalline depths, she could still see the predator lurking within him, but on the surface, he was all immaculate precision, gleaming and correct. She recalled how his smart red uniform had been bloodied and torn during the fight, but now his elegant civilian clothes were tailored to perfection. His white silk cravat was neatly tucked within the high-standing collar of his silver-gray waistcoat. He wore a dark blue tailcoat that snugly fitted his broad shoulders. His charcoal-colored breeches ran down into high, black riding boots that had not so much of a speck of dirt on them.

"Well, Miss FitzHubert, as I gather that is your name," he said with an aloof air, "it seems we meet again." He took a step toward her.

"Stay back!" she yelped, darting behind the large leather chair. "What are you doing here? What do you want? How did you find me?"

"Do not be afraid," he ordered, advancing slowly toward the chair. "I mean you no harm."

"Stay away from me," she warned, slipping around the desk, keeping the furniture between them like a barricade. "If you've come to make sure I keep quiet about last night, you needn't worry. I shall never tell a soul."

"That is not why I am here."

"I'm an honest girl!" she cried.

"Oh, Miranda, calm down," he said crossly. "I have not come to seduce you."

"Then why did you tell Mr. Reed you are my guardian? It's not going to work! My guardian is Major Sherbrooke of the Hundred and Thirty-sixth, and if you lay a hand on me, you'll have to answer to him!"

A fleeting look of anguish skimmed his face. "Try to listen for a moment, Miranda. It's because of your Uncle Jason that I'm here."

She froze and mentally retraced her last words. "How did you know his first name?" she demanded, a prickle of foreboding rushing down her spine. "I didn't say he was my uncle, either. How did you know that?"

"Perhaps you should sit down."

Miranda was bewildered. There was such gravity in his countenance, however, that she felt compelled to hear him out. She edged warily toward the chair and lowered herself onto it, ready to flee in a second. As he took a step closer, she noticed his black armband, then furrowed her brow to note that it was decorated with the insignia of her uncle's regiment.

Lord Winterley lifted his chin and clasped his hands behind his back. "I am the colonel of the Hundred and Thirty-sixth Regiment of Foot, Miss FitzHubert."

Her eyes widened.

"I was Major Sherbrooke's commanding officer in the Peninsula. I had the privilege of serving with your uncle for six years. He was my lieutenant from the days when I captained my first fusileer company." He paused, his gaze turning faraway. "We became close friends. The day he lost his arm at Albuera, I was by his side when the surgeons seared the wound."

She stared at him, on her guard. She was not disposed to believe a word the man said, but it sounded as though he really *did* know her uncle. Where the devil was the blackguard, then? she wanted to ask, but before she could speak, he continued in grim resolve.

"At Albuera, Jason asked me to look after you if he did not survive. I gave him my word that I would. He recovered from that wound, as you know, but our arrangement concerning you remained intact."

She shook her head in bafflement. "I don't understand. Did he send you to look in on me? Will I get to see him soon?"

"No, my dear," he said in a low, gentle tone. "I'm afraid there has been some very bad news."

She stared at him, brought up short by the solemnity in his voice. Everything in her went quiet with cold, sudden fear. There was some somber note in his tone that sent gooseflesh tingling down her arms, something that brought back a memory of sitting in the front pew of the dim chapel in Papa's country mansion, her feet dangling, not quite touching the floor, two coffins before her, a white one and a slightly larger one of mahogany. Uncle Jason had sat beside her protectively, holding her hand, while grown-ups she had never seen before went filing by—pale, stiff-faced men and ladies in black veils who would look at her in teary-eyed pity and murmur, "Poor little thing," and Uncle Jason would thank them for coming.

She stared at Lord Winterley. "What is it?" she asked, her voice gone hoarse.

"Miranda," he whispered with a soulful glance, then squared his broad shoulders and seemed to gather himself. He spoke with slow, deliberate formality. "It is my sad duty to inform you that Major Jason Sherbrooke was killed last Wednesday night, the twelfth of December, during a burglary at his lodgings in London. He was shot once in the heart."

Miranda barely heard the last part, her pulse roaring in her ears. Even his cultured baritone seemed muffled. The room spun sickeningly.

"What I told Mr. Reed was the truth. Jason appointed me your guardian in his will. I am so very sorry, Miranda."

A moment passed in utter silence.

Her mind reeled. She stared unseeingly at him until her eyes glazed over. Black rings exploded silently before her field of vision. She gripped the chair arm so hard her nails dug into the smooth leather.

"Miranda?" He approached hesitantly, crouching down beside her chair. He scanned her face in worry. "Are you all right? Shall I send for the headmistress to sit with you for a moment?"

She did not answer. She could not.

"My dear, you are so pale." He reached to steady her. "Let me call for smelling salts—"

"*Don't . . . touch me,*" she hissed, jerking away from him. She drew back, staring at him in loathing, her whole body trembling. "This . . . is not true. This," she whispered, "is the cruelest, lowest trick I have ever beheld in my life."

He tilted his head back with a startled look as she swept to her feet before him.

"You're a fraud!" she wrenched out, tears leaping

into her eyes. "Do you take me for a fool? Uncle Jason isn't dead! He did not survive six years of war only to be shot in his own home by a b-burglar! He could defend himself against any stupid thief!"

"He was drunk," he whispered.

"It's a lie! He's coming for me! He *is*! Why don't you admit what you really want, you disgusting brute? My answer is still the same!"

He rose, his face etched with taut self-control, as though he was determined to set aside her insults and show mercy. "Jason was my friend. One of the few I had left. I would never lie about such a thing. I have no designs on you. Our meeting last night was merest chance. Such things are banished between us now. You are my ward. If you had only told me your name last night, I never would have touched you."

"I didn't tell you, but you found me anyway!"

"I wasn't looking for you, Miranda," he said wearily. "I was too busy having a bullet extracted from my arm." He reached into his waistcoat, pulled out a folded letter, and handed it to her. "Here, if you don't believe me."

"What is it?"

"See for yourself."

Her hands were shaking so badly she could barely unfold the letter; her mind was in such a tumult that she barely comprehended what she read. Still, she concentrated long enough to gather that the document purported to be a page copied from Uncle Jason's will and an explanation from his solicitor.

"Meaningless. It could be a forgery," she said

tautly, thrusting the papers back into Lord Winterley's hands.

He stared at her in astonishment.

She swallowed hard, facing him in defiance, though she was only on eye level with his cravat pin. "If you were really such great friends with my uncle, he would've mentioned you in his letters. He used to write to me about all his fellow officers, but he never spoke of anyone by the name of Lord Winterley. Never!"

"I was only given the title a month ago. If Jason ever wrote to you about me, he would have referred to me as Damien Knight."

She froze and stared at him, wide-eyed, as the world lurched violently. The blood drained from her face. "Damien . . . Knight?"

"Ah, so you have heard of me," he murmured, his eyes narrowing in satisfaction.

"Damien—the captain of the grenadier company?" she forced out.

"Used to be. Colonel now."

"Damien . . . with the twin brother?"

He nodded, looking relieved. "Yes, that would be Lucien."

Miranda stared at him, at a loss. Captain Lord Damien Knight had been her uncle's idol. In his letters, the Knight twins had stood out larger than life, but it had always been Damien, the elder of the pair, like some storybook prince, who had been the hero of the tales. Damien—storming the walls of an ancient Spanish citadel, recapturing cannons stolen by the French, facing down perilous cavalry charges, pulling wounded comrades off the field under a hail of artillery fire.

"Ask me something about Jason, if you don't believe me. I knew your uncle as well as I know myself. As a matter of fact, there's a lot I know about you, too."

"Me?" She looked up quickly, her face ashen. "Like what?"

"I know you don't want to accept this because you've already suffered the loss of your parents," he said softly. "You saw them drown."

She sucked in her breath and backed away from him, the hairs on her nape standing on end. "How do you know that?"

"Jason used to talk about you all the time. He used to read us your letters in the mess at night because we were all so . . . damned homesick." With a sudden thoughtful look, he tapped his lips for a moment. "Do you remember a doll he sent you from the bazaar at Lisbon one year? I think it was, er, a Spanish lady sort of doll with a lace mantilla."

She nodded, scarcely comprehending.

"I picked it out for you."

"*What?*"

"Well, my brother and I both did," he amended. "We were sending one home to our little sister and we thought of you, as well, because ever since Albuera, Sherbrooke was, er, I'm afraid he was a little forgetful."

*Yes, he was.* "No!" she cried in shock, sweeping her hands up to cover her mouth as the truth hit her with overwhelming force. This was real. This was no sinister ploy for her seduction. Her dear uncle was dead.

Barely aware of Damien's hands steadying her, she sank back down to the chair, her head reeling. She was senseless to his whispered words of comfort, but she reached blindly for his handkerchief when he offered it to her. While she wept with shocked grief, trying to absorb the unfairness of her uncle's death, Damien crouched at her knee like some great, savage guard dog, bristling with fierce protectiveness.

"I will find the man who did this, Miranda. I swear it to you."

"And do what? Kill him, too?" she cried, tears streaming down her cheeks. "Don't you ever get tired of so much death?"

He paled at her angry outburst, staring at her. "I am more tired of it than you can possibly comprehend," he said hollowly after a pause. "My friend is dead."

The heartsick tone of his voice took her aback. She stopped crying abruptly, realizing she was not the only one in this room who had lost a loved one. In that moment, she looked into Damien's eyes, seeing past his archangel's beauty to the soul within, harrowed with pain; even now, she could feel the razor-edged tension in him, could see it in the broad, stiff lines of his shoulders.

He watched her with wolflike wariness, his high cheekbones shadowing the narrow planes of his cheeks, his fierce eyes guarded beneath the sweep of his inky lashes. He had the bleak, embittered gaze of a man who has lost more of his comrades than he can count. She had lost her uncle, but she hadn't even seen Jason in ages; this man had lost a friend who had been in his company nearly every hour of every day for the past six years. She understood now why he had come looking for a girl last night to comfort him.

As fresh tears rose in her eyes, she lifted her hand and touched the small scar that nicked the corner of his left eyebrow, then, without a word, pulled him into her arms.

She felt him tense uncertainly, the muscles in his back hardening with rigid grief, then, hesitantly, he accepted her embrace, sliding his arms around her waist. She squeezed her eyes shut. For several minutes, they clung to each other like two castaways washed up on a foreign shore, the sole survivors of some shipwreck. She could almost feel the crystallized anger pulsating within him. His big, powerful, warrior's body shook with the effort to contain it. With a vague, sorrowful wince, she pressed his head against her bosom and stroked his silky black hair, calming him, brushing aside the knowledge that the man she held in her arms could turn into a virtual killing machine in the blink of an eye. He was also the man who had saved her life.

"Damien Knight, I know he thought the world of you," she whispered.

He suddenly pulled back and stared at her for a second, consternation written across his angular features, as though his own response to her solace had confused him. Their faces were mere inches apart. At this close range, she saw the fear in his eyes. Without forethought, she touched his cheek gently, easing him with a little caress.

His glance dipped longingly to her lips, and the hunger in him that she had tasted last night was suddenly there once more between them, alive, electric, crackling like lightning. She pulled back abruptly; his startled gaze flew back up to her eyes, as though her movement had jarred him out of the trance. Mumbling a gruff apology, he swept to his feet, his vulnerable expression vanishing. He turned away and paced restlessly across the room. Miranda watched him, her heart pounding.

After a moment, he cleared his throat. "I propose we make a pact to forget last night ever happened."

"How can we?" she whispered.

Perhaps he had not heard her question, for he ignored it. "I shall be taking you to London where we will spend Christmas with my family. One of my kinswomen will act as your chaperon. You shall want for nothing. I know this all comes as a shock, but you have a whole new life ahead of you. Try to think of that. You'll have all the things you young ladies like— ball gowns and suitors and whatnot. There will be a large number of social occasions between Christmas and Twelfth Night. Parties, concerts, dances. Society will be a bit thin this time of year; nevertheless, I have every confidence that we can swiftly find you a suitable husband."

"A husband?" she echoed in astonishment.

"Of course." He pivoted, his chin high, his expression guarded and aloof. "That's what Jason wanted for you. I daresay you're old enough. I gave your uncle my word that I would see you respectably settled in life, and that is exactly what I intend to do. Now then, if you are quite composed, run along and pack your things. The journey to London takes two days. Bring only what you need. We'll travel light and post the rest to Knight House—that is the home of my eldest brother, the duke of Hawkscliffe. I have a sister about your age who lives there, as well. Her governess will help look after you."

Miranda stared at him, scarcely comprehending. This was all moving much too fast.

"Everything's going to be all right, Miranda. Go and get your things together," he prodded softly. "Keep moving, love. That's your best remedy. We can still reach Coventry by dark."

"Obviously, I owe you my thanks," she said, struggling for clarity, "for saving me from those ruffians last night, for your friendship to my uncle, for your generous offer. But I do not wish to go to London. I shall be staying here with my friends."

She dared not blindly entrust herself to this elemental warrior; the image of him standing on that snowy ridge, barbaric and magnificent, bathed in moonlight, streaked with blood, would be forever imprinted on her mind. Besides, the minute she left Yardley, she knew what would happen to Amy.

For a fraction of an instant, she considered telling Damien about Mr. Reed's unnatural proclivities, but discarded the notion with a shudder. She could not possibly bring herself to tell a virtual stranger something so personal and so humiliating.

He was shaking his head at her warily. "This is nonsense, Miranda. You can't stay here. You're too old to be at school. It's time to move on. Look at this dismal place. You don't really want to be here." He paused, resting his hands on his lean waist. "I daresay the only reason you could possibly wish to stay is so that you can keep sneaking out to the Pavilion. Isn't that right?"

She said nothing, bristling at his condescending tone.

"Miranda, Miranda, it seems you and I need to have a little chat. Put first things first." Sauntering over to Mr. Reed's desk, he sat casually on the corner of it, one foot braced on the floor. Loosely clasping his hands on his thigh, he held her in a penetrating stare, looking every inch the despotic army colonel. "Listen very carefully, my dear. Your playacting days are over; you have taken your final bow. You may be accustomed to duping your caretakers and running around the countryside half naked, but mademoiselle, you are my ward now. I will not tolerate insubordination."

Her nostrils flared as she inhaled sharply with indignation. She lifted her chin, but managed to hold her tongue.

"Oh, you don't like that, eh?" he taunted softly. "Well, glare all you want. Be advised, however, that I've turned some two thousand ignorant, malingering farm boys into disciplined soldiers capable of whipping Soult, Massena, and Boney himself, so I assure you, you can't win. You don't scare me, and I already know every trick in the book. Lord, if Jason could have seen you on that stage last night, he would have thrown you in a convent. I'm half tempted to myself. But in light of how you have been allowed to run wild,

I am prepared to give you a fair chance to start anew. From now on, you will conduct yourself in a manner befitting a respectable young lady. You will not embarrass me, my family, or your uncle's memory. Is that perfectly clear?"

"No!"

"Pardon?"

His arrogance incensed her. "For your information, I am nineteen years old and I don't need a guardian!"

"Oh? That's not how it looked last night. You flung yourself headlong into a highly dangerous situation. Where was your head, girl? Do you know how foolish that was? Do you have any inkling what could have happened to you if I hadn't been there?"

She huffed and looked away. "The Mud City people never bothered me before."

When he grasped her chin with the firm, gentle touch she remembered all too well, forcing her to look at him, she was shocked by her body's instant feverish response to the contact of his fingertips on her skin. Her pulse fluttered in her artery as she met his gleaming silver gaze in mingled fear and desire.

"Those men would have raped you and left you for dead," he said in a hard, quiet tone. "They got exactly what they deserved. I'm sorry you had to see it, but I don't for one second regret what I did. Aye, especially now that I know you are mine to protect." His light hold on her face became a caress. He trailed his knuckle along the line of her jaw, mesmerizing her with his touch. He held her in a masterful stare as his voice dropped to a lulling murmur. "You have nothing to fear, beauty. I think you and I are going to get along . . . just fine. These people don't know how to handle you, but I know exactly what you need."

"What's that?" she asked in defiance. Somehow her voice came out breathlessly.

"An iron hand in a velvet glove. Yes," he mused in a whisper, "that ought to tame your wild ways."

She was weak-kneed with his touch. The feelings he roused in her shocked and bewildered her. The man was violence incarnate, arrogant to the point of insult, yet his touch filled her with desire.

His sensual mouth curved in a slight, wicked smile as if he knew precisely his effect on her. Seduction gleamed in his light-tricked eyes. "Run along, my pet. Don't keep me waiting." As he brushed by her to the door, she cursed herself for letting him get the better of her again.

He turned back to her with one hand on the doorknob, then raised his eyebrows blandly. "Is there a question?"

"I still have not agreed to any of this."

"Your agreement would be welcome, but it is by no means necessary."

"You cannot make me go with you against my will! You have no right to march in here giving orders and trying to take control of my life."

"On the contrary, I have every legal right to do just that. You are under my authority until you reach the age of twenty-one. Or marry."

"I don't care. I'm not going anywhere with you!"

"You can't stay here," he said bluntly. "Mr. Reed has discharged you."

"*What?*" Why, that skulking pervert had already

schemed to get rid of her—the one obstacle blocking his path to Amy! She clenched her jaw and looked away, her eyes blazing with fury. She knew what she had to do. If Mr. Reed wanted her out, she would go, but she was taking Amy with her, she thought in grim resolve. Together they would catch up to Mr. Chipping's acting troupe at Leicester, the next stop on the circuit. She would accept the role of juvenile lead and would be able to support herself and Amy with her pay. But how was she to get rid of her formidable guardian first, when he appeared so staunchly determined to fulfill his duty to her uncle?

She could not simply dash away and outrun him. He was much faster and stronger than she, as his display of prowess last night had vastly proved. Indeed, she scarcely dared argue much more for fear of provoking his wrath. *Well, you are an actress, are you not?* she said to herself. She could go through the motions, make a show of obedience. When she had lulled the gray-eyed beast into a false sense of security, she would seize the first possible chance to flee back to Yardley and collect Amy; then they could catch up to Mr. Chipping's players. With any luck, the high and mighty Colonel Lord Winterley would not deem it worth his while to keep searching for a girl who wanted no part of his boring, respectable world of rules, rules, rules.

"Now then, Miss FitzHubert," he said, clasping his hands behind his back with an air of authority, "if you are quite through, go and get your things in order. Do be quick about it, please. Daylight is short."

She somehow leashed her pride and nodded stiffly, giving him an outward show of submission while her mind was already churning over her escape. His eyes flickered with gratification at her obedience as he opened the door and held it for her. Miranda forced her chin up and marched past him out of the office.

In the hallway, Mr. Reed and Miss Brocklehurst came out of the parlor across the entrance hall where they had been waiting.

"We will leave as soon as Miss FitzHubert has collected her belongings," Lord Winterley announced.

"Very good, sir," Mr. Reed answered, looking impressed by how quickly His Lordship had managed to bring the rebel of Yardley School to heel. "Miss Brocklehurst, would you be so good as to attend FitzHubert in preparing for her journey?"

"Gladly, Reverend."

With the thunderous Brocklehurst watching her every move, Miranda walked upstairs and into the dormitory, guarding her expression as she exchanged a glance with Amy. The child's blue eyes were wide with worry. The other girls looked on anxiously. Miranda kept her mouth shut as she folded her few belongings and placed them in her large calfskin satchel. She did not dare produce her theater costume from beneath her straw pallet. She would have to get it later when she returned for Amy.

"If you please, Miss Brocklehurst," Amy asked, unable to hold her tongue, "why must Miranda pack her things?"

"Because, Perkins, she is leaving Yardley today," the woman replied in smug satisfaction.

"Because of the Wedgwood doggy?" Amy cried, aghast.

"No, Perkins. FitzHubert's guardian has come to collect her."

Amy looked at Miranda in panic. "Your Uncle Jason's come at last?"

"No. He's dead. It's somebody else," Miranda said tautly, then slid Amy a firm, bolstering look. "Come, Amy. We must be brave and meet our futures without trembling."

"Dead? Oh, Miranda—but you can't leave me!"

"That is quite enough, Perkins."

"Sorry, Miss Brocklehurst." Amy stifled her anxious questions, but hovered by Miranda's elbow as she put on her ragged mantle and bonnet and slung the satchel over her shoulder.

"Come along, ladies," the headmistress said. "You may say good-bye to FitzHubert downstairs."

With Brocklehurst in the lead, the girls paraded sadly down the stairs, Jane and Sally following behind Miranda and Amy.

In the stairwell, Miranda put her arm around Amy and bent her head to the child's ear. "I am coming back for you tonight," she whispered quickly. "Don't go to sleep—and whatever you do, don't cross paths with Mr. Reed. You take my meaning?"

Amy nodded gravely.

"I'll throw a pebble at the window when I come; then you must use my knotted rope to climb down."

"Where will we go?" Amy asked, wide-eyed.

"We'll catch up to Mr. Chipping's players in Leicester and join the circuit."

Amy gasped. "Do you mean it? Am I to be an actress, too?"

"Shh!" Miranda glanced over her shoulder to make sure the others hadn't heard. "I'm sure Mr. Chipping can find you a small part every now and then. Are you game?"

"Am I?" she exclaimed. "Yes! Oh, Miranda, I can't wait to get out of here! You are the best, dearest—"

"Hush! I know you're excited, but you mustn't let it show. If Reed or the head witch find out, we're doomed. When I come, don't forget my costume and slippers. I left them under my cot so Brocklehurst wouldn't see."

Amy nodded somberly, then noticed Lord Winterley standing below and let out a gasp. "Is that your new guardian? Oh, I think I shall swoon! He's divine!"

Miranda rolled her eyes and went ahead, pulling on her gloves. Damien's shoulders looked even wider now that he had put on his caped greatcoat. As she came to the bottom of the steps and joined him in the entrance hall, his steely gaze assessed her, impersonal as a commander's inspecting his troops. He took her satchel from her.

"I've asked Mr. Reed to have the rest of your things sent to Knight House on Green Park, where you will be staying."

"This is all I have," she retorted, blushing at her poverty, but she lifted her chin as her bravado returned in full force.

"I see." He turned away, appearing a trifle nonplussed. "This way, then. Unfortunately, we've missed the London coach from Birmingham. The whole trip is about a hundred miles, but we might as well take a small bite out of it today."

She followed him outside, but upon stepping out into the bleak, snowy courtyard, she stopped. There was no carriage to be seen, only a large white steed that pawed the ground and snorted steam and appeared every bit as haughty and intimidating as Lord Winterley himself.

"We'll have to share my horse until we reach Coventry," he clipped out as he marched over to the magnificent beast and began tying her bag to the saddle.

Amy minced outside, tiptoed through the snow, and came to stand beside her with a conspiratorial giggle. The little imp looked at Damien, then at Miranda, elbowing her in the ribs.

"Stop it," Miranda hissed.

"We should be there in two or three hours," he continued, unaware of their exchange, for his back was to them. "We'll take lodgings at the coaching inn. In the morning, I shall put you on the stagecoach and follow you on Zeus." He gave the horse's flank a hearty slap and turned back to her. "Ready?"

"I don't ride," Miranda said, eyeing the fierce-looking stallion in trepidation.

He shrugged. "You do now."

Amy giggled again, drawing the colonel's glance. When he looked at the child, Amy gave him a dimpled smile and curtseyed. He lifted one charcoal-black eyebrow in stern perplexity.

"This is Miss Perkins," Miranda explained.

His gaze softened slightly with amusement. He gave the little girl a slight bow. "Mademoiselle."

Amy let out a small squeal of delight and dashed back inside. Miranda looked heavenward and prayed for patience, but her guardian merely chuckled a bit. Untying the horse's reins from the post, he swung up into the saddle.

"Come. Climb up onto the mounting block."

Miranda grumbled in protest under her breath, but did as he said. The squat, square stone was slippery with ice. The earl guided his horse over to the mounting block and held out his hand to her, maneuvering the stirrup in her direction with the toe of his shiny black boot.

"There you are; take my hand."

Nervously, she gripped his large, gloved hand and nudged her foot into the stirrup. He slid his arm around her waist and pulled her, sidesaddle, across his lap. She held onto him for dear life while the stallion sidestepped and tossed its head impatiently, its ivory mane flying. Then, suddenly, it was time to go.

As Miranda gazed at the old, slate-roofed farmhouse and the ragged group of girls waving good-bye, a lump rose in her throat. Unhappy as she had been here, in a way, it had been home. Her life was indeed about to change, though not in the way her imperious guardian had decreed.

Without further ado, he guided the stallion out of the walled courtyard at a docile walk. They crossed the tree-lined drive, which was deep with mud, and

cut across the flat, snowy field, beyond which lay the
Coventry Road. As they started across the open expanse, the sun emerged for the first time seemingly in
weeks.

Miranda drew in her breath as its brilliant light
transformed the world around them, as though a
dingy veil were being lifted from the earth, restoring
the blue of the sky's wide dome, whitewashing the
snow so that it sparkled with promise anew. Damien
clucked to his horse. Miranda let out a small shriek of
alarm, clutching his lean waist in fright as the bone-
jarring trot nearly bounced her headlong off of the
horse's back.

Damien's soft laugh misted in a cloud around
her. He tightened his hold around her midriff and
urged the horse into a canter—and suddenly her fear
changed to wonder. It was like flying. The horse's
strides were effortless, soaring over yards of ground.
The smoothness of the swift, rocking gait made her
breathless. The snow sprayed up in glittering plumes
from the stallion's mighty hoofs, while the wind from
their speed nipped at her nose and cheeks, turning
them rosy. Damien's athletic body was strong and sure
against her.

When she looked at him in amazement, he slipped
her a devilish glance, the sun warming his vibrantly
bronzed face, lighting the crystalline depths of his eyes
so they turned the pale, pure blue of the sky.

"Hold on," he murmured.

Her eyes widened as she spotted the hedgerow
straight ahead. She felt Zeus's mighty launch and
held her breath half in terror as they soared over the

hedgerow, landing neatly on the other side. The animal's supple body absorbed the impact with surefooted ease. With another little leap down the embankment, the stallion was on the road, carrying them toward an uncertain future.

# ⇥ CHAPTER ⇤
# FOUR

They rode for a long time in awkward silence, no sound between them but the whispering wind that blew the snow like desert sands and made the ice-coated branches of the trees clack. Holding the reins on either side of her slender waist, Damien did his best to distract his mind from the lush, warm softness of her body in his arms, the curve of her backside snug against his lap, rocking slowly against him with the horse's plodding steps. Contrary to what the schoolmaster had said, Miranda wasn't so very hard to manage, he thought with a measure of self-satisfaction. Once she had realized that he was in control, she had behaved like a perfect angel.

When she shivered again, he unbuttoned his great-coat and wrapped the ends of it around her, ignoring her huff of protest. The threadbare state of her cloak made him want to thrash his friend for neglecting her for so long. *Badly done, Jason. Badly done.* The temperature was dropping, and that was all she had to wear. She was a viscount's daughter, for God's sake. Her shoes should have been cast off on the rag-and-bone man long ago. When he thought of the whole roomful of gowns and another roomful of shoes that his seventeen-year-old sister owned, he could only shake his head. All of Miranda's belongings fit into one pitiful leather sack, but she had uttered no complaint. She was, he thought, a good little soldier.

He held her around her waist with protective care; they shared each other's body heat for the rest of the ride. He was mulling over the exacting standards by which he intended to measure her suitors when her voice broke into his thoughts.

"I thought colonels were supposed to be old."

"I *am* old," he said with a smile. "I feel old, anyway."

"You're not old. I mean elderly."

"Actually, you're right—it can take a man's whole career to make colonel. I was fortunate enough to enjoy a certain amount of preferment due to my family name, but I dared not take on too large a command until I had a good deal of experience. There's nothing worse than a green officer."

"Uncle Jason told me in his letters that you were the captain of the elite grenadier company of the Hundred Thirty-sixth."

He nodded. "I spent most of my years in Spain at that post, but after my brother left the army in '12, I was advanced rapidly to major, then lieutenant colonel, as my superiors died in the field. Officers, you see, have a dismally high mortality rate."

"Why is that?"

"Shoot the officers first. The rank and file are lost without leadership."

She shuddered slightly in his arms. "Weren't you ever frightened of being a target?"

"Somebody has to lead. Of course I was scared." He shrugged. "Fear makes a better soldier. You get used to it and do what needs to be done. That's all."

"I don't think I could get used to it. I'd run away."

"Then I would have to shoot you for desertion," he replied in morbid humor.

Her twin braids slid over her shoulders like dark, silken ropes as she turned to him, peeking uncertainly at him past the brim of her bonnet. "You wouldn't really shoot your own men for deserting?"

He just looked at her.

"Oh, Damien," she said with a wince.

"Those are the rules."

She shook her head. "You're a hard man."

He could not tell if it was a compliment or an insult. Then she changed the subject.

"How is your arm?"

"Not too bad."

"I feel terrible about that."

"Don't."

"You could have been killed—"

"You're safe. That's all that matters."

She was silent for a moment, perhaps mulling on his words.

"Damien? Sorry—I mean Lord Winterley."

Hearing his name on her tongue caused a curious little flutter of pleasure low in his belly. "I don't mind if you call me Damien," he murmured, "but only when we're alone. Publicly, it's best if we're more formal."

"I understand. What exactly do you think those horrid men wanted last night?"

His expression darkened. He held her more securely in the saddle. "Whatever they could get, I'm afraid."

"But they didn't take my money. I had just gotten paid from the theater."

"They didn't have time." He paused grimly. "Unfortunately, my dear, I don't think it was your money they were after." He was very glad that he had killed them.

"Perhaps, but it's hard to imagine that mere vagrants from Mud City should be so well organized. They even had horses."

"The horses were probably stolen. Miranda, did you recognize any of those men?"

She shuddered. "No. But, Damien—" She turned and stared at him, wide-eyed and somber. "What if they were white slavers?" she asked in a confidential tone. "You know—that catch girls and sell them to brothels?"

Taken aback by her earnest stare, he chuckled. "Oh, Miranda, you've been in too many melodramas."

"What do you mean?" she retorted. "Miss Brocklehurst says if we're bad, she'll make us stay out all night and the white slavers will get us!"

"And you believed her?"

"Yes."

Laughing softly, he gave her a light, comforting squeeze around her waist. What a strange blend of bravado, mistrust, and naivete she was. "Never fear, Miranda. If more white slavers come, I'll fight them off for you again, I promise." With that, he clucked to his horse and smiled at her happy exclamation as Zeus surged into a swift, gliding canter down the next stretch of road.

It was just past four o'clock but already dark with the early twilight of winter when they reached the coaching inn at Coventry. Miranda was nestled drowsily against him as the busy inn came into sight through the bare branches of the black trees. Warm lights gleamed in the windows. Smoke curled in wisps from the chimneys, and the smell of good things to eat carried to them on the night air, mingled with the horsey smell from the livery stable. Zeus whickered hungrily.

Miranda lifted her head from Damien's shoulder. "Ye Olde Red Cow." The name of the inn was painted in bold, block letters across the top of the building's entrance. "It looks busy. I hope they have room for us."

"They will," he murmured.

He halted his horse in the graveled yard and swung down from the saddle. Slipping the reins over Zeus's head, he returned for Miranda. A wave of desire moved through him as she braced her hands on his shoulders and slid down his body until her feet touched the ground. He released her and quickly turned away as a groom hurried over to attend them.

" 'Evening, sir. Stallion there?"

"Yes. Have you got a box stall open? He'll need quarters a bit away from the other horses, if possible."

The groom nodded efficiently. "Bring him this way, sir."

Damien glanced at Miranda. "Do you want to wait inside? This won't take long."

She shook her head. "I'll come with you." She followed near Zeus's flank as Damien led the animal inside through the wide barn doors.

The stable bustled with at least two dozen grooms mucking the stalls and caring for the countless livery horses. Many of the more docile creatures were simply tethered on a long line of rope, but there were box stalls to be had for a fee. Miranda wrinkled her nose at the smell as she loosened the ribbons of her bonnet around her throat and slipped it off of her head, letting it hang down her back. The wiry groom showed him to a stall at the end of the aisle, with an empty one beside it to give the kingly stallion plenty of privacy.

Damien dismissed the groom with a nod and took over the task of seeing to his horse's comforts personally. He unfastened the saddlebags and handed her satchel out to her, making a small pile of their baggage in the dimly lit aisle.

"Do all earls see to their own horses?" his ward asked quizzically. Grasping the bars that ran from the top of the stall's planks up to the ceiling, she swung back idly, watching him.

He glanced at her as he lifted the saddle off Zeus's back and carried it out of the stall. "He doesn't like strangers."

"He seems friendly enough to me."

"He likes you. He told me so," he said with a twinkle in his eyes. The truth was he liked tending to his horse himself. He found it relaxing. He took a currycomb out of one of the saddlebags and brushed Zeus's back vigorously where the saddle had sat. Slowly, he became aware of Miranda watching his hands moving with firm, sure gentleness over the animal's coat.

He glanced warily at her over his shoulder and felt the heat in her stare. He lowered his gaze, shaken by the force of the forbidden attraction between them. As he leaned against his horse for a moment, he wished he could apologize again for having propositioned her the night before and for kissing her like some rough brigand out there behind the theater, but it seemed unwise to bring the matter up. It was best forgotten. Besides, he was not sure that he was entirely sorry.

"Why do you keep a stallion if he's such a handful?"

Zeus swung his head around and nuzzled at Damien's coat pocket for a treat. "Get out of here," he muttered fondly, shoving away the animal's noble head. The stallion snorted in disdain. "He is going to sire great colts one day, that's why."

"For racing?"

"Or polo."

"He's got a very pretty face," she said.

"Did you hear that, old boy? The lady thinks you're quite the beau." Damien grasped the horse's delicate muzzle. Against his pearly coat, darker, blue-gray shadows surrounded the stallion's great, brown eyes. "He is a beauty, isn't he? That's his Arabian bloodlines showing through. He's half Hanoverian, which gives him his height and his speed, but on his dam's side, he's descended from the desert horses of the sheiks. Built for endurance." He patted the animal's neck. "Now all he needs is a wife. Or a harem, like the sheiks do," he added with a boyish smile.

She laughed softly. "Why didn't you go into the cavalry if you're so horse-mad?"

"That's precisely why I didn't go into the cavalry. It's bad enough seeing men get blown to bits. Horses don't even know what the fight's about." His smile faded.

Miranda sat down on a hay bale to wait, and rested her cheek on her hand while he quickly finished seeing to his horse. When Zeus was munching his grain at last in noisy, equine pleasure, Damien picked up their baggage and jerked a nod at Miranda to follow. Hurrying to keep up with his longer strides, she trailed him outside, across the yard, up the few steps, and through the door beneath the sign of Ye Olde Red Cow. Inside, a pleasant commotion filled the air. To the left of the cheerful, yellow-painted lobby was a dim, cozy pub; to the right, a quieter, more genteel dining room.

"Sir, madam! How do you do? Over here, please," a courteous little man greeted them from behind the counter.

Damien walked over to him, blinking against the illumination of the modest chandelier, while a porter shut the door behind them, barring the gust of wintry cold air that followed them in. Miranda peeled off her gloves and followed him over to the desk.

The concierge handed Damien the guest register. "You may sign for both yourself and your wife, sir."

"The young lady is my ward," he said gruffly, rebuking the man with a glower; then he bent his head, dipped the quill in the inkpot, and dashed out his neat, slanted signature. "Two rooms, please, and I'll need a seat for her on the London stagecoach tomorrow morning."

"Er, yes, of course, sir. Pardon my error." The concierge did not look convinced as to the nature of the relationship between Damien and his young companion. Pursing his lips, he took the register back. "Two rooms and one ticket to London, then, Mr. er—good heavens!" The concierge looked up from Damien's name on the register. "Colonel Lord Winterley! Sir, what an honor to have you as our guest!"

"Thanks," he muttered, tugging self-consciously at his cravat.

Several bystanders had heard the man's exclamation and were craning their necks to have a look at him.

Miranda raised an eyebrow at him. He sent her a distracted frown, then looked around with a tautly strained smile as the various guests and servants in earshot stared and bowed to him. *Here we go again,* he thought, wishing he could turn invisible.

"Good evening," he mumbled, nodding politely to the people who were staring at him.

Miranda glanced around at the onlookers in curious amusement, but the concierge could scarcely contain himself.

"May I just say, well done, my lord, well done!"

"Thank you."

The man handed him a pair of numbered room keys, then gave him back the gold sovereigns with which Damien had already paid for their night's room and board. "Now there, my lord, I won't take tuppence from you. I wish I had the finest rooms to give you and the young lady, but I'm afraid they've already been let. Roads are crowded, what with all the holiday visitors going to and fro."

"That's perfectly all right. Please, take it." He pushed the coins back across the counter. "It's only fair."

The little man grinned. "Not a chance, Colonel."

Damien laughed. "Very well, then. Send the lads in the pub a round or two with my compliments."

"Very good, sir, as you wish," the maitre d' said with a hearty chuckle. "Please, call on us if there is anything you require. The stagecoach leaves tomorrow morning at seven sharp. We begin serving breakfast at half-past six. Miss."

Miranda returned the man's nod.

"Hungry?" Damien asked her as they left the counter and walked toward the staircase, followed by two porters who carried their bags.

"Starved," she said.

"Let's settle in, then get something to eat."

She nodded at his suggestion, looking askance at him. Her green eyes danced at the staff's continued compliments behind them in the lobby as they went up the stairs.

"What a fine fellow."

"Now, there goes an Englishman!"

"Blood will tell!" the people said.

He could feel them watching his every move.

"Goodness, Damien, you didn't tell me you beat Napoleon single-handedly," Miranda whispered as they turned onto the landing and started up the next portion of the stairs.

"I thought you already knew," he said wryly.

"Do people always fawn on you like that?"

"No."

"Yes, they do. You're just being modest," she chided in a playful tone, studying him closely. "But you hate all the attention, don't you? Why? You deserve it."

"Not any more than the rest of my men. Not any more than the ones who died."

"Pshaw. There's nothing wrong with taking a bow every now and then when you've earned it," she scoffed.

"You'd be the expert on that."

She shot him a quelling smile at his jibe.

When they came to the third floor, the porters showed them to their rooms, which were situated across the hallway from each other. Miranda unlocked her door, back to back with Damien while he did the same; then the porters carried their bags into their respective chambers and lit the candles for them.

"I'll wait for you downstairs," Damien said in the hallway. "Pub or dining room?"

"Your choice."

He tossed her a narrow, teasing smile. "And to think Mr. Reed called you a difficult girl."

With a saucy little half smile, she shut the door in his face.

He really wasn't half bad when he wasn't barking orders or chopping people's heads off. Leaning against the door with a sigh, Miranda turned around and surveyed the compact but pretty room her guardian had taken for her. Her gaze traveled over the sturdy oak furniture and inviting sleigh bed, the neat fireplace of whitewashed brick, and the flower-printed curtains. She could barely remember the last time she had had a whole bedchamber all to herself. A foggy memory filtered back to her through the mist of years—her childhood bedroom in Papa's country mansion. She remembered a light blue canopy over her high, frilly bed and wallpaper printed with beautiful birds.

She closed her eyes, her shoulders drooping slowly with a pang of loss, not just for her uncle, but for the loss of this chance to walk through the door Damien had opened for her into a new life: a door into her father's glittering world of elegance and privilege. Lord Winterley moved in that world, belonged in it. For a second, she let herself imagine what it would be like beyond that threshold. *London* ... Parties, balls, suitors. Oh, that was what she really wanted, she thought in longing. The tinselly world of the stage was only a sham of the *beau monde* that she still recalled through the rosy haze of her childhood memories. Hadn't her mother's one burning wish been to see her daughter become a real lady, as she, herself, the notorious Fanny Blair, had never been?

But even if Miranda were to let Damien lead her through that door into the glittering world of elegant people that was London high society, once there, she would never fit in. She was not fine enough, and this arguing with herself was a waste of time. Her pensive expression hardened.

Her first priority was saving Amy. Until the child was safe, nothing else mattered—not her own dreams of a beautiful life, nor her disturbing attraction to her guardian. Pushing away from the door, she hurried to freshen up for dinner.

When she went back downstairs half an hour later, the noise of cheers and manly laughter from the pub advised her of the war hero's location without her having to ask the concierge. Shaking her head to herself in amusement, Miranda walked into the dim pub and saw him at once.

He was seated on a large, rough-hewn table near the fireplace, surrounded by a crowd of overfed, ruddy-cheeked John Bulls buoyed up with patriotism and liquor. They were buying him bumpers of ale and clamoring to hear his stories of battle. Stories, she judged by his uneasy smile, that he had no interest in telling.

As she strode toward him, the buxom blond tavern wench carried over a round of pewter tankards on a tray, stopping to whisper something in Damien's ear just as he looked past the crowd and saw Miranda coming. The barmaid made a point of thrusting her breasts practically in Damien's face as she handed out her pints before hurrying back to her duties. Miranda sent a guarded scowl after the little hussy while Damien rose to his feet.

"Excuse me, gentlemen. I have the pleasant duty of escorting this young lady to dinner."

A collective groan of disappointment went up from the men.

"Don't let me interrupt your fun," she muttered under her breath as he captured her hand and tucked it in the crook of his elbow.

"Perfectly all right, my dear. It is hardly proper for young ladies to loiter in taverns."

As he led her out of the taproom with guilty haste, the tavern wench crossed in front of their path. Miranda's smile withered at the implicit look Damien and the barmaid furtively exchanged; her heart balled up as tightly as a hedgehog in self-defense at the hungry way his gaze followed the girl, much as he had eyed *her* the night before, when he had mistaken her for another sort of woman. Actress that she was, she pretended not to have noticed.

Obviously, he had already made up his mind to use that girl tonight, but what did she care? she thought in disdain, more stung than she cared to admit. With him distracted, bedding his little tramp, her escape would be all the easier.

*Damn,* Damien cursed mentally. She had caught him red-handed planning his assignation with the barmaid. Now she was pouting like a jealous wife, as though she did not realize that his current state of frustration was her fault. The sweet torment of holding her on his lap for three hours had driven him to distraction.

She turned to him in the lobby, her emerald eyes snapping sparks. "Why don't I just go back upstairs and eat in my room and leave you here with your little friend?"

"I don't know what you're talking about, my dear," he said in bland superiority. "Come, the dining room is this way."

They went in, sat down, and ordered dinner. The waiter brought out wine and poured it, and still Miranda barely made eye contact with him. Damien drew a mental line in the sand, refusing to grovel, refusing to explain himself. She ignored him for a while longer, punishing him for his transgression. He had no idea why he felt guilty. He rested his elbow on the table and drummed his fingers by the base of his wineglass. She stared across the dining room at the mediocre paintings on the wall, watercolor landscapes and fox-hunting scenes.

"Miranda," he said dully at last.

"What?" She turned to him.

He gave her a knowing half smile.

She curled her lip in disdain and veiled her gaze with her long, black lashes, looking away. She took a judicious sip of her red wine. Carefully setting her glass back down, she leaned across the table toward him, crooking her finger at him to come closer.

He obliged.

"I think it's only fair someone should warn you"— her tone was prim and confidential—"a lot of the girls I knew from the Pavilion sell their bodies like your friend in the pub. Let me just say—you could catch a disease."

"Miranda!" he whispered, scandalized. He glanced

around to make sure no one sitting near them had heard. "I am not going to discuss this with you."

"Why not?"

"You're my ward."

"You're certainly singing a different tune than last night," she needled him.

He narrowed his eyes at her in warning and shook his head. What an outrageous chit she was.

"Perhaps you already have the French disease," she said sagely. "There must have been a lot of camp followers at the war. You seem to go in for that sort of thing."

"Perdition, girl! I do not have the French disease," he retorted in a whisper. "For your information, I'm careful."

She lifted her eyebrows, apparently enjoying his discomfiture. "What do you mean? You only bed virgins?" She took a sip of wine and innocently added, "I'm a virgin."

Mid-swallow, he coughed on his wine. Devil take the little hellion, she was toying with him! How dare she?

Ah, he knew what was going on here, he thought, recovering quickly. If they had been alone, she would not have dared act so cheeky, but the presence of the other hotel guests seated at their tables around the dining room had emboldened her past her healthy respect of him. His interest in another female had pricked her vanity and so she was back to rebellion, back to testing and challenging him like a cocksure fresh recruit who saw no reason to listen to his drill sergeant. Well, the headmaster had warned him of this, had he not? Damien could not decide if he was

vexed or amused at her jealousy over him, but he preferred to indulge her rather than to risk scaring her
again.

"I am delighted to hear it, Miss FitzHubert," he
said mildly.

"I did have a beau once who almost changed that,
though," she remarked with studied nonchalance, her
eyes flashing. "He was in the cavalry."

He scowled. "What's his name?"

"Trick."

"What the devil kind of name is that?"

"A nickname for Patrick."

"Patrick who?"

"I forget. He had a blue uniform, though. I thought
him very dashing."

"You're lying, my love."

"Why shouldn't I have had a beau? I wanted to believe that *someone* cared about me, since your Major
Sherbrooke obviously forgot I existed."

He looked away, unsettled by the bleakness in her
eyes, all at odds with her false, brittle smile. "What
happened to your beau, then?" he grumbled.

"I refused to give him what he wanted, and he never
came back. I was sixteen." She lowered her lashes, sitting very still.

He shook his head, simmering. "Cavalry's useless."

She looked up with a roguish smile. "Aye, that he
was. But he was a good kisser."

He clamped his jaw and turned away, then looked
at her again, quite incensed. "Stop it."

"My lord?"

"You are deliberately baiting me."

She tilted her head with an innocent smile. "Oh, don't be cross, Damien. He didn't kiss half as well as you do, though. I imagine you've had more practice."

"I shall turn you over my knee if you don't start showing some respect for your elders, my girl."

She laughed at him with a look in her eyes that suggested she just might enjoy that. Holding his gaze, she took a slow, lingering sip of her wine. He stared at her like a starved man, half blinded by the memory of her in that skimpy lavender gown, the paper-thin muslin giving him brief, tantalizing glimpses of her luscious curves. God, he wanted to lay her down and kiss her entire body from head to toe, consume every inch of her until she writhed with pleasure.

The timely arrival of the waiters with the meal dispersed the tension that charged the air around their table. A feast was set before them of beef steaks, pigeon pie, muffin pudding, and an assortment of vegetables.

When the staff had withdrawn, Miranda offered up grace before the meal. She closed her eyes and bowed her head, reciting the short prayer. As Damien gazed at her, somehow her nearness routed any lingering thoughts he might have had about the barmaid. It had been an unworthy impulse, after all. He knew that perfectly well. But as Miranda swept her green eyes open again and murmured, "Amen," he concealed his change of mind about the tryst.

She did not need to know she had that kind of power over him.

*    *    *

After dinner, they returned to their respective rooms and said a cordial good night in the hallway, though it was only seven. Damien claimed he was tired. She did not refute him, but she knew the real reason he was retiring so early. He could barely wait to get that harlot from the pub into his bed, Miranda thought, brooding on it as she slid under the covers of the sleigh bed, alone.

Exhausted from having gotten no rest the previous night, she slept soundly, but the urgency of her mission woke her two hours later. Better fed than she was rested, she dragged herself out of the warm, cozy bed at nine o'clock, knowing it was time to make her escape.

After last night's run-in with the outlaws from Mud City, she was not looking forward to the journey in the dark, in the cold, without Damien's protection. She had no choice. She still had her three shillings' pay from the Pavilion, and now that she had ridden on the mighty Zeus, she felt brave enough to try to manage one of the docile hack horses from the livery stable. A horse's slowest, safest gait would still be faster than her own two feet, but she realized that her guardian's fame might hamper her escape. The whole staff of Ye Olde Red Cow was groveling to the war hero and had noted her presence by his side. If she tried to hire a horse, the grooms would probably insist on detaining her until he could be consulted. It wouldn't work.

Well, it seemed her acting skills would be called upon yet again today, she thought as she fixed her hair before the chipped mirror on the stand. Hastily donning her cloak, pulling the leather strap of her satchel up over her shoulder, she opened the door a crack and peered into the hallway. Finding it empty, she sneaked out of her room.

She tiptoed past Damien's door and glided silently down the hallway to the stairs. Putting on her most demure expression, she made her way back to the dining room, pausing to steal a peek into the pub. She breathed a sigh of relief to see that Damien was not there, then furrowed her brow to see the blond barmaid darting among the men with her tray.

Were they through with their act of lust, or had the tramp not yet gone up to his room? she wondered, then shrugged off the question. It did not signify. She had said her good-byes to Damien Knight.

When she glanced into the dining room, she found it almost empty. Her gaze homed in at once on her marks—a pair of pimple-faced university lads about seventeen years old, accompanied by a slightly older fellow with the bearing of an upper servant. Their tutor, she guessed. She had not seen them earlier.

Perfect, she thought. She ventured to hope that the two young lads were later arrivals and would not realize she was under the protection of the hotel's famous guest this night. If she played her hand skillfully, they could provide her with transportation back to Yardley within two hours.

Mentally riffling through her repertoire of melodramas for a plot that would suit her purposes, the tale of *The Wayward Heiress* came to mind. Ah, yes, she thought with a wily smile skimming her lips, that one was lovely. Mr. Chipping had almost given her the role of Laura, the heroine, but at the last minute had relegated her to second lady. She had played Katherine, the heroine's cousin.

Summoning a grief-stricken air, which was not difficult when she thought of Uncle Jason, she walked with dirgelike steps into the dining room and went to sit at a small table by the fireplace, conspicuously dabbing at her eyes with her handkerchief. The boys gazed at her when she walked in, as boys were wont to do.

The waiter came over to her, looking surprised to see her again. She asked for a cup of tea and biscuits and pretended not to notice the stares of the two lads. She could hear their tutor scolding them in hushed tones to quit gawking at her, but when she glanced at them out of the corner of her eye, he was staring at her, too. She turned her face toward the fireplace as though to hide a piteous sob.

This proved more than the first lad could take. In an instant, the young Oxford gentleman was standing by her table, all alarmed youthful chivalry.

"Excuse me. Miss?"

Miranda knew as much basic etiquette as any young lady. It was not permissible to accept the address of any young man to whom she had not been properly introduced. He had done exactly what she wanted, but she slanted him a wary, affronted look.

"Forgive me," he said with a blush. "We could not help noticing that you seem to be in some sort of distress, and we were just wondering—" His voice cracked, screeching upward an octave.

Miranda hid her wince.

"That is," he tried again, "is there anything the three of us can do to help?"

She gave her lashes a shy flutter and offered the boy a tremulous smile.

It worked. The shorter boy and the sobersides tutor were there in a trice, surrounding her with their gallantries.

"Poor, dear lady—"

"What seems to be the trouble?"

"I'm sure you're very kind. I do not know what else to do!" She summoned a few choice tears. "I received word that my old nurse is on her deathbed. I must see her. I love her dearly. She has no one else. I must go to her, but my parents refused me permission. I confess, I—I've run away so I might reach her in time to say good-bye!"

"Dear me, miss, it was not wise to flee your parents," the tutor said, frowning. He was only about twenty-three or twenty-four himself.

"Why did they refuse to let you go?" the second boy asked, wide-eyed.

Miranda sniffled. "They would not allow me to leave because this very night they have arranged for a meeting between myself and the odious, old . . . colonel they are forcing me to marry!"

The two lads gasped with naive indignation, but their tutor eyed her skeptically.

"They would force you to marry him against your will?" the first boy exclaimed.

"No wonder you ran off!" the second chimed in.

They stared dazedly at her as she dabbed at the corners of her eyes. "I know, I know. But all that matters now is my poor old nurse. Somehow I must get to Yardley village before it is too late," she said with her best melodramatic flair. She put her cup of tea aside and started to rise to her feet. "If you good gentlemen will excuse me, I must press on."

"Let us call your carriage for you!" said the first.

"I have no carriage."

"Your horse—" offered the second.

"I have no horse. I could not risk taking one of my father's mounts, lest I be discovered."

The two boys exchanged a businesslike glance. "Right," they said, then looked at her. "If you will permit us, Miss, we will conduct you swiftly and safely to Yardley village."

"Oh, I couldn't possibly impose upon your generosity," she started, but remarkably, the two trusting lads soon managed to persuade her.


*Damien saw a field of corpses.*

The guns had gone silent. Peasants crept stealthily out of the nooks and crannies of the dusty Spanish town and stole out onto the surrounding battlefields. Ravens waited on nearby branches, cawing hungrily. The peasants picked their way among the bodies, robbing the dead of whatever valuables they could find, stripping them even of their clothes. In the floating fog of dawn, they left the slain, oppressors and liberators alike, naked and bereft of their dignity.

He saw soldiers at work piling their fallen comrades into mass graves on one side of the field; he heard someone calling his name. It was Lucien.

His brother was searching for him through the sea of bodies, but Damien found himself unable to move, unable to call out to his twin or to anyone. He gradually realized that he was badly wounded, pinned beneath a mound of corpses. The angel who had come to carry him up to heaven sat nearby perched on a wagon wheel, her chin resting on her fist, wings folded demurely. She had luxurious sable tresses and spring-green eyes that seemed to peer into the very soul of him. She just sat there watching him.

*Help me,* he tried to beg her, but he could not speak. She seemed to be waiting for something, some signal from him that he could not give because he was paralyzed, half dead.

Then he felt one of the peasants plucking at his clothes, come to rob his body. Horror welled up, choking him. He could not move to defend himself, as though his very limbs had frozen. He tried to scream, but he was mute. *Get your hands off me, I'm not dead. I'm still here. I'm still alive, damn it!*

He awoke suddenly and sat up, covered in a cold sweat. His breathing was ragged, deafening in the silence of the pitch-dark room.

For a moment, he did not know where he was.

Slowly, his head cleared and the vicious past scuttled back under the bed like a monster in a child's obsession, releasing him from its jaws for now.

He swung his legs off the bed and sat up and reached toward the bedside table to light a candle. His hands shook slightly; he fumbled with the tinderbox. The fire in the hearth had gone out, and the room was freezing.

Failing on his first attempt to catch a spark, he gave up and slowly put the tinderbox back on the table, his gaze heavy with the futility of it all. *You bastard, Jason. You're the lucky one,* he thought.

He rubbed his face with both hands for a moment, then rose restlessly and put his waistcoat back on but did not button it, nor did he bother with his cravat. He was otherwise still dressed, for it had been too early to retire for the night. He glanced at his fob watch: half-past nine.

*Miranda.*

The thought of her dragged him back firmly into the land of the living. He decided to check on her, in no humor to be left to his own grim company. With nightmare images still haunting his brain, he thought to order tea and a light repast, then to check on Zeus. He left his room and went across the hallway to see if she wanted something to eat or needed anything, but when he knocked softly on her door, he got no answer.

*Must be sleeping,* he thought. He started to walk away, leaving her to her slumber, when a faint tickle of intuition, or premonition, made him pause—that same sixth sense that had made him look back last night just in time to spy her attackers materializing out of the darkness. Narrowing his eyes suspiciously, he walked back to her door and knocked again a bit more loudly.

"Miranda?"

Still, no reply.

He pounded on the door. "Are you in there?" God, what if something was wrong? "Miranda, answer me!" His sense of danger fully alerted now, he grasped the knob and thrust open the door. His eyes widened. The room was dark, the bed scarcely rumpled.

She was gone.

With a curse under his breath, he spun around and without thinking twice, grabbed his sword from his room, knowing her penchant for getting herself into trouble. A moment later, he was running down the stairs, dashing across the hotel lobby, heedless of the guests and servants who stared at him in shock as he passed. He threw open the front door with a bang and plunged out into the darkness, his chest heaving, his heart pounding wildly.

The light snow that had begun falling struck his face as his stare homed in on the sleek curricle in the graveled yard. It was not yet in motion, but nearly so, the groom making a final check of the harness. There, on the driver's seat, nestled between two beardless youths, was his ward.

Damien's nostrils flared in fury as he realized she had ditched him again. He marched toward the carriage in wrath.

# ⋊ CHAPTER ⋉
# FIVE

"I say, stand aside!" the first boy yelled.

"Who's this?" the tutor murmured.

But Miranda could only stare in dread. The moonlight outlined the big, broad-shouldered silhouette of a man standing in the road, sword in hand—six feet of powerful, angry male—a tough, taciturn force of destruction. His breath clouded around him in puffs of steam, shrouding him in mist like some warrior out of legend.

"Halt!" his deep voice bellowed.

"Do as he says," she blurted out, terrified that he might go on the rampage as he had last night.

"You know him?" the second boy exclaimed.

"It's . . . the colonel," she said faintly.

The curricle had hardly stopped, but Damien was already stalking over to it.

"You said he was old!"

"What is going on here?" their tutor demanded.

"Now, look here—!" The first boy gulped, swallowing his protests, as he stared down Damien's sword, the tip of which suddenly hovered an inch away from the throat.

"Winterley! Don't hurt him; it's my fault!" Miranda cried, aghast.

"Colonel . . . Lord Winterley?" their tutor breathed in dread.

Damien's steely gaze swung from him to Miranda.

She pointed to his weapon. "Put . . . that . . . *down*!" She held his stare unflinchingly, willing him to get control of his fury.

Slowly, the battle rage cleared from his eyes, but his lips twisted in a proud, defiant snarl. He lowered his sword and slammed it point-first into the muddy road, driving it several inches into the ground so that it stood where he left it, jutting out of the earth, vibrating with the force of his movement. Without a moment's hesitation, he reached up, lifted her bodily out of the carriage, and slung her over his shoulder.

Miranda shrieked as she swung down over his broad back.

"Give me her bag," he growled at the lads.

The tutor handed it over in awe. "Please forgive the boys, my lord. The young lady told quite a cock-and-bull story."

"I can imagine," he said through gritted teeth, then pivoted toward the inn.

"Damien, put me down!" Miranda cried, shaking her long hair out of her face, but his grip on her was iron. He went and retrieved his sword.

Carrying her effortlessly over his right shoulder, her satchel and his weapon in his left hand, he strode across the yard and back inside, not relenting even as he marched through the lobby, past the astonished maitre d' and up the stairs. She cringed with mortification, dreading what he might do to her the moment they were alone. She didn't have long to wait. All too soon, he was marching swiftly down the hallway on the third floor. He slammed the door of her room open and strode inside, kicking it shut behind him. Crossing the room in three strides, he threw her down on the bed.

She landed on her back on the soft mattress and stared up at him, her heart in her throat as he loomed over her, fierce and wild, the few top buttons of his shirt undone down his bronzed, heaving chest.

"You ungrateful . . . reckless little . . . hellion!" He pivoted on his heel and took a few paces away from her, turning his back on her.

Warily, she eased up to a seated position, not daring to take her eyes off of him. He lowered his head and rested his hands on his lean waist. She stared in fright at his giant shoulders rising and falling as he struggled to tame his wrath.

"Why did you run from me?" he asked in a numb tone, not turning around. "How did I possibly wrong you?"

She clung to her pretense. "I'm going to become an actress, and you can't stop me!"

He spun around and glared at her. "Do you think I want this any more than you do? Do you think I have nothing better to do with my time than play nurse-maid to you?"

"Let me go and be done with it, then!"

"Would it were possible, but I have a duty to your uncle. Good God, girl! Going off with strangers?"

"You're a stranger," she said in a low tone of defiance.

"You trust them more than you trust me? But, of course. You *don't* trust me, do you, Miranda? I only saved your life. I only took a bullet for you. That's why you spent the whole day lying to me. Well, that's your game, isn't it? The minute I turn my back, you run. Are you too much of a coward to confront me face-to-face?"

She started to protest, but he cut her off.

"No. No more lies. I understand you better than you realize, Miranda. You want to be an actress because you crave the applause, I know. You think your audience gives a damn for you, but I'm going to tell you the unvarnished truth: Those men only want to bed you," he said harshly. "Trust me when I say that men don't have the slightest respect for the kind of woman you want to become. Where will they be when your beauty fades? Do you know where actresses past their prime end up? In the gutter, that's where. Forgotten. Alone. Is that what you want?"

"You don't know what I want," she forced out, her whole body shaking at his tirade. He had seen through her with such devastating clarity. She looked away.

"Applause isn't love, Miranda."

"It's close enough for me."

"No, it's not. Lord, you are a vexing chit! You want someone who will stand by you. Care for you. Take up your battles for you. What you need is a husband, so quit bloody fighting me, come to London, and let me find you one!"

"Why do you even care what I do?" She jumped off

the bed and stood before him, out of patience. "Why don't you mind your own business? I don't want your help. I don't need a guardian. Leave me alone! As your ward, I hereby absolve you of all responsibility—"

"I have a legal responsibility to you that is not so easily shed, besides which, I'm not doing this for you. I'm doing it for Jason."

"He's not here to check up on you, if you haven't noticed. He's dead," she said bitterly.

"You watch your tone when you speak of my friend," he warned. "A promise is a promise, and I gave him my word. Now hand over your room key. I'm locking you in until morning."

"The devil you will!" She dove toward the small nightstand where she had left the numbered key and grabbed it.

Glowering sternly at her, Damien stretched out his hand in front of her. "Give it to me, Miranda."

She put it behind her back, her heart pounding. "You can't have it. I won't let you lock me in."

"Stop being a child!" He grabbed for it, seizing her wrist, trying to pry her fingers open. "Damn it, Miranda, I'm not going to let you throw your life away!" he said through gritted teeth as they struggled. "You're not going to be an actress; you're going to be a respectable woman, as Jason wanted! Yield, you insufferable shrew!"

With that, he easily overpowered her and pulled the key out of her hand.

She lost her hold on it with a wild cry. "I hate you!"

"I don't give a damn." He pivoted and stalked

toward the door. "I advise you to get some sleep. The coach leaves early."

Aghast at the realization that in mere seconds, she would be locked in, prevented from going to Amy's rescue, Miranda watched him striding toward the door. "Winterley! Don't do this!"

"You can't be trusted. You leave me no choice."

Tears jumped into her eyes. "Wait!"

He paused and glanced warily over his shoulder. "What do you want?"

She swallowed hard, her pulse slamming in her arteries. "I wasn't running away to be an actress."

"Yes, you were—"

"Yes, but only because I have no choice."

"What can you possibly mean?"

"I want to go to London with you. I want to be a lady. But I can't only think of myself. That's why I have to be an actress. But I had to go back to the school first."

"What? You're not making any sense."

"Oh, Damien," she whispered, shaking her head. "All is not right at that place. You don't understand. Please."

"What is the matter, Miranda?" he asked in a hard tone. "Come to the point."

She closed her eyes for a second, trembling. *I cannot believe I have to tell him this*. But he gave her no other choice. He probably wouldn't even believe her. It was her word against the vicar's, and she had already proved herself a bit of a liar.

But he had to believe. He had to.

She braced herself, took a deep breath, and flicked

her eyes open again, evenly meeting his penetrating gaze. "Do you remember the little girl with the golden ringlets? She curtseyed to you in the schoolyard."

He nodded skeptically.

"She's in serious danger," she choked out.

He rolled his eyes and started to turn away. "Another of your cock-and-bull tales."

"No! Damien, please listen to me! I have to go back and get her. You're right; I was lying to you today, pretending to do whatever you said. And I lied to those boys in the curricle. I was planning all day on going back and saving Amy."

"From what?"

She held him in a stare of stark, silent pleading. "Mr. Reed."

He shook his head blankly. "What do you mean?"

"What do you think I mean?" she whispered with failing bravado, shaking visibly now.

Staring at her, he walked back slowly toward the bed. He rested his hands on his lean hips and searched her face. "Go on."

"He . . . harms the girls. He is not . . . natural. Nobody else knows what's really going on inside those walls. He flogs us with a b-birch rod." She squeezed her eyes shut in disgust and forced herself to say it. "He . . . touches us. And himself."

When she forced herself to look at him again, there was murder in his eyes. He lowered himself to sit on the bed beside her, rubbing his mouth for a moment.

His voice was very quiet, very controlled. "I'm listening."

"It's the little ones he goes after. He likes them when

they're still flat-chested." Bitterness rose in her throat. "I think it's the only reason he started a girls' school in the first place. He's had his eye on Amy Perkins for months now, but so far, I've been able to keep her out of his path. Tonight, with me gone . . ." She faltered, fairly paralyzed with fear at the thought of what might be happening already. "Oh, Damien, please. We've got to help her. She's only twelve. He'll wait until the other girls go to bed—"

"I'll handle it," he whispered. Reaching out, he took her hand and held it for a minute between both of his. "You're telling me the truth? Because I'm going to put my reputation behind this. My honor on the line."

"Yes," she whispered with an imploring sob, then quickly wiped away a tear.

He reached out and cupped her cheek in his hand, staring fiercely into her eyes. His voice was brusque, the underlying rage tautly controlled. "Nobody hurts you anymore, do you understand? You are under my protection now—"

She moved into his arms before he could finish, hugging him tightly around his neck. She clung to him, pressing her shivering body flat against his. His arms encircled her hesitantly. He stroked her hair for a moment, then just held her.

"Angel, I know you're scared of me after last night," he whispered, "but no matter what happens, you can trust me. Just give me one chance to show you that."

She squeezed her eyes shut, too moved by his words even to address them. Knowing that time was of the essence, she somehow pulled back and looked into his eyes. "I want to come with you," she said in a shaky voice. "The girls will need me."

He nodded and rose, but she reached for his hand, staying him.

"Damien, please, no more bloodshed. I know he deserves it, but I don't think I can bear it."

He lifted her hand to his lips and bowed his head, pressing a kiss into her palm. "Not for the world would I ever frighten you again." Tenderly, he closed her fingers into a fist, as though to save his little kiss for later. Releasing her hand, he prowled to the door and opened it. "Get yourself ready. I'll hire a carriage. A fast team can take us there in an hour and a half," he said, the light from the hallway glimmering along his profile.

She nodded, too choked up to voice her gratitude. Then he went out, leaving her holding her curled fist against her chest and trembling in the dark with the frightening newness of having someone on her side.

Soon, they were storming up the road in the light, fast four-in-hand that Damien had hired from the livery stable and which he drove with the cold, steady control of an ancient Roman charioteer. Rage bristled in the broad lines of his shoulders and in the smooth, emotionless mask of his face. With a groom posted on the boot, Miranda sat beside him on the driver's seat, shivering with foreboding and the chill of the wintry night. He drove the horses relentlessly, sweeping up the curving road. His hard face in the moonlight was unflinching, but the enraged glitter in his eyes told her that the headmaster was in dire peril.

When at last they turned off the road onto the drive of Yardley School, Miranda scanned the old farmhouse anxiously. The windows were dark, but a light gleamed from Miss Brocklehurst's parlor. Damien pulled the horses to a halt, leaped down from the driver's seat, and strode to the front door. The groom scrambled down from the back to mind the horses.

The night reverberated with the pounding of her guardian's leather-gloved fist on the thick oaken door. Miranda sat paralyzed on the driver's seat, her heart slamming in her chest. The curtain in the parlor window moved, and Brocklehurst peered through the glass. The sight of the headmistress's hateful face snapped Miranda into action. She had to think of Amy. This was no time to freeze up over her own hurt and confusion. There was still time to save the child, and that was all that mattered. She jumped down from the carriage and ran after Damien, coming up behind him just as Miss Brocklehurst answered the door.

"Lord Winterley, whatever brings you—"

"Where is he?" Damien growled.

"Check his office," Miranda said as Damien brushed past the headmistress and went marching across the entrance hall.

"Reed!" he thundered.

"What is the meaning of this?" Brocklehurst cried.

"You know full well," Miranda muttered, then ran to the bottom of the stairs. "Amy! Sally! Jane!" she shouted.

As Damien threw open the closed door to Mr. Reed's office, Miranda froze at the sound of Amy's shriek coming from inside. With an explosive curse, Damien disappeared into the office. Miranda was only a step or two behind him, but Miss Brocklehurst tried to block her path.

"What do you think you're doing, missy?"

Miranda shoved the woman out of her way. "Stay away from me! Amy!"

She flung into the office just as Amy jumped up from Mr. Reed's sofa by the wall and came hurtling across the office with a hysterical cry, fleeing, wild-eyed, into Miranda's arms.

Miranda hugged the girl hard, watching in fierce protectiveness as Damien advanced upon the head-master. Mr. Reed's face was a rictus of fear as he backed away, his shirtsleeves rolled up, his waistcoat unbuttoned, his greasy hair mussed, his collar un-done. She and Amy clung to each other, both flinching as Damien threw the man up against the wall and punched him in the face with a shattering blow. He picked him up and hit him again. Brocklehurst gasped from the doorway as Mr. Reed slithered down the door in a dazed heap, blood running from his nose.

Clenching his jaw, his nostrils flared in barbaric fury, Damien stared down at the semiconscious man as though he longed to skewer him. "Fetch Mrs. Warren," he ordered Miranda. "Tell her to take the carriage into Birmingham and bring the constable and the magistrate. The groom from the inn can drive her."

Miranda nodded. "Come, sweeting," she murmured to Amy, but the child broke free of her embrace and ran over to Mr. Reed's sprawled form.

"Yah!" Amy cried as she dealt the man a kick in the groin.

Startled, Miranda quickly retrieved her, then brought her back to the kitchens to fetch Yardley's dear, old cook, Mrs. Warren, as Damien had ordered.

The girls huddled together in the dormitory, staring at each other, too scared to speak, when the constable came and led Mr. Reed away in manacles. Miss Brocklehurst was forced to go with the authorities, as well, to answer their questions. What their fate would be, Miranda did not know.

The next few hours passed in a blur of anxiety. Two sweet-faced ladies from a children's charity came up and questioned them, shaking their heads as the girls haltingly explained their sordid ordeals. One of the ladies was the magistrate's wife; the other was his sister. Miranda said little at first, frightened of the repercussions in case the ladies did not believe them, but from their reactions, she gained a new respect for her guardian's standing in the world. Colonel Lord Winterley was an earl and a war hero, particularly known, she gathered, for his integrity. Now it was no longer the girls' word against Mr. Reed's; the great Winterley had taken up their cause. He had seen Mr. Reed's wrongdoing with his own eyes, and that, Miranda realized in awe, was as good as a noose around the corrupt minister's neck.

Downstairs, the officials confiscated Mr. Reed's ledger books upon Damien's suspicions that the man had been misappropriating funds, judging by the ragged state of the girls' clothes and shoes, by their insufficiently heated rooms, and by Mrs. Warren's stated disgust at the poor quality of the food she was ordered to prepare when the school's tuition was more than sufficient to afford better.

At last, their hero came up the steps and knocked gingerly on the door of the dormitory. Miranda let him in. Like a tamed lion, Damien sat down with the girls, tenderly asking each one in turn if she was all right. Amy hugged him hard and cried a bit on his shoulder.

Miranda watched his every move in silence, trying to reconcile this strong, caring knight with the savage warrior who had torn four criminals to shreds on Bordesley Green. He was the deadliest man she had ever encountered and, in his way, she thought, the gentlest. Then the crusading gentlewomen from the charity took matters in hand.

They agreed with Damien that the matter was best handled quietly for the sake of the girls, who had already suffered enough. The older lady, a childless widow, insisted that Amy, Sally, and Jane stay at her nice house in town for the rest of the Christmas break. The magistrate's wife volunteered for the task of hiring new teachers and preparing a letter to the families of the students to explain the removal of Mr. Reed and Miss Brocklehurst. At long last, Miranda felt that she could leave knowing her friends were in good hands—and that meant, to her amazement, that she was free to venture through the door into the new life that Damien had opened for her, the life her mother had wanted for her.

She hugged Sally, Jane, and Amy each in turn for a long moment, promised to write to them from London, then followed Damien out to the carriage in a state of physical and mental exhaustion. It was already two in the morning. The stagecoach would leave Coventry in five hours.

Outside, the night was clear and the air was sharp. She paused and looked up at the onyx sky, thickly seeded with stars. She wondered if, behind their distant, dancing lights, Uncle Jason and her parents were looking down on her.

"Are you coming?"

She looked over at Damien's softly spoken question. He stood waiting to assist her into the carriage, the starlight glimmering over the chiseled lines of his face.

Holding his gaze in the silvery darkness, she felt a fierce, instinctual loyalty to this man deep in her blood for what he had done for her tonight. The profundity of her gratitude shook her. He knew her shameful secret now about how she had suffered, and that was a dangerous weapon in a person's hands. She wondered warily what he might want from her in return for the debt she now owed him. But her fears barely surfaced before logic and her newfound faith in him laid them to rest. Uncle Jason had indeed chosen well. It seemed that Damien Knight really wanted nothing from her but a little cooperation so that he could fulfill his sworn duty to her uncle.

"Perhaps you might begin to trust me now," he

said, his cultured baritone deep and steady in the inky stillness of the winter night.

Miranda could not find her voice to answer, staring at him in mingled longing and trepidation. He had saved her life; he had saved her friends; he had proved himself the hero the world proclaimed him. And yet her words of thanks lodged in her throat, blocked by the bravado that had been her sole defense for so many years.

She felt so strange. A quiet, womanly acquiescence settled over her with a willingness to set aside her childish ways; her tinselly, adolescent dreams of the-atrical fame; and all her angry, headstrong willfulness. Instead, she would accept this strong, just man's rule, as though his very gentleness had already begun to tame her. The rebel in her kicked against it—this was not the destiny she had envisioned. But when Damien held out his hand to her, waiting to help her into the carriage, she could not fight the pull of her heart.

She lifted her chin, squared her shoulders, and went to him.


Algernon, Lord Hubert, could not sleep. It was not his conscience that plagued him, however, nor his dreams of what he would do with the money once enough time had passed to draw discreetly from Miranda's account, but practical worry. The unsavory fellows he had sent to get rid of his bastard niece, dis-reputable but useful creatures who lived in one of his tenement houses, should have reported back to him by now to collect their pay. They had not come.

He sat in his oak-paneled study, the door open, giving him a clear view of the entrance hall. The grandfather clock chimed two, and still Crispin was not home from the gaming hells. The thought of his son filled him with a pulsation of mingled disappointment and helpless doting. He loved his son better than any creature in the world, better than his insipid daughters, Daisy and Parthenia, whom he had long since given up on as a pair of twits; aye, better even than he loved his empty-eyed wife. If only he could tell Crispin that he was doing all of this for *him*. Algernon stared into the candle's flame while his servant huddled in the corner with the dogs, awaiting his next order.

He sipped a glass of warm cream with a shot of whisky in it to help make him drowsy, but sleep had grown even more difficult ever since he had learned from Jason's solicitor that the man his brother had appointed as Miranda's guardian was none other than the universally feared and esteemed Colonel Lord Winterley.

Algernon had sent his four hired criminals to Birmingham as swiftly as possible to get to Miranda before Winterley did, but he could only conclude they had failed. Perhaps they had fled their task, abandoning the promised gold rather than risk crossing the steely-eyed earl, he mused. If Winterley had already collected Miranda, Algernon knew he was going to have to devise some alternative solution.

"Egann," he said, glancing toward the corner.

"Yes, master? I am here." His slight-framed, balding valet came shuffling out of the shadows, dragging his clubfoot after him.

"I want you to go and watch Knight House. If our men in Birmingham have failed, Lord Winterley will in all likelihood bring my niece to his family head-quarters," he said with a faint sneer of envy. "I wish to know the moment they arrive. Be discreet. Don't let them notice you."

"I understand, sir." Egann bowed and limped out to do his bidding.

Algernon felt more secure about his predicament after his reliable servant had gone. Soon, he assured himself, he would have matters well in hand. At least he did not have to worry about the Bow Street officers who had come to question him as a matter of proce-dure. The officers had asked if he and his brother had been on good terms. No, they had not been close, he had said, but they had always been cordial. The bonds of blood, of course.

Algernon had answered the questions with im-punity, confident in his rank and in his certainty that he had not been seen by a soul when he had slipped out the back door of Jason's lodging house into the seedy environs where he had roamed in his dissipated youth from one low tavern, brothel, or gaming hell to the next. He had purposely arrived by hackney coach, leaving his fine carriage emblazoned with his coat of arms at home so that he could not be identified. Let the police search as they may; the case of his younger brother's murder would never be solved. The authori-ties had never figured out the truth about Richard's and Fanny's deaths, after all. Indeed, he was getting rather good at this, he mused, taking a satisfied sip of his scotch and cream. Major Jason Sherbrooke would merely go down as a casualty of the terrible neighborhood in which he had chosen to reside.

Just then, he heard the front door creak open and Crispin come stumbling in, home at last from his revelries. The dogs rushed out to greet the handsome twenty-five-year-old, their tails wagging, their nails clicking excitedly over the marble entrance hall. Algernon looked toward the door of his study with a frown.

"Hullo, hullo, boy! There's a good boy!" the lad whispered in drunken good cheer.

Well, thank God, Algernon thought. His good mood meant that Crispin had won at the tables, or at any rate, had not lost too badly.

"Crispin!" he called sternly.

"Ah, Father! I did well!" He strode in, the candlelight gleaming on his curly golden hair. With a roguish grin, he plunked a handful of gold sovereigns down on Algernon's desk.

Algernon had to fight not to smile. "I told you to stay away from the gaming hells, did I not?"

Reeking of smoke and ale, Crispin gave him a hearty wink, easily seeing through his disapproval. "You told me not to lose. So I didn't. G'night, Father."

He shook his head and sighed. "Goodnight, Son."

The thing that nagged him most was how sharply Crispin reminded him of his elder brother, Richard. It was the twinkle in his eyes and the cocksure levity of his grin. Crispin did not worry about himself, but Algernon worried about him. Algernon worried about everything. He worried about Miranda and Lord Winterley. He worried about his silly daughters and his oblivious wife. He worried about his house, his title, the latest bill in Parliament, the Corn Laws, the 'Change, Napoleon, and the weather; and it had irked him unbearably that Richard, head of the family, had never worried about a thing.

Algernon blew out the candle and sat wide awake in the dark, listening to the dogs settle down again in the corner.

# ⊰ CHAPTER ⊱
## SIX

The next day, the sky had only begun to lighten with December's tardy dawn, but already excitement charged the frosty morning air. The graveled yard of Ye Olde Red Cow bustled with activity and rang with the cheerful voices of travelers journeying to see their kin for Christmas, only five days away. The shiny black coach waited in the yard, its roof piled with hampers and baskets, parcels and packages. Its gold-and-red lettering proclaimed it part of the Star Line, while its team of four horses pawed the ground and snorted steam, their docked tails twitching. The coachman greeted the boarding passengers, while the guard, his long horn in hand, climbed up to his post on top, keeping watch that no one trifled with the luggage.

Perhaps it was the result of too little sleep, but Miranda's mood was giddy as she parted from Damien outside the inn and walked to the coach while he went to fetch Zeus from the stable. Climbing into the stagecoach with the other five passengers, Miranda was not too shy to claim a seat by the window, eager as she was to see the world. She watched Damien lead his tall white stallion out of the barn and admired the ease with which he stepped up on the stirrup, his dark woolen greatcoat swirling out gracefully behind him as he swung up into the saddle. The grooms gave the harness one last check; the coachman clanged his bell; then they were off.

For a while, she exchanged pleasantries with the other passengers, who described their holiday plans. Within the hour, the day grew bright, the morning sun gilding the fields of snow, but soon the rhythmic rocking of the coach lulled her. She dozed, resting her temple against the window until the guard's horn brought her sharply awake, announcing the first stop: Rugby.

Damien rode Zeus over to the halted coach, leaned over, and knocked on the window. "Wake up!" he teased her, his deep voice muffled through the glass.

She smiled at him. Some passengers climbed off and others got on. The grooms harnessed fresh horses from the livery stable, and the coach rolled into motion again. Miranda blew Damien an impertinent kiss as the coach pulled ahead, leaving him behind where he had dismounted to tighten Zeus's girth. It was not long, however, before he went streaking by on a flash of white, racing against the coach and beating it easily.

With a flutter of girlish admiration in her heart, she watched him and Zeus go galloping past. She shook her head to herself with a wry smile. *Show-off.*

The stagecoach only caught up to him at the next stop. She peered through the window and saw him leaning against the post where he had tied the stallion. He toasted her with the cup of coffee he was drinking, sending her an arrogant nod of victory. She laughed, unaware of the nosy passengers watching their exchange. She got out of the coach to stretch her limbs, and he bought her a pastry from the coaching inn's restaurant since she had slept through breakfast. She asked him if he was keeping warm, gave Zeus a pat on the neck, then climbed back into the coach. Once more, they were under way.

Thirty miles into the trip, she was restless to escape the confinement of the coach and begged Damien to let her ride with him for a while. He obliged her for the next stretch, sweeping down the even roadway at an easy canter, his arm wrapped securely around her waist. Miranda held on tightly to Zeus's mane, glorying in the freedom of it, the gold December sun beaming on her face, the brisk wind rushing through her hair. At the next stop, she returned obediently to the coach, pink-cheeked, her eyes sparkling with exhilaration. She settled happily back into her seat and noticed the rather scandalized looks of the more matronly passengers. Privately, she gave a little laugh at their disapproval. It excited her to let them think that Damien and she were more than merely guardian and ward.

After another twenty miles, their day's journey ended at an inn called the Jolly Rogue, just outside of Milton Keynes. If Ye Olde Red Cow had been busy, the Jolly Rogue was positively chaotic. Probably because they were so much closer to London, Miranda thought. In the yard, there was a great, dizzying shuffle of livery horses being changed out and coaches, post chaises, and carriages of all descriptions coming and

going, while the various arriving stagecoaches dis-
gorged hordes of fretful, hungry travelers. Unfortunately, by the time Damien had tended to his horse's
comforts, they walked into the lobby and were told
by the harried concierge that there were no more
vacancies—not even a stool left to sit on in the tavern.
Miranda waited by the wall with their piled bags while
Colonel Lord Winterley made himself known.

As if by magic, a room opened up about ten minutes
later. He prowled back across the crowded lobby to
her and picked up their bags. "Come."

"Have they got rooms for us?" she asked, holding
her breath.

"One—and that, only after a sizable bribe," he
muttered under his breath.

"Oh," she said, swallowing her protest, but a mild
jolt of alarm startled her maidenly sensibilities. Surely
they were not going to *share* a room for the night?

There was no time to ask. Damien grasped her wrist
and pulled her through the crowded lobby and up the
stairs behind one of the servants, who lit the way to
their quarters with a candle branch. She kept her
mouth shut and followed, only glad to leave the crush
below, for there were many people who would have to
spend the night sitting in the lobby on their luggage.

The clamor below receded as the footman led them
up to the shadowy top floor of the galleried inn and
unlocked the last door at the end of the hallway for
them. The chamber was neither as large nor as pretty
as the one Miranda had slept in last night. Her heart
pounded as she eyed the bed. It seemed awfully small.

The servant bowed out. "My lord. Madam. A chambermaid will attend you shortly. You may wish to sup here, as the dining room is exceedingly crowded at present."

"Thank you for that advice," Damien growled, giving the man his coin.

Miranda offered the servant a hapless smile and closed the door. A trifle nervous, she turned around as Damien dropped their bags in the corner and slipped off his greatcoat with an air of irritation. He draped his coat over the chair by the window. She peeled off her gloves and carefully took off her bonnet.

"Well, this is all very cozy," she remarked, trying to lighten his scowl with good humor, though she realized he was exhausted.

"Cozy? To be sure, I shall enjoy sleeping on the floor. You know, if there is one thing I cannot abide, it is poor planning. I apologize for this. If I had known you were coming with me, I could have arranged for better accommodations."

She laughed softly at his ire and hung her bonnet on the bedpost, tossing her gloves on the small table by the wall. "Nonsense. We shall fare perfectly well here. It's just one night."

"I suppose. But you had better not tell anyone about this," he warned, falling wearily onto the bed. He lay back and closed his eyes, his booted feet still planted on the floor.

Miranda went around to the other side of the bed and laid across it on her belly, propping herself up on her elbows. She smiled as she studied him, then ventured a brief caress upon his silky hair, soothing him.

"You take the bed tonight. I'll take the armchair. I was able to sleep on the coach—"

"No." His eyes were closed, but he seemed to be enjoying her light stroking on his hair. "I can always bed down in the stable, if need be."

"Don't be absurd. Our national hero?"

He opened his eyes and looked at her sardonically.

She tugged a lock of his hair, giving him a teasing smile. "I have put you out enough already, my lord. I'll not throw you out into the cold with the animals, too."

He merely sighed and closed his eyes again. "You haven't put me out, Miranda."

Her smile softened as she watched the tension ease from his angular face under her touch. "You rest a while," she murmured. "I'll find the maid and order our supper. What would you like?"

"Anything's fine, as long as they bring it soon."

"Done." She climbed off the bed and glanced back fondly at him over her shoulder, then withdrew to find the servant.

When she left the room, Damien quickly shed his tailcoat and waistcoat, thinking he would use the few minutes that she was gone to clean his wound and to change the bandages on his arm. He was tired and hungry, but in truth it felt good to be needed again. He poured water from the pitcher into the basin, lifted his shirt off over his head, then dug around in his haversack for the rolled length of bandages that the surgeon from Morris's garrison had given him.

He winced as he peeled the old bandage off his

wound. A thread stuck to the scab that was just beginning to form. He cursed as it pulled. In his haste to
finish the task of cleaning and redressing his wound
before Miranda returned to find him half naked, he
skipped heating the water and scarcely took time to
use soap. He was wrapping his arm, the other end of
the linen bandage secured between his teeth, when her
light knock sounded on the door. He froze, his heart
skipping a beat.

She opened the door and stepped in. "Your dinner
is on its way—oh, my." Her eyes widened as she took
in the sight of him standing, shirtless, by the table.

Damien dropped the bandage from between his
teeth, his cheeks flushing with embarrassment. "If
you'll give me a moment, please, I have to see to my
wound."

Her gaze traveled slowly over his bare torso. She
tilted her head with a naughty little smile, closed the
door, and leaned against it for a second, staring at him.

"Do you mind?" he scoffed, but even as he protested, his bandage came unwound. "Damn it," he
muttered.

She laughed gently and crossed the room to him.
"Let me help you, you poor thing."

"I don't need any help." He watched the enticing
sway of her hips as she came toward him, then forced
his stare to the floor, ferociously aware of her. "You
should leave until I'm decent."

"Should, should, should. I'm not about to let you
stand there bleeding, when it's my fault this happened
to you in the first place." She pushed him back with
firm, managing care until he leaned his hips against

the table behind him. "Stay," she ordered. "Does it hurt very badly?"

"I've had worse."

She reached up and cupped his cheek fondly. "You wouldn't tell me even if it did, would you?"

"No," he admitted with a rueful half smile. He felt no pain, only the pleasure of her simple touch.

"Well, the wine should dull the sting a little. Our dinner should be here any minute. The bill of fare is duck, pork pies, and roast beef with potatoes, by the way, so I hope you're hungry."

*Starved,* he thought. His gaze drifted down to her lips. As she moved to his side and inspected his wound, he eyed the creamy expanse of her chest and caught a tantalizing glimpse of her ripe, womanly cleavage. He swallowed hard and looked away, fighting temptation for all he was worth, his heartbeat slamming.

Miranda did her best to hide her reaction, but from the moment she had walked into the room, she had been dazzled by the sight of his bare, bronzed body and rippling muscles. The warm, velvety smoothness of his flesh made her hands tingle with the need to caress him, but she tamped down the impulse, grasping one end of the cotton bandage.

She secured it over the wound. "Hold this end in place, will you?"

He cooperated, his stare fixed on her face.

She wound the length of clean cotton around his astonishingly large left biceps, hoping he did not sense her yearning to explore every inch of his magnificent body. She let her stare travel discreetly along the sleek arc of his throat to the broad planes of his shoulders and chest, delighting in the small, dusky circles of his nipples. Her gaze followed the center groove that ran down his stomach amid undulating ridges of muscle, ending at his ineffably cute navel.

She wanted to cover his beautiful chest and sculpted belly in light, nibbling kisses, pleasure him in all the ways that Trick had taught her three years ago in secret. The fleeting fantasy made her light-headed. She had not shared such intimacies with anyone since then; indeed, she had been ashamed of what she knew about men, their bodies, their desires. As a trusting sixteen-year-old, she had only obliged her handsome young cavalryman because she had wanted him to love her, but with Damien, it was totally different. Trick had cajoled her constantly each time or would accuse her of not caring about him until she reluctantly agreed to touch him, but Damien had merely to stand there and she could scarcely keep her hands to herself. He awoke her deep, genuine desire as no man ever had. She watched the play of candlelight and shadow flickering over his torso, then roused herself from the trance.

"You can let go of your end now," she murmured, avoiding his gaze.

He obeyed. "You realize, of course, that this is completely inappropriate."

She passed a wary glance over his face. "No one has to know."

He raised his eyebrow with a speculative look.

She shrugged. "Those people downstairs already think I am your mistress."

"I know. That's why I didn't tell them your name."

"Is this too tight?" she asked, poised to tie off the bandage into a knot.

He glanced down at his arm and flexed his muscle to test it. She gasped at the sheer girth of his biceps and tore her wide-eyed stare away, blushing profusely.

She snapped her jaw shut. "Sorry."

He let out a low, cocky laugh, looking altogether pleased with himself. "This will do fine."

"Right." She cleared her throat, avoiding his gaze. Her hands trembled slightly as she knotted the ends of the bandage. He murmured a low-toned thanks; she nodded, trailing a feverish glance over the hard, lean length of him as he walked away and slipped his loose white shirt back on. He left it unbuttoned, perhaps to indulge her.

Miranda was washing her hands, forbidding herself from gawking at him a second longer, when a knock at the door jarred her out of her daze. She hurried to answer it and admitted the maid, who wheeled in their dinner on a tea cart. Since there was only one chair, Damien slid the table over to the bed. Miranda kicked off her shoes and sat, cross-legged, on the mattress while they ate. The food and wine gave them something rather than each other to devour and helped disperse the lingering tension.

They ate at a leisurely pace, but by the time Damien opened the second bottle of red wine, Miranda's mood had turned to one of frisky levity. She pulled the ivory combs from her hair, shaking it out to its full length, then reclined on her elbow on the bed and rested her crossed heels on Damien's thigh. He did not seem to mind.

"So, my good Lord Winterley," she said in saucy cheer, picking up the conversation precisely where they had left off earlier. "*Do* you have a mistress?"

"Miranda." He looked at her flatly, then downed the rest of his wine.

"I only ask since everyone in this hotel thinks that I'm it."

"You can't ask me that." He set his glass down.

"What, are you married?" she exclaimed.

"No, I'm not married!" he scoffed.

"Then answer the question. I told you about my cavalry boy, didn't I?"

"I do not have a mistress."

"No? No wife, no mistress? I say, what *do* you have, Damien?"

"Just a brat of a ward to marry off to the highest bidder." He picked up the wine bottle and refilled his goblet. Reaching over their emptied plates, he topped off her wineglass, as well, then curled his hand around her ankle, stroking it with his fingertips through her white stockings.

"I see, so you mean to sell me?" she asked sagely. "How much am I worth on the marriage market, do you suppose?"

"All the gold of King Midas couldn't measure your worth, Miss FitzHubert." He lifted his glass to her and drank, then resumed eating.

"Well, that's a good deal better than the three

shillings a night I earned at the Pavilion," she replied, pleased.

He pointed at her sternly with his fork. "You are not to breathe a word about any of that once we reach London, do you understand? Not to anybody."

"Not even to my future husband?"

"Especially him."

"But marriage is built on trust—"

"Rubbish, it's built on gold and advancing one's family."

"Well, since I have neither fortune nor family, I don't suppose anyone's going to want me, then."

"Yes, they will. You have something else."

"What's that?"

"Beauty." He stared at her for a second. "You have beauty." Studiously avoiding her gaze, he continued eating.

"I hope it's enough."

"You will also have the support of my family, and that is no small advantage. My eldest brother is the duke of Hawkscliffe. The youngest, Alec, is the current darling of fashionable society. He knows every eligible bachelor in London. By the way, don't tell my family, either, about your career as Miss White. If it seems necessary for them to know, I'll tell them when the time is right."

"Very well. It'll be our secret. Just like the fact that you propositioned me," she added, poking him in his belly with the tip of her toe.

He rolled his eyes. "Must you keep bringing that up?"

She laughed with wicked merriment, taunting him.

"Well, you did! What if I had said yes? I almost did, you know. You were very persuasive—I'm jesting!" she said hastily when he blanched at the mere suggestion. She couldn't help but chuckle. "You are so amusing, Winterley. You needn't blush so."

"I do not blush."

"Yes, you do, but there's no need. You're not the first man ever to make me an indecent offer, and I sincerely hope you won't be the last."

"Miranda!"

"What?" She batted him with her pillow.

"Hoyden! Are you drunk?"

"I don't think so. I'm not sure. They never gave us wine at Yardley. I feel happy."

"Happy?" He grabbed a corner of the pillow as she whacked him again with it. "Stop it!"

"You're too serious, Winterley!" She reached for another pillow. "I will beat you until you smile!"

He ducked out of his chair with a rakish grin as she swung at him, then tackled her flat on the soft bed, both of them laughing.

"You are . . . impossible," he chided with a gentle sigh as he braced his elbows on either side of her head. He traced her cheekbones with the pads of his thumbs.

"Difficult, but not impossible." She wrapped her arms around him, relishing the weight of him atop her, the smoothness of his bare chest against her bodice. "It all depends on who's trying."

"That sounded distinctly like an invitation," he murmured.

"Maybe it was," she whispered, stroking his hair. "Are you going to accept?"

Her words made him go very still. His stare turned uncertain. "I don't know."

"Think hard," she breathed, but he offered no protest whatsoever as she slowly pulled his head down to her until their lips met. She cupped his cheek, begging him with her touch not to pull away. He did not.

She closed her eyes, breathless, savoring the satiny warmth of his mouth against hers, the hammering of his mighty heartbeat against her breasts. She felt the tremor that ran the length of his body, heard his breath catch in his throat like a trapped groan when she parted her lips and slid her tongue into his mouth.

Unleashing his agonized restraint, he responded with fierce passion, consuming her with a kiss full of wild, aching hunger. She surrendered blissfully, raking her fingers through his silky, black hair. *Yes*. Her spirit felt freed as her body arched beneath him. He groaned as her eager movement roused the full length of his hardness. Her skirts rustled as she spread her legs wider, letting his body settle more comfortably between them. She could feel his steely length throbbing against her pleasure center.

He clutched her breast almost frantically, dragging his thumb back and forth across her nipple, driving her wild. She could not get enough of him. Sliding her hand inside his shirt, she stroked his muscled back, glorying in his supple motion as he ground against her. She reached lower, grasping his compact buttock through his breeches.

"Oh, God, we have to stop," he groaned, tearing his mouth away from hers, his breathing ragged. "This can't happen."

"It *is* happening, Damien. You can't deny it," she whispered, trying to hold him, but he pressed up from lying atop her and turned away.

He went to sit on the edge of the bed, dragging his hand through his hair. "You don't know what you're saying, Miranda. You're very vulnerable right now. You've been through a lot these past few—" His words broke off as he noticed his open shirt. He hastily began buttoning it, cursing at himself under his breath. "We've both had a little too much to drink. It won't happen again."

She sat up with a twinge of resentful disappointment. She knew he was perfectly sober, but she supposed he had his reasons for stopping them. Still, she could not escape a vague, hurt sense of rejection.

Warily, he looked over his shoulder at her. She slid over to sit beside him. His expression was guarded, his lips still deliciously wet and pliant with her kisses, but she could see his longing for her in his eyes. They had turned the deep blue-gray of thunderclouds. Lowering his gaze, he reached for her hand and held it gently, studying her knuckles as he traced them with his fingertip.

"Why did you stop?"

"You're my ward, Miranda."

She paused. "So?"

He turned to her, looking into her eyes. "You're a beautiful girl. But I want you to have choices. If we continue, I'm your only option."

"There are worse fates," she said guardedly.

"You don't know me very well," he said, then

dropped his gaze to the floor. "Besides, your Uncle Jason would kill me."

She gave a soft, rueful laugh.

He sent her a cautious smile askance. "I think I should go."

"Where?"

"I'll find a place to bed down in the barn—"

"Damien!"

He rose. "It's no trouble. They probably have a hayloft where I can—"

"No!" She captured his wrist in both hands. "Stay! I'll be good. I give you my word."

He tilted his head, studying her with a hesitant smile. "I don't know. . . ."

"You're exhausted. You won't get a proper night's sleep in a stable. For shame! What kind of earl are you? Stay in here where it's warm. *You* take the bed. I'll sleep in the chair."

"Absolutely not. I am a gentleman," he said vehemently.

"Ah—wait! I have the perfect plan." She dashed off the bed abruptly and hurried over to the pile of luggage, retrieving the yet-unused length of cotton bandaging. She brought it over to the bed and unrolled it down the middle. "There. You can have that half of the bed, and I'll take this half. Whoever crosses the lines does so at his peril."

He looked skeptically at the bed, neatly divided down the middle, then at her. "Do you really think this is a good idea?"

"Of course. Why not? I have complete faith in your honor. Please don't sleep in the stable, Damien," she cajoled him. "I already feel guilty enough over your getting shot because of me. There, now, I will stay on my side, and you stay on yours. Good night." Pulling back the coverlet, she slid down under the sheet, rested her head on the pillow, and closed her eyes determinedly.

For the next minute or two, she listened to him pacing about in the room as though he couldn't make up his mind what he wanted to do. What a dear, absurd creature he was, she thought in fond amusement, holding very still so as not to scare him away. Just when she peeked with one eye to see what in the world he was about, he blew out the candle and took his place gingerly on the other side of the bed. He made a point of lying atop the coverlet rather than under it, where they might risk their bodies touching.

For a long moment, they lay together in the darkness, separated by the coverlet and the gauzy strip of cotton. Their intense physical awareness of each other thrummed in the air like violin strings tightened to the breaking point, but they were both perfectly silent. Blue-white moonlight streamed in through the large window.

"Stop fidgeting," he grumbled after a moment, rolling onto his side to face the far wall.

"Sorry." She looked at his broad back, then heaved an irked sigh because he was shivering. "I don't mind if you get under the covers, Damien, as long as you stay on your side of the bed."

"No," he said stoically.

"Why ever not? I know you're freezing cold."

"I'm fine."

"You're shaking the whole bed with your shivering. What's the matter? Are you worried I might cross the little boundary?" she asked in an impetuous surge of mischief, walking her fingers across the strip of cotton and up his side, tickling him.

"Behave yourself!" he scolded, trying to hold back a yelp of laughter, but when he glanced over his shoulder at her, he was smiling. "Good night, Miranda."

She withdrew her hand and slipped it under her pillow, her eyes shining as she held his gaze for a moment. "Good night, Damien. God bless you."

His smile softened in the darkness; then he turned away again and very quickly went to sleep. Soon, his breathing had slowed and deepened. The sound lulled her. His shoulders rose and fell in a gentle rhythm. Some lazy, instinctual part of her only wanted to snuggle up close to him for warmth and sleep away the cold winter's night in his arms, sharing their body heat.

Drifting off, she did not know how much time had passed when he woke her with his muttering. She could not make out the words.

She squinted wearily and looked over as he jerked with agitation, as though in the grip of some fitful dream. She held perfectly still, trying to discern his unconscious movement in the darkness. Was he shaking? Twitching? Perhaps he was fighting some long-past battle in his slumber. Careful to avoid his bandaged wound, she reached out to try to quiet him, touching his shoulder.

"Damien," she started in a whisper.

But in the next instant, she did not know what hit her. He was upon her, slamming her back onto the mattress with a snarl, crushing her beneath his muscled weight. He pinned her wrists above her head and reached for her throat, choking her.

"Damien!" she shrieked in terror, struggling for air.

She had never seen anything more terrifying than his face in that split second before he came back to his senses.

Immediately he released his choke hold on her throat. "Jesus Christ." He lifted himself off of her at once and swept out of the bed, stalking across the moonlit room.

Miranda scrambled to a seated position, one hand on her throat.

He paced back to her, a cold sweat gleaming on his face, his eyes wild, luminous in the moonlight. "Are you all right?" he demanded in an agonized whisper. "Did I hurt you? Tell me you're all right."

"I'm . . . fine. You j-just scared me."

His chest heaving, he dropped his head. "What the hell were you doing? Why did you touch me? I could have killed you."

Tears of confusion rushed into her eyes at his harsh tone. "I was only trying to help. You were having a bad dream."

He just stared at her coldly for a moment, offered nothing—no reassurance, no explanation. Pivoting, he grabbed his greatcoat from off the chair and picked up his haversack, slinging it over his shoulder on his way to the door.

"I'm going to sleep in the barn."

"Damien!" She started to scramble out of bed to try

to stop him. "Don't leave. Tell me what's wrong. I want to help."

"You can't. Nobody can. Just stay the hell away from me." He stalked out, slamming the door behind him with a resolute bang that echoed through the dark.

# ⊰ CHAPTER ⊱
# SEVEN

London's sprawling outline came into sight upon the hazy blue horizon, but as Miranda stared out the coach window the next afternoon, most of the joy and excitement she had felt yesterday about starting her new life in the great city had eroded away in dread over Damien's welfare.

She sat, pale and brooding, while the other passengers exclaimed in admiration, craning their necks to look out the windows at it. Endless miles of buildings crowded around the gleaming dome of St. Paul's. Countless church spires and ships' masts bristled against the stone-white sky. There were glistening palaces, bold towers, too many streets to name. But she scarcely took note, for she knew now that her guardian, her rock amid the chaos, was battling demons of terrible power. She had seen them glaring out at her through his eyes last night when he had nearly choked the life out of her; she had seen them flex their might on Bordesley Green. And she was afraid, both *for* Damien, and *of* him.

She had gathered her courage to try to speak with him at each stop along the road today, but he was remote, utterly withdrawn, as though he had turned all his fury inward upon himself. He would barely make eye contact with her and had nothing to say but the usual perfunctory courtesies, along with a few details on practical matters regarding their arrival in London. Her attempts to broach the subject of what had happened last night met with icy silence. If she pressed him, he lashed out verbally to drive her off. No matter how she tried, she could not reach him.

She had never felt more alone.

Tranquil fields soon gave way to more densely populated villages as the stagecoach bore them southward over miles of undulating countryside, ever closer to the ancient capital. Very swiftly, they were in the heart of the noisy, dirty, clamoring city. A river of traffic and humanity moved in a rapid current up and down the street in each direction; shop signs swung on the cold breeze while flocks of pigeons swirled over the roofs.

The air rang with the clatter of many carriages and the cries of street vendors with their carts and baskets, selling everything imaginable. Sooty snow clumped in little mounds along the pavement, and ladies propped up on metal pattens went tripping by hither and thither. She could smell the river and the coal fires from untold thousands of chimneys. The stagecoach clattered down High Holborn to the raucous intersection with Fleet Market and passed the endless row of drab, rather dilapidated pavilions where meat and vegetables were sold. She glanced up dubiously at the severe facade of the formidable Fleet Prison as they rode by it.

"There's the river!" one of the passengers exclaimed a moment later.

She turned just in time to catch a glimpse of the gray Thames out the other window as they turned right into Ludgate Hill and made another hasty right into a passage between two narrow shops. She shuddered with relief that they had not been forced to cross one of the bridges over that vast body of deep, treacherous water; then the dark passage quickly deposited them in the immense, raucous inn yard of the Belle Sauvage, the terminus of their journey.

At last, the stagecoach rolled to a weary halt. A moment later, Miranda stepped down from the vehicle, looking around her, completely overwhelmed.

"Miss FitzHubert!" her guardian's deep voice called sharply. "Over here!"

She looked for him through the crowded inn yard, breathing a sigh of relief when she spotted him. He had already dismounted and was waiting for her, holding Zeus's reins. Since her passage had been paid for at the start, she collected her satchel and hurried across the chilly yard to him. She saw he had already secured a hackney coach for her. He avoided her gaze as he took her satchel from her.

Assisting her into the next carriage, he put the satchel in by her feet, then firmly closed the door and looked up at the driver, squinting against the overcast glare of the fading afternoon.

"Knight House on Green Park," he ordered.

"Aye, my lord," the driver said. With a flip of his whip, the carriage rolled into motion.

This journey was never going to end, Miranda

thought wearily. He swung back up into the saddle and trotted Zeus ahead of the hackney coach, leading the way, as ever. The stallion twitched his tail angrily, flexing his white neck in kingly irritation. Poor Zeus did not appear to like the hustle and bustle of the city any more than his stone-faced master did.

As they traveled west through Town, her surroundings became noticeably calmer, quieter, more refined, until at last the hackney coach turned onto the fabled St. James's Street, which even she knew was at the heart of London's most prestigious and aristocratic neighborhood. Mayfair was perhaps more fashionable, but St. James's meant old money and even older titles.

*Good Lord,* she thought, beginning to worry, *who are these people he is taking me to?* She knew from her uncle's letters that the illustrious Knight twins were younger sons of a duke, but the ramifications of that fact had not quite sunk in till now. How could she hope for such lofty personages ever to accept her? Then her jaw dropped as the hackney coach stopped in front of a mansion behind black wrought-iron gates.

A servant in dark blue livery came rushing out in answer to Damien's call, unlocked the heavy metal gates, and pulled them open, bowing to her guardian as he rode in. Her humble hackney coach rolled through the imposing entrance and up the short drive, past immaculate grounds, rolling to a halt in front of the massive baroque palace that towered before her in Palladian magnificence. Proudly overlooking Green

Park, the mansion had a round, columned portico with a heavy iron chandelier.

Miranda stared dazedly at it. The instant the carriage stopped, the door opened and a white-wigged groom appeared, efficiently let down the step, and bowed to her.

"May I assist you, ma'am?" he offered, extending one white-gloved hand.

Miranda stared at the servant, wondering if she was dreaming. Warily accepting the servant's help, she climbed down from the hackney coach while Damien paid the driver.

"May I take your parcel, ma'am?" the servant offered, bowing his head.

"No—thank you." She clutched her battered leather satchel tightly to her chest as she stared up at Knight House in wide-eyed awe. The huge, curved windows on the first floor reflected the sky and the wintry park beyond. Life-sized classical statues posed nobly at regular intervals along the edge of the roof. Meanwhile, behind her, Damien entrusted Zeus to one of the grooms.

He walked past her as though it were the most natural thing in the world to stroll casually into that regal home. Pausing on the few, broad steps up to the portico, he turned back to her. "Are you coming?"

Miranda realized abruptly that she was staring like the most provincial country bumpkin. She shook herself out of her daze and ran after him.

Even the butler who answered the door and greeted them seemed worlds above her station. He was tall and rather gaunt, with knife-hilt cheekbones and dignified gray sideburns. She gazed at him in abject terror, yet the minute she stepped into the entrance hall, she heard the most beautiful piano music pouring through the house.

Musical creature that she was, it eased her nerves by a few degrees. Someone was playing a charming Haydn sonata with a masterful hand. Unconsciously sidling up to her guardian, she stared in wonder at the soaring space of the white, marble entrance hall. The most sumptuous chandelier she had ever seen glittered overhead, heavy with its cloud of polished crystals. A curved staircase seemed to float up weightlessly to the next floor. To the right of the door stood an ancient, gleaming suit of armor, inlaid with jewels so bright they looked like candy.

"Good day, Mr. Walsh," Damien was saying to the butler. "I take it my brother is at home."

"Indeed, my lord. His grace is at his piano."

"And the duchess?" he asked, handing off his greatcoat.

"In the yellow drawing room, having tea with Lady Lucien. Shall I announce you?"

"Not necessary."

"Very good, sir. Your room has been made ready, as well. I trust you shall find everything in order."

"Thank you. See that a chamber is prepared for Miss FitzHubert, would you? She is my ward, lately come down from school. Miranda—"

Only half listening, she was gazing all around in wonder. Damien startled her out of her daze by prying her satchel out of her hands. He gave it to the butler, slanting her a scowl that ordered her to pay attention.

"Miranda, this is Mr. Walsh. He is the man to see if you need anything while you're here."

The butler bowed to her. "Miss. May I take your wrap?"

"Yes, thank you." Meekly, she handed over her rough woolen mantle, then cringed as she caught sight of herself in the pier glass by the wall. In her ill-fitting, beige Sunday uniform, rumpled from two days' travel, she looked pitifully low and out of place in these opulent surroundings. Her usual buoyant confidence dissolved in shame at her poverty. The refined creatures who dwelled in this earthly paradise would no doubt be horrified by her. She dreaded meeting them.

"Come along, my dear," Damien said briskly. "It is time to meet your fairy godmothers." He grasped her wrist and tugged her up the floating, curved staircase to the main floor.

It was all she could do to keep up as he led her down the corridor past tall white double doors and marble busts on pedestals. The exquisite cascade of rapid notes grew to a crescendo and faded as they passed the closed door to what must have been the music room.

"Who is that playing?" she whispered reverently.

"My eldest brother, Robert, the duke of Hawkscliffe," he replied, staring straight ahead as he marched down the hallway, pulling her by her hand. "The Tories must have roused his ire again. He always plays like that when he's fed up with politics.

And this is his house?"

"It is. And now you are about to meet his wife." With that, he swerved to the right, opened the next door they came to, and poked his head cautiously into the room. "Bel?"

"Winterley!"

"At last! Come in, come in, my dear, long-lost brother-in-law. *Now* the holidays can start."

Standing behind him in the hallway, quite on pins and needles, at first Miranda could only hear the two women who greeted him.

"Alice, it's good to see you," he said cordially as he opened the door wider. "I've brought someone to meet you both. Come along, Miranda."

Holding her chin high, her hands balled by her sides, she stepped stiffly into the doorway. Two ladies not much older than she sat on the sofa in the middle of the salon with a tea service and cakes spread out on the low table before them. They stared at her in curious surprise.

"Come closer," Damien prodded her.

Intimidated, she obeyed, taking a few steps into the room.

"Bel, Alice, allow me to present my ward, Major Sherbrooke's niece, Miss Miranda FitzHubert. Miranda, this is the duchess of Hawkscliffe and Lady Lucien Knight."

Miranda curtseyed to his kinswomen and lowered her gaze, struck shy. They were such lovely, elegant creatures. She so wanted them to accept her, but really had little hope of it.

"This is your ward?" the duchess exclaimed. She was about twenty-five years old and in the early stages of pregnancy; her high-waisted gown of powder-blue silk draped over the slight fullness of her belly. She was fair and lithe, with milky skin and wheat-blond hair swept up in a loose chignon.

Miranda cast a desperate glance at her guardian.

"Forgive me, Miss FitzHubert," the duchess amended blithely. "We were under the impression that Damien's ward was a mere child."

"As you can see, we were mistaken. I need help," he said flatly. "I don't even know where to begin with the girl. Chaperonage, wardrobe, introductions. Bel, Alice." He gave them a boyish, pleading glance.

They burst out laughing.

"What a pitiful sight you are, Winterley. Both of you, sit down and have some tea," the duchess commanded with a smile. "Let us see what can be done."

Miranda glanced uncertainly at Damien. He gestured toward the wing chair across from the women. She inched down onto it, moving with caution.

"I was so sorry to hear about your uncle, Miss FitzHubert," Lady Lucien said kindly, turning over an unused teacup and pouring out for her. "I knew Major Sherbrooke, though not very well. He was a friend of my brother's."

"Thank you, my lady," she said haltingly. Obviously, the second woman's title signaled that she was married to Damien's twin brother, Lucien, she thought. The duchess was ravishingly beautiful—a cool, pale goddess. But Lucien's wife was more delicate—a petite, ethereal, fey creature with hair the reddish gold of sunset and the most vivid blue eyes Miranda had ever seen.

Damien waved off the cup of tea that Lady Lucien offered him and gave a brief, sanitized account of his arrival at Yardley School. Finding her so grown up, he said, he had seen no point in leaving her there, though he'd had no time to make the necessary preparations. He told them nothing of the violent episode on Bordesley Green, the arrest of the schoolmaster, nor the fact that the two of them had shared a hotel bed for a while. Lady Lucien, for her part, seemed appalled that Miranda had been made to suffer the indignity of having to travel by public stagecoach.

"As you can see, she is of marriageable age," Damien went on. "It is my responsibility to see her settled in life, but frankly I am out of my depth. This is an area of ladies' expertise. That's why I need your help. I need her properly dressed, shod, chaperoned, and wedded," he said. "An engagement before Twelfth Night would be ideal."

"Why the hurry?"

"Because there's nowhere else for her to go," he said bluntly.

His words, though callous, were all too true. Miranda lowered her gaze with a pang in her heart. The pity she felt pouring from the women as they gazed at her was almost more than her pride could bear. She felt defenseless. Once more, she was nothing but a charity child, an unwanted orphan foisted off on strangers. The vulnerability was terrible, but her bravado was nowhere to be found. She kept her head down and prayed with pounding heart that they would not scorn her. She could not bear to be dealt a humiliating rejection in front of Damien.

"I see. Firstly, I have given the girls' governess leave

to go home to her family for the holidays." The duchess rested her elbow on the scrolled arm of the couch and gazed shrewdly at her. "Secondly, I would like to know what Miss FitzHubert has to say about all this."

Miranda looked up anxiously. "I do not wish to be a burden, Your Grace. I will do whatever Lord Winterley thinks best."

The two beautiful young wives looked at each other with an air of mischief.

"What say you, sister?" the duchess asked. "Shall we rise to the challenge?"

"Let's." Alice lifted her pert chin and turned to Miranda with a flourish. "We shall make you a toast, my dear! Winterley will have to fight to keep all your suitors at bay."

A smile spread slowly over Miranda's face. Glancing at Damien in tremulous joy, she caught him staring at her. He quickly assumed a bored expression and looked away, leaning on the chair, but as he stood in profile to her, pretending indifference, a telltale blush rose in his suntanned cheek above the clean, white line of his cravat.

Later that evening, after the impromptu welcome dinner that Bel had given to introduce Miranda to the rest of the family, Damien sat in the drawing room watching the others play charades. Only Robert sat out the game with him, smiling occasionally at their antics, casting an eye over the *Times*, and sipping his port in patriarchal tranquility. Lucien and Alice had come from their elegant townhouse on Upper Brooke

Street, bringing their three-year-old nephew, Harry, whom they were raising. Harry had become the reigning darling of the Knight clan and dashed from one doting auntie to another, collecting kisses. Even Alec, their golden-haired, rakish youngest brother, had graced them with his exclusive presence for the occasion, arriving from his fashionable bachelor lodgings on Curzon Street to dine with them rather than at his club. Between their seventeen-year-old sister, Jacinda's, squeals of excitement, her lady's companion, Lizzie Carlisle's, attempts to keep the game orderly, and Alec's irreverently witty observations, the evening had turned into something of a party.

Damien, however, sat quietly by the fire, a possessive glow in his eyes as he watched Miranda playing, her sincere, lovely face beaming with gratitude at the warm reception she had received at Knight House. By God, she was a tonic for his soul. It pleased him with a deep satisfaction to see how naturally she fit into his family. It had not taken very long for her shyness to wear off, and then she had charmed them easily.

Bel and Alice were taking her shopping on Bond Street tomorrow; he was preparing to go into debt. He knew that, luckily, the various merchants and shopkeepers would extend almost unlimited credit on the strength of his title alone. He would pay them off eventually. There was, of course, the possibility of taking a loan from Robert, but Damien had never asked any man to solve his problems for him and wasn't about to start now.

At any rate, he had told his sisters-in-law that he would not insist on Miranda's wearing black for the

next three months if she didn't want to. Though this
was the customary period of mourning for an uncle,
in his view that same uncle had neglected her past for-
giving and she had suffered shamefully as a result. Besides, as Bel had pointed out when they had discussed
it earlier, a girl had to look her best when she was husband hunting. To him, it merely seemed cruel to dress
such a colorful soul all in black when he knew full
well that she had never owned pretty clothes before.
He wanted her to be happy.

For now, he thought her beautiful in one of the
duchess's dinner gowns. Though it was too short in
the sleeves and around the hem, the dark blue satin
brought out the emerald splendor of Miranda's eyes
and made her skin glow like fresh cream. With her
glossy sable hair, she stood out exotically from his
brothers' fair-haired wives, his golden-blond sister,
and Lizzie's light brown tresses.

As he watched her laughing, his mind drifted. He
had distanced himself from her as of last night, and no
matter how much he wanted her, he intended to keep
it that way. Several times on the road earlier today, she
had tried to reach out to him, but he had stoically ignored her every soft plea to him to tell her what was
wrong. How could she even ask? *I could have killed
her,* he thought for the hundredth time since it had
happened. His creeping horror at the knowledge was
undimmed. A cold shudder ran through him to think
of how close he had come to snuffing out her sweet life
before he even knew what he was doing.

He should not have been in that bed with her, he
thought harshly, dragging his gaze away from her to

stare broodingly into the fire. He should never have permitted such familiarity between them. He could not believe he had kissed her again, fully knowing that she was his ward. The first time—behind the theater— at least he had had an excuse. He had mistaken her for an ordinary *fille de joie*, and she had done precious little to disabuse him of the notion. He had had no idea who she was then, but last night, in full knowledge— and quite sober, contrary to what he had told her— he had tasted her again. He had been unable to help himself.

He closed his eyes briefly at the torturous memory of her ardent response, her body arching gloriously under him, her soft arms wound tightly around his neck. He could still taste her on his tongue, but he refused to heed the provocative whisper of instinct in his blood, telling him that she was his, that he had a right to her because he had saved her life. He had promised Jason that he would find her a good husband, and so he would, but he was not that man. It did not matter what he felt for her. He was sworn to protect her— even from the beast within himself. The emotions stirring to life—rising like tiny, tender shoots from the frozen earth of his heart—were doomed to wither. He could not love. He was not fit for human society at all. He had made battle and victory his raison d'être, and now he was trapped within the steely armor he himself had forged.

After the debacle of last night, he longed to leave her in his family's care and let them oversee her courtship so that he could retreat to his sanctuary at Bayley House, but despite the sheer torment of it, he refused to abandon her. If her beauty had not made her enough of a target for seduction from amorous men, as the daughter of a notorious actress, she was sure to attract the most immoral rakes of the ton, with the most dishonorable intentions—men for whom pleasure was their sole pursuit in life. They would try to test her to see if she possessed her mother's easy virtue, but with the feared Colonel Lord Winterley by her side, watching over her, they would not dare. They would know that to insult her was suicide.

Just then, the butler glided into the drawing room and discreetly bent to whisper something in Lucien's ear. Lucien nodded and gently tumbled Harry onto Alice's arms, for the child was hanging on around his neck. While the raucous game continued, Damien rested his cheek on his fist and looked on curiously as his twin slipped out of the room.

About two minutes later, Lucien returned, nodding to Damien from the doorway to join him. Damien got up and strode out of the room, furrowing his brow.

In the hallway, he found Lucien's assistant from the Foreign Office, the intrepid young secret agent Marc Skipton.

Damien nodded to Marc as Lucien closed the salon door quietly behind him. "What is it?"

"They've made an arrest in the Sherbrooke case," the young man said grimly. "The suspect is a known thief and housebreaker in the area. They've got him in the holding cell at the magistrate's court, but we've got to hurry. He says he's got an alibi, and I don't know if they'll be able to keep him locked up."

Damien's eyes flared with vengeance. He knew Lucien had been putting a good deal of pressure on Bow Street to find Jason's killer. It appeared his efforts had paid off. "I'll get my coat."

Soon, the three men strode into the justice offices in Bow Street, but Lucien grabbed Damien's arm, holding him back a step as the constables led them past the small courtroom, busy even at this late hour, and down the dim corridor toward the holding cell.

"Try not to go mad on him quite yet, Demon," Lucien said under his breath. "The man has only been charged; he has not been convicted."

"Let him prove himself innocent, then." With a dark look, Damien shrugged him off and stalked after the guard.

"John Michael Boynton is his name, my lords." The constable set his oil lantern on a hook by the doorway.

By the lantern's light, Damien looked through the metal bars and beheld a thin, wiry, unkempt man in his late twenties. The prisoner's face was ashen but defiant.

"Known as 'Rooster,' " the guard continued. "Resident o' Seven Dials, not far from Major Sherbrooke's lodgings. We've been after this blackguard for ages on thieving and housebreaking charges. Now it seems he's graduated to murder."

"I didn't kill no one," the lanky, ill-kempt man snarled. "You got no right botherin' me."

"Where were you, Mr. Boyton, on Wednesday night, the twelfth of December?" Lucien asked coolly.

"Who the hell are you, my barrister?"

The constable struck the bars with his nightstick. "Mind your tongue!"

"Answer the question," Damien ordered through gritted teeth.

Boynton glanced uneasily from one twin to the other. "I was at my brother's house havin' supper with him, his wife, and his young ones. He'll be here directly to vouch for me!"

"To vouch for you," Lucien echoed skeptically.

"And why should we believe him?" Damien asked, the lust for vengeance turning his vision red. He rested his elbows on the crosswise bars, fixing the caged man in a predatory stare. "Let me in there with him, Officer. Just a minute or two is all I need."

"Keep this lunatic away from me!" the prisoner yelled, pacing along the back wall of his cell.

Damien let out a low, feral laugh. "You're a dead man, Boynton. I'll be there to see you hang."

"Enough," Lucien murmured, pulling him back from the bars. "His brother's just arrived. Look."

Damien turned and his heart sank as a young, anxious-looking Anglican minister in a white collar came rushing down the dim corridor. "John Michael? John Michael?"

"Andrew, I'm here!" the prisoner yelled.

*His alibi is a bloody priest?* Damien thought in shock.

The fresh-faced minister hurried into their midst, brushing by them to go to the guard. "John Michael, are you all right?"

"Get me out of here, Andrew. They're accusing me

of a murder the night I was at your house! Tell them, Andrew! Tell them!"

The minister turned to the guard in distress. "It's true. My brother couldn't have done it. He was with me and my wife and children. I must speak to the magistrate at once, please. This has all been a dreadful mistake!"

The guard glanced at Lucien, looking nonplussed. "Er, right away, Reverend. I'll see if I can get the magistrate to hear your side of the story before your brother is moved to the Old Bailey."

Damien felt his temper building like a volcano. "You can't simply release this vermin."

"If there's been a wrongful arrest, they most certainly can," the young priest said, turning to him indignantly. "I'll not have my brother go to the scaffold merely so some justice officer can collect a bounty. What is your interest in this, gentlemen, if I may ask?" He looked pugnaciously from Damien to Lucien.

"My brother was great friends with the victim," Lucien said quietly, gesturing toward Damien.

The young man turned to him. "I am so sorry, sir, but I can assure you, my brother could not have done it. John Michael may not be the most spotless of God's flock, but he was under my roof, at my table, on the night in question, and I will stake my good name on it."

"God damn it!" Damien exploded, out of patience.

"Sir!" the minister exclaimed.

"Let me at him, guard! I'll show you justice!"

"Stay away from me!"

"Damien!" Lucien wrenched him back from the bars

as he lunged his arm through them at the prisoner. "Calm yourself! He didn't do it!" Lucien pushed him back from the cell, his face flushed with anger. "Calm down. We have the wrong man. You know as well as I do they're telling the truth."

Damien yanked his arm free of his brother's hold, pivoted, and marched out with a cold look.

"Where are you going?" Lucien called after him as he stormed off down the corridor.

"Home," he said with a rude flick of his hand, not looking back.

Lucien paused. Damien could feel his brother's impatience with him.

"Don't you want to take the carriage with us?"

"I'll walk," he growled.

He pushed open the door and stalked out into the night, his pulse pounding with frustration and disgust. He raked his hand slowly through his hair.

Outside, the night was as cold and black as the devil's laughter. The street was quiet, with only an occasional carriage rumbling past. Damien turned up the collar of his greatcoat and started walking in the hopes that it would take the edge off his churning anger and impatience. He felt helpless over Jason's death and he hated it. He strode through the darkness of the street while, above him, lights glowed in the upper-story windows of the flat-fronted buildings.

He heard amiable voices and smelled the pungent aroma of coffee as he passed a busy coffeehouse across the street. When he came to the intersection, the night breeze stirred his hair and rippled through his coat. The misting cloud of his breath caught the light of the

lone street lamp on the corner. He looked left and saw
Drury Lane Theater a short distance away. A play
must have been in progress, for the street was lined
with waiting carriages. *I should take Miranda there,* he
thought, then walked the other direction.

Just down Russell Street lay Covent Garden. The
seedy markets in the center of the square were dark
and quiet, but in the somber shadow of St. Paul's
Church, the gaming hells were doing a brisk business.
Intoxicated young rakes yelled boisterously to each
other, coming and going, but as Damien sauntered
into the square, everywhere he looked he saw prostitutes. Most of them had their rooms in the tall,
terraced houses that flanked the square.

The assortment of whores was dizzying, from appallingly young neophytes to seasoned veterans of
the trade. There were blonds and brunettes; short
women and tall; thin, round, and every type in-
between; painted and shameless, like so many garish
flowers in a poison garden. He walked past them
slowly, aggressively eyeing each one, for he was certain that he could take no more of this cursed absti-
nence. He was only a man. It was the best thing for
him, the only thing that had ever worked for easing
what ailed him.

He stopped in front of a voluptuous redhead, chosen
almost by random. He just stared at her, keeping a taut
check on his desperation. He waited for her to take
control, to make his terrible, unceasing loneliness
go away.

"You look like you could do with a friend," she

murmured, shoving away from the wall where she had been leaning. "Do you want to come with me?"

He gave an almost imperceptible nod.

"This way." She took his hand.

He let her lead him through the darkness toward the door under the vaulted, Italian-style arcades. He hesitated at the threshold, he knew not why, but she turned to him, passing a glance over his face.

"You're a handsome one, aren't you? But why so sad?" She reached up and touched his cheek, and his whole being revolted at the prospect of making love to her.

He looked away, lowering his lashes; then he reached into his pocket and gave her a few guineas. "I'm sorry. I—I've changed my mind."

"Don't I please you?" she asked, accepting the coins.

"No, you're very pretty. Just take it."

"Come upstairs, then, love. Why don't you give me a chance? I can give you pleasure—"

But he was already walking away, his jaw clenched tightly at the dire realization that the only woman he wanted to touch him was Miranda. He strode through the city for an hour, trying to master his yearning for her. At last, he seemed to have walked off his confusion and achieved a cool equilibrium. When at last he climbed the front steps of Knight House, his heart leaped within him to wonder if she was still in the drawing room.

The night butler greeted him; Mr. Walsh had gone to bed. The house was mostly dark and very still. Damien shed his greatcoat, took a candle from the servant, and climbed the stairs, trying to pretend to himself that he was not disappointed to have missed out on bidding her good night. At the top of the stairs on the third floor, he headed to his boyhood rooms, then suddenly stopped. He turned by degrees, looking over his shoulder.

Drawn irresistibly, he silenced his footfalls as he prowled down the darkened hallway. He had noted earlier which room they had given her. Now he saw a faint light glimmering under her door.

His heart pounded wildly in the hush of the sleeping household as he reached for the doorknob, but his hand stopped before he reached it. He mustn't scare her. He knocked softly, thrice, upon her door.

No answer.

This took him aback. At once, his mind flew back to the last time he had knocked on her bedroom door—at the coaching inn, where she had tried to escape him. Surely she wouldn't have tried that trick again? Without thinking twice, he turned the doorknob and opened her door. "Miranda?"

His voice dropped to a whisper on the second syllable of her name.

She was fast asleep, with the candle burned down to a stub on the nightstand and an etiquette book lying, dog-eared, across her chest. The sight of her made his heart clench. He stepped into the room and closed the door silently behind him.

*Wake up.* His heartbeat pounded in the arteries in his throat as he stalked over to her. He stood beside her bed staring down at her, dazzled. She was clad in a white muslin night rail with a bit of lace around the neckline and the wrists. From the waist down, she was swathed in the scarlet, gold-embroidered blanket, but where her shift pulled tight across her breast, he could see the dusty-rose outline of her nipple. He wanted to kiss it and to nuzzle the soft blue vein of her wrist where her hand lay sweetly posed by her cheek.

Her rich, sable hair spilled luxuriously across her pillow, glistening by the candlelight. Her long, black lashes lay like the most delicate fans against her creamy, rose-tinged cheeks. Her ruby lips were parted slightly, her bosom rising, falling so peacefully. He wanted to lay his head there. He slowly lowered himself to his knees beside her, willing her to wake up. *I'm weak tonight, Miranda. Please.* His resistance was razor-thin, the hunger and loneliness pressing hard upon him. He knew that if she awoke and found him here, she would take him into her arms. They would lie together and kiss until they were on fire, and they would make love.

She slept on.

He did not touch her, yet merely being near her seemed to ease the pain. The demons inside of him quieted with the lulling rhythm of her breathing, and after a while, he was himself again. He gazed at her for one moment more, then blew out the candle and left.

"They have arrived, my lord, just as you said," Egann reported as Algernon walked into his dimly lit, oak-paneled office. "What would you have me do now?"

Algernon had just come home from dutifully taking his wife and insipid daughters to see the quite enjoy-able play at Drury Lane. Egann had been waiting anxiously to tell him the news. The viscount sat down at his desk and stroked his chin in thought.

What an excellent evening he was having. Everything was taking shape precisely as he had hoped. To his relief, none of his cronies at the club—indeed, not even his wife—yet suspected that he was on the brink of financial ruin. He had been able to fool them all, but the pressure he was under was tremendous, and now, at last, his niece's fortune was in arm's reach. He knew that Knight House—with its fences, gates, and watch dogs—was formidably well secured, but she could not stay in there forever; likewise, her guardian was a man of iron, but the war hero could not spend every waking moment with the girl. That would hardly be proper.

"Go back to Knight House and wait," he ordered coolly. "We must keep watch to discover our opportunity." He paused. "Can you do this, Egann? Those four men I sent to Birmingham failed me, but if you doubt yourself, I'll hire someone else."

"Count on me, master."

"It will require ruthlessness."

Egann smiled slyly. "I can be ruthless, as Your Lordship well knows."

Algernon smiled. Such loyalty—and it cost him so little. "Now, then, to the task at hand." He sat forward and interlocked his fingers, resting his elbows on the desk. "I want to know every move the girl makes, whither she goes, and when. Everything hangs upon the chance of finding her without her guardian by her side. Then we must strike without hesitation—and it must look like an accident, Egann. Do you understand?"

Egann gave a malevolent nod.

Algernon read the resolve in his servant's zealous stare and nodded. "Go."

Egann bowed and limped out of the study. Algernon watched him leave, his eyes narrowed with confident satisfaction.

Soon he would have fifty thousand pounds to dispose of as he saw fit and life would go back to normal, he assured himself. For the moment, it tickled his sense of irony to think that a weak and humble creature like Egann would thwart the mighty Lord Winterley. A cold smile curved his mouth.

*Soon.*

# ⊰ CHAPTER ⊱
# EIGHT

First thing the next morning, the duchess's hair-dresser, a haughty little Frenchman, arrived at Knight House with all the splendor of a visiting dignitary. With the passion of an artist, he cut two inches off of Miranda's long locks, trimmed her hair around her face, then swept the mass of it up into a topknot and curled the wispy hairs framing her face into fantastical ringlets. All the while, the duchess's lady's maid filed and buffed her nails into neat ovals, then used a collection of fine-scented creams to smooth away her calluses from scrubbing Yardley's floors and cooking pots.

This done, the duchess and Lady Lucien took Miranda to Bond Street, with young Lady Jacinda and the agreeable Miss Carlisle in tow. In the well-appointed shops, the women set about equipping her from head to foot at the milliner's, the corsetier's, the hosier's, the glover's, the linen draper's, and the cobbler's shops, in turn. Miranda did not at all mind being measured, poked, and prodded, basking in the attention, for when the duchess of Hawkscliffe sailed into a shop with her entourage, the place practically closed to all other customers. The staff waited on them hand and foot.

With cool expertise, they ordered up a dozen informal gowns on her behalf: morning gowns, walking gowns, afternoon and visiting gowns; a smart Skeffington-brown riding habit; a few half-dress promenade gowns, dinner gowns, and opera gowns in richer, jewel-toned fabrics. Then came the accessories. Guiding her in her choices, her two benefactresses ordered several varieties and colors of kid gloves, shoes, dainty silk pumps and delicate dancing slippers, boots, a pair of pattens for inclement weather; a beautiful pelisse trimmed with ermine to replace her rough, woolen cloak; hats and bonnets of all shapes and sizes; a generous supply of fine linen underthings and white silk stockings. But the most fun part of her shopping excursion was ordering the ball gowns. The duchess decreed that Miranda would need at least two or three formal evening dresses. With their rich satins and velvets, the two ball gowns cost as much as everything else put together.

For her pride's sake, Miranda desperately hoped that her Uncle Jason had left her a sum of money that was paying for her new wardrobe, but she could not bring herself to ask. She was slowly learning the rules of her new world, and it seemed that money was yet another one of those *verboten* topics that a lady of quality did not discuss. Heaven knew the duchess and Lady Lucien acted as though her fortune in new clothes all came for free.

Lady Jacinda managed to cajole the duchess into letting her order a new gown, too, so while she was being measured, Miranda asked permission to go down the street to the umbrella shop they had passed earlier. She had seen a pretty pink parasol in the display window that she wanted to buy and to send back to Yardley as a Christmas gift for Amy. After all, Damien had allotted her three guineas a week in pin money to spend however she chose. Sheer decadence, she thought happily. The duchess gave her leave to go, and Miss Carlisle, who insisted that Miranda call her Lizzie, offered to accompany her. The footman in the dark blue Hawkscliffe livery attended them for their convenience and protection. The girls slipped out, leaving the shop abuzz with the seamstresses and both elegant young wives fussing over the golden-haired, apple-cheeked Lady Jacinda.

Miranda liked the bookish, modest, ever-cheerful Lizzie Carlisle very much. Though they were opposites in temperament, they had several things in common: their lower rank amid the highborn Knight clan; their age; and the fact that they both were wards of the Knight family.

Lizzie's father had been the duke's estate manager, as had his father before him for several generations. When her father had died fifteen years ago, Lizzie had been taken into her guardian's family. She became the designated playmate and lady's companion to Lady Jacinda when they were both mere children in the nursery.

Since Miranda's arrival in London, Lizzie had quickly become her friend, ally, and sometime guide in the strange world of London aristocrats. When it was only the two of them, she felt like she could relax a bit, for she had been trying so hard to be on her best behavior.

They chatted idly as they browsed along Bond Street, the footman following at a respectful distance a couple of paces behind them. Miranda was enjoying herself immensely, but every now and then, she got the strange, prickling feeling along the back of her neck that someone was watching her.

She glanced casually over her shoulder. The street was busy with rich people buying Christmas presents, but nothing out of ordinary struck her. Wintry, late-morning sunshine glinted off the neat shop windows while phaetons, curricles, and other fashionable equipages dashed up and down the narrow street. Clusters of rakehelly young gentlemen, whom Lizzie termed "Bond Street Loungers," loitered here and there, laughing, smoking, and rudely quizzing the girls through their monocles as they passed. They laughed at the footman's rebukes and smiled at Lizzie's cold, scowling glances.

Miranda merely looked at them in curiosity as she walked on. Were these the sort of silly, obnoxious creatures that Damien expected her to accept as suitors? she wondered. The thought of her fierce guardian made her sigh.

She had not seen him much since they had arrived in London. He was doing a superb job of keeping a distance between them. She was lucky to get a glimpse of him at meals, but then, there were always other people present—and that was no doubt his intention. He would not give her a chance to try to talk to him about what had happened between them. Almost forty-eight hours had passed since he had accidentally pounced on her out of a dead sleep, and still, he was ignoring her.

Well, not literally, she admitted, but he barely made eye contact. He would not come within four feet of her; spoke to her only when it could not be avoided, and then, with cool, aloof courtesy that was enough to drive her mad. She felt so helpless, and she missed him terribly. She was worried sick about him. It was obvious that something was very wrong with this man who had done so much for her. He had saved her life, her friends. He had turned her life around. Somehow she had to help him, as he had helped her; but first, she would have to find a way to break down the invisible wall he had raised around him for the express purpose, it seemed, of shutting her out. She found herself walking on eggshells around him, though, for fear of doing anything wrong and driving him away all over again.

Coming to the quaint umbrella shop, she and Lizzie stepped inside and Miranda purchased the dainty parasol for Amy. "She's going to love it. I wish I could be there to see her face when she opens it," she exclaimed, smiling at Lizzie as they went back outside.

"Do you mind if I pop into the bookshop?" the latter asked, glancing longingly into the bookseller's domain. The dim, narrow shop was lined with shelves crammed with countless tomes.

"Not at all." On the pavement before them, a rack of books and a folding stand of various color prints for sale were positioned just outside the shop to entice customers inside. Miranda nodded to it. I think I'll look through these prints and see if I can find one to give to Lord Winterley for Christmas. He's been so kind to me."

"Very well. I won't be long." Lizzie gave her a nod and went into the shop.

Their footman positioned himself near the doorway, keeping a watchful eye on both of his charges. Miranda's reticule dangled from her wrist while she looked through the prints for a picture that Damien might like, perhaps one of a horse. Standing near the edge of the pavement, leafing idly through the paintings and aquatints, she was so engrossed in her musings about Damien and so lulled by the clattering noise of the traffic on the street that she took no note of the heavy rumbling of a large black coach barreling down the street straight toward her.

"Miss FitzHubert, beg your pardon, perhaps you'd best step back from the street—" the footman started.

She glanced up absently. He took a step toward her, his face going white as the tall coach swerved at her, taking her completely off guard.

"Watch out!" a passerby yelled.

She caught only a second's, horrified glimpse at the ugly, little, wizened driver whipping his horses as though he were deliberately trying to run her down. A chorus of male voices yelled from across the street. Miranda leaped out of the way, crashing into the footman as the carriage bumped up on two wheels onto the pavement and sent the aquatints and the books on the rack scattering.

The side of the carriage grazed her by a hair's

breadth; aghast, she felt the breeze from the heavy, spoked wheels that churned like grindstones. The coach shuddered on its springs as it crashed back down onto all four wheels and raced on, vanishing beyond the crook in the road.

Miranda was shaken and ashen faced as several young gentlemen came rushing over to her from all directions.

"Mademoiselle, are you hurt?"

"Do you require assistance?"

To her relief, Lizzie came rushing out of the shop. "Miranda! What happened?" she cried, embracing her.

"A deuced coach almost ran this poor, lovely creature down," one of the raffish young gentlemen declared indignantly.

"Are you all right?" Lizzie asked, anxiously searching her face.

"I think so," Miranda said, but she swallowed hard to realize how easily she could have been crushed beneath the horses' hooves or dragged under the heavy wheels.

"Did anybody see that blasted jehu's face?" a hefty young man demanded, while still another took it upon himself to upbraid the poor footman, as though it were his fault.

"Nary a glimpse of him," a lanky blond fellow answered. "Obviously, the lout lost control of his team. Unless, of course, Miss, someone's deliberately trying to kill you?" he suggested in a joking tone, trying to coax a smile from her, but Miranda blanched, her ordeal on Bordesley Green flooding back into her memory.

"I—I do not think so," she said weakly.

"Oh, for heaven's sake! Don't scare her worse, if you please," Lizzie scolded with the managing air of a born governess. "You all may run along, thank you. My friend will be all right."

The Bond Street Loungers withdrew with reluctant well-wishes. Miranda nodded her thanks, feeling like a foolish country bumpkin to find herself at the center of such a silly mishap. Still . . .

She turned anxiously to Lizzie, lowering her voice. "Do you think that little man really might have been trying to run me down?"

"Oh, don't listen to those idiotic boys, my dear. That is pure foolishness," Lizzie chided, patting her shoulder. "Everybody drives like a lunatic in London. You're just not used to it yet. Shall we go back to the mantua-maker's and see if Their Ladyships are ready to go home? I daresay we could both do with a spot of tea."

She nodded. "Don't tell Lord Winterley about this, please?" She glanced anxiously from Lizzie to the ashen-faced footman. More than the mere embarrassment of her blunder, she did not want to upset Damien or make him angry about anything in his precarious condition.

"I think we should, but if you don't want us to, I won't," Lizzie said reluctantly.

"Nor I, Miss," their manservant added, looking relieved.

When she realized that Damien would probably blame the poor footman for the incident, as the young gentleman had, she was glad to save the fellow from her guardian's terrifying wrath.

Then Lizzie retrieved Amy's parasol, which had flown out of Miranda's grasp. The crepe paper was torn, but the parasol itself was undamaged, to her relief. Lizzie helped the bookseller pick up his bruised tomes before they set out. The man whined bitterly over torn pages and ink blurred by contact with wet snow, though he scarcely seemed concerned that a woman had nearly been squashed to death by a runaway carriage outside his establishment.

Still shaken, Miranda walked with Lizzie back to the dressmaker's shop, where the duchess and Lady Lucien were giving the head seamstress a few final instructions. Miranda sat well out of harm's way and waited in silence as the footman went for the carriage, but she was haunted by the boy's absurd jest in spite of herself. She rubbed her arms against the day's chill. *I do wish Damien were here.*

The next night, they eased Miranda gently into her first experience of life amid the ton with an evening at Drury Lane Theater. In light of her secret career at the Pavilion, Damien watched his ward in knowing amusement. Miranda sat, enthralled, between Alice and Bel, her dutiful chaperons. Robert and Lucien had come out to see the Christmas pageant, as well. Robert was standing in the back of their box, chatting in a low tone with the constant stream of his fashionable Whig friends who stopped by, making the social rounds; Lucien, meanwhile, held an opera glass to his eye, boredly inspecting the audience rather than the dancers dressed as snowflakes on the stage.

Damien could not blame him. The pageant—with its spectacles, songs, and pantomimes—really was a very silly affair, which was why he found it much more entertaining to watch Miranda instead. He set aside his frustration with the fact that the police had still not caught Jason's killer. "Rooster" had been released into his brother the minister's custody. So they had caught the wrong man, he mused, but they would catch the right one eventually. He had to believe that. Then he put these dark thoughts out of his mind and turned his attention back to Miranda.

One would have thought that her night at Drury Lane was the absolute thrill of her life. Childlike wonder played across her face, every nuance of emotion visible in her eyes, in the rosy flush of her cheeks, in her quick, absorbed smiles. The sight of her both amused him in an aloof way and made him go all soft and warm inside. Perhaps it was merely the symptom of a poor digestion, he thought dryly. Certainly, the drain on his savings had brought about worthy results. He ran a furtive gaze over her. She had been a diamond to begin with, but Bel and Alice's efforts had polished her into dazzling beauty.

She was wearing the first of her new gowns to arrive from the dressmaker's shop. Bel must have bribed the modiste as an extra incentive to work quickly, he thought, for he could only wonder how many seamstresses it must have taken to finish the gown so fast. In any case, Miranda looked radiant. The dark green silk gave an added luster to the emerald of her eyes, while her low, heart-shaped neckline continually drew his eye. Bel had lent her a pretty cross necklace on a gold chain. Against Miranda's creamy skin, it twinkled in the bright illumination of the theater and nestled in the valley between her luscious breasts.

Damien dragged his stare away again, shifting restlessly in his seat. He folded his arms across his chest, then flicked a piece of lint off the scarlet sleeve of his uniform. At a burst of laughter behind him, he glanced over his shoulder at Robert's sociable Whigs, then ignored them in distaste. He did not care for their unpatriotic notions. They were the party, after all, who had protested the expense and duration of the war—as though England could realistically have ignored what was happening just a few miles across the Channel, Napoleon swallowing the Continent whole.

Fortunately, his brother had become an Independent upon leaving the Tory party several months ago. Robert's interest in Whiggish ideas centered on their efforts toward humanitarian reform, educating the children of the poor and so forth, to which Damien had no objections.

When intermission came, he braced himself for the onslaught of eligible bachelors who flooded their box on the pretense of paying their respects to the duke and duchess, but who were plainly angling for an introduction to the ravishing young lady in green. Bel and Alice doled out said introductions with unstinting generosity, much to Damien's annoyance.

Soon, Miranda was holding court with the ease of a born coquette, while Damien sat beside her, arms folded, scowling and stewing in what he feared was outright jealousy, or at least frustrated possessiveness. It seemed that the experience of actually marrying Miranda off was going to prove to be as different from his expectations as most men's notions of rushing into battle were from the reality of it.

The youngbloods hung on her every word and marveled aloud that they had never seen her before. Was she "out" or not? Damien tersely informed them she had been away at school. He told them she was his ward, Sherbrooke's niece, but did not go into the details of her parentage. The ton would find out soon enough exactly who she was, and then would come the test of his own standing in Society.

More young men crowded into the box, introducing their friends to Miranda, once the first round had gained access to her through her chaperons.

"How do you do, Miss FitzHubert?" the newest arrival was saying, bowing over her dainty, gloved hand. "I hope you are feeling better. What, don't you recognize us?"

"I don't think she remembers us, Ollie," his companion said with a smitten smile. He was a fair-haired youth, as lanky and anemically pale as his dark-haired friend was portly and ruddy faced. "She was rather shaken up, after all."

Miranda opened her mouth to speak, but "Ollie" beat her to it.

"We were there yesterday on Bond Street, when you were almost trampled by that coach," he told her. "By Jove, that was a close thing! I hope you are feeling better."

"I am . . . quite well, thank you," she said weakly, casting Damien a guilty glance.

Narrowing his eyes, he looked askance at his ward. "Whatever is he referring to, my dear?" he asked in a soft, imperious tone.

Her cheeks bloomed with a rush of color. "I had a bit of a, er, mishap yesterday when I was out."

"Do tell."

"It was my own fault—" she attempted, but he would hear none of it.

"Not at all, dear lady!" Ollie protested. "It was all that incompetent driver's fault." He looked at Damien, taking it upon himself to explain. "My lord, I do hope that bumbling footman was dismissed after his failure to look after the young lady better. I'd have fired him on the spot."

Damien stared quellingly at him. "And you are?"

"Oliver Quinn, my lord, at your service. This is the Honorable Nigel Stanhope." He jerked a gruff nod at his friend, who bowed to Damien with a hapless smile. The skinny one seemed to realize, if the husky one had not, that he verged on insult, daring to reproach the famed Colonel Lord Winterley on how he went about protecting his ward.

Or failed to, in this case. "I see."

"I wish I'd had my horse, I tell you," Ollie blustered on. "I'd have ridden after that carriage and found out who that driver was."

"I'm sure you're very gallant, Mr. Quinn," Miranda said with an uncomfortable smile. She soon managed to dismiss him as the signal sounded for the end of intermission.

"What happened?" Damien demanded in a low tone, leaning toward her as the young fops cleared the box.

"It was nothing, honestly," she whispered back. "When I was shopping on Bond Street yesterday, a runaway coach went by a bit close. I didn't know how madly people drive in Town."

"Miranda!"

"I was in no real danger, my lord."

"It sounds as though you could have been seriously injured."

"No, no, I was well out of the way. That's why I didn't mention it. There's no cause for alarm."

"You have to be on your guard in the city, Miranda. This isn't Yardley village."

"I know that now. I know I'm a provincial, but I'll get used to it. Please don't be cross."

He set his jaw, cursing himself for keeping a distance between them when it could have led to her being in danger. *Intolerable. I'm damned if I do and damned if I don't.* "I should have been with you," he said through gritted teeth.

She fluttered her borrowed fan. "No, you shouldn't."

"Why not?" he retorted.

"Because I was trying to buy you a Christmas present. If you had been there, I should not have been able to get you a surprise."

Her reply took him aback. When she smiled, gazing into his eyes, he dropped his gaze and shook his head, feeling his cheeks flush slightly. Maybe keeping her at arm's length was not the right thing to do, merely the easy thing. What did he know? For a man used to meeting dangerous situations with expertise, the girl had the power to reduce him to a bumbling fool.

"Everything you do surprises me," he muttered.

"Oh? You haven't seen anything yet," she murmured, sliding him a wicked look; then she settled back into her chair to watch the show.

Snow dusted London afresh outside their windows the next afternoon, but within, the delicious pungency of cinnamon and cloves from the wassail simmering in the kitchen permeated every room. Miranda had the unique pleasure of helping the duchess, Lizzie, and Lady Jacinda decorate the shelves and fireplace mantels of Knight House in preparation for the family's private Christmas Eve celebration on Saturday night. Together, the women of the house decked the mantels of every fireplace with evergreen boughs, pinecones, and clutches of holly berries tied with gold ribbons. They hung wreaths on the doors and set lacy illuminations in the windows.

Miranda draped ribbons and mistletoe over the grand, brass replica of the French eagle Damien had taken in battle, which was on display in the state room. The duchess made the butler tie a sprig of mistletoe over her husband's piano, merrily laying the trap for him; then Jacinda seized upon the idea of a parlor theatrical for after their dinner on Saturday night. Miranda chimed in with numerous suggestions, helping Jacinda plan the evening's comic entertainments.

As she did so, moving about the drawing room, she placed a few extra boughs on the carved white mantel in honor of the woman in the painting that hung above the fireplace. She had been told it was a portrait of Damien's mother, Georgiana, the last duchess of Hawkscliffe. Miranda studied the portrait for a moment. In her tall white wig and panniered gown with its plunging neckline, the late duchess looked like a force to be reckoned with. There was pride in the angle of her chin, a mysterious sparkling intelligence in her deep blue eyes, and a tart sort of humor in the star-shaped silk face patch so artfully placed near her sensual mouth.

Just then, Mr. Walsh came in to announce, to Miranda's delight, that more of her new clothes had just been delivered from the shops on Bond Street. The servants carried the thin, white boxes up to the elegant bedchamber she had been assigned, and Lizzie and Jacinda pounded up the stairs with her to see the finished products. She whipped off the lids and carefully pulled back the crepe paper, revealing three morning gowns in succession.

"What's in this one?" Lizzie asked in excitement.

Miranda opened a fourth box and drew in her breath. "Promenade, I think. It feels like Christmas already!"

"Open this one," Jacinda prodded, sliding the last unopened box across the bed to her.

She pulled off the lid and lifted the dress gently from the box. "Ooo! My riding habit!"

"Perhaps it's time you had your first riding lesson, then," a deep voice said from the doorway.

Her heart leaped with recognition. Pressing the smart brown bodice against her chest, she turned to find Damien leaning idly in the doorway, his thumb hooked in his waistcoat pocket. She blinked. Was she dreaming, or had he really come looking for her?

"Do you mean it?"

He nodded sagely. "Your education is sadly lacking until you can manage a horse."

A smile spread slowly across her face. "I'll be right there. Do you want to see my new clothes?"

He gave a boyishly shy shrug and sauntered into the room, nodding with probably pretended interest as she showed him her new dresses. Then he left so she could get changed.

A short while later, Damien took her out to Green Park for her very first riding lesson. She kept stealing little joyous glances at him. She couldn't believe he had sought her out. She was nervous about riding, but at the moment, she didn't care if she did break her neck. It would be worth it: Damien wanted to be with her at last.

While a groom stood in attendance, Colonel Lord Winterley turned all business, explaining the treacherous-looking sidesaddle to her. At length, he gave her a leg up onto the most docile animal in the duke's stable: a placid, cherry-bay pony called Apple-Jack. Tall as she was, her legs dangled comically off the potbellied pony as it went plodding through the light, powdery snow.

"Do you laugh at me, sir?" she demanded of her guardian, noting the slight twitching about one corner of his beautiful mouth.

"Absolutely not, my dear."

But she heard a distinct chuckle as she looked forward again. She scarcely minded. Her heart was light.

If appearing absurd was what it took in order to be with Damien for a while, she would gladly endure it.

He kept Apple-Jack on the lunge line while Miranda rode in a large circle, braving a trot. Bouncing everywhere, sans dignity, she scrambled to manage the reins without insulting the horse's sensitive mouth while trying to keep her seat centered at the same time. With each revolution around the circle, she could not help but steal a glance at Damien. The snow seemed to fall more gently around him. Bits of white clung in his black hair and stuck to his wool coat. As the half hour of instruction progressed, she applied herself to winning another coveted morsel of her riding master's praise, but her heart soared: She and Damien were on speaking terms again, and all was right with the world.

When the lesson was over, Miranda took care not to overstay her welcome with Damien—as Mr. Chipping always used to say to his actors, "Leave them wanting more." The groom held the gate open as they reentered the property. Miranda thanked her guardian for the lesson and accepted his offer of another on the morrow; then she parted ways with him in the graveled yard. This seemed to surprise him. He searched her face one last time as she nodded gracefully to him and turned back toward the house. With a puzzled glance over his shoulder, he led Apple-Jack back into the stable.

Exhilarated with her success and the fresh, brisk air, she swept off her veiled riding hat as she strode toward the house, then lifted her eyebrows to find Lord Lucien leaning against the stone balustrade of the veranda on the back of the house. His silvery eyes gleamed as he watched her come toward him. He moved toward her, sauntering around the snow-glazed statue of the blank-eyed stone cherub on its pedestal. Hands in his trouser pockets, he cast her a Machiavellian smile that made her a little uneasy. She realized he had been standing there for some time watching Damien and her together in the park just beyond the property.

"Good afternoon, my lord," she offered.

"Hullo, Miss FitzHubert," he drawled.

"Are you waiting for Damien—I mean Lord Winterley," she amended hastily, but she was too late.

He arched his eyebrow at her blunder. "Ah, 'Damien,' is it?"

She turned away sharply and swallowed hard, her heart pounding. "Pardon me. It was a simple mistake. If you'll excuse me, I must change for dinner—"

"No, my dear. Do indulge me with a moment of your time, please. I find this all very curious." He sauntered up behind her and dropped his smooth voice to a murmur. "I really have begun to wonder. What exactly is going on between you and my brother?"

"I don't know what you mean, I'm sure." Her heart pounded wildly.

"Miranda," he chided. "Do you think I'm as blind as everyone else around here?"

"It was a simple mistake," she repeated, her mouth going dry.

"Not so very simple, I think." He paused. "You would not lie to me, would you? That would be a very naughty thing to do. Besides, do you know I am a diplomat, Miss FitzHubert, professionally trained to ferret out the truth and drag it out into the light? You cannot hide anything from me, in the end."

Her body tensed. She realized in alarm that she was caught. Apparently not even her acting skills were enough to fool Lord Lucien. Not knowing what to say, she turned around slowly and forced herself to meet his scrutinizing stare. He studied her vulnerable expression for a moment in mingled pity and amusement.

"Does he know you're in love with him?" he asked.

She gazed at him, at a loss, then shook her head in despair. "Oh, I don't know. I don't know anything. I don't even know if I *am* in love with him. Please don't be angry at me. I can't help it. You're not going to tell him, are you? Promise you won't?"

"I promise nothing until I know all. Why do you say you aren't sure? It seems fairly obvious to me."

"What is the point?" she exclaimed, throwing up her hands and dropping them again to her sides. "He is too high above me, as I know perfectly well. I have no designs on your brother, my lord, if that is your worry. There may be a certain . . . affinity between us, but I know where I stand. He is an earl and a hero. I'm not even legitimate."

"You are talking like a fool, Miss FitzHubert. Come." He offered her his arm. "Take a turn about the gallery with me and let us try to sort this out."

She heaved a rebellious sigh but obeyed, trembling with the realization that her improper feelings toward her guardian, and his toward her, had been discovered. Lord Lucien did not seem exactly cross at her, but he was formidably determined to unveil her secrets, as though he sought to test her. She let him lead her back into the house, where they took a slow promenade down the long, narrow gallery where portraits of the Knight ancestors gazed down solemnly from the walls.

He began asking questions, and after an initial hesitation, Miranda told him everything. It was impossible to do otherwise. He was a shrewd, worldly-wise man who was shocked by nothing and impossible to fool. He asked such probing questions that he seemed to read her very mind. How Alice managed him so easily, she could not comprehend. But she had seen the strong bond between the twins, and she realized that if anyone would know how to help Damien fight his demons, Lucien would.

Reluctantly, she laid her cards down on the table in the hopes that he could read them better than she. She held back nothing: her career as Miss White; how Damien had mistaken her for a harlot; her attack by brigands on Bordesley Green and the savage way Damien had come to her rescue; his championing her and her friends against Mr. Reed at Yardley; and, finally, how he had lashed out when she had roused him from his slumber the night they had shared a bed at the hotel.

"Are you sure that's all that happened in that bed?" he asked calmly.

"All? He nearly choked the life out of me, my lord. I'm sure that's quite enough to have happened, is it not?"

He conceded this with a nod. "Yet you do not seem angry at him."

"How could I be? It's not his fault. All I want is to help the man. Surely you can see I owe him that." She sighed and shook her head. "He would be furious if he knew I had told you all this."

"Miranda, there are some things you should know about Damien. Come." He handed her down to sit on the viewing bench at the end of the picture gallery, then took his place beside her.

She turned to him, heeding him in full absorption.

"My brother was in nearly every major action of the war. I was there, and I saw the dark transformation it wrought in him. For example, he led storming parties at Ciudad Rodrigo and Badajoz. Only a handful of men served in both groups and lived to tell about it. You have seen him in action, so you know it is an awesome sight to behold. You may have heard about the insurrection among our troops after the fort at Badajoz was taken. Damien hunted down and executed those of his own men who had gone about raping and pillaging in the town. He was brutal. He felt betrayed by his men, and I suspect he felt personally responsible for losing control of them for those three days; but then, it had become a miniature war between the officers and the rank and file, by that point."

"It sounds like a very ugly experience."

"Ugly enough to disillusion me entirely about the way the war was being fought, but that is another story," he said softly. "It was all beginning to get to Damien. The carnage, the grief, the powerlessness and anger an officer feels at his inability to protect the men who entrust their lives to his command. It began to change Damien, as well you might imagine, for he is a leader in the finest sense of the word. He cares as other men do not. That is why, everywhere he goes, people love him. He may look tough, but he is all heart—and I watched that heart break in the Peninsula, Miranda. I saw him take refuge from the pain in apathy, as though he were the hardened captain of some blood-thirsty band of Hessian mercenaries. I tried to keep him human, civilized, tried to reason with him. He resented me for it." He shook his head. "It was easier for him to do his job by letting himself grow numb to it all. And he was good. By God, he's good. Born to it, you know. Fearless, mean as hell."

"I've seen," she murmured, nodding.

"At any rate, after Badajoz, as I said, I simply could take no more of the insanity. I decided to sell my commission in the army and join the Foreign Office instead. I tried to get Damien to leave with me before the war destroyed what remained of the brother I knew, but he would not hear of it. We had a great row. He called me a coward for leaving, if memory serves, but it did not deter me. For me, it was a matter of conscience to serve where I could be more useful. But the one great question that has haunted me ever since is, how much worse did Damien become as a result of my not being there?"

Lucien paused, and Miranda gazed at him, mystified.

"For a long time afterwards," he continued, "he wanted nothing to do with me, so I know how good he is at shutting a person out, especially those who care for him. That's why I'm giving you this." He reached into his waistcoat pocket and pulled out a small, rusty key, which he placed in her hand, curling her fingers around it with a gentle clasp. "Use only in case of emergency."

Her heart skipped a beat as she glanced at it, then looked at him, wide-eyed. "What does it open?"

He dodged the question with a cryptic smile. "The important thing is, you have his attention, and that is more than I can say for any other woman I've seen him with. Take heart: None of them have shown your mettle, else we would not be sitting here. He needs you, Miranda. You may be his last hope. I am only his brother. I can't do for him what you can."

"What can I do?" she asked in a hushed tone.

"Love him, *chérie*. You have my blessing." With that, he leaned toward her and kissed her on the forehead.

"Thank you, my lord, but I don't see how I *can* have your blessing," she said rather miserably, holding his amused gaze as he pulled back. "I know what I am. I'm not refined like the duchess, nor proper and good like your Lady Lucien—my lord?" He had risen to his feet and was casually sauntering away. She looked after him, bewildered. "My lord, where are you going?"

He did not answer. He only kept walking. What a strange, exasperating man!

"Lord Lucien? Wait! How I am to make him love me?"

He waved his hand with an idle gesture, ambling toward the large, open doorway. "That is your concern, Miranda. I am certainly not going to sit here listening to your litany of excuses of why it can't be done."

"But what happens if I approach him and he turns dangerous again? I told you what took place at the hotel. He could have killed me already."

"Stand up to him, girl," he said heartily. "Stand up to these demons that beset him as bravely as Damien faced down the French. You're a fighter, Miranda. I knew it from the minute I saw you, so fight to bring our brother back to us. Forget virtue and refinement; in this fight, your courage is the only measure of how 'worthy' you are."

Her shoulders slumped in dismay. He was no help. "Won't you at least tell me what door this key opens?"

His wicked laughter trailed after him, rebounding off the parquet floor and long walls of the gallery before he vanished from the doorway. "You'll figure it out, *chérie*. If you want him badly enough, you'll figure it all out in time."

# ⊰ CHAPTER ⊱
# NINE

When Christmas Eve arrived the next night, Lord Lucien suggested a sleigh ride in anticipation of their feast. He wanted to show little Harry the illuminations of the great houses in the neighborhood and on St. James's Square. The duke and duchess remained behind to visit with Belinda's bespectacled old father, Dr. Alfred Hamilton. Miranda soon found herself bundled up in her new coat and gloves as the team of horses with tinkling bells on their harness whisked them over the snow.

The sleigh was only intended for six, but they squeezed eight people in, merrily passing around flagons of mulled wine to help them keep warm. The evening was dark, but the stars danced brightly in the black velvet sky. Lucien and Alice held little Harry between them; Lady Jacinda and Lizzie sat on either side of the dashing Lord Alec; while Miranda sat nestled close to Damien.

As their jaunt took them through Hyde Park, Lucien hushed their laughter and called to the driver to halt in the middle of the deserted park as the strains of what seemed a heavenly chorus of angels reached them, floating softly across the frozen Serpentine. Somewhere an evening service was in progress. Even Harry sat in wide-eyed silence as they listened to the celestial melody of an old, familiar hymn. To Miranda, the moment felt oddly suspended in time.

*"Silent night, holy night, all is calm, all is bright . . ."*

She wanted to hold onto that moment—the precious, elusive sense of belonging—forever. She glanced at Damien and found him gazing at her.

*". . . Sleep in heavenly peace."*

In the darkness, she reached for his hand, but he only gave her fingers a brief squeeze, then put his arm around her and held her closer for warmth. A breathless silence settled over their cheerful company as the delicate music shivered into nothingness.

Damien quietly ordered the coachman to drive on.

Jacinda stared longingly at the frozen ornamental lake. "We must remember to go ice skating before the Serpentine melts. Lizzie, Miranda, shall we go on Monday?"

Miranda shuddered and shook her head. "Not me, thanks."

"Why not?" the girl protested. "It's fun."

"And good exercise," Lizzie chimed in.

"Why don't you try it?" Damien asked her in an intimate tone, his eyes aglow. No one seemed to mind or even to notice that he had his arm around her.

She shivered. "Not for me, thanks." None of their easy assurances could have talked her out of her utter phobia of the water.

Soon they viewed the illuminations at Apsley House,

stately Buckingham, and the prince regent's Carlton House behind its screen of Italianate columns.

Back at Knight House once more, they drank negus in the drawing room until Mr. Walsh, with a red carnation tucked in his buttonhole that did little to make festive his grave manner, announced that dinner was served. Their Graces led the way, followed by Lucien and Alice. Old Mr. Hamilton offered Lady Jacinda his frail arm; Lizzie went in with Alec, doting helplessly on the golden rogue every step of the way. Last of all, Damien offered Miranda his arm and escorted her in to dine. The chandelier blazed above; the room held the faint perfume of evergreen boughs. Miranda had never beheld a table so magnificently laden. It was bedecked with silver and exquisite china, yards of creamy white damask, and gleaming candles whose flames were reflected in the great mirrors on the walls.

They all joined hands around the table as the handsome young duke offered up a simple grace of thanks for God's gift of his Son this holy night; for their country's victory and peace after twenty years of war; and for the fact that, at last, Christmas found them together again. His prayer brought a lump up into Miranda's throat, though she had only known these people for a short while. She stared down at her shiny Sevres plate, then looked over at Damien as he gave her hand a gentle squeeze.

She thanked God most of all for her guardian—guardian angel, as she sometimes thought of him.

"And may our baby be healthy," the duchess added softly.

"Amen," her husband answered, leaning over to kiss her cheek.

"And God also bless Jack, wherever he is," Jacinda added, casting a brief, melancholic look around the table at her brothers.

"God bless Jack," Lucien and Alec echoed, but Robert and Damien remained silent, exchanging a grim glance.

The duchess gave the footmen a nod, and they began to wait on them.

"Who's Jack?" Miranda asked cautiously.

"He is our brother," Alec answered in a mellow, faraway tone. "He is the second-born, after Robert."

"He could not be with you tonight?"

"He does not live in England," Lizzie said delicately, giving her a warning glance.

The subject of their missing brother seemed to be an awkward one, so Miranda dropped it, turning her attention instead to the meal, which was sumptuous even by Knight House standards. A silver tureen of pease soup held pride of place in the center of the table. On one side, there was a roasted turkey with celery sauce; on the other, buttery cod and a rich, red chine of lamb. Mincemeat pie and fillet of pork with sharp sauce graced the foot of the table; at the head was fried sole, which Miranda did not fancy, and two whole chickens with broccoli. And this was only the first course of three.

"None of my new clothes are going to fit anymore," she told them with a laugh.

"They had better," Damien muttered, giving her a teasing look askance.

Next came apple puffs and startled-looking wood-cocks, arranged lifelike on the plate; pickled lambs' ears; galantine. The flaky sturgeon was done to per-fection, nearly as good as the hare with mushrooms. Miranda took one bite of a savory cake. It was deli-cious, but she could not finish it. She marveled at the days less than a fortnight ago when sometimes all she had had for dinner, provided she was not being pun-ished with starvation on any given night, was a hunk of stale bread and a tepid cup of tea.

Again, the four liveried footmen posted in the corners stepped forward, cleared the table, neatly brushed off the crumbs, and refilled the wineglasses. Miranda's thoughts drifted. She studied each face around the table, memorizing them, in her gratitude, and relishing the wonderful feelings this night had given her.

She took particular pleasure in simply looking at Damien and his collection of tall, handsome brothers. Though there was a family resemblance, it puzzled her that they did not look more alike. Robert, the eldest, was in his mid- to late thirties, with jet-black hair touched with silver at his temples and penetrating brown eyes. If he had not possessed such a kind smile, Miranda would have been impossibly intimidated by the duke. She did not need to know how many estates he owned or how many seats in Parliament he con-trolled to feel his aura of power, yet when he gazed at his wife, one could see him turn smitten.

She looked at Lord Alec next. *What a rogue.* She shook her head to herself with a wry smile. She quite adored him, for they were similar in nature, Alec and she—both flamboyant, provocative creatures who loved to be the center of attention. He was the youngest of the Knight brothers and the one Damien had called the current darling of Society. She could see why. Lord Alec was utterly gorgeous and knew it. He spoke his mind with frank, rapier wit and, like any true arbiter of fashion, took pleasure in his own eccentricity, dressing in rather loud colors, wearing his sun-streaked, dark gold hair shoulder-length, pulled back in a queue. He was the very sort of man she had mistaken Damien for the first night they met—the highborn, pleasure-hungry thrill seeker.

She knew she had found favor with the princely young rake and sensed that this was a rare privilege. When Alec had offered to introduce her to all of his friends in her search for a husband, Damien had promptly said, "No thank you." Alec had laughed. She had no doubt that when the golden charmer was not under Robert's stern eye, he was altogether wicked.

Finally, she turned her gaze to Lucien. She never tired of glancing from one twin to the other, fascinated by their identical appearance. One man so strikingly good-looking would have turned heads, but en suite, with their glossy black hair and gray eyes, the effect was irresistible. They looked like a pair of matched archangels, she mused, as the footmen brought out yet another course, setting half moon and potted larks on either side of her.

Feeling adventurous, she sampled the ox palates

with red currant sauce and fricassee of crawfish. Damien took a sip of his wine and eyed her askance as she ate a few of the fried oysters on a dainty fish fork. She brushed her napkin over her lips self-consciously.

"What is it?" she whispered.

He glanced at the oysters with a gleam in his eyes. "Nothing, my dear. Eat up."

She did, though heaven knew she would not be able to move soon. She picked at the fruits offered up at the end of the meal, Jargonel pears and China oranges, and the little tart lemon biscuits to clear the palate.

"I fear that we shall all burn for gluttony," Jacinda announced, pushing back from the table with a mild groan.

"And I, for one, am not a whit sorry," Dr. Hamilton replied with a chuckle.

At last, the ladies withdrew to the parlor while the men stayed at the table for a smoke and final glass of port.

"Don't be long," the duchess ordered her husband, father, and three brothers-in-law. "There are presents to be opened."

"Yes, ma'am," Robert answered, flashing her a conspiratorial smile.

Following Alice, Miranda glanced back at Damien. Again, she found him staring at her, his expression as tender as it was guarded; then the footman closed the door between them.

This was the moment Damien had waited for, the moment he had gone into debt for; the moment he could finally show Miranda beyond any doubt that there were people who did care about her. Uncharacteristically, she had been trying to make herself inconspicuous while the others exchanged gifts. The rounded line of her shoulders, the nervously twisting hands in her lap, every inch of her proclaimed her uneasiness as she waited for the entertainments to begin. It was obvious that she saw herself at this moment as an intruder upon their family holiday, but Damien went over to her, grasped both her hands, and pulled her up from her chair in the corner and led her over into their midst.

"Come, I have something for you."

Her cheeks turned bright red. "Oh, surely, Damien—I mean Lord Winterley—you shouldn't have."

"Damien," he corrected her softly, though the others heard. "I did. Now, sit."

She gave him a flustered yet adoring look and lowered herself to the ottoman near Bel's chair.

"First this," he said, handing her a small velvet box. She glanced at him uncertainly. "Go on," he murmured gently.

She took the lid off and gazed down reverently at the regimental medal inscribed to Major Jason Sherbrooke, awarded for valor at the Battle of Busaco.

She looked up at him with a sheen of crystal tears in her emerald eyes. "Thank you."

"Jason wanted you to have it. He is never far from us," he added softly.

She nodded, blinking the tears back with a delicate flutter of her long, black lashes.

"Now, then. It seems there are a few presents here that have not been claimed yet by their rightful owner."

She looked at him suspiciously, and he gave her a roguish smile, barely aware of anyone else in the brightly lit salon.

Lucien and Alice gave her a neat leather desk stocked with a very correct set of calling cards and stationery, indigo ink, and excellent writing utensils. Bel gave her a strand of white pearls with earrings to match. Lizzie had monogrammed Miranda's initials into a set of three fine handkerchiefs. Jacinda gave her an opera fan made of feathers with a little spyglass inserted into the handle. Alec gifted her with an oversized fur muff of sable, very fashionable. He had given one of spotted ermine to Jacinda, one of white rabbit to Lizzie. Even Mr. Hamilton had brought her a present, a book of Sir Walter Scott's verses, signed by the author, who had often dined at Robert's table.

Lastly, Damien gave her a piece of paper folded in triplet and sealed with a drop of red wax indented with his signet ring.

Her hands trembled slightly as she tore it open and read the message. She looked at him, wide-eyed. "You didn't."

He smiled.

"What does it say?" Jacinda exclaimed.

"Damien got me a blood-horse!" she cried, leaping to her feet.

"Aye, excellent stock." He beamed. "She's a liver-bay mare, sixteen hands, from Eclipse's line. Very gentle and moves like a dream. She'll be delivered here the day after Christmas. By then, I trust you'll be ready to graduate from Apple-Jack?"

"Oh, Damien, I don't believe it!" She launched out of her chair and threw her arms around his neck, hugging him hard. With one arm still wrapped tightly around his neck, she turned to the others with tears in her eyes. "I don't know what to say. I'm not sure I should accept such beautiful gifts—on the other hand, I don't think I could bear to give them back. I've never had a Christmas like this before. I don't know how I can ever thank you. You took me in. You all have been so generous and so uncommonly kind to me—and I have nothing to give you in return," she choked out, starting to break down as the others looked on fondly.

Damien let out a soft, chiding laugh and cupped her head gently against him. "There, there, darling, it was hardly our purpose to make you cry."

"Of course. I'm sorry," she said, sniffling. Chasing her tears away, she forced a tremulous smile, still clinging to him. She looked at Robert. "Your Grace, may I ask a favor of you?"

"What is it, Miss FitzHubert?"

She disengaged herself from Damien's light hold and hurried over to his eldest brother, bending to whisper something in his ear.

He smiled at her as she straightened up again. "Capital idea, my dear. Which key?"

"The key of C, please."

"Very good. Family, I am pleased to announce that Miss FitzHubert is going to give us a song," he said cheerfully, rising.

They exclaimed with pleasure at this announcement

as Robert escorted her over to his gleaming Broad-wood grand.

"I hope you will like it. It's not much, but it's all I have," she said, her cheeks turning nearly as red as the crimson roses arranged in a vase on the piano.

As Robert played a few introductory bars, Damien watched her, transfixed by her sweet face and shining eyes. He had never seen a prettier girl, nor a dearer one. Her stint as Miss White served her well when she stood up to sing before them, for her poise was as perfect as her pitch. The song she chose was the ancient Christmas hymn of "What Child Is This?" to the melody of "Greensleeves."

Nearly bursting with pride in her, Damien basked in the rich mellow alto of her voice, just as he had that night at the Pavilion.

When her performance came to an end, his family sat in charmed silence for a second as though she had cast a spell over them, but Damien, standing behind them, re-called her coquettish words to him on the night they had met: *"Humph! You didn't even clap for me."*

From the back of the room, he began slowly, loudly applauding.

She looked up and met his gaze, then glanced around, blushing with gratitude as the others joined in. The applause had a predictable effect on his lovely rose. She seemed to grow an inch before his very eyes.

"That was wonderful!" Alice exclaimed.

"What an exquisite voice you have," Bel agreed.

"Brava!" Alec shouted above the others, grinning at Damien in amazement at her talent.

"You're too kind, really." Miranda gave them a saucy little bow and skipped back to her seat, only to be called back a moment later for an encore.

It was midnight when Miranda went to bed in a delirium of happiness. Dreamily removing the combs and pins from her tresses, she held her hair up in back as the maid unfastened her dinner gown; then she slipped her night rail on over her head, her eyes watering with a contented yawn. It was the best Christmas of her life, but that had nothing to do with the gifts the Knight family had lavished on her. The real gift was the effort they had made to welcome and include her. Having been an outsider like her mother all her life, she had never experienced such a sense of belonging, certainly not at Yardley. She never wanted to let it go.

The maid curtseyed in the doorway on her way out. Miranda bade her a happy Christmas and good night. With a pervading sense of well-being, she sat on her bed and closed her eyes for a moment with a private, savoring smile.

*I can't believe he bought me a horse.* Flicking her eyes open again, she glanced at the scrolled print of some race horses that she had bought him, rolled up with a length of green ribbon that she had tied in a bow. It was such a paltry offering that she had been too embarrassed to give it to him in front of the others. Biting her lower lip in thought, she glanced at the door of her bedchamber, then promptly decided to deliver it to his room before he came upstairs. She had promised to surprise him, after all.

She jumped up and glided over to the dressing table, picked it up, then hesitated. Quickly scooping up the little key that Lord Lucien had given her yesterday, she stole out of her room and padded silently down the hallway, counting doors. She had made a mental note a few days ago which room was her guardian's: once around the corner and exactly eight doors down.

Beneath her slippered feet, the marble was cold; she trod on the plush Persian runner down its center. Candles were lit here and there along the dim corridor. They flickered in the draft. Scroll in one hand, key in the other, she crept up to the door of Damien's chamber and silently entered.

It was difficult to see much by the silvery moonlight, but from what she could make out, his domain was relatively spartan compared to the opulence throughout the rest of the house.

*My soldier,* she thought fondly. She rested the beribboned print on his pillow, then gazed at his bed for a moment with a flutter of desire in her belly. God, she missed his kiss. She glanced down at the little key in her hand, then tiptoed over to the door and tried the lock.

*Too small.*

That wasn't it. She frowned. What in blazes did the thing open? Casting another furtive glance around Damien's room, ignoring the fact that she was snooping shamelessly, she spied a fine mahogany box on the chest of drawers.

*Aha.* But when she tried the key in this lock, it was too large.

Suddenly, a shout of manly laughter startled her from outside, below Damien's bedroom window. It was followed by a clamor of yells, whooping cries, and the barking of dogs.

*What on earth?* Miranda furrowed her brow in utter bafflement. It sounded as though the house was being attacked by savages.

She knew she had to slip away before anyone discovered her here, but the sounds of hilarity drew her irresistibly to the window. When she peeked out the corner of the drape, her eyes widened. She clapped her hand over her mouth.

Good Lord, were they foxed? She could not believe her eyes.

A grand, jolly snowball battle had broken out across the grounds among the four Knight brothers. They skidded across the veranda, chasing Lord Alec, who had no doubt started it, yelling like a tribe of heathens. They dodged from tree to barren tree, leaped the evergreen parterres, and tackled each other like overgrown schoolboys without their coats on, snowballs whizzing back and forth. At first she thought it was the twins against Robert and Alec, but she soon realized it was every man for himself. All the while, the duke's big watchdogs leaped and barked all around them, tails wagging, and tried to catch the snowballs in their jaws.

Without warning, Alec let out a war cry like a Highlander and charged Lucien, diving on him. As they went tumbling onto the snowy ground, Robert foiled Alec's victory by stuffing snow down the back of his shirt; Damien, laughing, came to his youngest brother's rescue in turn, flattening Robert with a ready swipe of a kick to the back of his knees. The duke went down with a yelp; then the others scrambled. The snow flew once more, and the skirmish moved off around the corner of the house, where Miranda could no longer see.

She blinked in astonishment after they had gone. Had her eyes deceived her? Either it was Christmas bringing out the naughty children in them or they were all perfectly mad, she thought, her eyes twinkling, but she felt her heart lift with joy. As she raised her gaze to the night sky, she made a wish upon a star that she could win Damien's love and always be a part of this family.

Withdrawing silently, she went back to her own room and curled up contentedly in bed, feeling safer and more cared about than she had since her parents had been alive.

Holland House in Kensington was a grand Jacobean manor of dark brown brick edged with white piping. It was festooned for the Christmas party with candles, ribbons, and bows. From the distance of the surrounding park, Miranda thought it looked like an elaborate gingerbread palace. Her red satin ballgown had been delivered a mere hour before it was time to climb into the Hawkscliffes' town coach to go to her very first ball.

As the coach rolled up the lantern-lit drive, Damien and the duke argued idly over the political leanings of their hosts, for Lord and Lady Holland were leaders of Whig society, while Damien was a staunch Tory. Fortunately, members of the opposing parties were quite willing to socialize together, for they were still united by their exalted rank in the world.

As the gleaming black coach glided to a halt before the busy entrance of Holland House, Miranda glanced at Damien and thought him unbearably handsome in his full-dress uniform. Her heart raced in equal parts joy and dread of making some blunder as he assisted her down from the coach, then escorted her into the grand entrance, with the duke and duchess of Hawkscliffe a step ahead of them.

Scarcely able to believe she, the erstwhile rebel of Yardley School, was actually going to a real Society ball, Miranda clung to Damien's arm and hid her giddy lightheadedness. Wide-eyed and on her best behavior, she filed into the crowded entrance hall, where the guests had converged in great cheer. They were calling out greetings to each other as they handed off coats, hats, and wraps to the footmen. Some of the ladies had sat down on the bench by the wall and were exchanging their sturdy, warm shoes for dainty dancing slippers, while liveried servants offered each newly arrived guest a cup of delicious-smelling soup or negus, so they might warm themselves from the elements before ascending, red-nosed, to the ballroom.

Miranda allowed one of the Hollands' footmen to take her fur-lined pelisse and the luxurious muff that Lord Alec had given her for Christmas, then followed the duchess's lead, accepting a dainty cup of soup. She took only a few nervous sips before nodding her agreement that they go up to the party directly.

Above the music from the chamber orchestra and

the din of the gala in progress, they were announced to the gathering as they entered. In all her nineteen years, Miranda could remember no prouder moment than walking into the sprawling ballroom on the arm of her distinguished guardian.

Garlands of evergreen boughs adorned the long gallery, and sprigs of mistletoe hung from every carved doorway and glittering chandelier. Beyond the windows, flurries floated to earth like the sugar coating that sparkled on the magnificent plum cake, enthroned on a crystal dish in the center of the heavily laden refreshment table.

With Hawkscliffe and Damien in tow, the duchess led Miranda over to their hostess, a heavyset woman with dark curls and brilliant eyes that gleamed with sharp wit. As they approached, Miranda was astonished to overhear Lady Holland telling another guest how she and her husband had sent jars of jam and crates of books to Napoleon on Elba as a Christmas present. Incredulous, Miranda glanced at Damien in question. He did not notice her glance, but she knew that he had heard the woman's boast, for he bristled as he sauntered over.

When Lady Holland turned from her guest to greet them, the duchess presented Miranda to her. Miranda curtseyed and thanked the baroness for allowing her to come. The baroness gave her a cursory glance, nodded, and engaged the Hawkscliffes in conversation just as Lord and Lady Lucien came weaving through the crowd toward them, hand in hand.

After the newlyweds had greeted their hostess, the

four of them drifted away from the small, laughing crowd around Lady Holland. The twins were mobbed by people who gathered around and greeted them. Alice seemed to know everyone, too. Miranda stood beside Damien, trying not to look too visibly uncomfortable. It would have been an easy matter to strike up conversation with some of the people she was introduced to in rapid succession, but she was terrified of accidentally treading upon some rule of propriety that had not been listed in her etiquette book. She was desperate not to embarrass the Knight family, her sponsors.

"Griff!" Lucien exclaimed, reaching through the crowd that surrounded them to pull a tall, handsome man in formal black and white into their midst. "My God, Demon, would you look at this?" He slung his arm around the man, who had a forelock of wavy brown hair that tumbled over his brow. He had precisely chiseled features and brown eyes that gleamed with flecks of gold. "I don't believe my eyes!"

"Good God, Ian, is it really you?" With equally delighted surprise, Damien stepped forward and shook the man's hand.

"It's been a long time," the man said. "Congratulations on the title, Damien—or should I say Lord Winterley?"

Damien chuckled modestly.

The debonair man glanced at Lucien with a half smile. "Sorry I couldn't make your wedding, old boy. I just got back from Vienna."

"You crossed the Alps at this time of year? The overland journey must have been hell."

"Hell frozen over is more like it." Their friend shrugged. "I had no choice. My son was ill."

"And Catherine couldn't bear to tend him without you?" Damien asked with a knowing smile.

Lucien winced. "Forgive my brother, Ian. I don't think he was ever told. Damien, Lady Griffith passed away two years ago."

Watching their exchange, Miranda and Alice both widened their eyes, but the flicker of pain in the handsome man's tawny eyes was fleeting.

"Oh, my God." Damien wilted at his blunder, looking perfectly appalled. "Griff, I am so very sorry. I had no idea—"

"It's all right," the man murmured. "You've been off fighting a war."

"What happened?" he asked, at a loss. "Was she ill?"

"She died in childbirth," he replied, then took a drink of his wine, looking off across the ballroom. His gaze passed Alice and came to rest upon Miranda.

She stared soberly at him.

"I hope your boy has recovered?" Lucien said delicately.

A sardonic smile crooked the man's mouth. "Measles. He's doing better, thanks. But enough of this grim talk, you two scoundrels. Tell me which of these beautiful creatures belongs to whom."

"This is my wife, Alice," Lucien said with warm pride, turning to the petite blond. "Darling, allow me to introduce our boyhood friend, Ian Prescott, Lord Griffith. His family has owned the estate adjoining Hawkscliffe Hall for centuries."

Lord Griffith bowed to her. "Madam. I needn't tell you, I am sure, what an excellent man you have married."

Alice smiled at him, then looked askance at her husband. "Indeed, my lord. He has his moments."

"And what of you, Monsieur Earl?" he asked Damien in good-natured mockery. "Is this your bride? For I did not receive an invitation to the wedding—"

"No! No. That is—she is my ward, Miss Fitz-Hubert. She's the niece of one of my lately fallen officers. Miss FitzHubert, allow me to present Lord Griffith. As Lucien said, we wandered many an idle summer's day through the north country fells with this rogue when we were but lads."

Lord Griffith bowed to her, catching her eye again with a subtle look of interest. "Miss FitzHubert. I am sorry for your loss."

"As I am for yours. Pleased to meet you, my lord." She offered him a rather meek curtsy.

Just then, the duke and duchess rejoined them. Hawkscliffe greeted Lord Griffith with the same enthusiasm the twins had shown. After introducing him to his wife, in turn, the two young matrons took matters in hand.

"You gentlemen may reminisce on your squandered youths, but we are going to introduce Miss Fitz-Hubert around," Alice announced, hooking her arm through Miranda's with a determined air.

"Enjoy," Lucien said mildly.

"Behave," Damien ordered.

For nearly the next hour, Alice and Belinda showed

her how to go about among the ton, and soon Miranda found herself easing into the role. It took all her theatrical skill to hide her nervousness, but with her two patronesses flanking her protectively, she managed to hold her own. She was anxious, and rightly so, about the reception she would find among the ton on account of her being illegitimate and only half aristocratic on her father's side, but she met many people who nodded in approval at the mention of the former Lord Hubert, her papa. She behaved with such demure meekness that even Brocklehurst would have been amazed.

Then, to her relief, the dancing was announced. She turned and felt her heart skip a beat to see Damien striding toward her through the crowd.

"Come," he ordered when he reached her side. He tucked her hand into the crook of his muscular arm.

"You want to dance with me?" she exclaimed, holding her breath.

"It's just a formality," he said in a lofty tone. "No one else here will feel free to do so unless I do so first. Besides, Lady Holland had got hold of me and Lucien, and was bragging her head off again about her great friend, Bonaparte. Intolerable," he muttered under his breath.

Depositing her in her place for the dance, he did not answer the question. They each aligned themselves with the appropriate sides, ladies facing gentlemen.

One would have thought he was going through military maneuvers as he executed a very correct salute and retreat. Miranda smiled at Damien, coaxing an answering smile from him in return as they drew together once more. She placed her hands in his, turning with him in the center; he released her and they both returned to their places in time with the beat. They watched in pleasure and awaited their next figure as the alternate couples promenaded a few stately steps up the set, then cast off and wove around the stationary couples, who then echoed their movement. The dance progressed and the divertimento lilted. They went hand-over-hand with their neighbors, Lucien and Alice, then revolved in a star-four with them, only to be paired together again in a romantic turn á la gypsy. She was aware of nothing but him as they revolved slowly, staring into each other's eyes. For a second, the music seemed eons away. There was only his touch, his hand on hers . . . and the memory of his arms around her, his hands stroking her, his mouth ravishing hers in the most intimate kiss she had ever felt or even imagined. Then the moment passed as fleetingly as it had come. They retreated to their designated sides and the dance moved on.

Later that night, she danced twice with Lord Griffith, then with Lord Alec, who showed up fashionably late. She also stood up with a few young officers from the regiment who had known her uncle. She did her best to muster up a smile when she ran into the boys who had rushed to her aid on Bond Street, and who had introduced themselves that night at Drury Lane as Ollie Quinn and Nigel Stanhope.

When they each asked her to dance, there was no graceful way to refuse, despite the fact that the boorish Mr. Quinn would not stop ogling her chest.

Yet even this did not annoy her as much as seeing Damien dutifully standing up to dance with other ladies. Of course, he could not have done otherwise without appearing unforgivably rude, but she felt a twinge of jealousy, nonetheless. At length, she escaped Mr. Quinn and Mr. Stanhope by accepting Alec's invitation to visit the refreshment table with him and Lord Griffith. The pregnant duchess was already there, nibbling at the sumptuous offerings; Lucien and Alice were dancing.

Miranda joined the duchess and, at her bidding, took a taste of pineapple for the first time in her life. The spiky-topped fruit was the height of extravagance, the enduring symbol of hospitality imported from some exotic, sunny land. She exclaimed fervently over the juicy, tangy fruit until Lord Griffith, watching her, laughed outright at her enthusiasms.

"Wherever did Damien find you?" he asked, regarding her with growing interest in his unusual, tawny-gold eyes.

"I'll never tell," she replied with a tart smile, then turned to inspect the more traditional fare that spanned the table. "Aren't you eating anything, my lord? How can you resist? It all looks and smells delicious."

"Indeed," he murmured, gazing at her.

Standing off to the side, Alec looked from Lord Griffith to her, then lifted his eyebrow and gave her a slight nod of approval. Miranda blushed slightly, shot him a scolding look, and turned her attention willfully back to the food. She had barely eaten all day in her nervousness over the ball, but now that she had settled into it, there was much to tempt her—trestles of syllabub in several varieties, the quintessential Christmas pudding, endless cakes and trays of delicate biscuits, festive red pippins and orange wedges, as well as innumerable meat pies and brawns for those who wished for a light supper. Lord Griffith turned away to speak to a few guests who had greeted him, and Miranda sampled an almond syllabub. Just as she started to lift another sweet spoonful to her lips, somebody tapped her on the shoulder.

She turned around; then her eyes widened and her face paled. Standing before her in the full regalia of the Eleventh Dragoon Guards was a young cavalry officer with straight, sandy-brown hair. His high cheekbones tapered down to his narrow, slightly cleft chin. The boyish smirk she remembered so well still lingered on his lascivious mouth, but grown his dark green eyes had harder.

"Trick!" she breathed.

"Hullo, kitten." He gave her that satyric crook of his eyebrow that used to make her heart race, but which struck her now as altogether practiced and calculated.

She stared at him in amazement. *He's changed.* She could not believe the dissipation she saw in her old beau. His hair was slightly greasy and askew. He reeked of drink and was not terribly steady on his feet.

"God, look at you. When did you become this goddess? Where did you learn to dance so beautifully? Damn my eyes, but you're ravishing," he purred, slurring his words slightly.

"And you are in need of a shave," she replied, folding her arms across her chest.

With a laugh, he touched the stubbled gruff that roughened his jaw. "Haven't been home since the day before yesterday. I've been going from one party to the next. What are you doing here? You're a long way from Birmingham—and that farmer's shed where we used to meet." He flashed her a smile that made her whole body stiffen with alarm. "You haven't forgotten, I trust."

She looked away, blushing. "Please do not speak of it."

"Don't be embarrassed my pet. You guarded your virtue well. God knows I tried everything short of taking you by force."

She looked away with a wave of remembered hurt and anger rushing through her. "You certainly did. You even promised marriage."

"I would have promised anything to lift your skirts. What can I say? I was young and foolish."

"So was I," she whispered.

He lifted his eyebrow with a look of distaste, then wobbled on his feet with drunken, arrogant indifference. "Surely you know better than to take me seriously, M'randa. You knew I was going off to war. Why so bitter? It wasn't as though you didn't enjoy it."

She steeled herself. "Good-bye, Trick. Our acquaintance has long been over."

"My, what a fine lady we've become!" He grasped her arm, stopping her. "Are you too good for me now?"

"Trick, you horse's arse, I always was. Let go of me."

"Don't you walk away from me. You might be something fine now, but I remember when you were little better than a peasant girl. You have to admit we had fun, Miranda. What say you to another rendezvous for old times' sake?"

"When hell freezes over." She flicked a contemptuous glance at his white-gloved hand locked around her upper arm. "Let go of me, Trick. You are playing roulette with your life."

He scoffed. "As I recall, that uncle of yours didn't pose much threat last time I had my hands on you, so why should I . . ." His bold words withered and his face paled. His hand dropped from her arm and he took a step backward, staring at a spot just behind her.

"Miranda, my darling, you must introduce me to your friend."

Relief poured through her at the sound of Damien's voice. She glanced over her shoulder and found him standing behind her, his body tensed for a fight, but before she even had time to worry that violence might break out in the middle of the ballroom, Damien took another tack.

Moving up behind her so close that their bodies touched, he leaned down protectively, claiming her by placing one hand gently on her waist, linking his fingers through hers with the other hand. Nuzzling her temple like the most devoted lover, he bristled with danger, holding Trick in a narrow-eyed stare.

Miranda stood in her guardian's light embrace, bewildered, but thrilled by his scandalous show of possessive affection. "M-my lord, this is Captain Patrick Slidell of the Eleventh Dragoons. I'm sure you will recall me telling you about him."

"Yes, of course. So, this is 'Trick,'" he mused aloud, his tone silken. He studied the younger man as though he were an insect under a microscope, one he was contemplating squashing.

"Trick, this is my new guardian, Colonel Lord Winterley. I trust you've heard of him."

Trick stammered a greeting to Damien, made a hasty excuse, and fled. With a dark, low laugh, Damien released his hold on her waist, but kept hold of her other hand. Miranda turned to him and let out a sigh of relief.

"You scared me. I thought you were going to kill him."

"So did I," he said dryly, tucking her hand into the crook of his arm. "Now then, if you'll permit me, I've come to claim you for a second dance."

"I would be honored." As he escorted her to the dance floor, she gazed at him in adoration. He gave her a private smile in answer, and she was suddenly very glad that Trick had never made good on his offer of marriage.

They joined the newly forming set, taking their places across from each other once more. Miranda savored every moment of their second dance, knowing there could not be another tonight. Even she knew it was not permissible for a young lady to dance three times in one night with the same gentleman. She was soaking in the pleasure of the movement and the graceful beauty of the ladies' gowns as they stepped forward in a line and circled their smartly dressed partners, pale silks and shimmering satins swirling. Her hand rested lightly in Damien's, he was watching her every move, smiling fondly at her, when suddenly, not far behind him, someone opened a champagne bottle.

The cork loosed with a pop like a gunshot; before her eyes, Damien froze. In the middle of the dance, he spun around, searching the crowd, his hand grazing his side as though to reach for a sword that, thank God, he was not wearing.

"Lord Winterley?" she called anxiously over the music.

When he whirled back to her, his face was stark and white, his stare a million miles away. It was the same, wild look she had seen in his eyes on Bordesley Green and that night in the hotel, when he had nearly strangled her.

The dance moved on, turning to chaos as Damien just stood there as though he were suddenly lost. Miranda gazed helplessly at him, deafened by the pounding of her pulse in her ears. If she did not do something, he would be humiliated. People were beginning to stare.

*Think fast,* she told herself.

"Ow!" she cried suddenly, reaching down toward her ankle. "Ow, ow!" Her plaintive cries drew the dancers' stares away from him to herself. "Oh, I've twisted my ankle! How clumsy of me!" she went on, summoning forth every ounce of her acting skills, though she knew she was making herself look like a perfect fool. "My lord, would you please—"

"Of course," he said brusquely, startled out of his dark spell by her cries. The beast vanishing from the glittering depths of his eyes. Broadshouldered and gleamingly correct in all his martial splendor, he gave no outward sign of the pain and confusion that she knew roiled within him.

Leaning on his arm, assuring her well-wishers that she would be perfectly all right, she limped as Damien led her out of the ballroom and into the corridor as hastily as possible. She kept up the charade, hobbling a short distance down the corridor with his help. The spectacle she had made of herself at her very first Society ball quite chagrined her, but if she had helped her guardian save face, she thought, it was worth it.

At last, they ducked discreetly into a statuary alcove where a marble goddess in the classical style reigned from her pedestal. Some clever soul had dangled a sprig of mistletoe from the statue's gracefully posed fingers.

The moment they were alone in the alcove, Miranda turned to Damien. "Are you all right?"

"You're the one injured. Sit down," he ordered, avoiding her searching stare. "You must take your weight off of it. Shall I get you some ice?"

"Oh, Damien, I was acting," she said impatiently, brushing off his hand as he tried to assist her in sitting down on the cushioned bench behind her.

He gazed at her for a second, his emotionless mask

falling away; then his wide shoulders slumped. He hung his head. "Thanks," he muttered.

"You're welcome." She stared at him in distress. "I'm here for you, Damien. Everything's going to be all right."

"No, it's not," he bit back, dragging his hand through his hair. "I'm losing my mind, if you haven't noticed."

With a soft sound of sympathy, she reached out and started to caress his forearm. "I won't let you lose your mind."

"Would you stop it?" he cried, knocking her hand away. "Stop touching me!"

She took a step back, wide-eyed.

He glared at her. "I appreciate what you did for me just now, but for God's sake, save your touches for somebody else, someone who isn't a threat to your damned safety. Your future husband, for example."

Her eyes flared with hurt surprise at his outburst. "Damien—"

He grasped her shoulders and searched her eyes with fevered desperation. "Don't you see you're making this worse for me? Why must you tempt me?" he whispered. There is enough chaos in my head already without your enticements. If you care for me at all, get back in that ballroom and choose a damned husband, so I can go home and be done with this torture."

"But you're the one I want." The words slipped out traitorously as she held his ferocious stare, barely daring to breathe. Her words seemed to strike him like a rapier in the heart. Pain flickered in the steely depths of his eyes; then his face hardened with a warrior's resolve. "It is out of the question."

"Merry Christmas, Damien," she whispered, blinking back tears as he stalked off, leaving her alone beneath the mistletoe.

# ❧ CHAPTER ❧
## TEN

The next day, Damien held an audience in the drawing room with young, boorish Mr. Oliver Quinn, the rich merchant's son. Beads of sweat ran down his plump, ruddy face into his cravat as Damien folded his arms across his chest and locked him in a probing stare.

"As I've said, my lord, I find Miss FitzHubert a m-most excellent, b-beautiful young lady. I don't mind at all about her bastardy, nor does my father," Ollie blurted out, wetting his lips nervously. "She would be kept in the first stare of fashion, with every comfort her heart could desire."

Damien stroked his jaw. "Hmm," he growled, turning to glance out the window behind him at the elegant young woman exercising her mare in Green Park below. Two grooms minded Miranda carefully, but Damien would have felt better if he had stayed there to watch over her himself. She was still a very inexperienced rider and unfamiliar with her new horse.

Earlier today, the fine Thoroughbred mare, Milady's Fancy, had been delivered by handlers from Tattersall's. For as long as he lived, Damien would never

255

forget the amazement on his ward's face when she had
first laid eyes on the tall, leggy blood-horse that he
had bought for her. Together they had watched the
groom put the sleek liver-bay mare through her graceful paces. Though relations between them were still
strained after the awkwardness of the night before,
the presence of the grooms had warded off the intimate questions that he feared she burned to ask. He
had stood beside her, giving her numerous pointers
about how to handle the animal, how to watch for the
little quirks that signaled the mare's next reaction—
for every horse had its own personality, and mares
could be particularly feisty. Then he had helped her
mount up and had watched her for a while, pleased to
see that horse and rider were as well matched as he
had anticipated. Fancy was spirited enough to keep
Miranda entertained, but was still a safe, fairly docile
animal. His proud enjoyment in watching Miranda's
growing skill as a rider had been shadowed, however,
by the knowledge that he had wounded her feelings
last night.

She had given him little choice. He could have been
more tactful, no doubt, but his mad reaction to the
pop of a mere champagne cork had reminded him
afresh, in case he had forgotten, that he was not fit to
play the gentle lover; that, at heart, he was and always
would be a fiend, born on the killing fields, hungry for
blood, made for massacre and destruction. He should
not have ignored the warning signs last night, he
thought, recalling the thunder of rage that had
rumbled in the dark skies of his mind earlier on, when
he had seen "Trick" Slidell grab Miranda's arm.

Blood was exactly what he had wanted, knowing that that was the blackguard who had broken her young heart, who had made her promises he had never meant to keep, who had put his hands on her and had used her for his own pleasure.

Damien had fought with all his will to curb his wrath, for above all, he refused to scare her again. He had forced himself to be tame for her in that instance, but after the debacle of the champagne cork, he had been reminded anew that he could not always control his demons. It had made him face the hard fact that if he cared for Miranda, he had only one choice: to marry her off to someone worthy.

That someone, however, was not Oliver Quinn.

"So, ahem, my father has given me leave to offer a thousand guineas for her bride-price," the portly young dandy said judiciously, clearing his throat. "You must admit that is no mean sum for any girl without family or dowry."

Damien did not reply for a moment, keeping his face expressionless while he fought to keep a tight rein on the urge to knock the useless dandy on his lardy arse. "Mr. Quinn, I daresay your offer seems a bit premature."

"Sir?"

"I should doubt that you have even spoken to my ward for more than ten minutes total."

"We did have a dance."

"It is too soon for you to know if you would suit—" His words were cut off by a scream from beyond the window. He spun around and glanced out, his heart stopping in horror to see the liver-bay mare tearing off across the park, Miranda clinging on for dear life.

"My lord? My lord!" the lad called behind him, but Damien was already out of the room, running down the stairs before Ollie could even react.

He raced outside and across the yard, his heart pumping frantically.

"My lord, what is amiss?" one of the other grooms called, running toward him.

"Miranda's horse has bolted." Throwing back the wrought-iron gate, he sprinted into the park, dry-mouthed. He saw that she had dropped one of the reins and knew that if she fell off the treacherous sidesaddle, she could easily break her neck. *God preserve her.* He had told her what to do if a horse ever got spooked beneath her. As he raced after her, he saw that she had remembered his instruction.

Though clumsy, her action was effective. She hauled back on the left rein for all she was worth. The mare fought her, arcing her head to the side while still charging onward, but in a few more paces, the horse turned. Miranda held on tight, keeping her balance by some miracle. At last, she pulled the mare into a circle, winding in tighter with each revolution until the horse's fright was spent.

The animal stood on shaking legs, its coat darkened with sweat. Damien slowed to a walk as he approached, to avoid startling the mare again. When Miranda glanced over at him, her face was white. Her riding hat had fallen off, and the girth had loosened, the saddle hanging a bit skewed on the horse's back.

"Easy, easy, girl," Damien murmured, meaning it

for both woman and mare as he quickly grasped the fallen rein and laid hold of the bridle.

The groom was but a few steps behind him and took the horse's bridle, freeing him to move swiftly to Miranda. She slid down from the saddle into his embrace, her whole body shaking. He set her down so that her feet touched solid ground; then he held her hard. He could feel her heart pounding in time with his own.

He pulled back abruptly and cupped her face between his trembling hands, staring fiercely into her eyes. "Are you all right?"

She nodded, ashen.

"What happened?" he demanded almost harshly.

"I don't know. S-something spooked her."

Still holding Miranda protectively in his arms, he turned to the groom with a glower. "Get that animal out of my sight. Either take it back to the farm it came from or destroy it."

Miranda looked up at him in fear. He put his arm around her, tight-lipped with fury and belated fright. He walked her back to the house, where he ordered Ollie Quinn to leave.

Later that evening, Miranda wrapped her pelisse around her and slipped out the back of Knight House, going in search of Damien. Her feelings were still a bit bruised from his rejection last night, but the concern he had shown for her safety today after her debacle with the horse had renewed her hope of reaching him. In any case, she could not stay away from him, even though he had half-begged, half-ordered her to the previous night. Her breath clouding on the cold air, she stole across the graveled yard, hurrying past the carriage house to the stable, where lantern light spilled out onto the snow through the crack in the barn door.

When she stepped into the stable, her heart racing with anticipation, the only sound was the rhythmic munching of the horses at their grain. The sweetly pungent smell of oats mingled in her nostrils with the earthy, pleasant odors of horse and leather and hay. A striped barn cat came trotting out of the shadows and rubbed its nimble body against Miranda's legs, but the grooms had all gone to take their evening meal in the servants' dining hall. She stooped to scratch the cat's head for a moment, then straightened up again and walked slowly down the clean-swept aisle to Fancy's stall.

Damien was there, just where she had expected to find him. He turned and met her gaze soberly, his angular face gilded by the glow of the lantern overhead. His gray eyes were troubled. He gave her a slight nod in greeting, but said nothing, bending to run his leather-gloved hands down the mare's foreleg.

With a low murmur, he commanded Fancy to lift her hoof, which he braced firmly against his thigh. He inspected the hoof carefully, then released it and straightened up again. The mare snuffled and moved away from him, taking a mouthful of hay.

"Is she all right?"

Damien nodded, patted the horse soundly on the shoulder, and lowered his head, drawing off his thick leather gloves. "Are you?"

"I'm fine now. I had a nice, hot bath that soothed away the jolt to my shoulder and neck. I'm rather proud of myself, actually," she said, trying to coax a smile from him. "I didn't fall, and I managed to stop her, didn't I?"

He sent her a rueful half smile, the lantern casting the feathery shadow of his lashes over his high cheekbones.

"Are you still going to send Fancy back where she came from?" she asked wistfully. "She didn't mean any harm. I'm sure it was my fault." Miranda did not know what she had done to give the mare such a fright. They had been getting on capitally together, trotting tamely around in a circle, when all of a sudden the quiet, lovely mare had gone lunatic.

He glanced at the horse. "I suppose one instance of bad behavior may be forgiven her—that is, if you still find her acceptable."

"I do. I love her. Here, girl," she called softly. The mare came over to her and searched for sugar cubes, lipping at the hand Miranda stretched through the metal bars. "She says she's sorry. She promises not to do it again. It's just that she's not entirely used to her new life yet."

"You're not afraid to ride her again?" he asked in approval.

"Of course not. I managed, didn't I? Admit it, I was splendid." She flashed him a grin, and he smiled wanly. "I know you're blaming yourself about this because you bought her for me, but it wasn't your fault, Damien," she said in a shy, tender tone, avoiding his gaze as she stroked the horse's forehead. "No harm done."

He drifted over to the stall door, but instead of opening it, he grasped the metal bars and leaned his forehead against them. He stared at her through the bars like a prisoner looking out from his cell. Miranda waited, searching his eyes. They were so guarded, so full of longing.

"What is it?"

He sighed. "Oliver Quinn wants to marry you. Any interest?"

She looked at him in alarm. "No."

A cynical smile quirked his mouth. "Don't panic. I told him as much. But there will be more. Many more, I should think."

She stiffened, tearing her gaze away from his beautiful face. "You know where my affections lie, my lord."

"Miranda," he said in an anguished tone.

"I don't understand." She turned to him. "I know you're not indifferent to me. Why do you keep pushing me away?"

He looked into her eyes. "Why do you think I do?" he asked, and waited for her answer.

"I think it has to do with this problem of yours . . . your confusion last night, your nightmares. The same thing that caused you to attack me that night in the hotel room." She paused, not sure how much she ought to say. "I—I saw something in your eyes that night on Bordesley Green. . . ." Her voice trailed off as the memory came back to her.

"What did you see?" he murmured, watching her face closely.

"Something terrible. Some . . . part of you that is a

hell on earth." She glanced somberly at him. "It has to do with the war, doesn't it?"

He shook his head slowly. "I killed a great many men. I let flow a river of blood from my sword, and now I must pay."

"You did it for your country."

"I enjoyed it." His eyes gleamed, metallic gray, peering out at her from behind the bars. His face was shadowed in the dimness of the stall. "You don't know me, Miranda. Or, if you know, you choose not to believe."

"I believe in your goodness, Damien."

They stared at each other for a long moment. Her heart pounded in her eardrums.

"I want to help you as you helped me," she said.

"If you want to help me, then forget me. Your best bet is Lord Griffith, but I think you know that. He is a good man."

She searched his face in betrayal. "I don't want Lord Griffith. Don't you understand what I am trying to tell you? I'm in love with you, Damien."

He rested his head against the bars with a faint grimace of pain. "Why are you doing this to me? God help me, I can't risk destroying you."

She grasped the bars, holding him in an unflinching stare. "Why do you think that will happen? Why are you so scared? Tell me. You know the worst thing that ever happened to me. It can't be any worse than what Mr. Reed did. Talk to me. Why can't we be together?"

He closed his eyes with a pained expression, then hesitantly forced the words out. "Something . . . happened to me on Guy Fawkes Night, Miranda. The cannon salutes, the fireworks—I can't explain it." He dragged his eyes open and stared at her in despair. "I forgot where I was. I was in Knight House, sitting with Alice and Harry while Lucien was out on an errand—he had asked me to look after them—and something inside of me snapped."

"Snapped?"

"I thought I was back at the war. Don't ask me what happened, for I can't recall. All I know is that when I came back to myself, I had a knife in one hand and a loaded pistol in the other. I don't remember picking them up. Don't you see? I could have hurt someone, Miranda. I could have killed someone. Never mind Alice—a defenseless woman. I could have hurt Harry. I could have hurt the child," he whispered, his voice breaking with anguish.

Longing to take him into her arms to comfort him, she grasped the latch of the stall door and started to open it, but he stopped her, gripping her wrist through the bars.

Her startled gaze flew to his face.

He stared fiercely at her. "Go into the house. You know my reasons. Now go away."

"No," she said softly. "I want to help you."

"I don't want your help."

"I didn't want your help either, at first, but you have to trust me. This is the right thing to do. Let me hold you."

"Stay away from me," he whispered.

"Stop pushing me away!" she cried, her face flushing.

"What do you think, that you can nurse me back to

health, as though I had a cold?" He sneered. "I'll only drag you down with me. There is no cure. I should know. I've tried everything."

"By yourself! You haven't tried letting someone love you, take care of you."

"I don't need that. I never have."

"So arrogant," she whispered in outrage. "Heaven forfend that the great Winterley should ever need anyone. You stupid man! You're like a lion with a thorn in its paw that bites the person who comes to help it."

"I could do much more than bite you, my dear. I could reach through these bars and snap your lovely neck. Do you realize that?"

"You don't frighten me," she said. "I would rather take the risk than run and leave you here alone. You're not the only one who's looked death in the face, Damien Knight. I watched my parents die and was powerless to help them, but by God, I will not lose you. You must try. You must fight this—but not alone. You're an army man; you know our forces couldn't possibly have won without the men coordinating their efforts."

"The men. Precisely. We do not expose our women to such dangers."

"Why must you be so stubborn? You can't be all *that* mad, or Uncle Jason would not have named you my guardian."

"He didn't know. I hid it," he snarled. "I hid it from them all. Only Lucien knows. Alice has an inkling, for she was there, but you're the only one who's seen the ugly, unvarnished truth."

"Obviously, then, I am the only one who can help."

"God, why won't you listen?" he roared, shoving back from the stall door with an abrupt motion that startled the mare. "What's it going to take to get it through your head, girl? I've told you the truth. I can't make it any clearer."

"Yes, you've told me," she countered staunchly, "and I'm telling you, you're going to need a better reason than that to get rid of me."

"A better reason?" he exclaimed.

"Yes, because I still say we could beat this together. I *know* we could."

"Very well, then, here's one you might believe: You're beneath me, Miranda. How's that? You're penniless and illegitimate, and I'm an earl."

To every person there are certain words that must not be said; Damien knew what these words were for Miranda, who, until the day she had arrived at Knight House, had been rejected on all sides because of her mixed parentage. To him, the words were a last resort, chosen with deadly precision. He watched her courage crumble and the light of her faith in him extinguished in her eyes, but he could no more unsay them than a highwayman could call back a well-aimed bullet. He could only stand there, mute with pain at the wound he had inflicted, but holding firm for her sake against the river of remorse that nearly drowned him.

Slowly, she absorbed the cruel, cutting remark. For a long moment, she was silent, searching his face. Then she looked away and swallowed hard.

"You are right," she said, her voice rather choked but steady. She nodded stiffly. "These are facts that I cannot deny. Forgive me, Lord Winterley. I shall trouble you no more."

She was gone in a moment, pivoting with a slight dizziness in the motion, then walking quickly down the aisle of the barn.

He steeled himself against the urge to chase after her, catch her up in his arms, and never let her go. She slipped out the barn door. Once she was out of sight, he heard her light footfalls break into a run toward the house. He closed his eyes and lowered his head in a wave of suffering, while Fancy nudged with her velvety muzzle at his coat pocket.

"You incompetent bungler!" Algernon roared, cuffing his servant on the ear.

Egann yelped at the blow and went flying across the office, stumbling over his lame foot to sprawl on the floor in a whimpering heap. "I'm sorry, my lord. I did what you told me—"

"I did not tell you to fail, but so you did. Twice. You are useless. Get up and stop sniveling. I've got to think." Algernon paced in frustration, his hands braced on his hips. The stealth of his aim was compromised with each near miss, but worse was his own traitorous relief at the failure of Egann's second attempt on his niece's life.

Algernon had finally seen Miranda FitzHubert for himself at Lady Holland's Christmas party, though he had kept his distance and had left before she or any of the formidable Knight brothers had noticed him. He trembled with queer sensations flooding through him as the vision of the young, vibrant beauty haunted his mind—so full of life and freshness and zest. He had never seen a more exquisite, more graceful creature. She was a Botticelli goddess, with her laughing green eyes, her roundish, pink cheeks, and her sable ringlets falling in artful coils across her shoulders. She glowed with health; aye, he thought, she was made for throwing fine, strapping sons. She had all of Fanny's gaiety and Richard's fire.

*Fanny.*

Once upon a time, Algernon Sherbrooke had loved Fanny Blair. At twenty-five, he had thrown himself into his quest to win the famous actress as his mistress. He had been so attentive, so conscientious, but just when she had begun to flutter down into his grasp like some exotic butterfly, along came his elder brother, Richard, with his charm and popularity, his fortune, his good looks, his title. Richard had callously snatched her from his very grasp. That slut had gone willingly enough.

Later, they both had tried, Richard and she, to explain their feelings for each other in a way that would not wound him, but Algernon had simply swallowed his humiliation, conceding to their illicit union with gentlemanly grace . . . outwardly. He had learned his lesson about love that day. It was a bad investment.

But now there was young, luscious Miranda. He wished he had not seen her, for since the moment he had lain eyes on her, he had fought with himself in the hopes that perhaps there was some other way. The feelings she roused in him, her uncle, were appalling for obvious reasons, stirring the embers of a passion he had thought extinguished long ago. Yet she made him realize what a lonely, dried-up, old man he had become, though he was only forty-five, old before his time. Such a waste, such a waste, he thought, brooding, pacing in his office.

"Master—" Egann started meekly.

"Shut up."

Just then, the dogs let up a din in the entrance hall. Algernon stalked to the door of his office and flung it open, an order to the butler on the tip of his tongue to keep those damned animals quiet.

To his surprise, he saw that the reason for their clamoring was the arrival of their favorite, Crispin. Algernon narrowed his eyes as Crispin tried to slip past him and up the stairs without being seen.

"Crispin. Have you no manners, boy?"

Top hat in hand, his son halted and turned to him, scratching his eyebrow. "Er, hullo, Father."

It was most unusual to see the boy at this early hour of the evening.

"Dining at home tonight?" he asked suspiciously; then his face drained of blood. He looked at his son's pale countenance and felt sick to his stomach. "You've been at the gaming hells, haven't you?" he demanded in a voice that shook. "How much?"

"Father—"

"*How much did you lose?*" he roared, not caring if the deuced Frogs heard him all the way across the Channel.

He had expected the usual denials, excuses, the boyish attempts at charm, but the full peril of his son's latest losses hit him when Crispin threw his fine hat down on the floor, sat on the bottom stair, and buried his face in his hands in a pose of utter despair.

"Oh, you worthless cur," Algernon whispered.

"I'm sorry, Father," he wrenched out. "A thousand pounds. I lost it all."

Infuriated, Algernon seized his son by the arm and dragged him into his office, slamming the door behind him.

A second later, he heard his wife tapping timidly on the door. "My lord, is our son in there with you?"

"Leave us!" he bellowed through the door. With shaking hands, he shoved his charming, spoiled son into the chair.

Egann crawled over to Crispin and crouched like a dog by his polished boots—the best that money could buy.

Crispin rested his elbow on the chair arm and dragged his hand through his guinea-gold curls like a newly fallen angel. "I'm a failure, an utter failure," he whispered, still weeping. "I know it, Father. I cannot seem to do otherwise."

"Yes," Algernon snarled in his face, "you are a failure. You have brought this family to the brink of ruin. I hope you have not gone to another of those moneylenders for a loan, because I cannot repay it. Do you understand, Crispin? You have ruined me. You have ruined your father."

Tears filled Crispin's blue eyes. "I shall fix it, Father. I'll think of something. I'll find work—"

"Work?" He backhanded him hard across the face. "What do you think we are, middle class?"

Crispin looked up, startled, his cherubic face tearstained and red with the slap.

His heart pounding as inspiration gripped him, Algernon pointed a warning finger in his face. "I will tell you exactly what you are going to do, my boy, and if you utter so much as one syllable of complaint, I will leave you to the loan sharks to cut their pound of flesh from you as you deserve."

"Anything, Father," he whispered.

"There is a girl. An heiress. She has a fortune, Crispin, a fortune that no one else knows about but I . . . and Egann and now you, as well."

Crispin's tongue flicked over his lips. "A . . . substantial fortune?"

At last, an intelligent question from the fool. Algernon's lips thinned in a feral smile. "Does fifty thousand pounds sound significant to you?"

His son's eyes widened.

"Now, God may have denied you no more sense than he gave a hen, my boy, but he gave you looks. You will woo this girl and win her, or we are finished, Crispin. Do you understand? Me, you, your mother, your sisters. I mean debtor's prison."

Horror, then resolution, filled his youthful face. "I will win her, Father. If it is the last thing I do."

"She is well guarded. She has many suitors."

"I don't care if she were the sultan's virgin sister, nay, kept in an ivory palace with a horde of janissaries to protect her. I vow I shall win her somehow. I know I've failed you in the past, Father, but this I can do. Just tell me who she is and she is mine."

His hazel eyes hardened in satisfaction. "She is your

little bastard cousin, Crispin. Miss Miranda Fitz-Hubert. And I don't want to hear one word from you about marriage between first cousins becoming unfashionable. So help me, if you say it, I will put you through that window. It is an aristocratic tradition and perfectly legal."

Crispin searched his eyes. "I have heard of this girl. They say she is beautiful."

Algernon made no comment.

"Is she not the ward of Colonel Lord Winterley? His brother, Lord Alec Knight, is my good friend. I can gain an introduction through him—"

"No. You will do exactly as I say. Above all, we do not wish to appear overly eager. I see I shall have to conduct this affair for you from start to finish."

"Father?"

Algernon considered for a moment, studying the far wall absently; then he nodded, speaking rapidly under his breath, as though to himself. "We'll send your mother and sisters over to call on her, yes, the women-folk first. They'll be too suspicious if it comes from me. You will escort them. From there, we shall invite her to dine. A formal reception. Of course. We are her kin, are we not? It is proper that we accept her, even though she is illegitimate."

"If the Knight family has given her their blessing, we cannot fail to do the same."

"Exactly. Finally, you begin to see things my way. And Crispin, when she comes to dinner—"

"Yes, Father?"

"Dazzle her, if you know what's good for you." With a hard, warning look, he straightened up, turned his back on his son, and walked out to give his vapid twit of a wife her orders.

A short while after Miranda had fled the stable, Damien had collected himself and had saddled one of Robert's more manageable geldings, in no mood to fight with his temperamental stallion. As he guided the horse through the darkened streets of Town, heading for Lucien's home in Upper Brooke Street, he turned his thoughts away from brooding upon the painful exchange between him and his ward, returning instead to the suspicions that had begun taking shape in his mind before Miranda had come into the stable.

That horse should not have bolted on her. He had taken pains to be certain of the mare's steady temperament before buying it, but today the animal had run as though it had been stung by a bee or struck by some small missile, such as a rock or a pebble from a slingshot. He had checked the mare from head to hoof, but had found no mark or injury to suggest such an attack. Of course, it would have taken a hard blow indeed to have penetrated the horse's thick, protective winter coat.

He had questioned the grooms who had been watching Miranda, but they had not noticed anything out of the ordinary, yet they vouched that Miranda had done nothing to spook the horse, either. Lately the near misses and mishaps were becoming too numerous to discount as mere coincidence. Absurd as it sounded, he was beginning to wonder if someone was out to get Miranda. First she had been attacked on

Bordesley Green by men he had assumed were Mud City outlaws; then she had nearly been run down by a carriage on Bond Street, again, another seeming accident; now her docile mare had bolted off under her like a streak of lightning. It didn't make sense. That was why he was going to talk to Lucien.

This sort of intrigue was just his spy brother's area of expertise, and Damien was the first to admit that his own thinking was less than crystal clear of late. He meant to speak to his twin about all of it; if nothing else, Lucien would reassure him that he was merely suffering from overprotective paranoia.

The only two people that he could think of who had reason to despise Miranda were Mr. Reed and Mistress Brocklehurst of Yardley School, for revealing the abuse of the students that had been going on there, but their involvement seemed unlikely; the timing of the mishaps did not fit. The attack on Bordesley Green had occurred well before he had turned the headmaster over to justice. Indeed, the dangers had begun rolling at her shortly after Jason's death.

The parallel he drew chilled him to the marrow. Could the person who murdered Jason now be after Miranda? But why? Surely his half-demented brain was playing tricks on him, he thought, but at least he had managed to hide his concerns from her. There was no point in alarming the girl, on top of everything else. He worried a little about leaving her alone at the moment, if indeed someone were trying to harm her, but he felt she would be safe behind the formidable gates of Knight House, with the half dozen guard dogs and the staff of over three dozen servants to watch over her. Besides, Robert was at home, and for his part, Damien did not expect to be gone for more than a couple of hours.

Arriving in Upper Brooke Street before Lucien and Alice's elegant, flat-fronted townhouse, with its richly carved doorway, brass lamps, and delicate wrought-iron balconies on the upper windows, he swung down from his mount and called for one of Lucien's grooms. Leaving the animal with the servant, he was admitted into the entrance hall by Alice's excellent butler, Mr. Hattersley.

The little bald man took his coat and invited him upstairs to wait while he went to summon Lord Lucien. Damien went up to the drawing room and made himself at home. When a quarter hour had passed, however, and still his brother did not appear, he inquired impatiently with the butler.

Mr. Hattersley turned bright red and stammered that Lord Lucien had shouted from inside his lady's locked bedchamber that he would come soon.

*Bloody newlyweds,* Damien thought. Mr. Hattersley offered him a brandy, which he accepted, along with the day's issue of the *Times*. He skimmed the newspaper, trying to take his mind off the crushed look in Miranda's beautiful green eyes after he had dashed any chance of a future between them upon the rocks of his own hard nature.

At last, Lucien sauntered into the drawing room, barefooted, wearing nothing but black trousers and a voluminous dressing gown of dark orange silk. It lay open down his bare chest and billowed behind him with flamelike grace as he prowled into the room, his skin flushed, his hair tousled, his eyes glowing like pewter. His lazy smile was totally satisfied, totally relaxed.

Damien took one look at his brother and remembered anew how deprived he, himself, was. "Took you long enough," he remarked with a glower.

Lucien chuckled, sighed, and poured himself a brandy. "Damn me if I have not begotten a son this night." He tossed back his brandy and turned to him languidly. "What brings you to my nest of connubial bliss, brother?"

"I need your skills."

"What's afoot?"

Damien folded the paper, cast it onto the couch beside him, and stood. "I think someone may be trying to harm Miranda."

Lucien furrowed his brow. Damien told him about how the mare had bolted, then retraced the whole story, starting with the attack on Bordesley Green. He told him about the schoolmaster's crimes against the girls at Yardley, in case that sounded to Lucien like a possible source of the trouble, as well as the mysterious runaway carriage on Bond Street that had nearly run Miranda down.

"Miranda told me about the men on Bordesley Green," Lucien began.

"When?" Damien cut him off in surprise.

"A couple of days ago. I wanted to talk to her privately."

"What for?"

Lucien smiled angelically. "To see if she was good enough for you, of course."

Damien scowled at him in warning.

"It was a thorough interrogation. Don't you wish to know my ruling?"

"No."

Lucien shrugged it off. "She said the men who attacked her were outlaws. Do you have reason to suppose differently?"

"Well, it's all quite coincidental, don't you think? Especially considering that these mishaps began shortly after Jason's murder—a murder in which the killer still hasn't been found."

Lucien stroked his jaw. "Was Jason involved in any illegal or unseemly activities before his death? We both know he had been drinking heavily. Men can sometimes go astray—"

"Not Jason—certainly not criminal activity. He had a few favorite whores who visited him on regular occasions, that's all."

"Do you know who these women are?"

"Bow Street has already questioned them. I'm sure they have nothing to do with it."

"I recall after you met with Jason's solicitor after the memorial service, you mentioned your dismay upon learning that Jason had spent the whole five thousand pounds that Miranda's father left for her."

"Yes."

"What did he spend it on?"

Damien glanced at the floor, searching his mind. "I don't know. He lived in a hellhole. He didn't gamble to any large degree. He didn't love finery. Perhaps on the women? But that doesn't seem likely. They're low street prostitutes, not courtesans."

Lucien shook his head and began pacing. "You're right. Something isn't adding up. This is all beginning to sound damned strange. Start over again from the beginning. I want to know every detail you can recall, no matter how small or insignificant."

Damien did his best to piece a fuller picture together for his brother, answering Lucien's rapid-fire questions as well as his memory served. He scratched his eyebrow, racking his brain as Lucien questioned him on the Pavilion theater, the makeup of the audience, whether or not Mr. Reed was known to have any family who might seek revenge, and on Miranda's relationship with "Trick" Slidell. Had there been any other beaux she had mentioned? No, he told him.

"What of those men you killed in Birmingham?"

"Why do you keep coming back to them?"

"Indulge me. There were four, you say?"

"Yes. They were armed with pistols and knives," Damien repeated wearily. "One had a sword. They each had horses, thus my first thought was that they were highwaymen."

"Seems a logical conclusion. Was Colonel Morris able to identify them with any certainty?"

"No."

"What did they look like?"

He shrugged, sending him a dark look.

"Ah, you beat them beyond recognition. Well, then," Lucien said, his eyes glittering with intrigue over the puzzle. "Did you hear their voices long enough to pick up any accents?"

"General sort of low Cockney, I guess. I couldn't identify a region."

"Was there *anything* about these poor bleeders to distinguish them?"

"Let me think." He had been so deeply immersed in his battle mode that it was difficult now to recall details. "I believe one had a gold tooth. Another had a tattoo of an eagle or something."

"An eagle?"

"An eagle or a hawk. It was holding something in its talons. What the devil was it?" He snapped his fingers as the picture flashed back to him. "A dagger. That's it. It was some bird of prey clutching a dagger in its talons."

Lucien had gone very still. "Are you sure of this? Did you see it clearly?"

He nodded uneasily. "I saw it perfectly before they buried the sod. Why?"

Lucien paused and set down his drink, then looked at him, bracing his hands on his waist. "That's the insignia of a criminal gang based in the East End, not far," he said slowly, "from where Jason was killed."

# ☆ CHAPTER ☆
# ELEVEN

The hairs on Damien's nape prickled with danger, but his voice was steely. "What are they called?"

"The Raptors."

"Let's pay them a visit."

Lucien passed a dark glance over his face, no doubt knowing that if he declined, Damien would simply go alone. He nodded resolutely then went to get dressed.

"How the devil do you know about London gangs, anyway?" Damien asked a short while later as Lucien tossed him a sword, hilt first. Damien caught it out of the air and accepted a pistol from his brother, as well.

"If you really want to know, we occasionally use their ilk as informants," Lucien answered, strapping on his sword. Having been recalled from his "diplomatic" post on the Continent after the fall of Napoleon, Lucien had been assigned to an ongoing counter-espionage effort. It brought him in contact with a great many unsavory characters. One thing Damien could say for his brother: For his country's sake, Lucien was not afraid to walk along the edge of what most honor-obsessed gentlemen of their class would have consid-ered despicable conduct. It was only Alice's virtuous influence that had stopped Lucien from becoming tainted by the darkness he flirted with.

"There are certain pockets of these people to whose activities—within reason—we turn a blind eye," he explained. "One young cutthroat in particular has been most forthcoming when I need information. He was sentenced to the gallows, but I had him freed. He's more useful to me alive. He is known as 'Billy Blade.' "

"Billy Blade?" Damien echoed in a dubious tone, tucking the pistol into the waistband of his trousers.

Lucien flashed him a wily grin. "If I told you his real name—which I can't—but if I could, you'd be shocked."

"Who is he?"

"Sorry, can't tell you that, old chap. Suffice to say that Billy Blade heads a rival gang known as the Tomahawks."

"Wild savages?"

"Indeed. He'll know what's going on with the Raptors. These gangs spy on each other like countries and run their own little districts like medieval warlords. They have their own armies, their own black-market industries, their own codes of respect. My friend, you are about to enter an England you never knew you were fighting for."

Damien shrugged as they stalked out to the carriage. "As long as they're bribable."

"It is their most endearing trait." Lucien jangled the small leather purse of coins he had brought along for that purpose. "They are also territorial, treacherous as rats, and highly dangerous, so don't lose your temper. Let me do the talking."

"I've been doing that since we were four," he muttered.

Seemingly out of thin air, Lucien had conjured two of his young secret agents, Marc Skipton and Kyle Stewart, to drive them into the brick-and-mortar jungle of the East End and to guard the carriage while they were meeting with the mysterious leader of the gang. Without further ado, they climbed into Lucien's unmarked black coach and were under way.

The crescent moon hung over the dark rooftops, while below, the labyrinth of nameless streets in London's poorest regions crawled with corruption and the constant threat of violence. The dilapidated tenement houses and shadowed, filth-strewn alleys were fraught with danger. Through this stinking, un-inhabitable maze of poverty, disease, and degradation, they soon arrived at a raucous gin shop, where a low and drunken rabble had gathered to lay wagers on a dogfight.

Lucien beckoned Damien out of the carriage and nodded to Marc to drive on, having already arranged for where they would meet in half an hour. His battle-honed senses on high alert, Damien followed as his brother marched grimly ahead of him. They went around the building where another lively operation was in progress: a few burly men loading sealed wooden cartons onto a wagon.

"Stolen goods," Lucien explained under his breath. "They do their thieving in London and hawk whatever

they can up north and in the West Country, where it's
harder to trace."

"Charming," Damien murmured.

"Who's there? What do ye want?" one of the big
workmen called pugnaciously as they approached.

"I'm looking for Blade. Is he here?"

"Maybe." The man rested his fists on his waist,
blocking their path. "Who's askin'?"

"Tell him Lucifer is here."

Damien looked askance at him in dark amusement.
As wild youngbloods on the Town before they had entered the military, the Knight twins had been dubbed
Lucifer and Demon by their carousing friends. The
nicknames had followed them into the army, gaining
new meaning once their respective talents in battle
had been discovered. Lucien had headed up the regiment's swift, stealthy light infantry company, expert
sharpshooters and scouts who could move like ghosts
through the sparse terrain; Damien had captained the
stalwart, unflinching grenadiers, the shock troops of
the regiment, first into every battle.

"Lucifer, eh? And who's that?" The man nodded
toward Damien.

"That's Demon," his brother said smoothly. "Go
and tell Blade that we are here."

Damien stood beside him, at the ready, as Lucien
stared the brute down.

"Wait 'ere," the big man grunted after a tense moment, then slouched off into the shadows and disappeared through the door. He returned a few minutes
later and waved them over. "Blade says he'll see you."

"What an honor," Damien muttered under his breath. Lucien went ahead of him.

Scanning his surroundings as they crossed to the back entrance, Damien took a quick mental count of the lawless men loading the wagons or simply loitering around the area. Fifteen. He counted another dozen when the big, lumbering fellow led them into the seedy countinghouse that backed the gin shop, and up the cramped stairs to the second floor. They proceeded down a narrow hallway with peeling paint on the walls to the back room, where they were ushered into the presence of the gang's illustrious leader.

"Billy." Lucien greeted him with his most charming smile.

Damien hid his astonishment. 'Blade' was appallingly young, scarcely five-and-twenty—but then, life in this environment was short, nasty, and brutish. Dressed with rough-and-tumble flamboyance, he was a handsome youth with shrewd eyes and a jaded smirk of a smile. He wore black leather trousers and no cravat, but a loose-fitting jacket of abused black velvet with a red carnation tucked in the boutonniere. Beneath his coat, a garish, red-and-purple waistcoat and a dirty shirt of natural linen hugged his lean, sinewy frame. Thick gold rings, some set with jewels, gleamed on his nimble fingers as he toyed with his dagger, his warning stare removing all doubt that he was cock of the walk. A solid gold watch-chain winked against the gaudy superfine of his vest and disappeared into his waistcoat pocket, as though in brazen invitation to any of his cutthroat associates to dare try to take it from him.

He did not trouble himself to rise at their entrance, but kicked the chair across from him in Lucien's direction, offering him a seat with an insolent nod. "Well, I'll be damned," the hell-born babe drawled, glancing from one twin's face to the other. "There's two of you, Luce. You twins?"

Lucien nodded.

"Me mum was a twin. Not identical, though. Who's firstborn?"

"Demon is," Lucien said, nodding toward him, "but this is not a social call, Blade. May we speak privately?"

Blade sneered faintly, but obliged him, dismissing a few of his shadowy cronies with a princely flick of his hand, keeping only two very treacherous-looking ones on either side of him.

When the door had closed, the lad's hard-eyed gaze slid from it to Lucien.

Lucien set the purse of gold on the table between them.

Blade picked it up, weighing it in his palm. "If you're here about that dead army swell, I already told you, nobody seen a damned thing. They arrested Rooster, but I 'eard they let him go."

Lucien nodded. "We know that. No, I've come to ask you about your old friends, the Raptors."

Blade growled and narrowed his eyes. "Wot about 'em?"

"Four of them turned up dead in Birmingham. Did your men do it?"

Damien realized his brother was first testing the young cutthroat. Blade stared at him for a long moment, then shook his head and glanced at his two companions, who chuckled gruffly at the news.

"Those mother-lovin' sods. I wish we had."

"Do you know what they were doing up there?"

"No," he said with a malevolent gleam in his eyes. He took a swig from his flask and wiped his mouth with the back of his hand. "But give me a few days and I'll find out."

The next morning, Miranda feigned a headache, too humiliated by Damien's rejection to come out of her room. As a girl who prided herself on never crying, she did not want him to see her with her eyes all red and her nose stuffed up, for he would know she had wept over him all night like a blasted watering pot. Her self-respect had suffered enough without that added shame.

She knew she deserved it, though. That was the worst part. Like some brash poacher in an orchard, she had reached for forbidden fruit that hung too far above her head and had toppled to the ground for her folly.

He was an earl and a hero of the nation. She was penniless, illegitimate. The fine clothes she had been given to wear and the elegant surroundings of the mansion had caused her to forget herself, but he had put her back in her place. As Reed and Brocklehurst had taken such pains to teach her, she was nobody. She would not forget it again. As dear as the people at Knight House had become to her, Damien's bludgeoning words had reminded her that she did not really belong here, either, no more than she had belonged at Yardley.

Pacing in her room, she considered running away and joining one of the great London theaters, but now that she had become associated with the Knight family in the eyes of the ton, it would only make them look bad, and that was a poor way to repay all their kindness.

She only wished Damien would have told her the truth in the first place instead of trying to talk around it with a lot of nonsense about his "going mad." Having looked his demons in the eyes herself, she knew his problem was serious, but he was a fool to say there was no cure. She also rather wished he would have spoken up before she had declared herself like a lovesick country bumpkin.

Just then, a courteous knock sounded at her chamber door.

"Who is it?"

"Mr. Walsh, Miss."

She opened the door and looked inquiringly at the tall, dignified butler.

"Good day, Mr. Walsh."

He bowed his head. "Pardon my intrusion, Miss FitzHubert. Some visitors have just arrived to call on you. I know you are not feeling well, but in this case, I thought perhaps you might wish to see them." With a tender look of gravity, he offered her a calling card on his small silver tray. "I shall send them away at once if you are not up to it."

Miranda took the card from the tray and looked

at the name engraved on it. *Anne Sherbrooke, Viscountess Hubert.*

"My aunt," she breathed, her eyes widening. Why, it was Uncle Algernon's wife! Uncle Jason had occasionally mentioned the middle brother, Algernon, who had become Lord Hubert after Papa's death—the uncle who wanted nothing to do with her on account of her bastardy. Uncle Jason had always said that "Algy" was a cold fish.

"Her Ladyship has brought her children with her," Mr. Walsh added.

"I have cousins?" she exclaimed, wide-eyed.

"Indeed, Miss, there are three—two young ladies, one gentleman."

"Three cousins! Oh, I think I shall have to see them," she murmured, her heart beginning to pound with nervousness, yet she could not help but feel a bit cynical. It figured. Now that she had proven that she could acquit herself respectably in Society, her relatives must have deemed it safe to acknowledge her. She had half a mind to thumb her nose at them, but there was a faint glimmer of hope in her heart that maybe, among her own kin, she would finally find the place where she belonged.

"Shall I advise Her Grace that you could use reinforcements?" the butler asked gently.

Her gaze flew to his lined face. "Bless you, Mr. Walsh. I should be forever grateful if the duchess would go in with me."

He gave her a knowing smile and nodded.

"Oh, Mr. Walsh," she called as he started to close the door. She picked up the little key Lord Lucien had given her and showed it to him. "Do you happen to know what this opens?"

"Hmm, may I?"

She handed it to him. He held it up and examined it closely, then shook his head.

"I'm afraid I do not recognize it." He gave it back to her.

She nodded. "Thank you."

He bowed and went to fetch the duchess. Miranda hurried to the mirror and smoothed her hair. Her eyes were still a bit red, but they were no longer swollen. She thought of changing into a fancier gown, then dismissed the idea. She would have to do as she was. She was not about to trouble herself trying to impress the very people who had left her to rot up at Yardley while Uncle Jason had been away at the war.

A few minutes later, she walked into the drawing room with the duchess of Hawkscliffe by her side. Miranda's posture was stiff, her palms sweating with the jitters, but her patroness looked as serene as always, as their guests rose from their chairs and greeted them. Her first impression was one of deep surprise—the mother and both daughters were dressed all in black, in mourning, she realized, for Uncle Jason. The young man wore a black armband.

She was instantly ashamed of herself for choosing pretty colors for her wardrobe, eschewing the three-month mourning rule. On the other hand, she thought, her heart pounding, in light of her illegitimate status, perhaps her relatives had appreciated her distancing herself from the family by not presuming to wear mourning for poor Uncle Jason. As his legitimate kin, they might deem that their prerogative. As for Lady Hubert, Miranda was half prepared to be afraid of the aunt who had rejected her along with Uncle Cold Fish, but Lady Hubert looked even more nervous than she was. The fiftyish viscountess was a small, birdlike woman with papery skin and an air of frailty. She smiled wanly at Miranda, but even her smile did not remove her constant expression of vague, startled dismay. Curtsying to her, Miranda instinctively felt sorry for the woman.

Lady Hubert then presented her daughters, the Honorable Misses Daisy and Parthenia Sherbrooke, a pair of proud, pale, thin-lipped girls who rolled their eyes at their hapless, fluttering mother. Miranda nodded to them, uneasy with the way their dissecting glances flicked, scalpellike, over her.

Lastly, she was introduced to their rakish-looking elder brother, the Honorable Mr. Crispin Sherbrooke, a splendid young dandy in a bottle-green morning coat and sparkling black riding boots. He had guinea-gold curls and a roguish twinkle in his blue eyes, and the perfection of his snowy cravat made her suspect that his valet worked on it for an hour and a half.

Rather amused, she offered him a curtsy, but Crispin took her hand and bowed over it, pressing a gallant kiss to her knuckles. "Hullo, coz," he murmured, flashing her a grin as though he had known her all her life.

She smiled gratefully at him, feeling as though she had just found a much-needed friend.

*  *  *

The next evening, Damien escorted Miranda to a private chamber music concert in the home of some old friends, Lord and Lady Carteret. Folding his arms across his chest, he eased back into his chair and tried to take solace from the rich, sonorous strains of the Mozart wind serenade that poured through the candlelit drawing room. Try as he may, however, it was impossible to relax when his protective instincts were in a state of high alert. He was still waiting for that scoundrelly lad, Billy Blade, to report back with information about the men he had killed outside of Birmingham.

Following the twins' visit to the East End on Monday night, Damien had stopped at the Guards' Club, the gentlemen's club for military men. There, he had convened with a few of his most trusted officers from the regiment, gaining all the help he needed to ensure Miranda's security whenever he elected to take her outside the gates of Knight House. They had resolutely pledged their assistance, for she was Sherbrooke's niece and the major had been one of their own. Even now, they sat in strategic locations around the drawing room, smartly dressed in their scarlet uniforms, ready to spring into action if there was any sign of another mysterious "accident" befalling Miranda.

She was utterly innocent of the pains being taken to protect her, indeed, she had no idea that he suspected she might be in danger. That was exactly how Damien wanted it, at least until they knew anything for certain. It was bad enough that he had hurt her. He did not wish to frighten her unnecessarily with the possibility that she might be a murderer's next target.

Last night, he had made excuses to keep her at home rather than attending a large subscription ball at the Argyle Rooms, which she had been anticipating for days. The building was quite large, public, and difficult to secure, even with his men's help. It was too easy for any sort of person to buy a subscription and gain entry to the ball. A private concert in the home of a good friend was a much safer affair, with its smaller gathering of carefully selected guests, which was why he had relented tonight.

After all, he thought in self-directed bitterness, he had ordered her to find a husband. She could hardly carry out his command if he continued to keep her locked within the gates of Knight House. His gaze was drawn back to her irresistibly, and his stare turned sour.

Griff seemed to be making fine progress. Seated on the other side of her, the widowed marquis leaned over and whispered again in Miranda's ear. She nodded in apparent agreement with his murmured comment on the performance.

Damien hid his faint scowl and returned his attention to the musicians. Where the devil was Alice, anyway? he thought with a bit of a sulk. She wasn't doing a very good job as chaperon, or she would have noticed their old chum getting a bit too close. He glanced over his shoulder at Lucien and his wife, who were seated right behind them. Perhaps he was overreacting, for Alice was a woman of exacting moral standards, and she seemed to have no concern about Lord Griffith's attentions to the girl.

He heaved a grumbling sigh and, with folded arms, flicked his white-gloved fingers in brooding patience on his opposite biceps. Better Griff, anyway, than the likes of Ollie Quinn, but it really was starting to grate on him—the male adoration that followed his luscious ward everywhere she went.

He was unable to stop himself from glancing furtively at her again and felt a curious constriction in his chest at the sight of her that was part distress, part longing. She looked so beautiful tonight. He would not have thought that such a quiet, pink-pearl color would have flattered her so well, but her silken gown shimmered in the candlelight, its pale hue making the green of her eyes look all the more brilliant and deep. The soft, tender curve of her upper arms enticed him beyond bearing; he wanted to skim his lips along that small stretch of her bare skin between the short, puffed sleeves of her gown and her high, white gloves. That innocent region seemed so much more permissible than the splendor of her chest above the delicate neckline of her gown. He dragged his gaze away in misery. He knew he had brought this on himself, but he had not foreseen what a very cold place the world could be when someone as sunny and warm as Miranda FitzHubert treated one with cool reserve.

When the performance was over, he got up and went to check in with his fellow officers. Each discreetly reported that he had seen nothing out of the ordinary. Satisfied, he took a glass of wine from a passing waiter's tray just as Griff ambled over to him with a smile. Damien was unprepared for the jolt of jealous hostility he felt as his old friend joined him, clinking his glass with his own.

"Cheers."

Damien forced a taut smile and looked away, shaking off the strange impulse. Steeling himself, he looked at Griff in question. "Well?"

"Well, what?"

Damien crooked a brow at him.

"Ah. Possibly," he murmured with a sly half smile. "Very possibly, indeed. She is delightful."

"What's holding you back?" he asked with his usual soldier's bluntness.

"Are you so eager to get rid of her?"

He clamped his jaw judiciously for a moment, then lifted his chin. "I want to see her settled in life. That is all."

"I see. Well, it is too soon—for me, and, I suspect, for her."

"Don't wait too long. Look," Damien growled, nodding toward Miranda and Crispin, who were standing side by side, admiring a dramatic Turner landscape on the wall. "The cousins have got their heads together again."

Griff chuckled.

"Jason always said that lad is a fool," Damien muttered. "What the devil can he be talking to her about so intensely, do you think?"

The marquess shrugged idly, swirling his wine in his glass. "Who knows?"

"Aren't you going to do anything? That lad might be angling for her."

"Let him angle. She can handle herself. Better, I daresay, than most of the young ladies in this room. She is an original," Griff declared. "I find her quite refreshing."

"Well, if she's so damned refreshing, maybe you had better go over there and interrupt?"

Griff looked askance at him.

"What?" Damien asked, a bit put off by his friend's penetrating stare.

"Crispin Sherbrooke may be in love with her, but he's not the one who worries me." Griff gave him a hard look, then sauntered away to mingle politely with the guests.

"You mean you don't know?" Crispin asked, his blue eyes twinkling with wicked glee. "Oh, Lord, child, the tale is too delicious."

"Tell!" Miranda giggled.

"Perhaps I should make you wait until after you come to dinner at our house tomorrow night."

"You would be an infamous cad to do so. Tell me the gossip!"

"You will be scandalized," he warned playfully.

"No, I won't."

"Your guardian will lop my head off if he finds out I told you."

"I won't breathe a word. Crispin, you are torturing me. Tell."

"All right, but only because you are so pretty. Not the eldest brother, Hawkscliffe, nor that lovely morsel, Lady Jacinda—they are of the true blood. But the rest of them—that devil, Lord Jack; the twins; and my own *bon ami*, Alec—are, every one of them, cuckoos in the nest, the results of their mother's peccadilloes. And everybody knows it."

"No!" she exclaimed in a whisper, smacking him with her fan.

"I swear on my luck it's true." His eyes danced merrily as he took a sip of his wine. "Their mother, Georgiana, had so many lovers that she used to be known as the Hawkscliffe Harlot."

Miranda gasped, torn between fascination and guilt at listening to gossip about the people who had been so kind to her.

"Who is the twins' real father?" she whispered.

"*Ma petite,* so innocent! Don't you know anything, little chuckle-head? Their father was Georgiana's longtime devotee, the marquess of Carnarthen."

"Is he here?"

"He's dead. He was Welsh and a high-ranking navy man. He was so devoted to Georgiana—another man's wife—that he never married and died without legal issue."

"Oh, that is so sad!"

"That is why Parliament created your guardian Lord Winterley," Crispin went on in a conspiratorial whisper. "Carnarthen was very powerful and very well liked. As the elder of the twins, Damien is in actuality Lord Carnarthen's firstborn son. Since Carnarthen's title went defunct after his death, some of his friends in Parliament banded together to have a new title created and given to Damien so that the bloodlines would survive."

"I thought he was made an earl for his war victories!"

"Heavens, not an earl, no. Even Wellington's top men were only raised to viscounts."

" 'Only' viscounts," she scoffed merrily. "That's easy for you to say. You'll be one someday."

They laughed, but anger and shock began simmering in Miranda's veins. Of all the nerve!

That blackguard had sliced her heart open, casting her aside on the grounds of her illegitimacy, and all the while, he, too, was a bastard! Her eyes flashing, she scanned the room until she picked him out in his smart, scarlet uniform.

He was standing alone, staring at her.

She felt the familiar, soul-deep shock of the impact as their gazes collided and locked. With a withering look, she turned away and drew on her acting skills to summon a gay laugh. She took her cousin's arm and went to look at the next fine painting.

The next evening, Algernon looked down his long dining table with a shadowed smile to himself of complacency. Not only could he boast some of the brightest luminaries of the ton at his table this night, such as the great Lord Winterley and his elder brother, the powerful duke of Hawkscliffe and his radiant duchess—which made the night a social coup for a generally unpopular man like him—but, more importantly, his son was carrying out his task to perfection. The boy might just make him proud, after all. By virtue of their kinship, Crispin had already slipped under the defenses that Winterley had mounted around his ward to keep the rest of her suitors at bay.

Seated across from the fair Miranda, Crispin was at his most charming. He even had the duchess laughing. Only Winterley seemed unimpressed by the lad's wit.

Stern and unsmiling, sitting at attention beside Miranda, his huge shoulders rigid, the earl was a dark, brooding presence at the table. Recalling the sorry state Jason had been in before he had left this world, Algernon was not altogether surprised.

It was a bad business, soldiering, he thought, then ignored the gloom that surrounded the colonel and stole another surreptitious glance at Miranda.

Perhaps she felt his study, for her glance crept toward him—inch by shy, virginal inch—meeting his nervously from down the table. Ah, she enchanted him. Such pink cheeks, such green eyes. Her skin was as succulent as the petals of a lily. His heart beat faster with exhilaration. Though he was certain no one noticed, he held her stare for one second longer than perhaps was proper, then flicked his tongue over his dry lips and, ever so patiently, took a sip of his wine.

Early the next day, Damien stood in the drive, conversing with the head groom, a diminutive ex-jockey, who sat perched atop Zeus, having just come back from taking the stallion out for a gallop in Hyde Park. It was a brilliant December day, winter sunlight sparkling on the snow, the sky azure.

"Aye, he's in fine wind, my lord," the little man reported, giving the stallion's flexed neck a sound pat.

"I am glad to hear it," Damien answered, pleased with his stallion's high humor.

He would have liked to have taken Zeus out himself, but he was reluctant to leave Miranda unprotected even for a moment. Fortunately, there had been no accidents and no mishaps since Fancy had bolted on her four days ago. Either his vigilance in watching over his ward was paying off, or the danger was all in his head.

He had allowed Miranda to attend the dinner last night because it was important to know one's kin, however objectionable, but he knew she was too clever to be fooled about the Huberts' motives. If she had not received his family's support, or if she had not made such a good impression on the ton, her aunt and uncle would have upheld their policy of pretending she didn't exist. They were social climbers, plain and simple. As for her cousins, the two haughty girls had stared at her the whole night in withering jealousy—when they had not been staring at Robert and him, that was. Crispin was the only one who seemed to feel a genuine liking for Miranda, Damien thought just as a ruckus arose at the tall, wrought-iron gates of Knight House.

"Keep moving! You've got no business 'ere," the gatekeepers were saying.

Instantly on alert, Damien looked over. He could not see their would-be visitor, for the servants stood in the way. He glanced at the groom, nodding his dismissal. The weathered jockey turned Zeus and rode him at a walk around the house toward the stable as a piercing whistle split the air.

" 'Ay! Lordship!" somebody yelled from the gates. "Do you want to let me in or not?"

Damien marched over, curling his lip in disdain. It was that hell-born babe, Billy Blade. He had grasped the wrought-iron bars above his head and was leaning idly against the gate, his mouth stretched in a jaded, satyric smirk that was possibly the most insolent sight Damien had ever beheld.

Here was a young man who could have done with a few weeks of army discipline, Damien thought with a stern frown. "Let him in," he ordered the gatekeepers.

"Sir?" They turned to him, looking startled.

He gave a curt nod. "Do it."

"Ay, ye got some sense, after all." Blade pushed away from the gate, hitched up his black leather breeches as he waited, then swaggered in grandly through the gates. He tipped his cockade hat to the gatekeepers, who eyed him dubiously.

"You've got a hell of a lot of nerve coming here," Damien growled.

"Wot, should I have come scratching at the servant's gate?" he retorted.

"You should've gone to Lucien's. You are his acquaintance. Not mine."

"I tried. He wasn't 'ome. You're the one that came to me for help. I'm here to give it, but if you ain't gonna be gentlemanlike, I'll take my information elsewhere."

"This way, you detestable creature," Damien muttered under his breath.

Blade laughed in amusement and followed him in through the front door. At least he had the couth to doff his hat. "Not bad, not bad a'tall," he remarked, glancing around at the gleaming marble entrance hall of Knight House, but he did not look overly impressed. "This your house?"

The coxcomb was probably eyeing up the place for

the prospect of a future burglary, he thought. "No, my brother's. This way, Mr. Blade."

He led him to the small utilitarian office on the back of the first floor. It was used by the butler and housekeeper for the management of the household. He offered Blade a wooden chair well away from the butler's silver-safe. Rather than sitting, the lad planted his foot on the chair and draped his arm over his bent knee. His expression hardened.

"I'd say you've got trouble, gov."

"What did you learn?"

"Let me ask you somethin' first. You kill all four of them bleeders yourself up in Brum?"

Damien deemed it best not to answer.

Blade grinned. "That didn't sound like a 'no.' How'd you do it? I've killed me two at once, but never four."

Damien could not resist an oblique smile. "It's all a matter of rhythm."

"Rhythm. Right. I. Well, then." The lad's shrewd eyes turned grim. "Here's what I've got. Those four sows you skewered up north were hired in London by a rich man about three weeks ago. Nobody knows the chap's name, but there's a rumor going around he's a landlord that owns a few of the tenement houses in Seven Dials."

"What exactly did he hire them to do?"

Blade shook his head. "The rest of the gang don't know. All the man said was that he needed them to 'do a job' for him up north. He was to pay them a hundred guineas each."

"No mean sum," he murmured, a chill running

down his spine to realize that, indeed, those four men had been deliberately sent to get Miranda—whether to abduct or kill her, he did not know. He shuddered at the realization of what a near thing it had been. If his instincts had not warned him to turn around one last time to look at her, he wouldn't have been there to save her. They must have been watching the school, waiting for their chance. No doubt they had been perplexed about how to grab her, with the tight rein that Miss Brocklehurst had kept over the girls at Yardley. By dashing out that night to the theater, she must have taken them off guard.

Undoubtedly the enemy had more of his underlings watching Knight House even now, he thought darkly. His first thought was to remove her to one of the family's remote country estates, but he brushed off the idea. She would be safest right here in Knight House in the heart of London, where there were plenty of loyal eyes and ears to keep watch. Here the defenses were already in place, his brothers and his officers from the regiment on hand to assist, if need be.

He stroked his jaw broodingly. "So, how can I find out who this man is?" he mused aloud.

"Lucien should have better luck than I, on that point," Blade replied. "Most of those miserable buildings are owned by men with great names and titles, but they hide behind their gentlemen of business, who are under orders not to reveal their employers' identities. Secrecy's a virtue in my part o' Town."

"Did you hear anything about the man returning to hire more of the gang members to finish this 'job'?"

Blade shook his head firmly. "No. Would be too

risky for him, wouldn't it? Besides, if the first batch failed, why would he go back to them? If I were him, I reckon I'd change tactics."

"He already has. He's a bloody coward, too, trying to run down a young girl with a carriage," he murmured, thinking aloud.

Blade let out a low whistle. "That's low. I do not envy you, Colonel. Nothing worse than an enemy who refuses to show himself. Call on me again if I can be of help."

At his words, Damien's stare homed in on Blade's face, because, for the slightest moment, it seemed as though his thick Cockney accent had fallen away, a more cultured tone showing through underneath. Clearly, the young man did not realize he had betrayed this odd quirk. Come to think of it, Damien mused, he noticed a certain mark of high birth in the lad's knife-hilt cheekbones and sulky mouth.

"Have you always lived in Seven Dials, Mr. Blade?"

Blade's guarded smirk returned in the blink of an eye. He lowered his foot from the chair just as a trio of high-pitched voices floated back to them from the entrance hall.

Damien heard his little sister's crisp voice.

"Mr. Walsh, please tell Her Grace we shall be back in an hour. We are going walking in the park."

Damien jumped up out of his chair and strode out of the office to stop them. "Miranda!" he called sharply. Wrapped in her fur-lined pelisse, she turned around. "You may not go out."

"My lord?" she asked through gritted teeth, lifting her chin.

"I did not give you permission to leave the property."

"Damien, you brute, leave her alone," Jacinda scoffed, putting her arm around Miranda. "Look how sunny it is out. Enough of your arbitrary orders. We are not going to waste this day. Come, Miranda, Lizzie—"

"No," he growled, seizing his ward's wrist, but he instantly let go when Miranda muttered, "Ow."

"Leave her alone!" Jacinda tugged Miranda back to her side.

"I'd do as he says, if I were you, my lady."

They all turned as Billy Blade sauntered into the entrance hall, a wicked smile curving his lips.

Jacinda glanced over at him and blinked, wide-eyed. A look of withering hauteur crept over her elfin face. "I beg your pardon," she uttered, drawing herself up and looking every inch the blue-blooded daughter of a duke.

"Blade," Damien warned.

His glance flicked insolently over Jacinda. "I'm leavin'," he drawled, swaggering toward the front door.

Mr. Walsh opened it for him automatically, staring at the flamboyant, ragged creature with a quite shocked expression.

"Who—no, what—was that?" Jacinda demanded, spinning around to face at Damien the moment the door closed.

"Never you mind," he started, but before he could say another word, Jacinda grabbed Lizzie and Miranda's hands and rushed up the stairs, dragging them after her.

"Er, girls?" He promptly found himself left alone at

the foot of the stairs, scratching his head, but at least he had managed to keep them indoors.

"Jacinda? What on earth?" Miranda and Lizzie protested, laughing, as the girl raced down the corridor, half dragging them each by the hand. She flung into the music room that overlooked the drive and ran over to the window, planting her hands against the glass.

"Oh, look at him, he's *soooo* horrid," Jacinda whispered, staring in fascinated revulsion out the window as the gatekeepers opened the gates before the odd young man. "What did Damien call him? Blade?"

"I think so. What sort of name is that?" Lizzie asked as the girls huddled in the window.

"A perfect ruffian and just as bold as you please. Did you see how he looked at me?" Jacinda breathed. "*What* is he?"

"A Nasty Man, that's what," Lizzie said flatly. "I'm sure Her Grace would not at all approve. Damien certainly didn't. For heaven's sake, Jacinda, stop staring before he sees you!"

Even as Lizzie said it, Jacinda's white-gloved fingers flew to her lips as Blade turned back to look at the house and noticed her in the window. He flashed her a grin and swept off his hat, bowing to her with a flourish as though he were a French courtier at Versailles. Blade clapped his hat onto his head again, pivoted smoothly, and ambled away with slow, long-legged strides, as though he hadn't a care in the world.

"What a silly, ridiculous fool!" Jacinda scoffed, her

apple-cheeks flooding with color, but Lizzie and Miranda exchanged a bemused look, for her voice was breathless when she said it. Jacinda pressed her forehead against the glass, eagerly watching Blade through the window until he had disappeared down the street.

# ❧ CHAPTER ❧
# TWELVE

Miranda jerked awake at the sound of a distant explosion late the next night. As she scrambled up from her pillow, the book she had been reading before she drowsed off toppled off her chest. Whisked out of dreamland, she looked around in confusion. Her chamber was dim, the curtains drawn; the candle had burned down to a stub. She sat up, rubbing her eyes as the sounds continued like far-off thunder. When she glanced at the clock, she realized the reason for all the noise. The birth of the new year, 1815, was only twenty minutes away.

With a yawn, she threw off the coverlet and pushed up from the bed, padding across the cold floor to peer out the window. As she pulled the heavy damask curtain back and looked out, her lonely sigh misted the windowpane. Spending the holiday by herself was worse than spending it at Yardley, she thought as she stared at the fireworks painting the sky in flashes of colored light, illuminating the snowy rooftops of London.

So, this was what it was like to live in the regent's capital. In Birmingham, they did not have fireworks very often. She watched them for a moment in drowsy pleasure, her eyes heavy-lidded. Earlier, Damien and Lucien had explained to her about the danger they suspected she might be in. They seemed to feel that some of the accidents that had happened to her might not have been accidents at all. She was not particularly alarmed, for she knew that they would protect her. They said it was nothing to worry about and that she was safe, and she believed them. She only felt rather glum that she had not been allowed to go to the New Year's Eve party with the others.

Then again, she was not totally alone tonight, she thought. Somewhere in the house, her guardian was home, perhaps feeling every bit as lonely as she. Damien, too, had stayed in. Warily, she glanced over her shoulder at her chamber door, debating the notion of going to wish him a happy New Year. They had not spoken since that night in the stable, except for the practicalities, and even then, their conversations had been stilted and strained. That was no way to start a new year. She studied the door for a moment, gnawing her lip. She doubted he was sleeping at this hour. Who could sleep with all the noise—?

Her train of thought suddenly broke off. The fog of sleep fell away instantly as she remembered.

*Fireworks!*

She turned back to the window, her heart in her throat as the memory of his tortured confession in the stable flooded back into her now fully awake mind. Whirling away from the window, she grabbed her dressing gown from off its peg, pulled it on, and prayed he was all right as she picked up her taper and strode out into the hallway. Damien had specifically said that the noise of fireworks and festival cannons—like the ones that were firing even now—had triggered his terrifying experience on Guy Fawkes Night. He was probably fine, she told herself, but she had to check on him just to make sure.

Holding up her candle in the darkened hallway, she counted doors around the corner until she came to his bedchamber. Her courage wavered as she raised her fist to knock on the door. He had told her that he had not been aware of his own actions that night, that he had had a knife in one hand and a gun in the other. What if he *was* dangerous? She swallowed hard as the vision flashed through her mind of Damien on that moonlit ridge, fierce, bloodied, and wild, sword in hand. Oh, yes, she knew what he was capable of.

She also knew that that man would never hurt her. No matter how much he believed he was a threat, she knew to the very core of her being that he was not capable of losing himself in his pain so completely that he would ever hurt a woman. Not Damien Knight. Bracing herself, she lifted her chin and knocked bravely on the door.

There was no answer.

"Damien?" she called softly, knocking again. She waited for another moment or two, then hurried off to look for him downstairs. She peered over the edge of the banister, but there was no sign of the night butler or hall porter, no one to ask where Damien was. With the artillery and fireworks booming in the distance, the house was eerily still. She went in search of him, moving silently from one grand, empty salon to the next.

Moonlight filtered in through the great windows, sparkling like quicksilver over the dark, opulent halls, glittering along the gilt mirror frames. Her heart pounded with trepidation. As her candle began to gutter, burning down to the wax, she saw ghosts in every pool of shadows, imaginary goblins darting behind the airy scroll couches and the duke's gleaming piano, but no Damien.

Perhaps he had gone out, she thought, when suddenly, she found a room with people in it. Two of his officer friends were playing cards in the library. She stepped into the doorway with her pewter candleholder in hand and gazed at them uncertainly.

"Pardon me."

At her softly spoken words, they threw down their cards, jumped to their feet, and stood at attention. "Miss FitzHubert," they greeted her, bowing stiffly.

They looked a bit nervous to find her in her dressing gown, but she smiled at them in embarrassment. She knew they were only here as a favor to Damien to help protect her.

"Good evening, gentlemen," she said hesitantly. "I am sorry to have ruined your New Year's Eve."

"Not at all, Miss FitzHubert," said Lieutenant Colonel MacHugh, a tall, red-haired Scotsman with piercing eyes and a fierce-looking scar on his face. "We are glad to do it. Winterley would do the same for us."

"You're very kind. Have you seen him?"

"He retired about an hour ago."

She furrowed her brow. "He is in his rooms? Are you sure?"

"He said he wasn't feeling well," Captain Sutherland offered. He was a dashing blond fellow with a carefully groomed moustache.

This did not sound good, she thought as she nodded to them, wished them health and luck in the new year, and retreated, going back upstairs. That scoundrel had been in his rooms the whole time. Why had he not spoken up when she had come knocking? Was he hiding from her?

A few minutes later, she was back where she had started her search. "Damien?" she called, knocking more insistently on his door. "I know you're in there. Sutherland and MacHugh told me so." She waited. "Damien, answer me!"

"Go away."

"Stop being a child. Are you ill?"

"Yes."

"Shall I send for the physician?"

"No."

Her gaze searched the floor as she listened for any hint of his condition in his voice. "Can I get you anything?"

"Go *away*."

"I will not go away. What kind of sickness are you feeling?"

He did not answer.

"It's not a sickness of the body, is it?" she asked grimly through the door. "Have you been drinking?"

Still, he said nothing.

"Damien, are you armed in there?"

His black, bitter laughter sent a chill down her spine as it reached her softly through the thick door.

"Let me in!" she cried, slamming the door with the heel of her fist, her heart pounding with dread that he might do violence to himself.

"Run away, Little Red Riding Hood," he whispered madly, "before you are eaten by the big, bad wolf."

She backed away from the door with a gulp. Staring at the door—the locked, solid barrier he had set between them—she knew that this was the moment of testing, the moment that counted. The moment, she realized, for which Lord Lucien had given her the key.

By God, this affliction was the real reason Damien had refused to let himself love her. It was time to do battle for him the way he had fought to save her on Bordesley Green. She ran off down the hallway to retrieve the key from her chamber.

*There.* He had scared her off. From behind the door, Damien listened to her light footfalls moving off down the corridor. He was shirtless, covered in sweat, high in his battle state, and fighting it for all he was worth. He clenched his jaw to stop himself from screaming out her name and rested his head slowly against the door, closing his eyes with a grimace as reality continued flashing between past and present with dizzying speed, like shutters flapping in a gale. Curious, how his very soul pleaded for her while his cold lips always uttered, *Go away.* His demons were tearing him to shreds tonight; in his brain was a maelstrom of anguish, grief, rage, and guilt. He sought to ride the storm, to master it by sheer will alone, but he could not.

Every scar on his body burned like a brand. The icy

armor of his numbness was dissolving, and he was in this room, drowning silently on the tears he refused to shed. The distant booming sounded like artillery, and he could swear that it was coming closer. Who was it? General Massena? General Soult? He could beat Soult easily, but Massena was a foe to be reckoned with.

"No," he muttered under his breath, pacing back and forth across the room like a caged animal. It was just the fireworks, and damn him if he did not kill the regent the next time he saw that crowned feeder hog for doing this to him. He had never gone to war for Prinny. King George was still the monarch, mad as a March hare. Like him. He picked up a Hepplewhite chair and smashed it against the wall.

Ah, it was so satisfying to hear that splintering of wood. If only he had his axe! But, no, no, he could not trust himself with sharp objects. He had hidden them all away in case he somehow slipped his cage. It eased him for a second, killing the chair; then more evil visions flooded back: a trio of ravens picking at the entrails of his most promising young ensign. The colors had changed hands five times that day, as one standard bearer after another had been cut down. His thoughts whirled faster as each distant burst of fireworks lit his darkened room in faint, sickly colors. There was a certain angle of artillery where one good-sized cannonball, if aimed correctly, could behead a whole line of foot soldiers as it came screaming in, tearing through the column. It was one of the few things at the war that had literally made him throw up.

His legs trembled beneath him as he marched to the

window and threw back the drapes, which he had
closed earlier. He stared in hatred at the distant lights
and explosions, trying to reason with himself, but it
was no good. He touched the window's frosted pane
and took comfort in the coldness, lifting his dewy
hand to his feverish brow, wiping the coldness against
his skin; then, with a sudden, evil inspiration, his gaze
zoomed in from the flashes of light in the distance
to the glass before him. This could all be over quickly,
he thought. The pain finished. He need only put his
fist through that glass, pick up a good long shard, and
slash his throat with it.

He stared at the feathery designs of ice on the glass,
fascinated, his pulse ticking in his temples. It would be
a horrid mess. But that's what servants were for.

*Do it,* hissed the serpent in his brain, and its power
was great, constricting him in its coils of pain, but
there was only one problem.

Who would take care of Miranda?

*Hurry,* she urged herself, grabbing the key from her
dresser, her hands shaking. She was certain now that
Lucien had entrusted it to her because it would give
her some secret access to Damien's chamber. This time
she was not going to stop until she found the way in
and reached him. *How could Lucien know about a
door that not even Mr. Walsh was aware of?* Her eyes
flared with inspiration. Lucien's room . . .

She ran back down the hall, going silently past
Damien's door. She did not want to give him any
warning that she was seeking another way in, lest he
bar her from entering there, as well. She tiptoed into

the bedroom next door to his, the key in one hand, her candle in the other. Holding up the light, she searched the dim chamber that she reasoned had been Lucien's boyhood room.

The bed looked as though it had not been slept in for ages. The room bore the stamp of Lucien's scholarly nature: The volumes on the bookshelves were neatly arranged by language—French, German, Latin, Greek. A microscope, a globe, and a pair of calipers sat out on display on the boy-sized writing table in the far right corner. On the left, a door opened into the dressing room. Since Damien's chamber was on the other side of the left wall, she searched that side, her imagination offering up visions of the twins as young boys playing here. Anyone could see that there was a deep bond between them. Recently, during a family conversation in the drawing room after dinner, Robert, the duke, had told her in amusement that, as children, whenever the twins were bad, the worst punishment that their parents or governess could inflict was to separate them. Neither knew quite what to do without the other. The pair, he had said, had always seemed to have their own language; they appeared to know what each other was thinking at any given moment. Lord Alec had agreed. They were, the youngest brother had drawled in his winsome way, like one person in two bodies.

She opened the wardrobe and pressed against the back of it, but there was no door there. She moved on, nearing Lucien's dressing room.

As boys, Alec had said, both twins had come down with influenza on the exact same day—though Damien had been miles away visiting some friends. Lucien was left-handed, Damien right. Lucien had a dimple only on his left cheek when he smiled, and Damien had the same dimple, only on his right cheek. Jacinda had told her that they were a phenomenon called "mirror twins."

At that very moment, Miranda opened the door of the dressing room, and instantly her gaze homed in on a full-length mirror on the back wall.

Her heart pounded as she walked toward the looking glass, ignoring her own pale reflection. Surrounded by a thick mahogany frame, the mirror was large and rectangular, with a curved top. Putting the key in her pocket, she felt around the edge of it with her free hand, then drew in her breath as the whole frame creaked away from the wall, swinging toward her on unseen hinges. Behind it sat a low, narrow door.

Her mouth fell open with astonishment. She stared at it, wide-eyed. Why, the little devils must have knocked a hole in the wall without their parents knowing, thwarting the punishment of being kept apart. She snapped her jaw shut and reached into her pocket, her hands trembling as she fitted the key into the small, black lock.

A perfect match. Before she turned the key, however, she hesitated. It was no mischievous boy in the next room, but a hardened, violent warrior on the very knife edge of despair. She was taking her life in her hands going into that room. But had Damien hesitated for one instant when he had seen her attackers rushing at her on Bordesley Green? She thought. She took a deep breath and turned the key. At first, she tried to push the door open, but felt something blocking it and realized there was probably an identical mirror on Damien's side.

She pulled the little door toward her instead, then reached through and gingerly pressed her hand flat against the back of Damien's mirror.

Just as she had suspected, it swung open slowly. She had to duck her head under the low lintel as she stepped over the threshold into his dressing room.

"Damien?"

She shrieked as something grabbed her arm. The candle stub flew out of the pewter holder with the motion and fell to the floor, extinguished, as he flung her around and shoved her against the other wall.

She stared blindly into the darkness. She could not see a thing, could only hear his ragged panting in the room, very near.

"It's me, Damien. It's Miranda," she forced out, trying to sound as calm and rational as possible. "Everything is all right now, darling. I'm here now. I'm here to help you."

He let out a deafening, wordless roar in her face. She squeezed her eyes closed in terror and flinched away from him, but held her ground.

He fell silent. She flicked her eyes open, and slowly they adjusted to the darkness.

The first thing she could make out was his gleaming silver eyes, as pale and cold as moonlight. The rest of his magnificent body—the hard, angular severity of his face, the sculpted expanse of his bare chest and shoulders—materialized more slowly from the shadows.

"Lucien gave you his key," he said in disgust.

"Yes."

"It was very unwise of you to use it. I warned you to stay out." His muscles rippled as he spread his arms wide and planted his hands on the wall on either side of her, leaning down to her with a feral, threatening sort of smile. Their faces were inches apart. "But, now that you're here, whatever shall I do with you?"

Miranda swallowed hard. Sweat gleamed on his skin; tangled emotion harshened his features, but at least he had not made his plight worse by drinking, she thought, her heart in her throat. To her relief, she smelled no hard liquor on his breath, only a faint trace of wine.

He flinched as the far-off booming of the fireworks continued hammering away at the house. Damien glanced toward the sound. Tension rippled from him in waves. She could see it in the rigid line of his shoulders and the taut clenching of his jaw.

Here in the windowless dressing room, tucked into the house, the noise was muffled to a constant, dull thudding. It sounded to her very much like a battle, though she had never been at one. Indeed, it did not seem at all mad to her that a man who had spent six years on the front lines should suffer from the memories of his experiences to hear such a sound. Uncle Jason had said that in the thick of the fight there was no time for considering one's emotions, but though the soldiers could ignore their fear when the hour of their duty was at hand, surely it was bound to catch up with them later.

"I've come to help you," she said softly.

"Help me? Who are you to help me?" he asked with kingly contempt, like the lion of the forest.

"Shh," she whispered, touching his face, staring into his eyes.

He paused at her touch. His skin felt clammy. He closed his eyes tightly, trembling.

"Get out, Miranda."

"I will not leave you."

"Have you forgotten Bordesley Green?" He flicked his eyes open angrily again, and she found herself face-to-face with that immortal angel of death she had run from that night.

This time there was nowhere to run. Nor would she.

His silvery eyes gleamed like the blade of a sword, but she lifted her chin and met his gaze steadily. "I am not afraid of you. I will not be chased off this time, not even if you roar at me. Not even if you try another dirty trick like the one you played in the stable, my fellow *bastard*."

His eyes narrowed. "So, you've found me out. You gave me no alternative."

"I know that now, but I didn't come here to argue with you. Hand over whatever weapons you have in this room, right now."

"Or what?" he taunted her.

"Or I am going downstairs to get MacHugh and Sutherland to come in here and beat you back into your right mind, Damien. Then your whole regiment will find out about this, and I don't think you want that. Where are they? Guns? Knives? Now," she ordered.

His eyes mocked her. "I put them elsewhere before I locked myself in."

"Is this the truth?" she demanded.

"Yes," he said, relenting slightly.

"Then why didn't you answer me when I asked you before if you were armed?"

"I've still got these." He held up his hands before her with a bitter smile.

Her heart sank at the feverish pain in his eyes. "Oh, Damien," she murmured, capturing his hands in her own. His harsh stare wavered as she kissed his hands one by one. "I have also seen your gentleness, my love. You are tender with children, kind to animals, chivalrous toward women, patient with fools. Do not tell me you are a killer. You are a decorated officer of His Majesty's Infantry, and I am proud of you."

"What do you want with me?" he whispered in a shaken tone, his bravado draining away, leaving his face stark with suffering.

"All I want," she said as she laid her hand on his smooth, bare chest, caressing him slowly, "is to take away the pain."

He held very still, tilting his head back slightly as she ran her hand up his shoulder and cupped the side of his neck.

"Where are you, Damien? Portugal? Spain?"

He nodded.

"How do you feel?"

"Angry," he growled.

"Tell me why."

He did not answer for a long moment, fighting with his pride, drawn ever more deeply into his suffering. "You finally get to know a chap, and he gets his bloody head blown off." he said all of a sudden. His voice fell to a faraway whisper. "It isn't fair. I don't know why I'm here anymore, and everything is ugly and cruel."

"The ugliness and cruelty, these make you angry?"

"And sad. So sad I could die." He shook his head slightly. "But there's no time to grieve. Not for me."

"Why?"

"Details, Miranda. Always minutiae. Dead to be buried. Orders from headquarters to march the troops to the next battle. Supplies and materiel's to be gotten and guarded. Wounded to be transported to hospital. Promotions to be recommended to replace the officers I just lost in the field, deserters to be punished, displaced civilians to look after. It never ends. Never."

"And how does that make you feel?"

He stood before her, silent for a long moment as he searched himself. "Relieved. I'd rather work than feel the pain—" He stopped himself with a sharp inhalation. She could feel him holding back, refusing to go any deeper into his memories, yet she knew with an instinctive certainty that he wanted to be rid of it.

"The only way out of the pain is through it, darling," she whispered. "I'm here."

"I don't want any of the ugliness in me to touch you," he breathed, barely audibly.

"I'm strong. I can take it," she answered. "I want you to tell me the very worst thing that happened over there."

"You don't want to know this."

"Tell me anyway. Try me. Trust me."

He looked at her for a long moment, bleary-eyed, then sagged against the wall as his gaze slowly fell. Leaning his back against the wall, he slid down it a few inches, his broad shoulders slumping. "We had a skirmish one evening with French outposts in some high, scrub country. I was just a subaltern, still green. I'd brought this horse over that I owned before Zeus, a real Tattersall beauty, I tell you," he said wistfully, his gaze a thousand miles away. "His name was Presto. He was a good, tall sorrel with four white socks. Sweet-tempered, fast. I rode him for years." He paused, and she noticed that his chin began to tremble. "The skirmish started as nothing, really, but then the gunfire drew a few volleys from their artillery. My horse was hit. I was thrown and knocked unconscious against a rock like a damned fool. When I came to my senses, it was dark, my head was bleeding, and I had been left behind by my men, who had scattered, thinking me dead."

She shook her head with a wordless murmur of sympathy.

"I heard this terrible sound and looked over, and there was Presto. His back legs had been blown off, but he kept trying to get up." He brushed away a tear that rushed down the stark plane of his cheek. "Damned horse kept looking at me like he wanted me to help him. I sat there on the ground and watched him for half an hour before I could bring myself to go over there and shoot him. I had killed at least a dozen men in battle by that time, but I just . . . couldn't work up my nerve." His voice was hollow. "Finally, I went over to him and told him how sorry I was for bringing him to the war when some fop could have been riding him in Hyde Park. Then I put him out of his misery. And he finally died. And so did a part of me, inside, I think. But the rest of me, the outside part, just kept getting up and going on, and sometimes I think it would be best if I put myself out of my misery, too. I'm tired of being in pain." He looked at her like a drowning man. "Oh, God, Miranda, there's so much pain. Make it go away."

"Come back from there, my love. Stay with me," she whispered, pulling him into her arms.

He clenched her to his chest, taking her mouth with a desperate, almost frantic kiss. She stroked his cheek and his hair, trying to ease him, but his every touch told her that his need was too deep for mere kisses. She pressed him gently against the wall, wanting nothing but to give him solace. He leaned his head back, his fingers tangled in her hair as she wove a trail of silken kisses down the elegant curve of his neck to his muscled shoulder, caressing his chest and belly. He let his hands fall to his sides, but his chest rose and fell rapidly as she tilted her head back and met his veiled stare. Slowly, she tugged her dressing gown open.

His eyes flickered in the darkness. She took a step back. Letting her robe fall away behind her, she unbuttoned her white muslin night rail and watched his glittering gaze slide down her chest. She withdrew her arms from the sleeves and pushed the night rail down to her waist, baring her breasts for him. His stare was riveted to her chest. His tongue flicked over his lips.

She stepped toward him and wound her arms
around his neck, hugging him in adoration, clinging
to him, pressing her bare skin to his. Staring into her
eyes, he ran his fingertips slowly up her back from her
waist, tangling his hands in her hair. He held her like
that for a second, his angular face fierce with passion.

Then he lowered his head, closed his eyes, and
claimed her mouth. She yielded, parting her lips to let
him taste of her deeply. His tongue tasted of a sweet
dessert wine that he must have been drinking earlier.
Madeira, perhaps. As he mesmerized her with his
melting kisses, her body trembled against his. Her
heart pounded. She was acutely aware of the strength
in his powerful arms, the steely hardness of muscle beneath his smooth, velvet skin. She prayed he would
not push her away. Then his hand swept up her side
and cupped her breast.

He ended the kiss, his eyes hazy with passion. His
voice was hoarse as he whispered her name. *"Miranda."* He dropped slowly to his knees and closed his
long-lashed eyes, as beautiful as one of God's warrior
angels as he kissed her breast, taking her nipple into
his warm, wet mouth. She moaned with desire, stroking his night-black hair as he suckled her. Somehow
she refrained from confessing how badly she had
yearned for this from that night in the hotel. He
kneaded her backside in his large, strong—deadly—
hands. But instead of fear, the thought of his dangerous power heightened her instinctual excitement
for him. Her arousal climbed.

He pulled her night rail down lower on one side, exploring the curve of her hip; then his mouth left her

breast, his lips swollen with kissing. He skimmed his lips, feather-lightly, across her chest to taste her other breast, petting her belly softly while his tongue licked her nipple to turgid arousal. His hands did not venture beneath her night rail, but he touched her mound of Venus through the thin cloth, lightly caressing her—so unlike Trick, who had always been in such a hurry. Breathless with want, scarely able to believe it was finally happening, she braced herself weakly against his massive shoulders, but did not allow him to sweep her away with pleasure. Not yet.

She cupped his jaw and pulled him again up to kiss her.

"Stay with me, Damien. I know exactly what you need," she murmured. "Concentrate, just concentrate on my hands, my lips. On my touching you."

His breathing deepened and his big body quivered as she kissed his tiny nipple. He touched her hair ever so lightly, pulling it back from her face so he could watch as she kissed her way down his belly, flicking her tongue into his navel. He leaned back weakly against the wall as she went down on her knees, unfastening his black trousers.

"Oh, God, Miranda," he groaned.

"Are you still with me, Damien?" she whispered, freeing his enormous manhood.

"Yes," he rasped. He was rock-solid as she wrapped her fingers around his wieldy silken shaft and stroked him. "Do I have your full attention?" she asked wickedly as she licked her lips in anticipation, glancing up at him.

"I . . . *unh*." He didn't finish the sentence, dropping

his head back helplessly against the wall as she took him into her mouth.

She licked him slowly from base to tip, then stroked him for a moment. "Oh, you've needed this, haven't you?" she whispered.

"Please," he groaned.

She bent her head and obliged him. She held nothing back, taking pleasure in the pleasure she gave, loving him in ferocious tenderness with mouth and hands. She did not know how much time passed, as she reveled in his splendid body, caressing his throbbing shaft firmly and sucked on the smooth head of his cock. To steady himself, he wrapped his hand around one of the clothing pegs that jutted out from the wall above his head. She ran her other hand over the lean, athletic curve of his buttock and teased his tautened scrotum with her fingertips, opening her throat to receive him as he thrust more deeply into her mouth. He drew his breath in sharply when she raked his sculpted stomach with her nails. His groans clamped down into hard, primal grunts that came ever more quickly. Her jaw ached, thrust open wide by his frenzy. He ravished her lips. She could feel him pulsating against her tongue; she stroked him harder, faster with her hand as he swelled so large she could barely get her fingers around him.

"Miranda, oh, God, darling, you must stop," he panted, but she ignored him, pressing his backside to keep him from pulling away. She was delirious with passion and could not be satisfied until he was spent; her greedy insistence drove him over the edge. He exploded in her mouth, a sumptuous feast of virility, his hot seed coursing down the back of her throat. Her body was afire. Spasms of pleasure heaved through her woman's core as she drank him down with each mighty pulsation, consuming every salty, creamy drop of his warrior's potency.

Drunk with him, she uncurled her hand from around his still-hard member and rested her forehead against his flat abdomen. He gripped her shoulders and bent down over her, trembling. He kissed the top of her head and draped his arms around her, encircling her. She nestled her face against his sleek body. "Oh, Damien, I'm so in love with you," she panted, still shaking and breathless with passion. "I can't help myself. I love you now and I always will."

Racked by the exquisite pain of her love, she glanced up at his face, trying to read him. His beautiful mouth was slack, his eyes sensual and heavy-lidded, but the wildness had ebbed from their gray depths, and his gaze was tender.

Tilting her chin upward with his fingertips, Damien slowly kissed her eyelids and the tip of her nose, cuddling her a little; then he lifted her, sweeping her up in his powerful arms. He brushed the tip of his nose against her cheek, nuzzling her, as he carried her into his dimly-lit bedchamber. He placed her gently upon his high, chilly bed then turned and walked away. She reached toward him anxiously.

"Where are you going? Won't you please say something?"

"Drink?" he offered softly, glancing over his shoulder at her from across the room as he poured two glasses of the sweet Madeira wine. He brought them over and gave her one, then clinked his goblet against hers with an intimate half smile. He lowered his lashes in knowing silence as she accepted the wine and took a sip, the honeyed flavor washing down the musky taste of him.

He sat down beside her and began stroking her hair, his gaze following his hand. Her heart thumped nervously in her chest as she sipped her wine and waited for him to say something, anything, in reply to her desperate confession.

"I owe you an apology," he whispered. Lifting her hand from her lap, he kissed it.

"What for?" she asked in surprise.

"I was cruel to you in the stable in my effort to drive you away."

Flinching slightly at the reminder, she looked away from his steady, penetrating stare. "You merely spoke the truth."

He shook his head. "No, only a part of it."

"You mean the fact that you hid it from me that you, too, were born on the wrong side of the blanket? I can hardly mind that. I know how embarrassing it is. I was angry when I first found out, but not anymore. I could never stay angry at you," she whispered, melting as she stole a glance at him.

He wrapped his arm around her shoulders, kissing her forehead. "I wasn't speaking of that." He paused, letting out a small sigh against her brow. "Ah, Miranda. Driving you away that night was the very last thing I wanted to do."

Her lips trembled as she swept her lashes upward, looking into his eyes. "What did you want to do?"

"This." He touched her face, staring into her eyes; then he tilted his head, and kissed her. The slow, caressing contact of his lips on hers dizzied her. Her heart hammered wildly as his tongue entered her mouth, exploring, stroking. She reached her arms around his neck, her body going soft and yielding as he laid her down gently on the bed and eased partly atop her.

When he pulled back a small space a few minutes later and gazed at her, there was a light shining in his eyes that she had never seen before, and a bemused smile on his lips.

"What is it?" she asked.

"Having you in my arms feels even better than I remembered. You're so soft, so warm."

"Oh, Damien," she sighed, her toes curling with pleasure at his doting gaze, but then her expression sobered. "I can't let you make love to me, you know. You're not ready for that yet and if you're not ready, I'm not ready. You weren't expecting any of this and I want you to have choices, as you once said to me."

"God, you are a sweet, lovely creature," he murmured, searching her face with a rather love-struck gaze. "Very well, my darling." He ran his hand down her body. "I shall merely have to pleasure you without the deflowering."

"Mmm," she purred, shifting restlessly under his gliding touch.

"Do you trust me?"

"Completely."

"Spread your legs," he whispered, his eyes turning a beautiful, mysterious color of smoky gray.

He helped her to obey his command, pressing her bent knees apart gently. Her breath caught with rising excitement and unsatisfied longing as he brushed the hem of her night rail up over her hips. He ran his hand along the inside of her thigh, up and down; his touch was so warm, so soothing. She licked her lips, feeling herself grow wet again with anticipation. As he stroked her legs, he gazed as though spellbound at her pink, dew-slicked womanhood. He slipped his thick, strong fingers into her wet passage for a moment, resting his thumb on her mound.

"I could never let another man have you, Miranda," he whispered. "That is the truth of it. I would kill anyone who tried to take you from me."

"Damien," she gasped, shivering with want, dying for him, but he withdrew his hand and lifted it to his lips, slowly licking the taste of her from his finger.

She watched him in hazy-eyed longing. This was definitely not Trick's way, she thought; then all recollection of her former beau dissolved as Damien lay down beside her and kissed her again and again, dizzying her senses and her heart with his tenderness. He began to move lower, but she held him around his neck to keep him near, moaning softly against his cheek, arching against him as he pleasured her with slow, deep caresses.

"Look at me," he whispered as she neared her climax.

She dragged her eyes open. Panting and weak, enervated with the rising pleasure, she held his stormy stare as her control dissolved, letting him gaze into her eyes, into her very spirit as she surrendered to his touch. He must have seen her helpless adoration of him shining in her eyes, for anguished sweetness flitted over his face and he lowered his mouth to hers, capturing her gasps on his tongue.

"So beautiful, my wild, red rose," he whispered as he gathered her into his arms. He sat against the headboard, holding her to him, stroking her hair. Lying, spent, against his bare chest, his muscled arms wrapped around her, Miranda gradually realized that the battlelike sounds in the distance had gone quiet. "I'm sorry you have suffered so, Damien," she said pensively after a moment. "But now perhaps you'll see that you don't have to face the pain alone. It's easier when there's someone by your side who loves you and cares for you."

He squeezed her more tightly and kissed her brow. "You're very good for me, my girl," he whispered. "Do you know that?"

"I am, aren't I?" she agreed, pulling back to smile wryly at him, joy sparkling in her eyes.

"Rascal," he scolded with a chuckle.

"You're good for me, too, Damien," she sighed, snuggling against him in contentment. "Maybe Uncle Jason knew we would be good for each other."

"Maybe so , Miranda," he echoed softly. "Maybe so."

The next day, Damien took out the box of papers that Jason Sherbrooke had left behind among his personal effects and spent the whole afternoon, in the painstaking process of sorting through the major's letters and bank receipts, creditors' bills and gambling IOUs, trying to figure out exactly how Jason had spent Miranda's inheritance money. Lucien had insisted on the importance of unearthing this piece of information. Lucien, meanwhile, was slowly but surely uncovering the identities of the Seven Dials' landlords, though the process of doing so, he reported, was akin to a great shell game, one he was playing most delicately so that the guilty party would not find out that someone was making inquiries.

In the middle of checking the sum on the bill from Jason's boot maker, Damien once more caught himself daydreaming. He cast the bill of sale aside, sighing to realize he'd have to do that one over. He took a short break, lifting his cup of coffee to his lips, then grimaced. It had gone cold. Lord, his mind must have wandered right out the window while he had been sitting here, he thought. That had been happening a lot since New Year's Eve. . . .

Ah, but he had never been in love before. The thought of his luscious ward made his nerve-endings tingle with odd, quivery sensations and left him rather breathless, his heart racing with crazed joy. He was still a little shocked at what had happened last night, but he supposed he should have realized it was only a matter of time before Miranda splintered the barriers he had tried to raise between them. And when at last she had, bursting into his darkness like an angel of light to rescue him from his demons, he had been unable to resist her. Almost as if by magic, she had made everything all right. She had pleasured him until he was empty, then had sung him softly to sleep at the end of their glorious night together, sending him to dreamland with whispered lullabies and caresses on his hair. Her beautiful face was the last thing he had seen before he had drifted off, sated and peaceful down into his very soul. Now he wanted nothing but to surrender everything to her. He would marry her, of course. It was what he wanted as well as the only honorable thing to do.

It was a new year, a new world free of war, and he knew it was time to make a new life. But he had to be sure that he was cleansed of the frightening urges he had felt before she had come into his room, that he was fit to take a wife.

Just then, Mr. Walsh broke into his thoughts as he marched into the library and gave him a bow. "Pardon, sir. Lord Hubert and his son, Mr. Crispin Sherbrooke, are here to see you. Are you at home?"

*Algernon and Crispin?* he thought, furrowing his brow as he nodded. "I will see them. Escort them to the drawing room, please. I'll be right there."

"Very good, sir."

Damien set Jason's papers aside and abandoned his cold coffee, striding into the drawing room a few minutes later. Crispin shook his hand enthusiastically, but the straitlaced, unsmiling viscount sufficed with a cool bow.

"Winterley."

"Hubert," he replied with a nod. "Have a seat, gentlemen," he offered, gesturing toward the furniture in the center of the salon.

Crispin swung down onto a cavalry chair off to the

side, his legs sprawled over the armless corners. Algernon lowered himself to the couch with considerably more ceremony. Damien took a seat in the wing chair across from them. He sat back, crossing one knee over the other, rested his elbows on the chair arms, and waited with a lordly stare over his steepled fingers for them to state the purpose of their visit.

It was only out of respect for Miranda that he received them at all, but they did not appear to realize that. Did they expect his friendship? he wondered. Surely not. Perhaps his ward was willing to forgive her kin for ignoring her all those years, but he was not.

"Well, then, I understand you military chaps are not much for small talk, so I shall come straight to the point," Algernon said, giving him a bland, artificial smile.

Crispin tittered nervously like a hapless cherub, while Damien raised his eyebrows with an arrogant stare.

"My son and I are here because, you see, Winterley, we would like to make it up to Miss FitzHubert for our—well, let us not mince words—neglectful treatment of her in days gone by."

"Ah, yes, when you left her to rot in Yardley, you mean." He matched the viscount's bland aloof smile with one of his own.

Lord Hubert dropped his gaze to the floor and nodded in chagrin, the very picture of contrition, but no brother of Lucien Knight could hear such smooth talk and fail to realize that someone was trying to finesse him.

"Ahem, yes. Well, what, with her mother's reputation, it's just that we did not grasp the quality of the girl herself. We did not wish to endanger the reputations of our own daughters by association. I'm sure you understand."

"Hmm," Damien said, keeping his tone noncommittal. *Why, these sons of bitches.* "What did you have in mind for her in terms of reparations?" He supposed grudgingly that if they wanted to give a formal reception or ball for Miranda, he could allow that.

Algernon glanced at Crispin, whose cheeks turned red. The lad jumped to his feet and took a step forward.

"Um, my lord," he said, clearing his throat. He clasped his hands behind his back like a schoolboy reciting a bit of Petrarch from memory. "Since I have met my fair cousin, all other young ladies hold no interest for me whatsoever."

"Really," Damien said mildly.

"Yes, my lord. I hold Miss FitzHubert in the very highest esteem. She is as spirited and clever as she is lovely. We get on quite well together. I do believe she's fond of me. She says I make her laugh, and I do. And she makes me laugh, a-all the time," he stammered, coloring again. Damien's eyes narrowed in a quelling stare. Crispin paused. "She's not like any of the other young ladies at all."

"No, she's not."

The lad cast a quick glance at his father, who gave him a nod of encouragement. Crispin clenched and unclenched his fists a few times by his sides, as though working up his courage. Damien stared at him intently, offering nothing.

"I have my father's blessing to offer for her. I now

seek your permission, sir, to ask for Miss FitzHubert's hand in marriage."

Damien tapped his lips for a moment, incensed. He chose his words carefully, then shrugged and looked up at the lad. "No."

Crispin's china-blue eyes widened. "My lord?"

"Winterley?" Algernon demanded.

"Over my dead body." He swept to his feet and sauntered toward Crispin, glaring at him as though he were a recalcitrant new recruit. "My ward will never marry a spineless boy who cannot undertake a man's business unless he brings his parent to help him along. If you cannot even propose without your papa looking over your shoulder, how can I possibly trust you to take care of my ward? You make her laugh, you say? Aye, with you as her husband, you'll laugh yourselves hungry, laugh yourselves homeless, laugh yourself right into debtor's prison," he finished vehemently.

Crispin gasped in affront. "I say!"

His father attempted to intervene with oily finesse. "Lord Winterley, we are a family of means. There is no need to grow insulting."

"I *am* insulted by this offer," he replied. "It is disgraceful after the way you've treated her."

"We wish to make amends. Isn't that clear? She is an orphan, and we are her kin. We are trying to do our Christian duty by her."

"And where have your morals been for the past nineteen years?" he asked sharply, pointing to Crispin. "Your son is a spoiled fop who only wants Miranda because she is the toast of the moment—"

"That is not true," the lad cried. "I care for her!"

"Yes, it is; no, you don't; and do not interrupt me again, Mr. Sherbrooke. You, sir," he said to the father, "have created this man-boy by indulging his every whim. He wouldn't last a day in my regiment. Perhaps in a month or two I could make a man of him, but you shall not be able to buy this particular bauble for your little heir. Even if Miranda wished the match, which I know she does not, I would never consent to it after the shameful way your family has treated her."

Algernon stared assessingly into his eyes. "You make your point most passionately, my lord. Perhaps the great Winterley desires to keep my niece for himself."

Damien lifted his chin. "Get out of this house."

"Gladly," Algernon said. "Come along, Crispin."

The boy sent Damien a glare of humiliated rage and went storming out, his father walking at a stately pace after him. Damien was surprised to find himself trembling with anger and very much in need of his pretty ward's soothing company.

The whole carriage ride home, Crispin prated in fury about Winterley's intolerable arrogance, bad grace, and ill temper, while Algernon sat in enraged silence, his hand white-knuckled on the head of his showy walking cane.

"I don't understand!" Crispin fumed. "I did it perfectly. I spoke it exactly as we rehearsed. Did you hear how he insulted me? I had half a mind to call him out!"

"Don't be a fool." Algernon flicked a scornful look at his son.

"Can you believe his outrageous possessiveness

over Miranda? Do you really suppose there is something going on between the two of them? It's not natural, the way he keeps her locked in that house all the time—"

"He has to bring her back out into Society sometime," he answered impassively, watching the city roll by out the carriage window.

"Do you really think he is angling for her himself?"

"He need not 'angle' if he wants her, you fool. He is her guardian. He can do with her whatever he likes. But, no, Winterley might want her, but firstly, he is obsessed with honor. For Jason's sake, he would never touch her because he knows he would never marry her. To wed such a woman—impoverished, a bastard— would be madness for a man of his rank."

Crispin sighed disgustedly as their carriage halted. They both climbed out and went up the front steps into the entrance hall. Crispin turned to him wearily.

"What do we do now, Father?"

"Simple," he answered, handing off his cane and gloves to his butler. He gave his son a silencing look until the servant had withdrawn; then he lowered his voice. "You must wait for the next time he brings her into Society and simply arrange to be found with the girl in a compromising position. Then Winterley will have to approve the match or Miranda will be disgraced."

"You want me to compromise her—deliberately?" Crispin asked, wrinkling his aristocratic nose.

"That is what I just said, is it not?"

Crispin stared at him for a long moment. "I cannot do that, Father."

Algernon lifted his chin. "I beg your pardon, Sir?"

"Miranda is my friend. She is a sweet, trusting young lady. It would be dishonorable to us both—"

Before he could complete the sentence, Algernon hauled back and punched Crispin across the face as hard as he could. His son went stumbling across the entrance hall and sprawled on his rear end with a stunned look. He raised his pampered fingertips to touch the trickle of blood on the corner of his mouth, then looked at his father in frightened astonishment.

Algernon strode toward him and leaned down into his face. "You ungrateful, stinking whelp. Don't you dare contradict me. You're the reason I'm in this predicament, but I have had my fill of you, sir! Winterley was right, you know. You're nothing but a parasite. Now, you will do as I have told you. Get her alone, tear her clothing, make her scream, if you wish—"

"Father, I cannot believe you wish me to carry out such a vile bit of business!"

"If you argue, so help me, Crispin, I will disown you."

"But Winterley will kill me if I do it!"

"And I will kill you if you don't." He took in his son's look of horror with a bitter smile. "You think you are finer than me with your dandyish ways. Oh, you are just like your Uncle Richard, but let me tell you something, my pretty fellow: I got rid of him and your brave Uncle Jason, to boot, and if you cross me, I will do the same to you." He straightened up and kicked his son in the stomach for good measure.

As Crispin grunted with pain, Algernon stepped over his curled-up body and went into his office across the way, slamming the door behind him.

# ≈ CHAPTER ≈
# THIRTEEN

Damien and Miranda returned to Holland House to attend the baroness's Twelfth Night Ball one week later. It was the grand finale of the winter social season. After Twelfth Night, the Christmas decorations would be taken down from all the houses, Parliament would begin sessions again, and life would return to the workaday world. It would be a long, gray, dreary wait for spring, when the social whirl would start anew.

Miranda gazed across the ballroom at Damien, where he stood chatting with some of his acquaintances, a glass of wine in one hand, the other thrust boyishly into his pocket. He had worn civilian clothing this evening, one small but important outward sign that he was making an effort to let go of his old army life. In his formal black tailcoat and white brocade waistcoat, he was dressed so similarly to Lucien that only a handful of people could tell them apart, a fact the twins seemed to find tremendously diverting.

With a sigh of lovelorn misery, she tore her stare away before anyone noticed her ogling the beautiful man.

One question had obsessed her for the past seven

days and seven nights: *What is Damien going to do?*
He was a strong man of few words, but, Lord, how
she wished he would say what he was thinking and
feeling, for her very fate was in his hands. The matter
rested with him now. She had done all she could to
prove her case, that they were better together than either of them was apart. Penniless, illegitimate, she
knew she was unsuitable for a man of his rank and
consequence. That was why she had denied him the
full consummation of their passion—she had left him
a way out if he chose to take it. She would not force
her honor-bound guardian into marrying her if he did
not want to, but she was certain that no other woman
could ever love him as fiercely as she did. Surely that
counted for something. His silence and his delaying
made her anxious because if he planned on marrying
her, shouldn't he have said something by now? Still,
she was determined to be patient until he was ready to
make his decision about her, and, she told herself, if he
chose not to have her in his life, somehow she would
find the strength to accept that.

Shrugging off her nagging uncertainty, she turned
her attention to the festivities in progress around her.
Tonight, all she wanted was to dance and to laugh, to
enjoy her new friends, and to play the silly, traditional
Twelfth Night games, forgetting her cares in merriment.

Mingling among the guests, greeting friends throughout the room, she caught sight of her cousin, Crispin,
looking very glum. She knew that he and his father
had come to Knight House and had proposed a match
between herself and Crispin, but Damien had told

her that he had soundly refused them on the grounds of their past treatment of her. Knowing how harsh her guardian could be when his protective instincts were riled, she was anxious to make sure that Crispin was not hurt or angry at her, that they were still friends.

It was absurd of him to have proposed in the first place, she thought, as she made her way toward him through the ballroom. She was sure he had merely done it on a whim, or perhaps because he worried that no one else would want her because of illegitimacy. He was rather silly, but he was not an unkind lad and Miranda knew that he was indeed fond of her. She plucked two wineglasses off the tray of a passing waiter and brought them over to him, offering one as a peace offering.

He gave her a sulky look but accepted it, clinking her glass with his own. "What are you doing in public?" he asked.

"What do you mean?"

"Winterley locks you away like you are his private treasure. Why won't he share you with the rest of the world?" he whined. "What do the two of you do together, locked up in that house day after day?"

"Wouldn't you like to know?" she drawled, giving him a sly, teasing smile.

"What, are you in love with him?" he cried indignantly.

"My guardian? Heavens, no. Crispin, tell me you are not pouting."

"I am pouting," he retorted. "And you know deuced

well why. May we speak of this in private? It's embarrassing enough without anyone overhearing about how my pretty cousin jilted me."

She smacked him with her folded fan. "Don't be daft, I didn't jilt you. My guardian did. I thought it was sweet of you."

"*He* didn't."

"I know," she said, taking his arm as they strolled down the same hallway she had walked down with Damien at the last ball. "But, there, there, my dear, think of it. We would never have suited." She tried to cajole a smile out of him. "I would have bossed you around constantly until you fled into the arms of some mistress, and it all would have been a most unpleasant row. This way, we shall always be friends."

"Aha, friends. In that case, I take it that he was right. Even if I had been granted permission to ask you, you would have given me the jilt."

"Not necessarily," she chided, trying to soften the blow. Heavens, he seemed genuinely put out. Of course, he was very spoiled and coddled, used to getting his way. "It all depends."

"On what?" he demanded, opening a side door and sauntering into a dimly lit salon.

Miranda leaned in the doorway. "On how prettily you would have asked me, of course. Would you have complimented my eyes, for example? Waxed poetic on the roses of my cheeks?"

"How could I not? And the stygian splendor of your hair, your alabaster forehead, fine nose, regal chin, et cetera, on down to your lovely ankles—"

"You have never seen my ankles, coz," she interrupted, swirling her wine jauntily in the glass.

"I can imagine," he said with a half smile.

"Don't," she said flatly.

"Ah, Miranda, you silly creature." He set his glass down on the small table by the couch and hooked his thumbs into his waistcoat, shaking his head as he gazed at her. "You make me smile just thinking of you."

She returned his stare for a long moment, studying him. There was a troubled look behind his blue eyes. "Is something wrong? Have you been honest with me? You are upset, aren't you?"

"No, it's not that." He came and took her hands, drawing her farther into the room.

"What, then, my dear boy?"

"I am not a boy," he murmured.

"Crispin—"

He shoved the door closed with one hand and slipped the other around her waist. "Kiss me, Miranda. Just once, let me taste your lips."

"Don't be an idiot."

"I've dreamed of their sweetness."

"For heaven's sake, Crispin! If I've given you the wrong impression, I am sorry—"

"I want you, Miranda."

"Stop it! Crispin, you are beginning to scare me."

"Good," he whispered, grasping the edge of her gown as though he meant to rip it off of her. "Perhaps then you'll take me seriously."

"Crispin!" Her heart beating frantically, she clutched the fabric to stop him from ripping it, knowing that if he succeeded, it meant her ruin. Her fragile reputation would never survive it. With her mother's scarlet past, she knew all of Society was watching and waiting for some scandalous folly to overtake her. Furiously unwilling to taint the Knight family with scandal, she held on fast to the satin, pushing her amorous cousin away with her other hand.

He strained toward her, forcibly trying to kiss her. "I will have you, my sweet girl," he panted.

"Stop this indecency!" She let go of her gown and slapped him across the face with a resounding *crack*.

"That wasn't very smart," he said through gritted teeth, snaking his other arm around her, pinning her wrist up behind her back. He swooped his mouth down violently onto hers, bruising her lips against her teeth with the urgent force of his kiss just as the door banged open explosively.

In the next instant, Damien was between them, hauling Crispin back by his collar. Enraged, Crispin took a swing at him. Miranda gasped, but Damien caught Crispin's fist in his white-gloved hand in mid-air and held it in an iron grip, glaring at him.

"Damien, no!" she cried, terrified that he would kill him on the spot. He glanced blackly at her, saw for himself that she was only a bit tousled, not harmed; then his stare returned to her cousin.

"You spoiled little shit." He knocked Crispin to the floor, knocking his legs out from under him with a sweeping kick. He swept the fire poker out of its holder and held the sharpened tip of it to Crispin's throat like a sword. "This is your final warning, laddie. Come near her again and you die." Then his glance homed in on Miranda for the first time seemingly in days. "Let's get out of here," he said tautly.

She drew in her breath, her heart lifting like a bird on the wing. She gave a swift nod, ready to follow him anywhere.

Algernon knew something had gone wrong. He felt it in his bones even before Crispin finally came home hours later, drunk and insolent, his cravat hanging open around his neck.

"Where the hell have you been?" he demanded.

"At my club."

"You failed."

"I hate you for making me do that," Crispin said, glaring at him. "I hate myself for being a part of it. Let it go, Father. They are in love with each other."

"What?" he asked sharply, with a galling twinge of betrayal in his heart, the memory still fresh of how Miranda's beautiful mother had chosen his brother over him. Now it seemed the daughter had chosen Winterley over his son, and somehow that brought back the rage and indignation he had suffered all those years ago.

"For God's sake," Crispin was saying, "forget the money. Let the two of them be."

Algernon shook his head in disgust at his son's drunken sentimentality and walked away from him across his office. "Every time I think I have plumbed your depths, you sink lower."

"At least I have never stooped to fratricide," Crispin said softly.

Algernon turned to him, tempted to draw his pistol

on him, but he shrugged off the urge. "What happened? How do you know they are in love?"

"I just know. I know Miranda. I had her alone; then Winterley barged in and would have beaten me senseless if she hadn't told him not to. He obeys her as a man only obeys the woman he worships."

"Is that so?" he murmured to himself, stroking his chin. "What happened then?"

"They left the party."

"Alone?"

"I think so. It was rather hard to tell from where I had been knocked onto the floor," he muttered in sarcasm, pouring himself a drink.

Egann burst in the front door at that moment and hurried into his office. "Master! Master!"

"What is it?" He shut the door quickly behind his servant.

Egann bobbed a bow, his voice breathless with his haste. "I was in the carriage watching Knight House, just as you ordered, when I saw Lord Winterley and Miss FitzHubert come back from the ball, then leave again at once in the sleigh."

"Did you follow them?"

He nodded eagerly. "I followed them to the edge of town. They went out onto the Bath Road."

Algernon's mind whirled. By God, was Crispin right? Were they running off together, eloping? He knew that Winterley's country seat lay to the west, in Berkshire, not far, he believed, from Windsor Castle, if memory served. It had been in all the papers when Parliament had bestowed the earl's title and lands on him this past November.

If they married, Miranda's fortune would become Winterley's property by law.

"I've got to stop them," he said aloud, almost to himself.

"Father," Crispin pleaded, turning to him.

"Shut up," he ground out. He turned and began pacing, racking his brain for one last-ditch solution. His four thugs had failed; Egann had failed; Crispin had failed. Now it was clearly time for him to take matters into his own hands. He had no hope, of course, of battling the likes of Winterley man-to-man, but he surmised that the rest of the Raptor gang would certainly relish the chance to take revenge on the man who had slaughtered their four mates up in Birmingham.

A cruel smile flicked over Algernon's mouth. He still knew where to find those Cockney scum. Yes, he mused, he'd let the so-called Raptors deal with Winterley, but as for his luscious little niece, he'd take care of her personally. He would enjoy the favors that her mother had so cruelly denied him. Then he would cut her pretty throat.

He pushed Crispin out of his way and stalked out to the entrance hall, throwing on his greatcoat as he strode out into the black, chilly night.

There was a magical quality to their escape that night, the high, full moon glittering on the packed snow as the fast, light sleigh flew behind the galloping horses, whisking almost soundlessly over the white highway that stretched for miles ahead of them in a corridor between broad, snowcapped hills and whispering woods. She sat near him on the driver's seat, sharing her warmth beneath the lap rug, but they did not speak. They did not need to. They *knew*.

Half standing in the driver's seat, his greatcoat billowing behind him, he drove the horses on with vigor, miles and miles of the Bath Road falling away beneath them while the wind stung his cheeks. His mood was strange: a fierce joy infused with all the power of his will, and an aching to be one with her always. The moment he had seen Crispin Sherbrooke trying to kiss Miranda, absolute, unflinching conviction had exploded within him, blowing all his uncertainty and hesitation of the past few days to smithereens. She would not wait forever for him to make his move, nor should she have to, after all that she had done for him. She had been steadfast, reaching out to him again and again, coming back to hold out another chance for him to take her hand each time he had shoved her away. Her patience had gentled him just like a wild horse. He glanced at her to make sure she was all right, bundled in her coat and scarf, a few curls flying in the wind behind her, beneath her warm, velvet bonnet. She was keeping her hands warm in the giant fur muff that Alec had given her. She gave him a tremulous smile when he looked at her. Aye, she knew, he thought, turning forward again with a smile, his body thrilling to her nearness.

He had not forgotten the danger to her, of course, though it had not reared its ugly head since the day of her riding "accident." Just to be safe, he was well armed, but he was not worried because they had slipped away under the cover of darkness, telling no one that they were leaving or where they were going.

Thank God Miranda was not the sort of woman who needed an entourage of servants to accompany her everywhere she went, he thought. He wanted to be totally alone with her to tell her how he felt.

It was a clear night, not overly frigid. The road was good, there was no traffic to slow them, and the full moon gave them light. Thus it took them only four hours to traverse the forty miles from London, past the busy town of Maidenhead, to the village of Littlewick Green. He turned north and drove another two and a half miles, arriving at last at the snowy drive of Bayley House. Damien slowed the horses to a trot as they approached the large, ramshackle house. He sighed to himself as he drew the team to a halt. It still looked like a mausoleum, gleaming in the silvered darkness.

He looped the reins around the holder and turned to her. She was staring at his house.

He waved a vague gesture at the mansion. "Perhaps you cannot tell from here, but it's rather run down. It's in a sorry state on the inside. Now that I've warned you, would you like to go in?"

She turned to him with great, soulful eyes. "Damien, I cannot stand another second of this suspense. I'm not budging from this seat until you tell me why you've brought me here."

He laughed softly, taken aback by her imploring tone. "Will you take off your bonnet? I want to see your face in the moonlight."

She withdrew her gloved hands from the muff, but

her fingers must have been trembling with her discomfiture. She fumbled with the ribbons. He smiled softly and helped her with them. She took off her hat, whose large brim had shadowed her face. Likewise, he took off his top hat and flicked it into the seat behind them with the baskets of food stores he had hastily packed from the kitchen pantry at Knight House.

Slyly, he reached his hand into the nearest hamper and pulled out a crimson rose that he had swiped from the bouquet in the entrance hall.

He trailed the petals down her cheek, then gave it to her, holding her starry-eyed gaze. Her skin was alabaster in the moon's white glow; her hair was as dark as shadows. The mother-of-pearl combs in the dark, silky mass of her tresses winked in the illumination of a moonbeam. Miranda swallowed hard, staring somberly at him. He succumbed to a faint smile and wondered if she had any idea how adorable she was even when she wasn't trying.

"Yes?" she prodded him.

"So impatient," he chided, running his fingertips along her arm.

"I've been exceedingly patient. For me, anyway."

"You have." He cupped her cheek in his leather-gloved hand. "I thank you for it."

"Please," she squeaked, tears clouding her eyes. "Just say it, one way or the other, Damien. Please just tell me—"

"I love you," he whispered. "I love you, Miranda."

She sobbed and started toward him, but he laid his fingertip over her lips, hushing her until he was finished.

"That is why I have decided to turn away all of your suitors, every last one: Ollie, Nigel, Crispin, even Griff. I have decided to keep you for myself. I am sorry if you object, but you see, I cannot do without you. You silly girl, why are you crying?"

She couldn't seem to speak. Tears streamed down her cheeks like liquid diamonds in the moonlight, and she was staring at him like she would die of love; her face so ardent, so lovely that it summoned up answering tears in him, too, as though the ice in the core of him was melting so fast that it welled up from his very eyes. "I have loved you from the moment you strode into Mr. Reed's office in your white gloves and schoolgirl braids, your chin up high, ready to take on the world," he murmured. "I loved you when you tricked those witless lads at the hotel trying to escape me—of all men!"

"I'm sorry about that," she slipped out with a trembling, penitent smile through her tears.

"Don't be, my red rose. You could never do anything that requires an apology, and even if you did, I would forgive you without your having to ask."

"You would?" she whispered.

"Yes. I loved you riding that fat, ridiculous pony, trying so hard to do everything right just to please me. I loved you faking a sprained ankle to save my pride . . . and I want to love you for the rest of our lives, if you'll have me. Miranda, will you be my wife?"

She launched across the driver's seat, flinging herself into his arms, weeping as she sobbed out, "Yes, yes!" Clinging around his neck, she covered his face in her eager kisses and joyful tears, until he captured her lips with his own.

He could feel her trembling in his arms as she yielded, taking his tongue into her sweet mouth. Her fingertips skimmed his cheek, and she pulled back, desire welling in her eyes.

"Damien, make love to me."

A shock of need coursed through him in response. "Let's go inside."

She nodded.

He closed his eyes and cupped the back of her head, kissing her once more in slow, rich promise before releasing her and jumping down lightly from the sleigh. He helped her down after him and pulled one of the lanterns out of its secure holder, handing it to her.

He quickly led the leader of his four-horse team into the barn, pulling the sleigh behind. He unharnessed them in the barn for the night, leaving them water and hay, then lifted out of the back the baskets of food and the satchels of extra clothes that both of them had brought. His uncomplaining future countess helped him carry the parcels across the open area, up the snowy front stairs, and into the deserted Bayley House.

Inside, the cavernous space was pitch-dark, freezing cold, and silent as a tomb. He took the lantern from her and led the way to the drawing room, where he had left his camp intact by the fireplace. All was just as he had left it on the day Lucien had come to tell him of Jason's death. Even his trusty wood-chopping axe still leaned against the wall. They set all their supplies down. Damien dusted off his hands.

"You have a real eye for decor," Miranda remarked, looking around at the cobwebs and swallows' nests.

He grinned. "Come and hold the light while I get wood to make our fire."

She obeyed, following him back outside. "Do your tenants pay their rents in cordwood?" she asked as he pulled back the oilskin from atop his giant woodpile and took a few logs.

"I chopped it myself."

"Ah, naturally," she answered wryly, looking mystified.

He chuckled, and soon they had a roaring bonfire in the drawing room hearth. It cast a ruddy circle of cheerful light and warmth over his little camp. He moved aside some loose floorboards, uncovering the well-concealed hidey-hole where he kept a store of expensive brandy for when the occasion called, along with some other provisions. Miranda peered curiously into it, then took out his mess kit and poured a draught into his unbreakable tumbler for them to share. Kneeling before the fire, Damien prodded the logs into place with a few final shoves of the fire poker. She came over to stand beside him, offering him the brandy. He took a sip, then looked up as she raked her fingers lovingly through his hair, her touch a summons. He kissed her wrist, desire flaming in his blood, then looked up and passed an assessing glance over her beloved face.

"Are you sure, my darling?" he murmured. "I can wait for our wedding night if you . . ." His voice trailed off hoarsely as she withdrew and drifted languidly to his bedroll, taking off the pale gold ball gown that she was still wearing from Lady Holland's party.

He could wait, he claimed? Who was he fooling? He stared at her, dry-mouthed with reverent awe. Firelight and shadows sculpted her delicate features, but the seriousness of her expression, the intelligence and intensity in her stare, the trust and loyalty in her eyes all bespoke her love for him. He knew that she would never let him down. In a short period of time, this headstrong young woman had become home to him. She understood him with a depth that needed no words and had become more of a companion to him than he had ever expected from a wife. She let down her long, rich, dark-chocolate brown hair and undressed for him by the firelight, all softness and abundant curves, a luminous white goddess with lush, pink nipples and enchantment in her emerald eyes. Letting him have his fill of gazing at her, she lowered herself slowly to the blankets and slid her long legs down into the bedroll, waiting for him between the blankets. He stared at her—mute, transfixed, and still. She held out her hand to him, waiting.

His movements were slow and dreamlike as he stood and went to her.

She tilted her head back, gazing up at him in perfect trust. "Will you always love me, Damien?" she murmured in a sensuous tone.

"Aye," he promised. "Always."

"You will never turn to another?"

"I am yours . . . completely." Taking her hand, he knelt down beside her and gathered her to him, kissing her mouth with savoring depth as her artful fingers plucked at the buttons of his waistcoat and shirt, undressing him. Then her hands were on his skin, running along his arms and shoulders, caressing his sides. Still kissing her, letting her long, thick mane spill through his fingers, he moved into the bedroll with her.

He took the rose that he had given her earlier and trailed it lightly over her skin until she quivered with desire for him. He bent his head, sucking her breast, then stroked her womanhood and found her ready. Her palm grazed his solid flesh, and he moaned softly. Her touch grew more insistent, her kisses ever more hungry. Her skin burned with the heat of her passion as he lay down atop her, feeling her wrap her legs around his hips. He was breathless, his heart slamming in his chest.

"My beloved," he whispered, throbbing with transcendent joy as he found his way to her silken threshold. He had never deflowered a virgin before and took pains to be gentle.

Her arms were around him, her head tipped back, her neck arched. Her black velvet lashes half veiled her eyes, which were glazed with longing as he kissed her throat. Her breasts heaved against his bare chest, and he held her more tenderly than he had ever touched a woman in his life. He ran his fingertips down her cheek and followed them with kisses.

"Oh, Damien," she groaned. "Oh, my love, make me yours . . . *forever*."

He closed his eyes in soul-deep obedience and took her, capturing her sharp gasp of pain on his lips.

"Shh," he whispered. "Shh." With his thumbs, he

wiped away the pair of tears that trickled from the corners of her eyes. He petted her, murmuring love words he had never before dared to utter as he waited for her fertile body to accept him.

"Oo, that hurt," she confessed after a moment, flicking her eyes open to meet his gaze anxiously. She looked very young and, indeed, she was.

He kissed her nose and gave her a sensual smile of reassurance. "Yes, my beauty, but now I'll make it all better."

Her eyes flickered with renewed desire as he ran his hand down her side and touched her between their bodies. Her moan was little more than a murmur of pleasure, but her sinuous movements were an unmistakable invitation. He rose up on his hands above her and rode her endlessly with slow, tender care; she arched beneath him in trembling desire, caressing the flexing muscles of his chest and abdomen, staring hotly into his eyes.

The dancing hearth flames cast the shadows of their lovemaking across the expanse of bare walls and ceiling in the once-elegant drawing room, and as Damien felt his control melting away, he caught a glimpse of future dreams; this house would live again, he thought, for his fiery Miranda would give it new life—color and laughter and music and warmth—all of the rich gifts she had given to him. Then all thought dissolved, great currents of emotion rolling up from the depths of his heart like a river rising. He clutched her to him, lost in kissing her, consuming the sweet cries of her climax as he spilled his seed inside of her body, making her a part of himself irrevocably.

When it was over, he collapsed on her and stayed like that, caressing her cheek and her hair while she held him. They stared in mystical silence into each other's eyes, both overcome by the depth of the passion they shared. At length, they drifted off to sleep, their bodies still entwined.

Algernon and fifteen members of the Raptors gang rode up to Bayley House as the red sun was glimmering on the eastern horizon.

"Surround the house and find them. Remember," he ordered, "no one is to touch the girl. She is mine."

Their swarthy ringleader gave him a surly nod and swung down from his horse, gesturing to the others to do the same.

One remained behind with him while the others darted off, slipping stealthily around the outer walls of the house. Algernon dismounted and jerked a nod to the remaining man to follow him to the front door. Creeping slowly up the front steps, he drew his pistol, then stood well off to the side as he tried the door.

Locked.

His heart pounding, he nodded again to the professional housebreaker next to him. The gang member pulled out a little metal pin from his ridiculous hat, knelt down smoothly, and picked the lock with the dextrous precision of a Swiss watchmaker. Less than a minute later, the thief turned the doorknob without a sound and pulled out a knife, then crept into the manor house ahead of him.

Following him into the tomblike silence of the huge, dilapidated house, Algernon passed a glance over the cobwebby entrance hall with its empty walls and peeling paint. The smell of a smoldering fire hung on the air. It seemed to be coming from somewhere upstairs. He nodded to his accomplice; then they stole silently toward the staircase.

Damien awoke with a start, though he didn't know why. He had not been having a nightmare; he did not think he had heard anything, but wakefulness zoomed into him, calling all of his battle-honed senses onto high alert. Miranda slept peacefully beside him in his bedroll. He was glad they had put on some of their clothes before bedding down for the night, for the vast drawing room had gone cold. The fire was nothing but embers.

An orange-red glow filled the large, arched windows, however, from the rising sun beyond the eastern hillocks.

*There.*

He heard something: an indistinct creaking. He held very still, listening with highly attuned senses. Perhaps it was just one of those noises peculiar to the old house, but he slid out of their warm lovers' nest to go make sure.

He was careful not to disturb Miranda's slumber as he left her alone. Her beauty caught at his heart, but he did not linger, stalking over silently to glance out the window. He drew in his breath at the sight of over a dozen riderless horses on the lawn. He turned his head swiftly, just in time to see two men dart by on the ground beneath his window, gliding toward the back of the house. *Who the hell were they?* He did not stop to ponder the question.

In the next second, he was dragging Miranda out of the bedroll, barely awake.

"They're here. Don't breathe a word," he whispered, half carrying her over to the wall by the main entrance of the drawing room. He ran back over to his camp around the fireplace and grabbed his weapons—pistols, sword, dagger—then returned to her and flattened his back against the wall.

She looked at him in bewilderment, sleep in her eyes. "Who's come?"

"Whoever's after you. We shall find out soon enough who it is, I warrant. Shh."

He slipped his knife silently out of its sheath while she cowered in terror beside him, covering her mouth with her hands. He could hear the men coming down the corridor. There was scarcely time to wonder how their faceless enemy had known they had left Knight House and had come here. The trespassers were closer now; he could hear their creeping steps.

He cocked his head, focusing on discerning the number, weight, and height of the men by their footfalls, gauging their size before he had even clapped eyes on them. He counted two. He knew he had to kill them quietly, or it would bring the rest running. He held his breath as he waited, a terrible thrumming blood lust pounding in his brain. *How dare they storm his house?* He had to protect Miranda. He could feel them getting closer, closer. He flicked his fingers over the hilt of his knife and ticked off the seconds in his mind. *Four, three, two, one.*

*Now.*

He whirled out of his hiding place as they stepped into the drawing room and swung out with the knife, slashing the first man's throat, stabbing the second in the belly with one smooth, dancelike motion. The second one managed to squeeze off his pistol before Damien swooped down and finished him off, but the bullet went wide, slamming up into the ceiling. As a flurry of plaster scattered down on Damien and Miranda, he paused only to wrench the dead man's sleeve up over his forearm. Sure enough, there was the tattoo of the bird of prey with a dagger in its talons. The Raptors. God damn it, what the hell did they want with him now? This was not going to be pleasant.

He reached over and seized Miranda's wrist, pulling her at a run across the drawing room to the place where he had pulled up the floorboards.

"Get down, get down!" He thrust one of his pistols into her hand and shoved her down into the hiding place under the floorboards. Tall as she was, she had to fold herself up to fit. "No matter what happens, stay down there. If anyone sees you, shoot him."

"Damien—"

"Quiet. I love you," he whispered, then fixed the floorboards back over the spot and threw the blankets they had been sleeping in over it to help disguise the breach. He drew his sword and rushed to meet the men who were pounding toward the drawing room from all directions in answer to the gunshot.

In the next moment, he was besieged on all sides as a dozen men crashed into the room, some hurtling in at him through the main entrance, others burst-

ing in through the white double door from the adjoining music room and sweeping up on him from
behind at a run. More plaster fell from the ceiling, and
a window shattered as bullets whizzed through the
drawing room. But miraculously, Damien was not hit.

Having saved his pistol until after they had emptied
theirs, he took cool, level aim at the first thug who
rushed at him with a sword. He squeezed the trigger,
killing the man instantly with a bullet between the
eyes. The others roared with fury and charged him.

He fought two at once with his sword, thrust his
dagger into the neck of another, kicked another man
away just in time to save himself from getting skewered. Another rushed up behind him, and he flipped
the man over his shoulder and drove his sword down
into his heart. While he was fighting for his life against
the gang, he noticed a shadowy movement in the
doorway; then Algernon, Lord Hubert, sauntered into
the room.

Damien's eyes turned red with fury when he saw
him. *He was the one behind all this?* "Hubert!" he
bellowed.

Algernon sent him a thin-lipped smile, but Damien
was unable to go after him, for he had to keep fighting
off the Raptors.

"How positively shocking, Winterley, to find you,
the flower of chivalry, here, debauching my niece."

"Go to hell!" Damien spat, fighting for his life.

"Ah, but then, I suppose you are not to be blamed.
Her mother was a thoroughgoing harlot, after all, and
the apple does not fall far from the tree. What else

could we expect of Fanny Blair's daughter, but to prove a lascivious slut like her mama?"

He let out a roar and drove his attackers back a step with a feint, then had to retreat himself a step or two, blades clanging furiously. Sweat streamed down his face.

The viscount snickered and took an idle stroll around the large drawing room, poking his head into Damien's tent. He gestured at the swarthy thug by his side to check the unused fireplace on the other end of the room. He drifted over to the sole piece of furniture the previous owners had left behind in the room, a great armoire, and opened it, peering inside. Damien knew they were looking for Miranda, and though he had no inkling why they were after her, he felt the full power of his rage rushing into his veins, doubling his determination to protect her.

He cut and slashed at the men who were trying to kill him, inching toward a more advantageous position in the corner of the room so that he would not have to watch his back as well as fight the onslaught in front of him.

"She's not here," the thug grunted, returning to Algernon after having checked the fireplace.

"Oh, she's here somewhere, the little hussy. We'll keep looking."

"You're a dead man, Hubert!" Damien roared after him as Algernon drifted toward the doorway.

"No, Winterley," the viscount replied with a smirk. "You are."

Damien shouted as one of the thugs cut him across

the leg, then bared his teeth and skewered the man on his sword.

It had been an exceedingly rude awakening, and now the floorboards shuddered and reverberated with the commotion as Miranda huddled in her cramped, musty hiding place. It sounded as though a full score of men were attacking her fiancé. She had heard her Uncle Algernon's voice—had heard him insulting her mother's memory. First Crispin had acted so irrationally at the ball, and now her uncle had arrived with an army of ruffians. But why? she wondered, her heart pounding in dread. What the devil was going on?

Damien suddenly let out a harsh, barbaric cry from somewhere above—she knew his voice. The blood drained from her face. Had he just been wounded? She did not know what that cry had meant. She strained to peer through the cracks in the floorboards, but could not see anything because he had covered up her hiding place with the blankets. She could only tell by the thunderous footsteps that he was badly outnumbered. If he had just gotten injured, that put him at an even greater disadvantage.

Her hands sweated with her indecision as she fingered the pistol. He had ordered her to stay here, but surely he had not expected to be beset so viciously. She had to help him. She was afraid, but she steeled herself. By God, as a child, she had watched helplessly while her parents drowned. She was not about to let her future husband die in the very room with her and do nothing to help him. If he was killed, she did not care what happened to her, but there was no reason to

think that was going to happen. Damien had a gift for
battle like the mythical Sir Lancelot, she reasoned,
and she, why, she had this gun.

She was quite certain that she could pull the trigger
if it meant saving her future husband's life. She quelled
the shaking of her hands by sheer dint of will and
rested the gun gingerly to the side, then pressed both
hands slowly against the boards. She moved silently to
avoid alerting the foe to her presence, knowing she
would need the element of surprise.

As she slipped out of her hiding place and reached
back down into the hole for the gun, one of the
hardened-looking thugs attacking Damien noticed
her. The man left Damien entangled with the others
and started toward her, leering. Miranda stood and
brought up the pistol. She trained it on the man's
chest, then looked him in his beady brown eyes. *God,
forgive me,* she thought, then fired.

"What the hell are you doing?" Damien roared at
her as the man dropped to the ground, stone-cold
dead. She had hit him in the heart.

Her fascinated stare zipped from her victim to her
lover. "Helping you, darling." She grabbed the fire
poker in both hands and ran over toward the fray,
cracking one of his assailants as hard as she could on
the back of his skull.

"Good God," Damien panted as the man dropped,
unconscious. "Hand me that, would you?"

She tossed him the fire poker and darted out of
the way as one of the thugs swung his sword at
her. Damien hurled the fire poker like a spear, im-
paling the next thug who came after her. Miranda

grimaced at the bloodcurdling scream; then the ruffian thunked down onto the floor. Damien was immediately embattled with the remaining five, until two broke away from him and stalked toward her. She backed away, glancing anxiously toward her guardian, waiting for him to tell her what to do. He glanced toward her between blows with a look of panic at the danger she was in.

The two, mangy, disreputable-looking brigands tracked her across the drawing room. She broke away from them and darted toward the fireplace, grabbing Damien's wood-chopping axe. Then she whirled to face them, holding them at bay with the big, deadly blade, but they grinned as though they knew she could barely hold the thing steady, it was so heavy. She was forced to take several backward steps as they stalked her through the drawing room.

"Miranda, behind you!" Damien yelled suddenly.

She whirled around and gasped to find her Uncle Algernon stalking up behind her from the adjoining music room. He held out his hands to her.

"Come and give your uncle a kiss, my dear," he said with a sinister smile; then he glanced in irritation at the pair of thugs coming after her. "Finish him," he ordered, pointing to Damien, who was surrounded by a growing pile of corpses.

They grumbled, but returned to face the earl. Uncle Algernon turned to her with an indulgent smile. "Now, then, my pet."

"Stay back!" she warned. "What do you want with me?"

"The same thing I wanted from your mother, *chérie*. When my men are through with your guardian, I shall take the pleasure from you that she denied me."

She swung at him with the axe, but it was so heavy and hard to lift that the blow was wild. He laughed at her.

"What do you know about my mother?" she demanded, shaken by his ruthlessness.

"Only that she made a poor choice when she chose your father over me. There was no future in it."

Miranda stared at him, paling with horror. "What do you mean by that? 'No future'?"

"Well," he said with a shrug.

"You killed them?" she breathed.

"Perhaps, indirectly," he said with a modest smile.

Miranda stood there, her mind reeling, when suddenly another voice broke into her thoughts.

"Father!"

She and her uncle both looked over as Crispin flung into the doorway, his guinea-gold curls tousled, his clothes disheveled. No longer trusting her cousin, Miranda swung back half a step to hold them both off.

"What are you doing here?" Algernon snarled at his son.

"I will not let you go through with this, Father! Call them off of Lord Winterley right now!" He glanced anxiously toward her. "Don't be afraid, Miranda. I don't deserve your forgiveness after my behavior, but I want you to know it was he who put me up to it," he said, nodding toward his father in contempt.

"Why?" she demanded shakily.

"Crispin," the viscount warned through gritted teeth.

His son ignored him. "Because of this." Reaching into his waistcoat, Crispin pulled out an official-looking document and held it toward her. Your inheritance. You're an heiress, Miranda. You've got a fortune worth fifty thousand pounds."

Her jaw dropped as Algernon swung out at Crispin with his dagger. "Traitor!" he bellowed.

Crispin jumped back nimbly out of reach. "It's too late, Father! I'm not going to let you spill more blood. I beg you, end this madness now before anything worse happens. Call your dogs off Winterley! He doesn't deserve it."

"Crispin, your father has just been boasting about killing my parents," Miranda said grimly, moving toward her uncle with the axe as Algernon slashed again at her cousin. "Were you aware of that?"

"Yes, he revealed it when he threatened my life as well if I refused to try to compromise you. And there's something else: It was he who killed our Uncle Jason. Agh!" Crispin cried as the knife made contact, slicing him open across his chest. He looked down at himself in horror, then at his sire. "Father, you have killed me!" he said in disbelief.

"Crispin!" Miranda screamed.

At that moment, Damien thrust off his final, dying adversary and stalked over the corpses of the gang, crossing the room toward them with kingly wrath in his eyes. He was bloodied and covered in sweat, but his eyes glowed silver with righteous fury. "You're mine now, Hubert. Get away from Miranda—"

"No," Crispin cried. Before he could stop him, Algernon swooped down and swiped the pistol that Crispin had tucked into the waistband of his trousers.

The viscount swept to his feet again, and Miranda heard him cock the gun with lethal intent as he took aim at Damien.

Her eyes widened. *Her mother. Her father. Uncle Jason.* Now he would shoot down her beloved in cold blood. She did not think. Something far more primal than reason overtook her. She lifted the axe with all her strength, a savage battle cry on her lips, and swung it on an upward angle like the warrior queen Boudicca, slamming it into her murderous uncle's middle. It stuck there, folding him forward as the bullet whizzed over Damien's head.

Algernon slumped to his knees and fell facedown on top of the axe. Miranda stared at what she had just done, disbelieving she had done it, while Crispin stammered wordlessly at the sight.

Then Damien came and wrapped his arms around her. She could feel him trembling after his exertions, but she could only stare at the spreading pool of blood pouring out from underneath her uncle.

"Is he dead?" Crispin whispered.

"He's dead," Damien panted, then glanced at Miranda. "Are you all right?"

"I—I—I'm sorry. I didn't—"

He clasped her around her waist and kissed her forehead, turning her away from the sight. "You had to. You saved my life. Everything's going to be all right, sweeting. Pay attention, now. Look at me."

She did, ignoring her odd, vague dizziness at the

nearness of so many dead men. She stared at his mouth, doing her best to focus her mind entirely on his words.

"Get the bandages from the trunk inside my tent," he ordered calmly. "We've got to bind your cousin's wounds before he loses any more blood. Crispin— Lord Hubert?" he addressed the young man with a grim, meaningful stare.

"Yes, sir?" he answered weakly.

"Off with your coat and shirt. Let's see how badly he got you." He stooped down and picked up the folded account papers, handing them slowly to Miranda before they were tainted by the spreading pool of blood. "Now, then, we are going to tell the authorities that we all four came into Bayley House together and found it occupied by trespassers, who attacked us. Algernon died fighting them. Do you understand?"

"Yes, my lord," Crispin murmured, slowly pulling off his coat. His face was ashen.

"Good." Damien turned to Miranda. "Bandages, angel," he reminded her softly.

She shook off her daze and ran to do as he said.

# ≒ CHAPTER ≒ FOURTEEN

They were married three weeks later on the last Sunday in January. Flurries dusted the Wren steeple, which jutted up into the gray sky from the heart of the fashionable Mayfair district. Inside, the flower girl, little Amy Perkins from Yardley School, scattered rose petals before Miranda as she proceeded down the aisle on the arm of the duke of Hawkscliffe, who had kindly offered to give her away. Lizzie Carlisle followed, minding the long train of Miranda's gown. She had chosen her lovable fellow ward as her bridesmaid.

Miranda clutched her bouquet of white, red, and pink roses a bit nervously as they passed the Society-page journalists, madly scribbling notes at the back of the church. Her and Damien's engagement had made quite a stir, especially when the whole world had heard how they had been attacked by the "bandits" who had dared to take up residence at Bayley House in its master's absence. Damien had been hailed as a hero all over again for his valor. Algernon's death was lamented by few, but Miranda understood why Damien had allowed Crispin to salvage his father's reputation.

The guilty party had been punished. If Algernon's

fratricides had been made known, Crispin would have been stripped of the title; the whole family would have been disgraced and, as the family was bankrupt, would have been cast out onto the street, if not thrown into debtor's prison. Now Crispin had a chance to start anew for the good of his family, who—like it or not—were Miranda's relatives, too.

Robert and she moved on at a stately pace past rows and rows of all the people Miranda had met on her adventures. All the members of the Knight family were present, except, of course, for the black sheep of the family, Lord Jack. She was thrilled to have been invited to call the duchess and Lady Lucien by their first names, now that she was to be their kinswoman. She saw Sally and Jane from Yardley and the kindly ladies from the charity who had taken them in; Lieutenant Colonel MacHugh, Captain Sutherland, and all the dashing officers of the Hundred and Thirty-sixth; fat Ollie Quinn and skinny Nigel Stanhope and a half dozen of her former suitors, looking downcast; Lord Griffith and his shy little boy; lastly, she passed Crispin and his mother and sisters. She sent her cousin a fond look as she went by him. She did not know what might have happened to her if he had not intervened that awful morning. She still shuddered at the thought of her evil uncle, but she cast out his memory, fixing her gaze and all her thoughts on Damien, waiting for her by the altar, magnificent in his military regalia. Lucien, his groomsman, stood by his side in a splendid gray morning coat.

The whole ceremony was a blur. Her heart raced, and her hand shook crazily when Damien tried to slip the ring onto her finger. It took him several tries, and he whispered to her to hold still. She laughed in front of everyone and quickly silenced herself. Then the minister pronounced them man and wife, and she turned to her husband with such a flood of happiness rushing from her heart she felt like she would burst.

"Lady Winterley," he murmured, gazing deeply into her eyes as he pulled her into his arms.

The whole church applauded thunderously as Damien kissed her. Brazen as ever, she flung her arms around his neck and returned his kiss wholeheartedly, not caring a fig if the whole world watched. He ended the kiss, laughing at her ardor, and they exited the church to more applause, Miranda holding her voluminous white skirts up as she ran.

Outside, the officers of his regiment stood in two rows and made a gleaming metal tunnel, holding up their crossed swords. Damien and she darted under it while the church bells pealed wildly. They climbed into the festooned, beribboned carriage, pulled by four white horses with plumes on their heads, and were in each other's arms before the coach door had scarcely shut.

The reception at Knight House lasted all day. Bel had hired French chefs to cook for the occasion, and these artists had created a mammoth bride cake to feed the throng of well-wishers who came and went until five. At seven, the house emptied and there was only time for a change of clothes and a brief rest before it was time for the more select dinner party, which lasted well into the night. Afterward, Damien and Miranda spent their wedding night in a luxurious suite at the elegant Pulteney Hotel on Piccadilly, since the smart Mayfair townhouse they had taken was not yet ready for them to move in.

They lay facing each other, staring into each other's eyes. Miranda stroked his hair gently while Damien drew circles with his fingertip around the beauty mark on her left hip.

"Lady Winterley," he whispered with a slightly dazed smile.

"I love when you say that," she purred, snuggling closer. "I love *you*."

"I love you, too. I can barely believe I get to spend the rest of my life with you, my mighty, magnificent Miranda."

"Doting Damien," she teased, hugging him.

"Aye, that I am." He slipped his arms around her waist and rolled her atop him. "Kiss me, wife," he commanded.

She did, and soon felt the evidence of his response.

"Someone's waking up," she murmured in a naughty little singsong.

"What a temptress you are. I'm going to like being married to you."

She let out a happy shout as he rolled over, tumbling her onto her back, and moved atop her, kissing her deeply. She ran her hands all over his velvety skin.

"Do you know I adore you?" he whispered, pausing to stare into her eyes.

Burning for him, she pulled him down to kiss her. "Show me."

"Mm," he said, kissing his way down her neck, her

chest, her belly, moving down lower still over her heated, quivering body.

With one hand on his hair, the other grasping the satin sheet beneath her, Miranda closed her eyes and arched her back with pleasure as he parted her thighs and licked her with a slow, savoring kiss.

*Ah, this man,* she thought, panting with delight. Then her sweet, wicked husband proceeded to redefine the words *matrimonial bliss.*

All through February and into March, Bayley House was besieged by an army of carpenters, stonemasons, roofers, plasterers, painters, glaziers, cabinetmakers, and groundskeepers, with the great and much sought-after architect Matthew Wyatt as their commanding general. Since it was Miranda's gold that resurrected the place, it was given to her to rename the property. She called it Winterhaven. Rounding the property, the river swelled as it melted in the spring sunshine.

She and Damien made regular jaunts from their graceful townhouse in Mayfair to the Berkshire countryside to monitor the workers' progress. When a suite in the east wing was ready, they were able to stay for a few days at a time.

Damien's cottagers fixed their roofs, and the legion of new laborers he had hired turned over the soil for planting. The smell of fresh earth and growing things carried on the balmy breezes as they rippled through the almond orchard on the ridge, scattering white petals on the air like a soft snow. It was Miranda's favorite place on earth.

The stable was livable for horses well before the house was livable for people. Damien began buying broodmares for Zeus's harem, as Miranda laughingly called it. The horses would be bred in the autumn, and the mares would drop their foals next spring.

In London, Jacinda and Lizzie finished their final term at Mrs. Hall's Academy for Young Ladies and began readying themselves to make their entree into Society in late April. Miranda used a portion of her inheritance to send Amy, Sally, and Jane to the same excellent boarding school in Islington where the two older girls were ending their education. Meanwhile, Bel entered her confinement for the final term of her pregnancy, due in May, while poor Robert worried himself into a knot as she steadily grew great with his child. Lucien and Alice announced a blessed event of their own to occur in September. Little Harry turned four.

Day by day, Damien's torturous memories slowly faded like the colors on an ancient battle pennant. But then, one day, news came that Miranda could never have foreseen—news that rang out like a death knell across all of England. In mid-March that news reached Winterhaven.

The unthinkable had happened.

Damien was inspecting the carpenters' work on the repaired staircase when he heard shouts from outside. He nodded his approval and told them to keep up the good work, then walked out onto the portico to find Sutherland and MacHugh riding hard up the muddy drive. They passed his groundskeepers, who were planting plane trees to line the drive. In a few years, the matured trees would look quite stately. A smile of pleasure crossed his face at the prospect of showing off the improvements to his house to his friends. He and Miranda had spent the past week at Winterhaven and were delighted with the progress that was being made throughout the property.

The uniformed officers leaped off their horses and came running toward him.

"Winterley!"

"You aren't in the city, lads. There's no need to hurry so," he drawled, leaning against the pillar with a half smile. "Welcome to my little paradise."

They glanced grimly at each other.

"What is it?" he asked, furrowing his brow.

"Winterley, Napoleon has escaped from Elba," Sutherland said in agitation. "Haven't you heard? He is marching on Paris, collecting an ever-growing throng of supporters as he goes. King Louis is preparing to flee."

"Good God," he whispered, shoving away from the pillar as his stomach plummeted with sickening swiftness.

"Wellington's already on his way back from the Congress of Vienna," MacHugh said. "He's going to need all the experienced officers he can get."

"Aye," Sutherland chimed in. "Dozens of 'em were shipped off weeks ago to command troops in America and India. We need whoever's left to go to Belgium. Do you see what this means?" Sutherland punched Damien's chest in brotherly excitement. "We're going back to war!"

He stared at them in shock.

"You *will* come back to London with us and help ready the regiment?" MacHugh asked.

Damien's head whirled. His answer ripped out harshly from his lips. "No!"

Both men froze and looked at him in disbelief.

"No!" he said again, anger flushing his face. His heart was pounding. "Look around you! Look at this house. Look there." He pointed at Miranda on the ridge some few hundred yards away, walking through the flowery orchard. "I will not come."

They glanced warily at each other as though he must have lost his mind.

"I have a new life now," he said in a shaky, impassioned voice. "I am a husband. She could be with child. I have my tenants to consider. I have responsibilities."

"Of course, my lord" MacHugh murmured, clearly shocked. He lowered his head.

Sutherland looked askance at the Scotsman and shifted his weight from one foot to the other. "Well, then, Colonel, what shall we tell the men?"

"How should I know?" Damien retorted.

"Because they're your men. You're the colonel."

"Not anymore. His Majesty's army has had enough of my blood. Ask your questions of MacHugh. He's next in rank. Let Wellington promote him."

Sutherland glanced at the big Scotsman. "Right."

MacHugh flushed slightly and avoided meeting Damien's gaze, as though he was embarrassed of his selfish, unsoldierly answer. He cleared his throat and looked at the captain. "Might as well go back to Town, then. There's much to be done."

Sutherland nodded, then saluted Damien out of

habit, but MacHugh did not give him that courtesy, only passing a guarded look of mingled puzzlement and reproach over his face that lanced Damien to the heart.

*Bloody hell,* he thought. *This can't be happening.*

His men turned around and walked slowly, rather dazedly, back to their horses, as though they did not know where to begin without him to tell them what to do. He closed his eyes, feeling his whole, bright, happy future spinning away from him in a trice.

Napoleon was on the march. If the emperor took back power in France, then everything they had fought for, everything that so many of their friends had died for, had been in vain.

"God damn it, they will not be happy until I'm dead," he said under his breath, then shouted, "Wait!"

They pivoted. "Sir?"

He glared at them as though it were their fault. "Wait for me in Town. Gather up our sergeants and see who you can recruit. I reckon we'll finish it properly this time."

Hearty, knowing grins spread over their faces. "Aye, Colonel!" they both said.

MacHugh swung up onto his horse and threw him a crisp salute. "It'll be just like old times, Winterley!"

"I so hope not," he replied, folding his arms across his chest, yet he could feel the drumbeat in his pulse, summoning him to battle. He glanced at the half-rebuilt house behind him, then scanned the fields, ripe for the sowing.

No, it was beyond his power to languish here when his country needed him.

His gaze wandered to the almond orchard, where Miranda was walking among the trees, clouds of white petals scattering around her, catching in her dark hair. He watched her as she held up her Paisley scarf over her head, letting the wind play with it like a kite. He exhaled slowly, quietly.

Then he went to tell her.

Miranda saw Damien walking toward her across the wet, marshy grass and moved to the brow of the ridge to wait for him. The wind whipped through her skirts and her hair and her Paisley scarf, but the sun warmed her. The afternoon light fell at a sharp angle; the sky behind him was the color of his eyes; tall, piled clouds with silver linings, pierced by silver beams of light.

"Can we have our salon out here?" she called playfully, sweeping a gesture toward the trees. "I cannot think of a prettier setting in which to receive our callers."

He flashed her an even, white smile, his complexion glowing a vibrant bronzed hue as the sunbeams lit his face; the wind ran rampant through his silky black hair. He was dressed with rustic simplicity in buff leather breeches and a short leather coat with a handsome plaid wool scarf wrapped around his neck. His high boots were flecked with mud. He came toward her, drawing off his thick leather work gloves.

"We can put the couch there." She pointed. "And the table there—and hang two swings from those branches instead of boring old chairs. What say you?"

"Where is your coat?"

"I'm not cold. I have a strong constitution," she boasted; then her grin faded as she noticed the troubled look in his gray eyes. "What is it, darling?" She danced over to him and touched his forearms gently, glancing up into his face.

He tucked his gloves in his coat pockets and took her hand in his, pausing to pluck a flower petal out of her hair. He let the wind take it, his gaze turning faraway as he watched the white petal fly.

Miranda touched his chest. "Damien?"

He lifted his chin, still avoiding her gaze. He stared toward the river. "MacHugh and Sutherland have been here," he said in a stiff voice that she had not heard him use in weeks. She noticed the tension in the broad line of his shoulders.

"Are they staying for supper? We shall have to take them to the inn at Littlewick—"

"They've gone."

"So quickly?"

"Yes."

"What did they want?"

He looked at her at last with anger and sorrow churning in his eyes. "They brought news from London."

"Bad news?" she murmured, sobering.

He nodded.

"What is it?"

"Napoleon has escaped the island of Elba," he said hesitantly. "He is marching on Paris. Wellington will be assembling an army—"

"No!" she gasped, pulling out of his light hold,

backing away, the color draining from her cheeks. "No, Damien. No."

Anguish flitted over his elegantly chiseled face. "I must go," he forced out. "You know they need me."

"I need you!" The wind carried her wail across the river.

He took a step toward her, pain in his eyes. "Miranda."

"You're not going, Damien! No! I forbid it!"

He said nothing.

She knew that his mind was already made up. Her mouth went dry with fear, her heart pounding. Her distress was so acute it dizzied her. She struggled for clarity. "Damien, I can't let you do this," she said with forced calm, though her voice trembled. "I cannot lose you. It took all of your strength and my love to help you find your way out of the darkness the last time. I almost lost you to it. If you go back and expose yourself to all of that violence and bloodshed again, it might happen all over again, and this time I may not be able to save you."

"It is my duty."

"I am your duty! I am your wife! You are my husband, and I need you here!"

"I have to finish this, Miranda. I fought too hard, sacrificed too much to see that Corsican monster once more on his throne."

"It's France! What do you care? It's not your country—"

"It's not that simple, my love," he whispered. "If we do not act to remove him at once, he will dig in his heels, become entrenched, and the whole damned thing will start all over again. Is that what you want for our children?"

"I want our children to know their father!" She whirled around and ran away from him, unable to bear another word.

She ran as far as the edge of the river, crying, blinded with tears. She slumped down by the reeds and stared at the rushing water, betrayed and terrified. He was leaving her. That was all she knew.

Damien walked up behind her, his step uncertain. "Miranda, be strong."

"Why?" she cried. "Why must I be strong when my husband of less than two months is abandoning me?"

"I'm not abandoning you," he whispered helplessly.

"Then stay." She turned to him on her knees, tears pouring down her face. "Promise me you will stay no matter what. Those were your vows, weren't they? You are finally healing, Damien. Look at the life we are building here. What of your horses? Our children? Our family? Doesn't it mean anything to you?"

He swallowed hard. "Miranda, my men will be lost in the field without me. They will be fighting for the security of England and their own lives. I cannot abandon them."

"And what of me?" she wailed. "You're abandoning me!"

"You're strong," he whispered pleadingly. "I need you to be strong, as only my Miranda can be."

She grabbed onto that strength within her and hardened it willfully to anger, staring at him. "If you go, I shall no longer be 'your' Miranda."

He paled. "What do you mean?"

"If you abandon me for the sake of your filthy war, I will never forgive you. Never."

"What's that supposed to mean?" he asked, his voice dark with warning. "I will never grant you a divorce."

"No need, when I will likely be a widow before the year is out." She shoved him out of her way as she marched past him toward the house on legs that shook beneath her.

They returned to their London townhouse, but Miranda refused to speak to him during the four-hour coach ride and for the entire week that followed. Four days into her silent treatment, Damien roared at her to stop it, but her only answer was an icy stare. Seeing it, he slammed out of the house and commenced returning her silence in kind. At night, she locked the door that joined their bedrooms, but he did not try to enter. Napoleon had caused their first fight as husband and wife, and it was a huge one, with equal stubbornness arrayed on both sides, each one absolutely certain that he or she was right.

On Thursday the sixteenth, he received the urgent request for his service by special dispatch from the War Office. They wanted him in Brussels by the third of April. Knowing that the orders would be coming, he had already sent out messages to gather up his men, who had scattered to the four corners of Britain. He had also begun ordering supplies and materiel for them, such as tents and canteens.

"You had better not use one penny of my inheritance to outfit your regiment," she had warned him bitterly.

"It's not your money anymore, wife, and I shall spend it however I damn well please," he had answered bitterly before going out the door to meet with his captains at the Guards' Club.

She sat in the parlor that overlooked the street, listening to the silence of the house. The dull sounds of the occasional traffic below were deafening in the newly furnished parlor. Was this how it would be when he was gone? she thought. The silence would drive her mad. Unable to stand another moment of it, she pulled on her bonnet and gloves, draped her Paisley shawl around her shoulders, and went out walking, brooding with every step. Perhaps she would not speak to Damien, but he was all she thought about, constantly. How would she survive his desertion?

*I shall take lovers,* she thought in defiance. Why, she would enjoy herself so heartily in his absence she would make the Hawkscliffe Harlot, his mother, look like a nun. It would serve him right. . . .

But her bold thoughts drained away, and her shoulders slumped in misery as she trailed her hand along the black wrought-iron bars of the fences that girded the elegant townhouses in her neighborhood. She didn't want anybody else. She would *never* want anybody else. She only wanted that cruel barbarian. Why didn't he love her enough to stay? Lucien wasn't going, she thought sullenly. Lucien was staying home with Alice, so why must Damien go?

Maybe if she were pregnant, as Alice was, he would stay home, too. But she knew she was fooling herself.

The man she had married, the man she loved still, was no more capable of turning his back on his men or ignoring his country's call to arms than she was capable of staying angry at him much longer. It was hard being a military wife, she thought. Vaguely ashamed of herself for handling this so poorly, she felt as though she did not even know herself anymore. She had never felt such deadening depression and despair. She knew she was making it all harder on him, but he was everything to her—her best friend, her guardian, her lover, and mate—and he was leaving her, probably to die. She knew he was not trying to betray her, but it still felt like it.

As she walked down the street, heavy-hearted and lonely, all around her the bustling city was abuzz. The mood in the streets was one of excitement over the coming war. For an hour, she meandered, letting her feet take her wherever they would. When she looked up, she found herself in front of Lucien and Alice's house on Upper Brooke Street. She stared at it for a long moment, then took a deep breath and shook off her self-pity for good. She squared her shoulders and lifted her chin, then went up the three front steps and banged the knocker.

To her surprise, Lucien answered the door himself instead of their butler.

"Why, Lady Winterley," he said, lifting his eyebrows in surprise. "Do come in."

She did, wandering restlessly into the entrance hall.

"Where is your carriage?"

"I walked."

"No footman? No maid?"

She gave him a warning look.

"I take it the domestic squabble is still going strong," he remarked, taking in her glum, introspective expression as he closed the door behind her.

As she turned to him, she caught a glimpse of herself in the hall mirror: a poor, homeless waif no more, but a countess, elegantly dressed, a woman of rank and position, who had a duty to her husband, just as her husband had a duty to his king.

She looked Lucien squarely in his eyes. "I need a favor," she said. "Tell me what I need to bring with me to the war."

A hearty smile spread slowly across his face. "Dare I ask you've decided to follow the drum?"

She tossed her head in a short, angry nod. "He gives me little choice, that blackguard."

"Brava, Lady Winterley. Brava, *bella*," he murmured, crossing the hall to enfold her in a brotherly hug.

"I still hate him for this," she muttered with a sniffle, grateful for his affection.

He chuckled fondly. "I knew you'd come around. Somebody's got to look after him over there."

"Don't tell him I've decided to come," she warned, her eyes misting briefly as she pulled back and glanced at him. "He'll never allow it if he knows in advance."

Lucien gave her shoulders a bracing squeeze. "Never fear, sister. I know how to keep a secret. Now, then. Let's think about what you'll need. . . ."

The days rolled by in hectic preparation, but Miranda gave Damien no sign that she had made up her mind to come with him for fear that if he caught wind of her plan, he would say it was too dangerous and forbid her to go.

Meanwhile, on Lucien's advice, she was amassing provisions of her own, stocking up on the appropriate clothing, getting her identification papers drawn up, and putting her affairs in order. She practiced riding her mare, Fancy, for long hours in the park to improve her equestrian skills; bought a pair of dueling pistols for self-protection; hired a servant woman who had followed the army before to act as her maid; and said private good-byes to the women of the Knight family, who regarded her decision in mingled awe and dread.

Then, at last, Monday dawned, the twenty-seventh of March—the day that Damien was to leave for the port of Ramsgate to sail across the Channel to Ostend.

Miranda rose at three-thirty in the morning to ensure that she would be awake and ready to go before he could even protest. Too nervous to eat breakfast, she had the carriage brought out in the predawn darkness. By lamplight, she oversaw the grooms who loaded the vehicle with her luggage.

All of a sudden, she heard Damien yelling for her from inside the house. "Miranda! Miranda! Damn that woman, where has she gone?" He suddenly flung into the doorway. "Miranda!"

She stiffened at his bewildered call and slowly turned around, braced to defy him. "Yes, my lord?"

He looked at little shocked to find her up and dressed. He glanced warily at the carriage. "What are you doing?"

"None of your business."

"You were trying to slip away to Winterhaven before I awoke," he accused her, his tone raw with hurt.

"No, I was not. Did you really think I would leave without saying good-bye?" she asked in reproach.

He stared at her. "Where are you going, then?"

She set her hands on her waist and lifted her chin a notch. "To Brussels. With you," she replied, her eyes ablaze, daring him to naysay her.

His jaw dropped. "With me?"

"Oh, yes, I am, sir, and if you have one word of protest, tell it to the wind." She turned her back on him and continued hurrying the grooms along at their task.

After a long moment, when there was still no sound from her husband, she chanced a look over her shoulder. He was still standing in the doorway, looking utterly routed.

"Is there a problem?" she asked haughtily.

He snapped his jaw shut. "No."

"Good."

"Well, then," he said to himself. Shaking his head a bit as if to clear it, he stepped back into the house and closed the door.

Miranda stood there gazing at the closed door, shocked by his lack of argument. He hadn't even put up a fight! she thought, her heart lifting to realize that she had gotten her way. She was going to the Continent; she would stay by his side!

The first battle was won.

They set out from London as the sun rose: Damien and she, her maid, his manservant, one of his regimental aides, and two grooms astride the riding horses—Fancy and a large, powerful bay gelding that

Damien had bought from Newmarket. Robert, Lucien, and Alec escorted them to Ramsgate to see them off. The brothers chatted in hearty tones along the way, but Damien and Miranda kept stealing furtive, uncertain glances at each other. She could not tell what he was thinking and was too busy in any case trying to hide her nervousness.

After a ride of several hours, they reached the port, from which innumerable ships were leaving, conveying members of the army to the Continent. They hastened to the pier to board the sloop on which Damien had secured their passage. The captain escorted him on board to ensure that the packet was large enough for their party. The ship looked seaworthy and the crew most able, but Miranda blanched when her husband came back with the revelation that the voyage to Ostend would take twenty-four hours. The captain was anxious to get under way, for the winds were ideal.

After loading the horses and baggage onto the boat, there was barely room for them, their five servants, and Damien's eager young aide. While he oversaw the horses being taken up the gangplank, Miranda hung back on solid ground, holding on anxiously to the arms of her brothers-in-law. She had not been on a boat since the day her parents had drowned and was terrified of what love now compelled her to do.

She exchanged heartfelt good-byes with his brothers, giving Lucien, her coconspirator, an especially long hug.

"Be brave," he murmured, giving her a kiss on her forehead.

She nodded, then marched down the dock with slow, dirgelike steps, trying not to look down at the water, though she could hear it slapping the mossy, barnacled posts. Damien was already on deck when she boarded the sloop with sweating palms and pounding heart. Her stomach was in knots and sweat broke out on her face as she walked up the gangplank. She went down to the hold at once with her maid, but Damien stayed at the rails, watching his brothers and England drifting out of sight.

When he came into the teakwood cabin, she was sitting balled up on the berth. Her grip was white-knuckled as she held onto a wooden shelf beside her to steady herself against the boat's uneasy rocking. Her maid sat beside her with smelling salts at the ready in a little round vinaigrette. Miranda glanced rather desperately at him as he entered the hold.

She knew that he could see in a glance that her defiance had dissolved; her face had the greenish pale cast of one suffering from mal de mer, but he knew full well that it was fear, not motion, that ailed her. Moving in time with the boat's gentle rocking, he crossed the tiny cabin to her and nodded her maid's dismissal, taking the smelling salts from the woman. He sat down on the berth and gathered Miranda onto his lap, stilling her feeble protest with a soft, "Hush, wife."

Though still uneasy after the bitterness that had held them apart for the past ten days, she gave in to the generous strength that he offered. Holding her against his chest, he stroked her hair and her back, calming her by degrees.

"God, it feels so good to hold you again," he whispered at length. He stopped petting her, closed his eyes, and rested his forehead against her temple. He shook his head with a sigh. "When I looked in your room this morning and you weren't in your bed, I thought you'd left me."

She gazed at him wordlessly, linking her fingers through his.

"I never want to fight with you again. It hurts too much." He lifted her hands, winding her arms around his neck as he pulled her more snugly into his embrace.

"I'm sorry for saying I would never forgive you," she whispered anxiously.

"It's all right—"

"No, it's not—"

"Miranda, I love you, and I know you love me. Your lips may claim that you hate me, but I know you. I know that your love for me is the only thing that could have possibly induced you to drag yourself out onto this boat."

Tears rushed into her eyes as she nodded, hugging him. "I thought you wouldn't allow me to come if I gave you any warning."

"Probably right," he agreed with a nod. "I can always send you home if the fighting gets too hot."

"I will do whatever you say, but I couldn't bear to be left behind. I would go mad without you, Damien. Lucien helped me get everything ready."

"I figured as much," he said wryly.

"You see? This way, if anything happens to you—if you are hurt—I will be there to take care of you. And whatever happens, I won't let you get lost in the darkness again."

"That couldn't happen with you by my side." He captured her face between his hands and kissed her with fierce, wild longing, easing her back onto the narrow, cushioned berth. "I need you," he breathed. "You've deprived me too long."

"Oh, Damien, I can't. I'm too scared and ill," she whispered, closing her eyes in helpless attraction as he caressed her breast through her clothing.

"This will help you," he promised in a dark, satiny whisper.

She caught her breath sharply as he kissed her earlobe, awakening her senses. "We mustn't. The whole crew will hear."

"No, we'll be very quiet," he breathed, slowly pinning her wrists above her head on the cushioned berth. "If you're going to join my regiment, I think it's best you learn your duties," he purred.

"Oh, you are a wicked man," she murmured, feeling her body's instantaneous response to his taunting, a wet surge of warmth.

"How many times do you think I can make you come before we reach Ostend?"

"Twenty-four hours?" she asked breathlessly as he reached under her skirts, enthralling her with his slow, insistent touch.

He never answered the question, for his mouth came down on hers in ravishing hunger. His lusty eagerness excited her to fever pitch, melting away her fear in her need of him. She felt him unfastening his black trousers with jerky haste; then he was inside her, big and throbbing, driving in to the hilt. He let out a whispered groan near her ear; she trembled under him in needy bliss. He took her roughly, just the way he liked it, staking his claim on her anew.

She devoured his passionate kisses and yielded utterly. Primal vigor fueled his every thrust as he pleasured her relentlessly, lest she forget to whom she belonged. All restraint shattered as they neared climax, panting and writhing frantically together as though they could not merge their bodies completely enough. She wrapped her legs around his sleek hips; he gripped her bared buttocks, dizzying her with wild, forbidden pleasure as he pressed his fingertip deeply in the cleft of her backside. He bit her earlobe just short of pain and ordered her in a harsh, rasping whisper to come for him.

She submitted, powerless to resist. A wave of release rushed through her, so complete and overwhelming that she was unconscious of the near screams of pleasure wrenching from her lips, rising up quite audibly to the entire crew and echoing out across the placid water of the Channel. In that moment, her whole universe was contained in blinding pleasure and passion, and at its center was her fierce warrior. His chiseled features were taut, his long-lashed eyes closed, his head tipped back. His splendid manhood, hot and hard, pulsated within her, sliding in her satiny wetness again and again until he collapsed on her, spent, his muscled body sweaty and quivering, leaden-heavy.

"Ohhh, *Damien*," she murmured after several minutes, draping her arms around his shoulders in indolent affection, a light sheen of sweat on her skin.

He smiled drowsily and rested his head on her chest. "I think," he said in a lazy purr, "that you and I ought to fight more often."

When the sloop finally reached the shallow approaches to Ostend the next day, the horses were let down into the water by a huge sling and had to swim to shore. The passengers climbed down into a long-boat, which a couple of crewmen then rowed to the beach. Damien picked her up and carried her to shore so she would not have to set foot in the deep, sucking sand. The country was very flat in all directions. Miranda thought the fort a rather dull, dreary place. It stank of too many horses, for the sandy beaches made it a useful disembarking point for cavalry.

They did not linger long, but packed their luggage onto some mules that Damien's aide located for them in the town, mounted up on their horses, and set out on the excellent paved road that ran alongside a canal for the entire two-hour ride. The bare, watery land-scape was so flat that they could see the tall windmills and church spires of the town from ten miles away. When they arrived at the neat, picturesque town, they had an early supper at the Hotel de Commerce. The concierge told them that it was about seven hours by horseback to Ghent, where King Louis had arrived with his court, having fled Paris at Napoleon's return. Heartened by their repast, they pressed on.

If Miranda was not enjoying her adventure tremen-dously already, she experienced the thrill of her hus-band's high regard in the army when the British infantry troops guarding the large, fine town sent up a cheer, recognizing Damien as he rode past the sentries. When he stopped to greet them, they told him that many of his friends were already there. They proceeded on into the fine, spacious town, took rooms for the night at the elegant Hotel de Flandre, and attended a formal reception that evening for the king. Miranda had never been in the presence of royalty before, but poor, gouty Louis XVIII did not quite match her expectations, wheezing and leaning his great bulk on his royal cane as though his heart might give out on him at any moment.

Though she had been married for two whole months now, it still awed her to hear the stately courtier beside the king present Damien and her formally to His Majesty as the earl and countess of Winterley.

*Am I actually a countess?* she wondered, holding back a laugh to think that it was true—she, the rebel of Yardley School!—but she behaved herself, executing a quite perfect, low curtsy while, beside her, Damien bowed to the overweight royal. They were lifted from their courtesies, thanked, and dismissed to go off and chat with Damien's highborn officer friends. He presented them to her one by one, and each of them praised him for his excellent taste. Miranda beamed at their gallant flatteries and hung on her husband's arm.

After a few pleasant hours at the reception, and a far more enjoyable interlude of Damien's athletic lovemaking in the luxurious hotel room, they slept soundly in each other's arms, woke at a leisurely hour, met up again with the other officers, and all set out merrily together for Brussels, where the duke of Wellington was amassing his army.

They stayed in Brussels for two and a half months, billeted in Gothic splendor at the Hotel de Ville, which was full of British officers. Their men, the rank and file, poured across the Channel in large transport ships, arriving by the tens of thousands. The officers sought quarters in the town, while the rank and file bivouacked in the surrounding countryside, a great mass of tough veterans and fresh-faced boys eager to get a taste of martial glory. Yet all could do nothing but wait for the action to begin.

April stretched on, flowers burgeoning; the rich Flanders countryside bloomed. More British civilians attached to the army and nobles from all the allied countries of the Coalition flooded into the city to join in the gaiety and excitement. There were parties and balls every night, and hardly anything was danced but the risqué waltz. There were nightly promenades of the fashionable in the park and comedies in the theaters; but the plays were all in French, so Miranda did not bother with them, for she barely understood a word. In any case, Damien and Miranda declined at least as many invitations as they accepted, preferring to spend every possible moment together, all their attentions focused on each other.

Though the atmosphere in Brussels was one of levity, a darker sense of restlessness pervaded it just under the surface; the men, at least, knew they were there for a war and that some of them were going to die. Damien knew it. Miranda brooded on it. The knowledge made their every moment together all the more precious.

For now, her beloved colonel's duties were light. While he drilled his men at their camp a couple of miles south of the city, Miranda kept busy to distract herself from the gnawing anxiety of what would happen when Napoleon had his army in order and was ready to fight. She toured the cathedral with the friends she had made of the other officers' wives and shopped for souvenirs of Brussels lace to send back to London for her kinswomen. Frequent, treasured letters from Alice, Bel, Lizzie, and Jacinda kept her well informed of the happenings at home.

At the end of April, Jacinda was presented at court and was now officially "out." She rhapsodized over the lavish gown she had worn before the regent and the queen, describing every detail, but complained bitterly that the resumption of hostilities had ruined the Season that she had longed for every day of her seventeen years. London, she wrote, was *devoid* of interesting young gentlemen. All she could hope for was better luck next year. She wanted to come to Brussels, where "everyone" had gone, but her brothers unanimously forbade her.

Alice sent her lists of both boys' and girls' names that she and Lucien were considering for their child, whose arrival was expected in September. Miranda had her twentieth birthday on the eleventh of May. Still there was no hint of battle. The waiting was growing nerve-racking. She did not know how the troops in the field could withstand it. She went out to visit them from time to time with Damien and made an effort to be particularly merry in order to lift their spirits.

In late May, word came that Bel had given birth to a robustly healthy boy. Both mother and son were thriving; Hawkscliffe could not have been prouder. They named him Robert William, of course, after his papa; the newborn's courtesy title was the earl of Morley.

As May gave way to June, Miranda could not seem to shake off a persistent nausea from the increasing heat and humidity. Nothing laid out on the lavish tables of the hostesses nor the meals offered at the hotel agreed with her. It went on for more than a fortnight. She did not complain of it to her husband, but finally sent for the doctor one day while he was off reviewing his troops. The estimable doctor then made the great revelation: She was not ill. She was pregnant.

Somehow, she was shocked to the marrow, though God knew she ought not have been, with Damien's insatiable appetites. She was waiting for the perfect moment to tell him when a Prussian messenger came tearing into the heart of Brussels and rushed straight to Wellington's headquarters. Shortly thereafter, the news spread like wildfire through the city that Napoleon had attacked the Prussian troops only half a day's ride southward.

South? she thought in horror, realizing that her husband was in that direction with his men. As she wove through the lobby of the grand hotel, the officers she knew tried to reassure her, saying that it might be nothing at all, just some outposts firing on each other. Yet Wellington sent out the order that the army be ready to march at a moment's notice. She was beside herself with anxiety, waiting for Damien to appear.

When he finally came, it was evening and a steady rain had been pounding the cobblestones of the plaza. She was waiting on a chair in the lobby of the hotel when she saw him, MacHugh, and Sutherland come riding into the square, mud-splattered, rain running off the brims of their shakos. Heedless of the weather, she was on her feet, running out the door to him, before he had even halted his horse in front of the hotel. She glanced at the other two. MacHugh was looking fierce, but Sutherland appeared shaken. Damien sprang down off his mount and stalked toward her, sweeping off his shako. She threw herself into his arms.

"Are you all right? I've been so worried. Were you near it?"

He did not answer, just held her hard for a moment. The wet and mud of his clothes soiled hers, but she didn't care. His skin was warm and his kiss tasted of rain. "We saw the retreat. Napoleon tore the Prussians to shreds. It's best you know now that this is going to be a large battle, Miranda. I can't stay."

"Can't you come in and have supper, at least?"

He waved off her suggestion. "No time."

His urgency increased her alarm. "Do you have all your provisions? Everything you need?"

He smiled at her then. "Almost," he said meaningfully, leaning down to steal a quick kiss. "Get back inside. I have to go."

"But why? Wellington is at the Richmonds' ball. Surely it's not that serious—"

"He has to put in an appearance there, love," he said as he walked her back into the hotel. "If he were to leave now, the city would panic. The civilians would flee north, and that would demoralize the soldiers. It's just for show. He'll be joining us soon at the front. My battalion has been ordered to be ready by the time he gets there. I don't know how long this will take, but I will do my best to keep you informed of where I am. You may need to evacuate to Antwerp. I'll let you know."

Tears suddenly flooded her eyes. This was the moment she had been dreading—the moment of parting. She almost couldn't believe it had come. She held onto him. "Damien."

He pulled her into his arms again. "Don't cry. I beg you, please, don't."

She knew he needed her to be strong for him now more than ever. She felt as though she could fall senseless with fear and grief or shatter into tiny pieces from sheer weakness, but somehow she steeled herself, reaching down into the depths of her being to pull up the resolve worthy of such a man. She swallowed hard, clung fast to her courage, and moved back a small space, glancing up to meet his gaze.

His face was stark, his gray eyes fierce with tortured love.

"I love you," she whispered. "We both do." As she said it, she took his hand gently, pressed it flat against her belly, and stared meaningfully into his eyes.

He blinked as though he was not sure he had heard her correctly; then his jaw dropped. "You mean—?"

She managed a rueful smile and nodded.

"Are you sure?" he breathed.

"Mm-hmm."

"When?"

"March."

"Oh, my God," he said dazedly. He encircled her in his arms and held her. She could feel him trembling at the news, though he had not so much as blinked an eye at the prospect of battle. He kissed her with hot, ardent devotion, then pulled back, staring into her eyes with a burning, white ferocity that made her very soul thrill. "I will come back to you," he vowed in a savage whisper.

"If God wills it," she said softly.

He shook his head. "I will come back."

She cried out as he abruptly pulled away from her and threw open the lobby doors, marching back to his horse. She followed to the doorway and watched him swing up into the saddle, renewed will and precision in his every movement. MacHugh and Sutherland nodded to her. Damien's gleaming, gray eyes flashed like a silvery blade as he kissed his fingertips to her, then reeled his tall horse around and galloped off with his men to fight the French.

Long after he was out of sight, Miranda stood right in the spot where he had left her, sobbing, until her maid came and led her back up to their rooms.

The rain fell harder.

Later that night, Miranda heard that another dispatch had come from General Blücher, delivered to Wellington at the Richmond ball. Whatever its contents, it had resulted in a great, swift exodus of officers and the commander himself from the very ballroom; by dawn, the whole army was marching south, where Damien and his battalion had already started. Many of the civilians were leaving Brussels for Antwerp, but Damien had not ordered Miranda to do so, nor had she any desire to remove herself one mile farther from where he was, even if it was dangerous to stay. Winterleys did not run, she told her maid.

By the time morning came, the rain had stopped, but the day remained overcast under moody skies. From her room high in the hotel, she could see the blue-gray smoke that rose far away over the battle, but when the windows and doors in her room continued rattling with the constant, far-off rumbling of artillery, she could no longer stand the sound and rushed out to a gathering of the officers' wives. She joined their efforts to prepare for the wounded before they began arriving and was glad to have something to do. She noticed from their nervous chatter that the other wives all seemed to think that love would protect their husbands from all harm. Miranda did not think that. Watching her parents drown had taught her that love was not powerful enough to keep boats afloat when they were going down, and she did not suppose it was powerful enough to deflect bullets. In fact, deep down, she dared not hope too much that she would ever see Damien alive again, despite his gallant promise.

Then a courier brought a message from him on Saturday night, and she wept with gratitude to read that he was safe. She kissed the paper that his hand had touched. He said they had fought General Ney at Quatre Bras and had given the French a sound beating, but the thing was far from over. That night, she did not sleep for more than an hour and prayed more than she had in her entire twenty years: *Please, Lord, let my baby know his father. Don't make him grow up an orphan as I did.*

Sunday, June the eighteenth, came and went. She went to service at the cathedral, and the priest tried to give them courage while the great stained windows rattled like the devil was outside trying to find a way in. Her maid was as impassive as the great sphinx of Egypt, but Miranda was raw and jittery with worry and exhaustion. By evening, word reached them of a great slaughter in a field called Waterloo. It was still going on.

Then the wounded started arriving. Miranda rushed out to see if her help was needed and to gather what news she could. Nobody seemed to have heard anything about the Hundred Thirty-sixth.

"The cavalry has seen much action," a man with his face bandaged from a saber cut told her. "We may all have to evacuate for Antwerp if Blücher does not send reinforcements soon."

She threw herself into helping the bloody, mangled masses streaming into the city by the cartload. The houses of the rich turned into hospitals. Miranda went among them for hours, giving them water, hiding her horror at their gruesome wounds, bandaging them when she could, murmuring praise to them for their bravery as they waited for their turn with the surgeon. Pale, shaking, clammy with sweat and fear, she ignored her own exhaustion and did her best to keep a check on the constant thoughts of Damien that agonized her.

Night deepened. She heard that her husband's regiment had held superbly before the advance of Napoleon's elite Imperial Guard, repulsing them near the end of the day, but the casualties had been high, someone said. Panic rose in her, but she tamped it down again and again.

New casualty lists were passed around, but she could not bring herself to look at them. One by one, she saw her friends among the officers' wives crumple as the news was brought to them of their husbands' deaths, or of wounds so desperate that they could not be moved from the little town called Waterloo, where the doctors were hastily tending them. Miranda hardened herself grimly for the news that, with every passing moment, seemed inevitable. She would have his child, she told herself. The baby would have to be enough.

Even the tidings of Wellington's great victory barely stirred her. Napoleon had been taken into custody, but even this meant nothing to her because she had not yet learned where Damien was, and all the while, the wounded kept coming, overflowing the town. A young cavalryman she gave water to begged her to stay by him because he was dying. His trusty mount had been destroyed under him, and he had been trampled in the cavalry charge, his legs crushed; then a

French lancer had punctured his lung to finish him off. Miranda wiped the boy's brow with a wet cloth and sang softly to him until he lost consciousness. She barely realized she was crying at her own helplessness to save him, to stop all of this. He died right before her eyes, and then she heard a soft, low, weary voice behind her.

"My lady."

She froze. Her heart missed a beat. She swept to her feet and spun around, barely daring to breathe.

*"Damien!"*

He was smeared with black powder and blood. His stare glittered with exhaustion. There was a cut on his cheek and his uniform was torn, but he was whole and alive and standing before her. When he opened his arms to her, she rushed into them with a wild cry, flinging her arms around his neck.

He gripped her hard, holding on tightly around her waist. She could feel his body shaking with the exertion of nine hours of battle and then the long gallop through the darkness to Brussels to come back to her.

"It's over now," he ground out in a choked whisper, stroking her hair. "This time it's over for good."

"I love you," she said again and again, standing on tiptoe to kiss his bruised, bloodied face.

Holding her around her waist, he closed his eyes and leaned his forehead against hers. "Sutherland's dead. I left MacHugh in charge of the regiment, what's left of it. He didn't like me leaving, but I told him I made you a promise." He buried his face in her hair. "Oh, Miranda, I want to go home."

She kissed him, tears streaming down her cheeks, fevered prayers of thanks spinning through her mind. "Yes, darling. Come with me." Holding him around his waist, she draped his arm across her shoulders and let him lean on her as they walked out slowly into the starry night.

# ⇥ EPILOGUE ⇤

*March, 1816*

"*Winterleyyyy!*"

The long, robust shout echoed out from an upper window of the gleaming white mansion of Winterhaven, with its triangular pediment atop four noble pillars. With perfect pitch and frightful lung power, the feminine war cry carried on the spring breeze over the green fields, over the neatly mended roofs of the cottagers' hamlet, to the white, split-rail fence where an extremely nervous Colonel Lord Winterley stood, dry-mouthed, waiting, while his brothers smoked with the worldly serenity of men who had been through this ordeal before. His heart pounded with dread and hope and worry, but Robert and Lucien merely watched the foals frolicking among the grazing mares, commenting on what fine stock they were.

"*Winterley, you bastard!*" the womanly bellow came again. "*I'm going to wring your neck for this!*"

He stared at the refurbished, repainted, redecorated house, then whirled to his brothers in distress. "I should go to her."

"I do not advise it," Robert said sagely, his brown eyes dancing at Damien's discomfiture. "Courage, man."

Lucien clapped him on the shoulder. "Leave it to the doctor, old chap. That's my advice."

He dragged his hand through his sun-warmed hair and stared helplessly at the house, scarcely able to remain where he was, yet afraid to go in. The Battle of Waterloo was nothing compared to Miranda's first birthing. Their babe had been in no hurry to come, and had no doubt grown to a great, strapping size, for her belly had swollen to such enormous girth she had boasted she was fatter than King Louis.

Just then, the four-year-old Harry came charging ahead of his elegant Aunt Jacinda, who was prepared to embark on her second Season next month. Lizzie and Alec strolled over together a bit more slowly. They all had come to wait with Damien through the excruciating hours of his firstborn's arrival. Harry climbed up onto the rail and held out his small hand, trying to lure a few of the colts over, to no avail. Lucien plucked the boy off the fence and set him up on his shoulders as Alice ambled over, carrying their six-month-old daughter, Phillipa, who gurgled and cooed with excitement when she saw her papa.

Robert turned with a possessive glow in his eyes as Bel joined them, hugging little Morley in her arms and telling him to look at the horsies. The small heir to their ancient lineage always wore the most thoughtful, curious expression for a tot not quite one year old.

Besotted as he was with his adorable niece and two

nephews, Damien was impatient to meet his own child.

"Do you think it's almost over?" he asked Bel and Alice in desperation.

Bel smiled wisely and murmured, "Soon."

"Don't worry," Alice told him. "She'll be fine."

"I don't think she'll ever forgive me."

"She will," Lucien said, leaning down to give his daughter a kiss on her downy-fine hair. The baby grabbed at his nose, and he laughed.

"My lord!"

Damien whirled around as the butler came hurrying out across the lawn.

"The doctor says you can see her now!"

The women exclaimed in excitement, but Damien was already running, tearing into the house. He froze in his tracks halfway up the stairs when he heard the tiny, angry wailing. Then he doubled his speed, arriving in their bedroom in a state of dazed awe. The physician nodded to him and stepped out of the way with a knowing twinkle in his old eyes.

"Miranda!"

She turned her head on the pillow and gazed at him from the bed, then held out her hand weakly to him. Her face was pale and covered in sweat. Tendrils of her sable hair stuck to her skin.

His heart pounded louder than Wellington's cannonades as he approached, staring at the tiny bundle sheltered in the crook of her arm. She glanced from it to him and gave him a smile full of mystery and adoration.

He approached slowly, took her hand, and lowered

himself to his knees beside the bed, staring at her, then at the baby.

"It's a boy," she whispered.

He glanced at her again in amazement. He couldn't speak. He could barely believe it was real, not some beautiful dream. When he looked down at his son, his eyes filled with tears. The baby was a red-faced, squirmy little thing with barely opened eyes and a tiny tuft of black hair.

Damien began laughing softly in sheer wonder and disbelief. He took a quick count of the child's fingers and toes and found them all accounted for.

Miranda touched his arm, her smile tremulous, tears welling in her eyes. "Isn't he the singularly most spectacular thing you have ever seen in your entire life?" she choked out.

"Yes." Awestruck, he leaned toward her and pressed a lingering kiss to her clammy brow. "I—I think I'm in shock."

Her smile widened fondly.

"How are you?" he whispered, petting her hair.

She gave him a reassuring nod. "I'm fine. Tell Bel and Alice I want to see them. I want them to see him," she started, then suddenly stopped, furrowing her brow.

"Miranda?" Damien paled as she blanched.

"Oh, no," she said. "Get the doctor."

"What is it?" he cried.

She looked at him in astonishment. "I think—I think there's another baby coming! No wonder I'm so fat, Damien—I'm having twins!"

He jumped to his feet. "You're jesting," he hissed.

Her bellow of pain assured him she was not. He

flew to get the doctor, but the man was already on his way in, rolling up his sleeves to bring the second-born into the world. The doctor scooped up the first baby and thrust him into Damien's arms, herding him quickly into the anteroom.

"Wait!" he protested. "I don't know how to hold a baby."

"My dear young fellow, you have just sired twins," the doctor said in amusement. "I suggest you learn."

With that, he shut the door firmly in his face.

Damien glanced down in perplexity at his tiny son in his arms and softened his grip as gently as possibly. "Well, then, my laddie," he whispered, "we shall have to wait here till your brother arrives, then Mama can tell us, all three, what to do." He eased down onto the nearby armchair, unable to stop staring at his child.

When a second burst of angry but healthy wailing reverberated through the walls, the doctor poked his head out of the room. "Boy," he announced curtly, then closed the door again.

"I knew it," Damien murmured, then closed his eyes with a prayer of thanksgiving, leaned his head back against the chair, and laughed, long and quietly.